Sircus of Impossible Magicks

Chosen

A novel by

Leslie Le Mon

© Leslie Le Mon, 2012

Table of Contents

Dedication 5

Prologue 7

Chapter One – Welcome to the Apocalypse 11

Chapter Two – Stranger on the Gold Line 29

Chapter Three – Magickal History Hunt 45

Chapter Four – The Sircus of Impossible Magicks 55

Chapter Five – The First Companion 67

Chapter Six – Magic Bags 79

Chapter Seven – Impossible Magicks 85

Chapter Eight – First Blood 95

Chapter Nine – Teulu 103

Chapter Ten – The Fortress 117

Chapter Eleven – The Tower 125

Chapter Twelve – Monsters in the Closet 143

Chapter Thirteen – The Haunted Forest 155

Chapter Fourteen – Winter Quarters 171

Chapter Fifteen – The White City 191

Chapter Sixteen – Battle 205

Chapter Seventeen – The Second Companion 217

Chapter Eighteen – Echoes 245

Chapter Nineteen – End of the Line 269

Chapter Twenty – Home 299

Appendix – Glossary By Alice Iztali 313

Acknowledgements 315

More Books By Leslie Le Mon 317

About the Author 319

Copyrights 321

Dedication

For my mother, who can do anything.

Prologue
June 22^{nd-ish} – Aelwyd

It was a clear, cool morning in the forest village of Teulu. The residents, from the youngest to the oldest, gathered around the fire pit, basking in its warmth, and fragrant wreaths of wood smoke.

It has been foretold, the chieftain told his people, *that in four years' time, we should greet the Chosen, and welcome them to our clan. On our behalf, they shall quest to retrieve the sacred touchstones, lost so very long ago, and finally restore them to our people.*

The villagers nodded to each other, and to their chieftain, and there was a general murmur of assent.

However, the chieftain continued, *Tanwen and I believe that the Hungry Ones have learned the identity of the Chosen. If this is true, then the Hungry Ones, by cunning or by force, will attempt to steal the touchstones for themselves. And they will not wait four years.*

A worried murmur swept among the villagers.

The chieftain's son, however, shrugged. He toyed idly with a razor-sharp dagger. *Let the Hungry Ones do as they will*, said the boy, *where it concerns the Chosen Ones. The Chosen Ones are rubbish.*

His father frowned magnificently. *The Chosen are not rubbish. We must do all in our power to assist the Chosen – and we shall.*

They're children, said the son. *Stupid, mortal children.*

You are a child, said the chieftain.

I am a warrior, said the boy, with a lift of his chin. *I am a magician. I am your son, and Tanwen's son. I am of the faery blood. The Chosen Ones –*

They, too, have magick in their blood, said the chieftain, *though they have been raised as mortals. And if the Hungry Ones know their identity, the Chosen are in terrible danger.*

The boy yawned.

We can wait no longer, the chieftain continued, turning to address his people. *We must welcome the Chosen Ones now. Though we cannot fully train the children, we can offer them guidance and support during their quest.* He looked hard at his son. *Guidance, and support*, the chieftain repeated significantly. *The Chosen must obtain the touchstones and deliver them to us, rather than to the Hungry Ones. For if the Hungry Ones obtained that magick, well …*

The chieftain let the terrible thought hang.

An elderly woman, who had been present many years past, at the battle of Nant Newyn, shuddered, and pulled her grandchildren closer.

None of us wish the Hungry Ones to gain possession of the touchstones, said the chieftain's son. *It's too important a matter to leave to the Chosen. I will quest for the touchstones.* He tossed his dagger into the air, catching it easily by its handle. *I am your son and heir. It is my duty – and my right – to restore the touchstones, father. Leave it to mortals, and they'll fail. I'll travel to Goror Du this very morning, and –*

You shall not! said his mother Tanwen, her voice sharp as a whip. *It has been foretold for centuries that the Chosen shall gather the touchstones, and return them to Aelwyd. It is the Chosen's quest, lad – not yours.*

Oh, this was foretold, and that was foretold, and blah, blah, blah, said the son. He tossed his dagger up in the air again, caught it gracefully. *Not everything foretold comes to pass – and even when it does, it is not always in the way we anticipated. Are we to protect ourselves sensibly, or to follow a pack of old mumbo-jumbo legends? Are we Clan Teulu, or sniveling fools?*

Take care with your tone, said the chieftain. *And remember that legend is truth. Though our interpretation is not always perfect, what is foretold shall come to pass. The Chosen will succeed – with our help. The Chosen are family.*

Not my family, said the boy.

They are of our family, the chieftain insisted quietly. *More than you understand. They are of the magick bloodline. They – and no other – shall restore the touchstones. And no one of Teulu –* he gave his son a hard glance – *will do ought but assist them.*

Aye, murmured many of the villagers, nodding at their chieftain, making clear their support.

The chieftain's son made a sour face.

Technically, said the boy, *even the Hungry Ones are family. Were family, until the Great Rift. There's family, and then there's family. The Chosen are a sad little mortal twig on our family's mighty tree. And, like a twig, they'll be easily broken.*

He hurled the dagger at a log in the fire pit; the blade sank deep into the wood. Sparks flew up from the blaze.

That's enough, his mother said grimly. *We'll hear not another word from you, lad.*

The boy scowled at her. *All are welcome to speak, mother. It is your own rule, I believe.*

Aye, she agreed, *and it is my own rule, as well, that there's a limit to the nonsense any one villager can babble at a single council. Your father will visit the Chosen Ones – and that, is that.*

Unless, said the chieftain, his dark eyes sweeping the gathering, *unless there are any other objections to the plan?*

Nay, said many of the villagers, shaking their heads. *No objections.*

Do what you must, called the blacksmith.

We trust you, called the potter.

Don't let them Hungry Ones get ten leagues near the touchstones, cried the old woman who remembered the battle of Nant Newyn. She held her grandchildren tighter. *You help them Chosen Ones!* she told the chieftain. *You gives them anything what they need!*

The chieftain's son put a hand to his head, and tapped it.

You're all mad, he told the villagers. *Placing our future in the hands of three nobodies. Mortal nobodies, at that.*

That's enough, Daith, his mother said firmly. *Your father will do as he must. And you and I shall have a little chat …*

Chapter One – Welcome to the Apocalypse
June 23rd – Los Angeles

In later years, when he was asked to tell how it all began, James would think back to the big Victorian house on Orange Grove Avenue in South Pasadena – the big house, with its tower and gables and stained glass windows, the house his father had repaired and restored over the years, sometimes with James' help, until it was the prettiest home on Orange Grove – at least in James' estimation.

It was the house where James had grown up, from the time he was born. There was a framed photo on the wall in the main stairwell, of his mother Roz and his father Sam, when they were young, standing in front of the big Victorian house, holding a tiny baby in their arms – the baby was James, and the photo was snapped when his parents brought him home from the hospital.

James had always been fond of the house, especially when he was old enough to help his father with sanding and painting and varnishing. When James wandered through the halls and rooms of the beautiful old place, he could see his own handiwork, as well as his dad's.

It was in this house, when James was sixteen, that the adventure that changed his life began without any warning. One minute he was plain old James Jones, on Orange Grove in South Pasadena, an ordinary boy and happy to be an ordinary boy. He didn't care much for school, loved to hang out with his friends, loved videogames, and hiking, and working with his hands. An ordinary kid … But before that day was through …

School had just ended. Summer was beginning. And James knew exactly how he was going to spend his time.

He was going to play videogames with his friends. Lots of videogames. He and his best friends were going to win the Mortal Quest tournament online. And he was going camping with his dad, like they always did in the summer time, building a shelter, and fishing, and swimming, and living off the land. His dad would be finished with a big construction job out-of-state soon, and, first thing when he got back, they were going up north, to the forest, to camp.

On the morning of June 23rd, James was fast asleep. He had been up all night playing Mortal Quest online with Tariq and Hisoka, his two best friends, known in the online gaming world as *thadude1055* and *rockemsockem99*, respectively. The trio had crushed all opponents and mastered the seemingly impossible Level 25.

It had taken until three in the morning to beat Level 25, and James, happy but exhausted, had dropped into a deep sleep ...

In the early hours, just after dawn, something woke him from a nightmare: a dream about a dark tunnel, a flickering torch, a shadowy figure that moved like a panther.

James squinted. The light in his room wasn't proper morning light; a grey and murky dawn light seeping between the curtains.

Something was tapping his forehead lightly, *tap, tap, tap*, an irritating sensation, but too gentle to be his little brother Aiden. *Tap, tap, tap ...*

James muttered and opened eyes gritty with sleep-sand.

In the dim light he saw his book shelf, filled with books on video games, and science fiction novels, and comic books. The alarm clock on the bookshelf said "7:00 a.m."

Next to the clock was a photo of James and his dad, Sam, taken last summer; they were holding a giant trout they'd caught. His dad was laughing, blue eyes bright, wavy red hair a little messy in the wind.

James looked from the photo to the person standing next to him, the incredibly annoying person tapping his forehead.

It was Alice, his little cousin, a mischievous smile on her face, one finger poised above his forehead. *Tap, tap, tap* went her finger.

"Good morning, dork," Alice said sweetly. She was dressed all rock-n-roll-Goth, as usual, black jeans, black sneakers, grey t-shirt, grey hoodie with a skull pattern, black-and-red painted nails, dark eyeliner.

James pushed her small hand out of his face and pulled his pillow over his head.

"Go away, demon child," he muttered.

"I'm sorry," Alice said sweetly, "I can't understand what you just said. I don't speak dorkish." She tapped the back of his head, where his hair was a dark mane of waves and cowlicks. "Come on, dork, get up. You're watching me today."

James sat up as if a jolt of electricity had shot down his spine.

"I'm *what*?"

"You're watching me today. Isn't that wonderful?"

"I'm *what*?"

Alice narrowed her eyes critically. "You're not very bright, are you? No – don't bother to answer. I said," she enunciated carefully, with long pauses between each word, "You ... are ... watching ... me ... today."

"No way!" said James. "No way, no way, no way."

He tossed aside his sheets and blanket, getting his legs tangled in them, almost falling as he climbed out of bed, but righting himself at the last moment.

He barged past Alice, into the hallway. "Mom? Mom? *Mom*?"

"What is it, James?" Roz' voice came from several floors below – from the kitchen, James thought. She sounded weary, annoyed – almost as weary and annoyed as her eldest son.

James charged down the hall, feet slapping on the hardwood floor, navigated several other corridors, and stairwells, and finally stormed into the kitchen.

The kitchen smelled like coffee and toast. All James registered at first was his mother, in her blue business suit, and his Aunt Peggy, in a brown business suit, sitting at the kitchen counter with mugs of coffee in front of them. His mother was a financial analyst and his aunt was a customer service supervisor. They both worked downtown and they always dressed up for work.

"I am *not* watching Alice today," James told his mother. "No way, no how, no way."

"Yes," said his mother in her clear, commanding voice, "you are."

"But, mom – "

"No 'But, moms' James. You sound like you're five years old. And we greet guests in this house. Say 'good morning' to Aunt Peggy."

"Good morning, Aunt Peggy," James said sulkily. And then, before he could lose momentum, "I'm sorry, Aunt Peggy, but I am *not* watching your demon-child today. Or *any* day, unless *maybe* it's some kind of apocalypse."

"Welcome to the apocalypse," his mother said drily. "Want a cup of coffee, James? You'll probably need it. Because you're watching Aiden too."

"*I'm* watching Aiden? He's supposed to go to camp. What the heck is going on around here?" James demanded.

He knew he sounded shrill, maybe not like a five-year-old, but more like a twelve-year old, like a kid Alice's age. But James didn't care. The unfairness of it all stung him. "This is my first day of vacation," he said. "I have a million things I wanna do!"

"You can play your little computer game tonight," his mother said dismissively. "Your cousin needs you today, and so does your brother. Alice and Aiden are more important than some game."

James sank onto the wooden stool next to Aunt Peggy.

He knew his mother, her tones of voice, how far he could push her before she got mad, and right now, that was *nada*.

Just now, his mother's voice was as cool as the snow that was lingering on the distant peaks of the Sierra range. Roz was never what anyone would call a softy, but there was even more steel in her today. James didn't understand it, and he didn't like it.

"Hi, James," Aunt Peggy said quietly.

For the first time since storming into the kitchen, James actually looked at his Aunt Peggy. She was a chunky, sweet-natured lady with big green eyes and a kind smile. Right now the smile was uncertain and the eyes were red-rimmed, as if she'd been crying. "I know Alice can be a handful," Peggy said apologetically, "but I would really appreciate your help."

James' mother handed him a cup of coffee. He accepted it absently, took a sip.

Alice, James knew, wasn't just a handful. Alice was an irritating, attention-grabbing know-it-all who had been making his life miserable for years. A day watching her would be exhausting and completely focused on *her*. All of his plans would be ruined.

But Aunt Peggy looked so sad ... and vulnerable ... and why did she need him to do this, anyway?

"So, I guess I can watch Alice for today," James said slowly, grudgingly, trying to be gracious. "I guess it won't *kill* me to watch her until her camp starts tomorrow." Every summer Alice's parents put her in a gifted-and-talented camp, where she and dozens of other little over-achieving geniuses did genius-type things. "I mean, if you really need my help today – "

"It's not a favor," his mother told him, sounding annoyed. "You don't need to be a martyr about it. Family does for family, James. We need your help today, and you're going to help. Period."

Great, thought James. *Not only is it going to be a rotten day, watching Alice, I don't even get any credit for it!*

"And don't make that face," said Roz.

"I'm not making a face," he said petulantly.

"You are making a face, and stop making it."

"But, mom – "

"I told you – No 'but, moms'."

"But why am I watching Aiden, too? Alice I can barely handle, but Aiden – "

"Aiden is your brother," said Roz.

"But he has camp. He starts Camp Happy Face today. How can he miss his first day?"

"Life is full of fun surprises," Roz said drily. "Now, your brother's not awake yet, but he will be soon. I've got a bowl of oatmeal in the microwave, all you have to do is heat it for one minute and put some milk in it before you give it to him. You can remember that, right?"

"Mom, I *think* I can make Aiden a bowl of oatmeal. I'm not an idiot."

"Great. Then your day should be a breeze."

James groaned.

"The first aid kit is in the bathroom cabinet, in case the kids need it," said Roz, "and you have my work number, and Aunt Peggy's. Bring the kids to Union Station at 5:30pm today. Got it? Not 5:45pm, James. 5:30 pm. Aunt Peggy will pick up Alice there, and I'll bring you and Aiden to McDonald's for supper."

"OK. Got it."

The logical part of James' brain was filing away his mother's comments. The rest of him felt like a big meteor had crashed through the kitchen roof and fallen on him, crushing his chest.

"Good. Thanks." His mother ruffled his hair, making it even messier. "I really do appreciate it, James."

"Me too," said Aunt Peggy. She gave James a big, squashy hug. She sniffled.

"It's going to be OK," Roz told Peggy quietly.

"What's going to be OK?" asked James.

"Nothing that concerns you," his mother said sharply. She placed the empty coffee mugs in the sink. "You guys can wash the dishes today. OK? OK. We're out of here."

Aunt Peggy gave her nephew another hug. Then the two women went out the front door, down the steps.

James wandered like a sleepwalker to the big bow window in the living room, watched his mother climb into her SUV and pull out smoothly, racing down the street, and then watched Aunt Peggy climb into her VW bug – it was almost a magic trick, how she folded herself up and crammed herself into the car – and slowly, carefully drive away.

"So," said Alice, making James jump.

Somehow she had crept up beside him, silent as fog.

"Here's how it's going to go today," said Alice.

"No," James interrupted, "*here*'s how it's going to go today. *This* is the summer Tariq and Hisoka and I are going to win the Mortal Quest tournament, and we have to practice every day. *Every day!* Including today. So you – "

Alice made a startlingly realistic imitation of static. "Excuse me, we interrupt this dorky transmission with a cool transmission from *me*. *Here*'s how it's going to go today, James. You're going to play your stupid, loser game with your stupid, loser friends, and I'm going to do my homework."

"We don't have homework in the summer."

"No, *you* don't have homework in the summer," Alice corrected him. "Those of us who are going to be world-famous lawyers and fashion designers have a lot of homework in the summer." She held up a thick paperback book with a green cover. It read "12th Grade Curriculum" in stark white letters.

"I thought you were starting 7th grade in September," James said.

"I am. Your point?"

He sighed. "So, basically what you're saying is, you're going to read this book and leave me alone so I can play Mortal Quest? Because I can *totally* live with that plan."

"As much as I dislike making you happy, yes, that is the plan," Alice agreed.

"All right. Cool." James pointed to the living room sofa. "You can sit there and read. Make yourself comfortable. Lots of chips in the kitchen and sodas in the fridge. Don't try to cook anything. If you want something cooked, get me."

Alice snorted. "Like *you* can cook!"

"I can heat soup," he said defensively. "And I can microwave things."

"So can I."

"Yeah, but you're still little, and this isn't your house, so *I'll* do the microwaving."

"Whatever." Alice walked over to the sofa, plopped down, opened her book to a page near the middle. She made a scornful shooing motion toward James. "Go away, dork. I can't stand people watching me while I study. It makes me nervous."

James made a face at her, and then bounded up the steps toward his room. When he finally got there – his room was high up on the third floor, near the tower – he threw himself on his bed and pulled the sheets up over his head.

A couple more hours of sleep, he thought, and then when he woke up, he'd call Tariq and Hisoka and see when they were going to hop online again.

"If we can win Mortal Quest," he thought drowsily, "*when* we win this, it's going to be awesome. A hundred grand a piece. A hundred grand a piece …"

He quickly drifted to sleep … and back into the nightmare.

* * *

The tunnel was narrow. It dead-ended in a massive mirror. Reflections of distant torches flickered on the silvery glass and danced on the damp stone walls. James and Alice stood in front of the mirror, staring at their reflections.

It had always been a matter of great distress for both of them that they looked so much alike. Strangers mistook them for brother and sister, instead of cousins.

At sixteen, James was substantially taller than twelve-year-old Alice, but other than height, they were uncannily alike. They both had thick, dark, wavy hair, a tousled mane on him, long tresses on her. They both had large dark eyes; features that were strong but had a regal delicacy; straight black brows; sensitive mouths. They were both slender rather than athletic in frame.

In the dream they were dressed in dead black cloaks fastened with something glittery – diamonds? – at their throats. They could see something in the mirror, some shadow *behind* them; it was human yet feline, slipping in and out of view. It seemed to be drawing closer.

"It's right behind us," Alice said quietly.

"Yes," James agreed, voice tense. "At least Aiden's safe. So … how do we play this?"

"I don't know. The mirror *looks* pretty sturdy." She pressed a small hand against it.

Startlingly, her hand plunged into it as if the mirror were made of some viscous liquid, like honey.

"James," she said, smiling, "it's not solid. It's not solid!"

"Yes, I see," he said.

"It's a way out!" she whispered excitedly.

"Or a trap."

Behind them, the menacing shadow drew closer, with a vague flutter like the shadow of wings.

* * *

"James, James, James, James, James, wake up James! JAAAAAAMES!!"

James groaned as something repeatedly thwacked his skull, not hard enough to hurt, but hard enough to annoy.

This, he knew, was not Alice. This was none other than his four-year-old little brother, Aiden.

"JAAAAAAMES! JAAAAAMES!"

James pulled the sheets down over his head, blinking against the bright sunlight spilling into his room. Aiden was hopping up and down on the bed, whacking James' skull with a red plastic pail, not in malice, apparently, but excitement.

Scattered across the blanket were beach toys, little plastic shovels and trowels and Nerf footballs that had apparently fallen out of the pail when Aiden started smacking it against James' head.

"Aiden, calm down," said James, sitting up. "Calm down, pal."

Aiden kept hopping up and down, but stopped hitting James with the pail. The little guy had obviously just woken up. His beautiful dark curls – his mother couldn't bear to cut them – framed his angelic face like a wild halo.

The little boy had obviously dressed himself; his red bathing suit was on backward, although his T-shirt, which read "Camp Happy Face," was neatly tucked into the backward trunks. His red flip-flops were on the wrong feet.

"Aidie go camp!" shouted Aiden, hopping around and swinging the red pail wildly. "Today Aidie camp day! Happy Camp!"

James rubbed his eyes. "Come on, Aiden, *please* calm down. James is very tired."

"Camp Happy Face!" shouted Aiden. "Hurray! Come on, James. Come on, brother. You bring Aidie camp." Aiden dropped his pail and gave James a monster hug.

"Why are you so crazy?" James asked affectionately.

He picked up his brother, held him over his head. Aiden laughed merrily.

"Aidie is airplane!" Aiden shouted. "Aidie is helcopter!"

"Hel-i-copter," James corrected patiently, gently shaking Aiden back and forth as if the little boy were, in fact, an airplane or helicopter hovering high above the ground.

"Yeah, Aidie helicopter! Zzzzzzoooooom!"

"Excuse me," said Alice coldly.

She stood in the doorway, scowling at James. As usual, she had appeared with the stealth of a ninja. "How am I supposed to study with all this commotion going on up here?"

"ALLIE!!" Aiden shouted exuberantly.

He wriggled out of James' grip, somersaulted on the blanket and all but leaped into Alice's arms. He hugged her tightly. "My Allle!"

Alice's face softened for a moment. She hugged the child.

"Hi, Aidie," she said kindly. Then, scowling over the little boy's head at James, she said "Aidie, you need to be quiet, OK? Allie is studying. You would think your brother would know better than to get you all out of control."

"Oh, of course," said James, scowling right back at her. "Yes, this whole commotion is *my* fault."

"So we agree." Alice knelt down, looked at Aiden with a soft look that she reserved only for her beloved small cousin. "Aiden, Allie has to read a book. So I need you to be very quiet. OK?"

"Quiet like mouse?"

"Yes, quiet like a mouse. Like the little mouse we read about last week. The *good* little mouse."

"Read me mouse! Read mouse *now*!"

"What a great idea," smiled James. "Aiden, get the mouse book. Allie would *love* to read it to you, right now."

"Hurray!" Aiden pushed past Alice, mismatched flip-flops flapping on the hardwood floor as he raced down the hall to his room.

Alice regarded James thoughtfully. "That was pretty good," she said.

"Thank you."

"You must be paying attention to me. You're not usually that clever."

"You do have a certain evil genius-ness that is not unimpressive."

"But you know I'm going to get you back, like, double."

"I know you're going to *try*," said James. "Now, if you don't mind – and even if you do – I need to call Tariq, and you need to read Aiden 'The Good Little Mouse'. You know Aiden likes to hear it, like, *twenty* times in a row, right?"

"I know."

Aiden barreled into the room, a colorful picture book, "The Good Little Mouse," clutched in one tiny hand. "Read, Allie! Read!"

"Not in here," said James. He grabbed his cell phone off his nightstand, tapped the touch screen. "Read it in the living room."

"Oh, no," Alice said in mock horror. "The living room? No, this is a *family* book. We're *all* going to enjoy it as a *family*."

"Family, yay!" shouted Aiden.

Alice gently took the book from the child, and crossed to the only chair in James' room. The chair was draped with jeans, swim trunks, sweatshirts and empty McDonald's wrappers. Alice coughed delicately and with a *swoosh* of one arm knocked everything onto the floor.

"Hey!" said James.

Alice raised her eyebrows in mock surprise.

"Aiden and I need to sit down," she said. "You don't want us to sit on the *floor*, do you?" She sat, and Aiden sat on her lap, nestling against her. She ran a hand through his angelic curls.

"'The Good Little Mouse, Chapter One'," Alice read aloud, "'Once upon a time, there was a very bad little mouse, a *very* bad little mouse indeed. He was always cross, and always cruel, and always, *always* mean.'" She turned a page, tapped the picture with her finger. "See, Aidie? That's the bad little mouse."

"Bad mouse!" Aidie shouted at the picture.

"No shouting, Aiden," said James.

"He's just enjoying the story," said Alice. "It's a very exciting story."

James resisted the urge to peg the cell phone at his cousin. He would've been in a ton of trouble with his mother if he did. Besides, it was a new phone. And it was ringing now. It rang five times before there was a click at the other end and he heard Tariq's impatient voice, so loud that it could be heard throughout James' room. You never needed speakerphone with Tariq.

"Dude, *where* have you been?" Tariq boomed cheerfully. "RockEmSockEm and I have been online for, like, *hours*."

"I was sleeping."

"Sleep is for losers. Do I need to go over there and kick your butt?"

"Please do!" shouted Alice.

"Who's that?" asked Tariq. "Did you get another player? Because, dude, you know we already analyzed this, our strategy is totally only going to work with three players. Trios win, quartets lose. Right? You know?"

"She's not another player," said James, "she's my evil cousin. I got stuck watching her today."

"Bummer!"

"I know."

"But don't let that mess up our practice, right? We need you, James. You're the best of us all, you're the key to our win."

Alice snorted.

"Wow, she really *is* mean, huh?" boomed Tariq. "Don't be negative, Ellis."

"Alice!" she shouted at the cell phone. "Alice, not Ellis!"

"Don't be negative, Alice," said Tariq. "Don't put any bad vibes on this. Mortal Quest might not be your groove, but it's *our* groove, you gotta respect that, right?"

"Alice understands," said James. "She's taking my brother downstairs to read him a book," said James. "So I can concentrate on Mortal Quest."

Alice made a face.

"Awesome," Tariq's voice boomed cheerfully from the phone. "Right on, little dudette!"

Alice stood, Aiden sliding gracefully to the floor. "Come on, Aiden," Alice said. "We're going to the living room, where there aren't any dorks or surfer geeks telling us what to do."

"Dorks!" laughed Aiden.

"Ouch!" laughed Tariq.

* * *

They beat Level 26 of Mortal Quest. It took them most of the day, but they did it.

Tariq was an eccentric guy, but he knew his strategy, and they were a tight trio, Tariq leaping ahead as the advanced guard, Hisoka covering the rear, ever alert and cautious, and James, the best shot, the best fighter, keeping it all together at the heart of the unit.

When James' game system was online he, Tariq and Hisoka could communicate while they played, their voices zipping instantly through the ether and through each other's game speakers while onscreen their avatars Night (James), ThaDude (Tariq) and RockEmSockEm (Hisoka) bested other strangers who were seated all over the planet in front of their own consoles.

It was exhilarating. When James' avatar, Night, blasted the final opponent, he and Tariq war-whooped at the same time, and even reserved Hisoka could be heard shouting "Way to go, guys!"

"Way to go team!" yelled Tariq. "Yeeeeeha!"

It was only a practice round, of course, the real tournament wasn't until August, but if they were starting out this strong, they reasoned, what on earth could possibly stop them in August?

After James powered down his game system and basked in the victory for a moment, it occurred to him that the sunlight trickling into his room was very weak, that his arms ached, that his legs were stiff, and that he was starving. He glanced at the clock on his nightstand. It was 4:30 pm.

James leaped up like a live current had zapped his feet.

It was 4:30pm! And he'd never even brushed his hair, or his teeth! And he'd forgotten about the kids, completely and utterly forgotten about the kids!

He flew down corridors and stairs, down to the living room, his feet barely touching the floor.

His heart stopped when he saw the mess.

What appeared to be every single one of Aiden's toys, books and Nerf balls were scattered around the living room floor in a veritable minefield.

Uncapped magic markers lay on the floor amid snowdrifts of paper. Varicolored drops and puddles of watercolor paints had dried on the scrubbed white floorboards.

Bowls of half-eaten oatmeal and macaroni-and -cheese sat on the coffee table, the contents congealing, crusting solid, so that only a sandblaster would be able to scour them from the bowls.

A can of cola had tipped over, staining the white boards.

I'm gonna kill her, thought James. *Gonna kill her, gonna kill her …*

Alice dozed on the sofa, snoring mightily, still clutching her "12th Grade Curriculum" book.

Aiden sat cross-legged on the cushion next to her, staring at the big screen television, on which a blood-curdling B-horror movie was unfolding. An octopus-like creature with giant tentacles was tearing apart a freighter.

Aiden watched, mesmerized, traumatized, as the octopus tore apart the ship.

He held a spoon and a big bowl of melted chocolate ice cream, not eating it, but, in his horrified trance, dripping ice cream all over the white sofa cushions in a demented Rorschach pattern.

"Aaaaaaaah!" screamed James.

Aiden jumped, startled, dropped the spoon, and started to wail.

Alice sat up, rubbing her eyes.

"What the heck …" she mumbled. She hugged Aiden. "Shh. What's wrong, Aidie?"

"'What's wrong *Aidie*?'" hollered James. "'What's wrong *Aidie*?' Look at this mess, Alice! My mother is going to kill me! No. First she's going to send me to a really horrible military school, where everyone is a psycho, and then if I survive that, *then* she's gonna kill me!"

Alice hugged Aiden tighter. "It's OK," she told her small cousin. His wail subsided into muffled hiccups. She tousled his curls. "That's right, Aidie," she said. "Good little mice don't cry."

Alice looked around at the mess, and then looked coolly at James.

"Well," she said, "you are officially the most irresponsible babysitter ever."

"*I'm* irresponsible?" James knew Alice was a demon-child, but this time she'd gone too far. "*I'm* irresponsible?"

"It's really annoying, James," said Alice, "when you repeat everything I say. Of course you're irresponsible. Just look at this place."

"I'm looking! I see. What the heck *happened* out here?"

Alice finally glanced at the television, where the tentacle monster was now wrenching apart a car full of teenagers. She gasped. "Oh my gosh! What the heck are you letting Aidie watch?" She grabbed the remote controller off the floor and jabbed buttons until she found a cartoon channel.

"What am *I* letting Aidie watch?" James demanded. "What am *I* letting Aidie watch? I repeat, Alice: what in the heck *happened* out here?"

"Look, I'm not the babysitter," said Alice. "I'm your adorable little cousin. I'm twelve years old. *You're* supposed to be taking care of *me*. In your neglectful absence," she shrugged, "I did the best I could."

"*This* is the best you could do?"

"No, you're right; that's a complete lie," Alice admitted. "I could actually run this place like a well-oiled machine, if I wanted to. Instead, I just let little Aidie run amok. I think he had a really great day. Till now."

"But why would you *do* that?"

"Because, dear cousin, I don't want to come back here to be babysat by you ever again. And since you let this happen," she swept her arm from left to right, encompassing the entire, chaotic living room, "there's no way your mother will let my mom leave me here again. Mission accomplished. You're welcome, dork."

James was glad he wasn't holding his cell phone because he really, *really* would have been tempted to peg it at Alice, no matter what the consequences were. With the living room this trashed, he was already in massive trouble anyway. James struggled to keep his temper.

"Aunt Peggy isn't going to bring you here again," he said through gritted teeth. "You're going to your stupid genius camp tomorrow. It always starts right after school ends. So this mess just seems … really mean. And pointless. Even for you."

"Or so it would seem to the average dork," said Alice. "But you don't know the whole story."

"What whole story?"

"Of why I'm here today, and why you're watching Aiden. And why my mom was crying this morning."

"I asked about that. My mother said it was none of my business."

Alice smacked her forehead in frustration. "For crying out loud, James, don't you know when a grownup tells you something's not your business, it must be super-serious and it must be one-thousand-million percent your business? And not in a happy way?"

"All I know is my mother said it's not my business what upset Aunt Peggy, and I'm going to be murdered if we don't clean this up in three minutes. So get those bowls, and those cups, and that soda can, and throw them in the sink. I mean, don't actually *throw* them – "

Alice rolled her eyes. "You're missing the point, which is I *don't* want to clean up the mess. I *want* Aunt Roz to find it, so you can't babysit me anymore …" She trailed off.

James was fixing her with a look she had never seen on his face before. It was partially a pleading look, and partially a threatening look, and she wasn't sure which was more disturbing.

Alice sighed. "All right, all right, I'll help. A little bit. Don't have a stroke or whatever."

Alice grudgingly placed the bowls and cups in the sink and filled them with water to soften up the calcified oatmeal and mac-and-cheese.

She threw the cola can in the trash bin, and wiped up the soda spill.

Then she sat in the rocking chair, Aiden on her lap, and quietly sang him a lullaby to keep him distracted and docile while James did the bulk of the cleanup.

James ran around like a chicken with his head cut off, grabbing big armfuls of Aiden's toys and books. He crammed them into the toy chest and under the sofa and under the easy chair. He even shoved some behind his mother's china cabinet.

He ran to the kitchen, soaked yards of paper towels in cool water, and scrubbed as much of the paint off the floorboards as he could. There were still a lot of cobalt and rose and sea foam-colored stains on the wood. They were lovely in an abstract way, but his mom would never see it that way.

"Just cover them with the rug from your room," Alice suggested impatiently. James raced upstairs, into his room, grabbed the black-and-white Navajo rug his dad had sent him from New Mexico. He raced back down the living room, threw the rug over the stains.

"Perfect," Alice said.

"Mom's gonna ask me why I put the rug there."

"You wanted to surprise her," said Alice. "You know how much she misses your dad since he went to work on that project, and now whenever she sees the rug, she'll think of him."

"She'll never buy that. I'm not that considerate," objected James.

"Of course you're not. But like all moms, Aunt Roz *wants* to believe you are. It'll work, dork. Trust me."

James was dubious. His mother was too smart to fall for a line of boloney like that, but he had no time to come up with anything else. He had to tackle the sofa.

He labored for five nerve-wracking minutes, but the chocolate-stained sofa cushions were hopeless. The wet paper towels just smeared the chocolate around, made the stains worse.

He froze, staring at them in horror. "Military school," he croaked. "Military school."

"Jeez, James, don't you *ever* do anything wrong?" asked Alice. "This is one of the oldest domestic disasters in the book. When you spill something on a sofa, you just flip the cushions over." Alice suited her actions to the word. James regarded the pristine white sofa cushion in amazement.

"But ... that's awesome!"

"Of course," Alice said, buffing her black- and-red-painted nails on her grey T-shirt.

"But what happens when mom flips over the cushions someday? She'll wring my neck."

"Hopefully, you'll be away at college by then. If not, just plead ignorance. She'll figure it was Aidie who ruined the cushions, which – newsflash, dork – it was!"

"But you were supposed to be watching him. *I* was supposed to be watching him. So it's actually our fault."

"Your fault. But who'll remember the details by the time your mom finds out? It's already a blur. I've already put it behind me. Don't live in the past, James."

James looked around the living room. It actually appeared fine, if you didn't know there were stuffed animals squashed behind the china cabinet, paint stains hidden by the Navajo rug, and chocolate stains on the flip-side of the cushions.

"OK, so, you get Aiden ready," said James. "I have to change." He bolted into his room before Alice had a chance to argue.

Alice regarded Aiden critically. "You look OK to me," she said, "just a little chocolaty."

She picked him up and carried him to the kitchen sink, where she scrubbed the ice cream from his face and wetted his curls. "Go get your brush, Aidie." He raced out of the room; she heard his flip-flops flapping up the stairs. He was back in a few minutes with a blue hair brush. He leaped up into her lap.

"Allie brush Aidie hair!"

"Yes, Allie is going to brush your hair."

When she was finished, she set him on the floor.

"OK, little guy, let's see. You've got to go put on some jeans."

He shook his head. "No. Aidie wear bathe suit. Aidie swim camp."

"Aidie, the day's already over," she said reasonably. "No camp today."

Aiden frowned. His small hands clenched. "Aidie go Happy Face Camp."

"Not today, Aiden."

Aiden squeezed his hands into tight fists. "AIDIE GO HAPPY CAMP! *NOW!*"

James rushed into the kitchen in clean jeans and a relatively clean blue T-shirt emblazoned with the Mortal Quest logo. He grabbed Aiden, and rushed back into the depths of the house, Aiden under his arm.

Alice heard James, several floors above, trying to explain something in a soothing, muffled voice, punctuated by Aiden's bellows of "HAPPY CAMP! HAAAPPY CAAAAMP!"

A few minutes later they reappeared, Aiden wearing a plain white tee and a pair of jeans and sneakers, his face red from bellowing, and damp with tears.

"Happy Face Camp," the little boy sobbed.

"Come on, Aiden," coaxed Alice, "today you went to Allie Camp. *That* was fun, right?"

Aiden sniffled dubiously.

"We painted … and we laughed … and we read 'Good Little Mouse' … and we ate ice cream …"

Aiden brightened. He gave one final, enormous sniff and then smiled dazzlingly. He reached toward Alice and James handed him to her.

"Aidie like Allie Camp!" Aiden said brightly. "Allie Camp good!"

James rolled his eyes. "For Pete's sake," he muttered. "Come on, come on, we're *totally* late. Let's go."

It was 5:15 pm. There was no way they'd make it to Union Station in fifteen minutes.

As they hurried along the sidewalk toward the Gold Line train platform, Aiden holding tight to Alice's hand, James flipped open his cell phone. He tapped out his mom's cell number. She answered after the first ring, as usual.

"Uh, hi, mom. Sorry, but we're gonna be a couple minutes late …"

Chapter Two – Stranger on the Gold Line
June 23rd – Los Angeles

In later years, when she was asked to tell how it all began, Alice would think back to the little bungalow on Silverwood Terrace in Silver Lake – the little bungalow, painted sunset orange, that her father Roberto had improved over the years with his paintings and his sculptures, the sun dial he had fashioned out of copper, the serpent-shaped water wheel he had designed and built for the little garden, basing it on Mayan hieroglyphs.

It was a tiny house, but, as her dad always said, "Who needs a big house? If we had a big house," he always joked, "I'd have to yell louder to call you to dinner, kid. I've have to walk farther to ask you how you're day went."

Alice's father was a designer, and though he sometimes taught classes at USC and UCLA, mostly he made things for movies and TV. He made paintings and sculptures and furniture and entire sets, and it was a good, if sometimes erratic, living. In the last year, though, there hadn't been many classes to teach, and there hadn't been many movies to design things for.

"It's this crazy economy, kid," Roberto told Alice, when he drove her to school the mornings he didn't have a job to go to. "They aren't hiring adjuncts like they used to and they aren't making all the shows and movies like they used to. And they do film something, studios are recycling everything – props, paintings, sets. But it's gonna turn around – you just wait and see, Alice." He would grin at her – his dazzling, always optimistic grin …

The day Alice's life changed – the day her whole family's life changed – was the 23rd of June. It was the day after school ended – the day she was supposed to start gifted-and-talented camp. She and her friends were going to learn a ton of history and chemistry, rack up more academic credits, and, in between classes, paint their nails, trade hair and makeup tips, and offer their advice to fashion-challenged peers. Because, as her friend Penny had put it best, "What does it matter if some chick is gonna be the next Madame Curie, if she's, like, a fashion tragedy? It's our duty to help the fashion-blind."

The summer was mapped out. It was going to be wonderful. So Alice had been surprised, and not in a good way, when Peggy woke her at dawn on the 23rd and told her she wasn't going to go to camp that day.

Peggy looked like she'd been crying, and there was a strained tone to her voice. Not going to camp that day was, Alice suspected, was just the tip of the ice berg.

Being babysat by James is gonna stink, thought Alice, *plain and simple.*

James was no fun at all. He was more boring than wallpaper. He was a goody-goody who only thought about was his stupid video games and his stupid friends.

Alice had had twelve years of practice at almost always getting her way, whether with a winning smile or a ballistic tantrum. So she considered launching into a dramatic tirade, absolutely refusing to go to James' house ... but the woebegone look in her mother's eyes stopped her.

Crud. Something is really, really wrong ...

Alice sighed, got dressed, splashed water on her face and grabbed her "12th Grade Curriculum" book.

Peggy *hated* to drive – she had grown up in a small town in Vermont, and L.A. traffic made her nervous – so Alice was surprised when it was Peggy, not Roberto, who drove to Aunt Roz' house.

"Is Dad teaching a class today?" asked Alice as their little VW bug turned onto Sunset Boulevard.

"Um ... Kind of," said her mom.

"What does that mean?"

"It means ... it means he's not teaching so much as, um, he's going to be learning."

"So ... He's *taking* a class?" Alice hazarded.

"Kind of," said Peggy.

"Kind of *what*?" asked Alice. She couldn't stand it when adults gave vague, patronizing answers. "Mom – where is dad this morning?"

Peggy made a little sobbing sound.

"Oh, my God," said Alice, alarmed. "Is he hurt? Is he in the hospital?"

"No, no," Peggy said hastily, maintaining control of her emotions. "I'm sorry, I don't want to worry you, sweetie. But your Dad had to go out of town for awhile."

"When?" Alice demanded. "Where?" *Dad's out of town? Why? How is this happening and nobody told me?*

"You know work has been a little slow for Daddy," said Peggy. "And, you know, we have our house payment, and everything. So, your dad has gone out to New Mexico, to work with your Tio Sam. Isn't that great?"

Peggy smiled a ghastly smile. She was trying to be a trooper for her daughter, but anyone could see that no, it wasn't great, and Peggy was barely keeping it together.

"That *sucks*," said Alice. "Oh my God! Dad's in New Mexico, and nobody told me?"

"We didn't want to upset you, sweetie."

"Well, too late! Somebody should've told me. And what does this mean? It's that desperate, dad has to go out-of-state to work? What's he going to *do*?"

"Tio Sam got him some work on the construction project. You know, design work. It's perfect for Daddy. It's just, you know, too bad," Peggy's voice caught a little, "that it's New Mexico, but, you know, better than nothing, right?"

Alice's eyes narrowed. "Mom – how bad is it? It's got to be really bad. Are we going to lose the house?"

"Don't worry, Alice. It's for big people to worry about those things, not kids."

"Don't worry?" Alice demanded. "How am I *not* going to worry? Can we even pay our mortgage this month? Do we have enough for groceries?"

"Alice, I … I don't want to talk about this now." A tear slid down Peggy's face. "It's all going to be OK."

"Mom, things don't just, you know, end up OK. It takes planning and, like, facing things head on."

"We're facing it head on," Peggy assured her. "I'm going to miss your dad like crazy and he's going to miss us, but with this work Tio Sam got lined up, we're really going to be OK."

"I just don't understand," said Alice, "how working one week in New Mexico is gonna make everything OK," said Alice. "Tio's project ends next week, right? When dad comes home, is that – "

"Alice," said her mother, "I can't talk any more about this right now. I'll explain more later."

"But – "

"Alice, you just have to trust me right now. I can't talk any more about this or I'm going to get really upset and crack up the car."

Alice had stopped asking questions – but her mind continued to race. *This is bad … This is not good, nope, not good at all …*

Alice's mother sniffled once in awhile during the drive to South Pasadena, hands white-knuckled on the steering wheel, eyes glued to the road. As Alice and Roberto always noted, Peggy drove like a turtle, very slowly, with no sudden turns and with many frequent pauses to look from the left to the right before deciding which way to go. It seemed like hours before they finally pulled up to Aunt Roz and Tio Sam's beautiful Victorian house on Orange Grove in South Pasadena.

Aunt Roz greeted them at the door with her usual brief, business-like hugs.

She had coffee ready, and handed a cup to Peggy. Aunt Roz was always so efficient. The kitchen was fragrant with fresh coffee and spotlessly clean – the entire house was spotlessly clean – and Aunt Roz' briefcase stood by the front door, ready for Roz to grab when it was time to leave for work.

"Why don't you go wake James?" Roz suggested to Alice. As with most of Roz' suggestions, it was really a command.

Alice slipped quietly from the kitchen. She went down halls and up staircases, marveling, always, at how huge the house was.

Finally she reached James' room on the third floor. His door was half-closed, adorned with a couple of novelty signs: "James' Room: Trespassers Will Be Shot (From a Cannon)" and "DANGER! Do Not Enter!" with a skull and crossbones under it.

Alice hesitated.

Muffled voices drifted up from the kitchen, her mother sounding tearful, rambling on about something, probably dad going to New Mexico, punctuated by Aunt Roz' matter-of-fact, confident tones.

What are we going to do? wondered Alice. *What if New Mexico doesn't work out? What if dad can't get another job?* There was so much in the news lately, lay-offs, unemployment, evictions. Like her dad told her – the crazy economy. What if they couldn't pay their mortgage? There was a girl at Alice's school, her parents had fallen behind on their mortgage, and they ended up moving to an awful little hotel on Sunset …

Alice felt dizzy suddenly. She swayed, put out a hand and steadied herself against the doorframe. It was stupid to dwell on the family finances. She would make herself crazy. Better to distract herself, she decided.

Quietly pushing the door open, she ghosted into James' room. He was dead to the world, snoring softly, one arm thrown over his eyes. A murky grey morning light slipped between the curtains.

Silently Alice placed her hand over his face, extended one finger and began to tap softly, maddeningly, on his forehead. *Tap, tap, tap. Tap, tap, tap.*

James mumbled, shifted. *Tap, tap, tap.* He mumbled again. Yes, as always, Alice thought sarcastically, her cousin James was a barrel of fun.

It was then that it occurred to Alice that with her dad out of work, gifted-and-talented camp was probably off the agenda, not just for one day, but for the summer.

She felt that dizzy sensation again, and even felt tears welling up. No camp, for the first time since, well, since she could remember? It was a horrible thought.

But an even more horrible thought took shape immediately.

Because if her parents couldn't afford camp, they had to find *someone* to take care of her all summer and that would probably be James. No. *That*, she couldn't accept. She had to scuttle that plan somehow.

"Good morning, dork," she said with mock sweetness.

James pushed her hand out of his face. He pulled a pillow over his head. "Go away, demon child."

"I'm sorry," Alice said sweetly, "I can't understand what you just said. I don't speak dorkish." She tapped the back of his head. "Come on, dork, get up. You're watching me today."

James sat up as if a jolt of electricity had shot down his spine.

"I'm *what*?"

"You're watching me today. Isn't that wonderful …"

* * *

Alice felt exhausted by the evening, even though she'd napped most of the afternoon. It had been exhausting, though fun, playing the day away with little Aiden, and it had been exhausting trying not to worry about her dad being out of work, about not going to camp, about spending her summer with el dorko James.

It was exhaustion, she decided, that had made her weak enough to relent and help James clean up the living room. She had done such a great job letting Aiden wreck the room, it was a shame to undo all that work.

But James had looked genuinely frightened of his mother finding that unbelievable chaos in the living room. He had looked so vulnerable. Alice was too tired to stick to her guns. And, truth be told, it had given her real satisfaction to help James cover up the worst of the mess. He was so clueless when it came to being devious, so helpless compared to her …

They only had to wait a few minutes on the South Pasadena platform before a south-bound Gold Line train pulled up and they climbed aboard. The passenger car was surprisingly empty for an evening rush hour train. Usually they would've had to stand, but there were plenty of empty seats.

Alice scooted across a bench, sitting, as she always did, near a window, holding Aiden on her lap. James sat on the bench in front of her. "No," she said, "sit next to me."

"I want my own seat," James said. "I'm not sitting next to a couple of little kids."

"You have to sit next to me," Alice insisted. "Mom always sits between me and the aisle, so no one can take me."

James rolled his eyes. "Who's going to take *you*?"

"Some weirdo. You never know." L.A. was full of characters and strange people, and most of them seemed to gravitate to L.A.'s network of buses and trains. Alice knew this well. Since Peggy was nervous about driving, she often took public transportation, and she'd been dragging a reluctant Alice along with her since Alice was a baby.

"Watch out for strangers," Peggy warned her daughter repeatedly. "People notice you, so always be alert."

And people *did* notice Alice. They always had. She was as uncannily pretty as her cousin James was handsome; the kids stood out even in Los Angeles, a city largely built on good looks. People had always noticed Alice, waving to her and smiling at her and asking Peggy how old the child was. Alice found it gratifying, but a little unnerving sometimes, especially when her admirer was one of L.A.'s assorted strange characters.

"Just get over here and sit next to me," Alice said to James. She felt strangely vulnerable with an empty seat next to her. *Anyone* could plop down there; anyone could lean over and sweep her and Aiden up and run out the door with them. "Please, James," said Alice.

James sighed. If his cousin was *actually* going to be polite, he realized, then she must really be scared. He stood up, reluctantly, and then sat down next to her with ill grace.

"You shouldn't worry," said James. "If anyone *did* take you, they'd give you right back. Like that story, 'The Ransom of Red Chief'."

"Ha, ha, ha," Alice said sarcastically. "You're so hilarious. You should have a show."

"I know."

They rode in silence for a moment. James checked his cell phone for texts from Tariq or Hisoka.

"So," said Alice, "how mad is Aunt Roz that we're late?"

"Not at all."

"Not at all? That's weird."

"I know."

"That's a bad sign, James. That means something's wrong."

"You're so dramatic."

"Think about it. Your mother is always mad when you're late – when *anyone's* late."

"She sounds tired, that's all," said James. "I don't care *why* she's not mad, I'm just glad she's not. If she doesn't notice the paint and the ice cream stains in the living room, I'm home free."

"Hmmm," Alice said thoughtfully.

"Don't do that," James said, annoyed. "Just let me have a few minutes of peace."

"Hmmm."

Elaborately ignoring his cousin, James put away his cell phone, took his PSP out of his pocket and began playing "Mortal Mission," the classic game that launched the "Mortal" series in 1995.

Equally elaborately, Alice took *her* PSP from her pocket and began reading a digital Manga book.

Aiden watched Alice read for a moment, then his eyelids began fluttering, and then closed, and then he was snored quietly, nestled against her.

Outside the big train windows, South Pasadena flashed past, its tree-shaded streets, bright flower beds, Victorian manors and quaint bungalows. James and Alice were oblivious to the landscape, deeply focused on their electronic devices, James in the calm, Zen-like trance that made him such a formidable gamer, Alice completely focused on finishing the Manga book she had begun reading the day before.

The Mayberry-like charm of South Pasadena transitioned into a more industrial landscape of windowless, fortress-like warehouses. The train glided over the Arroyo Seco railroad bridge, a heady hundred feet above the 110 freeway below.

The buildings along the tracks became smaller, older, tilting and sagging at funhouse angles. Paint peeled, bricks crumbled and many buildings and walls were tagged with graffiti. Blazing against the decay, however, were flowers, vines and citrus trees. Flocks of laughing kids kicked soccer balls and played tag on the streets and in the yards beyond the tracks.

The train paused at the Highland Park Station, and then continued on in the shadow of Mount Washington and the dramatic Mission Revival tower of the Southwest Museum. On again, through the increasingly graffiti-tagged landscape the train dashed, stopping at Heritage Square and Lincoln Park before plunging on toward China Town.

James and Alice had ridden the Gold Line many times before, with one or both of their parents, or with their classes on school trips. It held no particular excitement for them, so they remained immersed in their game and book. Until …

When the train slid into a tunnel, James' head snapped up automatically.

It was a reflex, an instant response to the knowledge that something was wrong.

Alice looked up, too, a couple of seconds later. Without speaking, they both slipped their PSPs into their pockets.

The train's interior lights were dim, a feeble, token counter to the pitch blackness of the tunnel outside the windows. Not only were the lights dim, but all of a sudden they were flickering and buzzing loudly, as if they were about to burn out at any instant.

James and Alice glanced around the train car, then at each other. There was no need to speak. However much they argued, they were cousins, and they knew each other's facial expressions.

The car was suddenly empty, except for them and one passenger in a black hoodie. Something was very, *very* wrong and they both knew it.

Without thinking, Alice drew Aiden closer against her. The child was still blissfully asleep.

Alice wouldn't go so far as to shrink against James; that was too babyish, and beneath her dignity. But she did slide marginally, almost infinitesimally closer to James, and he gave her the faintest, almost subliminal smile of reassurance.

"Where did everybody go?" Alice whispered.

"I don't know," he whispered back. "But I *do* know there's no tunnel on this part of the trip."

"No," she agreed, "there's not."

It should have been a clear, open-air ride from Lincoln Heights into China Town, on a narrow elevated track that first crossed the Los Angeles River. This leg of the journey was almost like a roller coaster ride, you were so high above the ground and sometimes raced so fast.

But here they were, *under* the ground somehow ... and the tunnel seemed never-ending.

The only other passenger in the car was a big, burly person in a loose black hoodie, sitting a few seats ahead of them. The person had the hood pulled up over their head, so from the back James and Alice couldn't even tell if it was a man or an Amazonian woman.

Suddenly the train sped up for a few seconds. James and Alice were pressed back against their seats by the acceleration. Then, just as suddenly, the train slowed dramatically and they pitched forward, Alice instinctively cradling Aiden's head so he didn't strike the seat in front of them.

There was a loud, horrible screech of metal grinding against metal and then the train juddered to a stop.

"What ... the ... heck?" hissed Alice. James said a less polite word under his breath. A muffled vibration, as of a straining motor, stuttered through the floor and then the train fell still and silent. The dim lights buzzed and blinked and then finally were extinguished.

It was dark, pitch dark. Neither James nor Alice had ever experienced such blackness. In the city there was always ambient light from streetlamps and houses and cars. And on the occasions they'd been camping with the family there had been moonlight, and starlight, and the reassuring flicker of the campfire.

This was utter darkness, not a sliver of light.

James felt Alice's hand on his arm, her fingernails digging through his sleeve. Someone was drawing a ragged, choking breath. He realized it was him.

Pow! The lights blazed on without warning.

James and Alice winced against the light, so bright and unexpected that it hurt their eyes.

The stranger in the black hoodie stood over them. Alice screamed. James shouted in surprise. He flung a protective arm around his cousin and brother.

"Sorry to startle you," said the stranger in a soft but resonant voice.

He was tall, even taller than James' father Sam, at least six-and-a-half feet. His black hoodie was much too big; it draped him almost like an old-fashioned cloak. But he was a burly guy, a muscular guy, you could tell even though he was swathed in folds of dark material.

From within the dark hood, a gaunt, handsome face peered down at them. The stranger's features were strong, but delicately chiseled. Dead-black sunglasses hid the eyes. He had a dashing little mustache, like Errol Flynn's in the old "Robin Hood" movie, but an ugly scar twisted from the right side of his nose down to his right jaw. You could just see that his hair was close-shorn, like an athlete's ("or a prisoner's," thought James), like a thin layer of black lamb's wool close against his skull beneath the hood.

All in all, he looked to James and to Alice like a homeless wanna-be actor, one of the thousands of good-looking young adults who flocked to Los Angeles every year, hoping to be the next big star. You could see them by the dozens in Hollywood and on the Red Line subway between Hollywood and Downtown, beautiful young people in clothes that looked mismatched or cast off, always too big or two small, their faces so lovely but thin with hunger or malnutrition.

Sometimes they busked for coins, singing a song or dancing or telling jokes. They always, somehow, drew attention to themselves; they were performers, after all; if no one was noticing them, they almost felt they didn't exist. Alice was always intrigued by them when she and her mom saw them around Silver Lake and Hollywood, but Peggy always told her not to stare.

"Seems we've been delayed," said the stranger. He had a wonderful voice, quiet but rich in timbre, a heroic voice and a winning smile to boot. Definitely an actor, thought James. Question was, was he a harmless ham or some kind of dangerous nut?

"I fear I'm frightening you," said the stranger.

Alice couldn't quite place his accent. It wasn't totally American and it wasn't totally British. It was some kind of blend of both, like an American actor playing a Brit in PBS production.

"We're fine," said James. Actually, his heart was hammering in his chest, but he maintained a poker face and a voice as quiet and calm as the stranger's. James had slipped into that adrenalized Zen zone from which he played his video games.

The stranger extended his hand. James instantly tightened his protective grip on Alice and Aiden and slid a few inches along the seat, away from the stranger, closer to the window.

The stranger laughed, a big, booming laugh, as if something was hilarious. He even threw his head back while he laughed.

OK, thought James, *a potentially dangerous nut.*

"I've no intention of harming you," said the stranger. "I merely wish to shake your hand, and make your acquaintance."

"Not necessary," said James. "Maybe you could just take your seat. I'm sure they'll be fixing the train any second now."

James felt Alice's fingernails digging into his arm again, probably not so much from fear but to keep from laughing hysterically. They had both been on Metro buses and trains when they broke down, and they were never, but *never*, fixed quickly.

The stranger hesitated, and then withdrew his hand. He seemed rather disappointed. He plunked his large frame down in the seat directly across from them.

"Of course, you don't know who I am," he said. "And the bloody thing, pardon, the blasted thing is that I can't tell you. But I assure you, I'm a friend."

"That's great," James said calmly, "but we don't need any friends. We're good. Really."

Alice kicked James' shin. Alice was – had always been – particularly good at kicking people. It hurt like heck, and James stoically stifled a yelp. He knew why she'd kicked him. She wanted him to shut up, not to antagonize a hooded stranger who could probably go from friendly to psycho, without warning, in 2.3 seconds.

The stranger continued to smile at them. He tilted his head and seemed to focus on Aiden for the first time. "What a perfect little lad," he said, "what a likely lad."

Alice drew closer to the window and shielded Aiden with her arm.

The stranger laughed, another booming, merry laugh that was engaging and disturbing at the same time. James glanced at Alice. "*Loco*," she mouthed. He nodded fractionally.

"You must think I'm crazy," said the stranger.

"Not at all," James lied politely.

"Nonsense! Though it's good of you to pretend. I'm sure I *seem* crazy. It's been a long time since I've been in Los Angeles, and I know I'm oddly dressed and my speech has been anglicized, rather, by my lengthy sojourn in other lands. Crazy – that's the portrait, doubtless, that I present."

"Not at all," James lied again. *Total wacko*, he thought.

"My name," said the stranger, "well, I'm afraid I can't share my name. It's a dead secret for now. But all will be revealed in due course. What matters is not my name, but *your* names."

"We don't give our names to strangers," James said courteously. "In fact, we don't talk to strangers." Alice kicked him in the shin again. He managed not to yelp, but he drew a deep breath and couldn't speak for a moment.

"You seem nice, though," Alice told the stranger, in her most engaging way. She had decided the best way to handle this nut was to charm him until the train was rolling again – charm him or at the very least *not* antagonize him. "We don't mind telling you our names. I'm Rosa, and he's Sebastian, and this little guy is Damian."

"What a marvelous little liar you are," said the stranger. He smiled warmly, as if he were impressed with Alice rather than annoyed.

"I'm sure I don't know what you mean," she said, irritated. Now it was James' turn to kick her shin. She kicked him back, hard.

"Now, children," said the stranger, "there's no need for this bad blood. In fact, you're going to have to behave rather well together if you're to accomplish your objectives. Rather well together, rather better than you normally behave."

"I behave just fine," said Alice, stung. "*He's* always a jerk to *me*."

"Really?" asked James softly. "You're complaining about me to a total … stranger?"

"Please," the stranger said pleasantly, "let's be candid. You're both generally horrible to each other."

"How would *you* know?" demanded Alice.

"I know a great many things," said the stranger. "For example, I know that you three are the champions that will recover the lost touchstones of my clan."

"Er – cool," said Alice. *Yup – total wacko.*

"I can see you believe me daft," said the stranger. "But I speak truth. I bring you greetings from a village that is not so very far from here, yet not so very near. And I bring you a warning." He drew a sheet of neon-blue paper from within his voluminous hoodie and held it up just out of their reach.

"L.A.'s MAGICKAL HISTORY HUNT!" read the flier in huge block letters above a rather murky, smudgy old photo of the L.A. City Hall and its iconic pyramid. Beneath the photo it said "FREE entry! Youngsters aged 4 to 16. Experience history first-hand! Entry Deadline: June 23rd."

"That's today," said James.

"Indeed," agreed the stranger. "Now, lad, mark my words well. If you see this flier, you must avoid it. You must avoid it, and any people who attempt to coax you to enter this competition. It could be a matter of life and death."

He whisked the blue flier back into the depths of his cloak.

James shook his head slowly. His head felt heavy, like it was full of sand, and his vision was blurring. The entire encounter was so bizarre; it felt like being awake in the middle of a weird dream. A tunnel that shouldn't exist, a weirdo telling them to find some touchstones, and not to join some weirdo competition …

"But what *is* L.A.'s Magickal History Hunt?" Alice demanded. She loved puzzles and riddles and history; her curiosity overrode her fear of the stranger.

"It is a trap," said the stranger, "best avoided."

The train's interior lights suddenly intensified to full power, so bright that James and Alice winced. The floor trembled as the train engine rumbled back to life.

"Three important pieces of information," the stranger said quickly, "before I must depart. One: Only you three children can retrieve the touchstones. Two: My people will be able to offer you limited assistance from time to time. And three," he paused, looking intently from James to Alice to Aiden sleeping on Alice's lap.

"Three," Alice prompted impatiently.

"Three … *WAKE UP!*" the stranger shouted.

And the lights went out, plunging them all in total darkness.

* * *

The darkness was as thick as ink. It was like being blind. Alice screamed, and screamed and then screamed some more.

And then they were out of the tunnel, instantly, as if they'd never been in it. The train raced along the elevated track high above the concrete canyon of the L.A. River bed. Sunlight streamed through the windows; the horned, red-tiled roofs of China Town were visible in the near distance.

The stranger was gone, and the train was full of passengers who were all looking at Alice like she was crazy.

James squeezed her arm. "Cut it out," he said. "We're OK."

Alice stopped shrieking as if a switch had been thrown. She hiccupped once, softly, and fell silent. Aiden stirred, sitting up slowly, his curls tousled. He blinked drowsily at Alice.

"Allie OK?" he asked.

"I'm fine, Aidie." She patted his back. He put his thumb in his mouth, closed his eyes and settled back against her.

"So what the heck just happened?" Alice demanded of James.

He shrugged helplessly. His eyes were gritty with sleep sand, as if he'd been taking a nap, and his head ached. He thumbed the grit out of his eyes. *How the heck did Aidie sleep through that craziness?* he wondered.

"Who was that guy?" asked Alice. "You saw him, right? Who *was* he?"

"Yes, I saw him. And how do *I* know who he was?" asked James. "A hypnotist, maybe. He, like, hypnotized us. Gave us both the same illusion: the tunnel, the train breaking down, all that stuff."

"You should have *protected* us," said Alice. "You should've kicked his butt."

"Did you *see* how big he was?" James demanded. His adrenalin was dwindling; he was trembling a bit now with reaction, and with relief that they were all OK. "That guy was like the Hulk. What was I supposed to do?"

"You should've done *something*. Ow." Alice put a hand to her forehead. "Ow. I've got a headache. Do you have a headache?"

"Yes," he said.

"Good! If I have a headache, you should too, dork. It must be a reaction from being hypnotized. I can't even *believe* you're supposed to be taking care of us. Anyone can just hypnotize us or mangle us and you do *nothing*."

James was silent. Usually he tuned Alice out, but this stung. It was unfair; what could he possibly have done? But she was right, too. He hadn't protected them. He couldn't protect them.

The train stopped at the elevated China Town platform. The doors slid open and passengers streamed out, new passengers streaming in, mostly tourists. The doors closed and the train dashed toward Union Station.

To the southwest gleamed L.A.'s white civic buildings, the courthouses and administrative centers and the monolithic City Hall, capped by a pyramid. Beyond the Civic Center rose the shining glass and metal towers of L.A.'s Financial District, the one area of the city where tall buildings were permitted, the one concentrated patch of land that resembled a mini-Manhattan.

That's where Roz and Peggy worked – the Financial District. But by now, James knew, they were both in Union Station, waiting impatiently for their children to arrive.

The train pulled alongside Platform One, just outside the Mission-Pueblo-style train station, with its famous tower, and tile mosaics, and pale mocha-colored walls.

James gently took Aiden from Alice and stood up, cradling Aiden against his shoulder. The little boy didn't wake. Alice stood too. They both knew the drill; Union Station was a major hub, the station where the most people boarded and the most people detrained, and not everyone was polite about it.

The cousins shouldered their way into the swirling crowd, the press of passengers, a wild hodgepodge of business people, teachers, kids, moms with strollers, elderly people leaning on walkers and canes and the general assortment of homeless, winos and criminal-types.

The mass of exiting passengers swept them out onto the platform and down the steps into the long corridor that connected both of the station terminals. They bore right, toward the original terminal, where their mothers were waiting.

"So," said Alice, "what do we tell our moms about the weirdo on the train?"

James considered it. "I'm fine with not telling them anything," he said.

Alice nodded. "OK," she said.

He was surprised. "Seriously? You're not going to throw me under the bus?"

"To tell you the truth," Alice said, "normally I'd love to, but in this case I just wanna forget the whole thing. And there'll be plenty of other chances for me to throw you under the bus this summer."

"Not really," he said. "I plan not to see you at all summer."

"Fourth of July," she said.

"Yeah. Yeah, that's unavoidable. But other than that, I'm going to be so busy with Mortal Quest and Tariq and Hisoka I'm going to forget I have a cousin."

"Promise?"

"You bet."

"Good. Because I'm going to be so busy at camp," – *if Mom and Dad can still afford to send me to camp*– "and with Penny and all my friends, I'm going to forget *I* have a cousin. In fact, I already forgot. Except Aidie, of course. I would never forget him. But my older, mean, dorky cousin – that's you – I've already forgotten."

"Great," James said absently. His mind was already on Level 27 of Mortal Quest and how he and the guys were going to get past the giant spiders.

Chapter Three – Magickal History Hunt
June 23rd – Los Angeles

Peggy and Roz sat in a couple of the tall, leather-upholstered chairs that marched in rows throughout the original terminal. They had chosen seats near the Information Booth, which was not staffed at this late hour. Peggy and Roz held paper cups of coffee; they were deep in conversation.

James knew immediately that something was very wrong, even more wrong than things had been that morning.

Aunt Peggy's eyes were so red from crying that it looked like she'd burst some blood vessels. Her nose was red too. She dabbed her eyes with a tissue when she saw the kids approaching, but it was too late to hide that she'd been crying hard.

What *really* freaked him out, though, was that when his mother saw them, she gave them a big, sweet smile.

James knew Roz loved him and Aiden, and her niece Alice too, but Roz was not the kind of sweet, sappy lady who gave people big smiles. Her way of showing how much she loved them was getting on their case about homework, grades, schedules, teeth-brushing, washing behind ears, sitting too close to the television, and other such things – the list was infinite.

James could sense Alice tensing beside him as she saw her mother's teary face and her aunt's out-of-character smile.

"It's OK," James whispered to Alice.

"Shut up, dork," she hissed back.

"Hi, kids," called Roz, "did you have a nice day?"

"Uh, it was great," said James. *Who are you and what have you done with my* real *mother?* he wondered.

"Good, good," said Roz. He could tell she wasn't really listening. He could've said "Alice and I joined the army and Aiden robbed a bank," and his mother still would've said "Good, good," in that frighteningly chipper voice.

"How was *your* day?" he asked.

"Good, good," said Roz. "Why don't you three gather around. Great. OK, you know I don't like to sugar-coat things, so here it is: there are going to be some changes to our summer plans."

"We kind of figured that," said James. "How about the good news first?"

"That'd be great," said Roz, "except there really *isn't* any good news. Dad is going to need to stay at the New Mexico site all summer. They ran into some delays, and there isn't any work out here right now anyway. And, well, we just can't make ends meet unless he works through the summer there."

James blinked. He felt like someone had just thrown a bucket of icy water in his face. He had been missing his dad so much, for so long now, and playing it off as no big deal. But it *was* a big deal. Dad was finally supposed to be coming home – and then the rug got yanked out from under their feet.

"I'm sorry, James," said Roz. "But it gets worse, so brace yourself. You're going to be seeing a lot less of me, too; I'm going to be working a lot of nights to help make ends meet. And, you," she took Alice's hand, "you need to know your mom's going to be working nights, too. And your dad … I'm sorry, Alice, but your Dad hasn't been able to find any work in L.A."

"I know," said Alice. "Mom told me. Is he …" *I will not cry,* Alice told herself sternly. *I will not cry.* "Aunt Roz – is my dad staying in New Mexico all summer like Tio Sam?"

"Yes," said Roz. "Your dad's in New Mexico and he's going to work with your Tio Sam all summer. So they'll have each other to hang around with. They won't be alone."

Alice bit her lip. *Dad – gone all summer. And I didn't even get a chance to say goodbye ….*

"It gets even better," Roz said drily, but not without sympathy. "There's not going to be any camp for anyone this summer. No Gifted Camp for you, Alice. Not even Happy Face Camp for Aiden."

"Aidie want Happy Camp!!" shouted Aiden, and then promptly burst into tears. When his mother reached out to touch his face he drew back, stamping his foot and crying harder. Alice knelt down and hugged him.

"It's OK, Aidie," she said, "we don't need dumb old camp."

"Camp not dumb," sniffled Aiden, burying his face against his cousin's shoulder.

An idea was forming in James' mind – a horrifying idea.

He turned his gaze slowly from Alice and Aiden to his mother. "So … if our dads are away, and our moms are working all the time, and there's no camp …"

"Yup," said Roz.

"Oh, *come on!*" wailed James.

"What?" asked Alice, only half-interested, drying Aiden's tears with her sleeve.

"*I* have to watch you all summer!" said James.

"No!" cried Alice. It was the fearful thought that had crossed her mind that morning – and now it was reality!

"Yay!" shouted Aiden. "Yay! Camp Brother! Brother Camp!"

"I guess that's about it," said Roz. She looked tired. She rubbed the dark circles under her eyes.

"That's it, all right!" said James. "It sure is!"

"This isn't going to be a picnic for any of us," said Roz. "Do you think Aunt Peggy and I want to work all these extra hours? Do you think we don't miss your dads? It'll be a tough summer, but we'll get through it together."

"Apart, you mean," James muttered.

"And when this is all behind us," Roz continued, "we're going to have great stories to tell about this summer. That's how it is. It's tough getting through it, but then you have stories for a lifetime."

"I'm good on stories," said James. "I've got plenty of stories. What I really would've liked this summer, is my dad."

"You'll have him back in September. Probably. All right," Roz sighed, "Aunt Peggy and I still have a few things to talk about, so why don't you kids stroll around for a few minutes."

James was speechless. *Stroll around?* In Union Station, which, despite being, architecturally speaking, an Art Deco treasure, was always brimming with transients and colorful characters? Usually his mother warned him *against* strolling around places like this. And now she was telling him to do just that.

Alice squeezed his arm hard. Alice was looking at her mother, real fear in her eyes.

Peggy was wiping her eyes with a handkerchief, head down, the picture of despair.

Alice started toward her mother, but Roz said sharply, "Go on, kids, take a walk. Come back in a few minutes. Or maybe ten. "

James took Alice's elbow and steered her toward the other end of the terminal, toward the food court. The scent of toasted pastries and brewed coffee drifting from the snack shops was intoxicating; James remembered he hadn't eaten yet today.

"Come on," he told Alice, "let's get something to eat."

She shook away James' hand, but followed him.

Aiden took a deep breath, inhaling the scent of the pastries, grinned, and slipped out of James' arms. He took one of Alice's hands and one of James' and accompanied them into the coffee shop.

"Aidie wants cookie," he said. "Chocolate chip. *Two* chocolate chips!"

* * *

James only had a five-dollar bill in his pocket, just enough for them all to split a big chocolate chip cookie and a bottle of juice. They sat at a table well away from Peggy and Roz. They noshed the cookie and passed the juice back and forth.

"So, this all totally sucks," said Alice.

"Yeah," James agreed.

"It wouldn't be so bad if you weren't such a dork," she said.

"Or if you weren't such a narcissistic brat," he said.

"I'm not a narcissist! I've never been a narcissist! How can you call me, of all people, a narcissist, when I'm 100 percent not?" Alice demanded.

James didn't answer. They subsided into a discontented silence.

They were sitting in the oldest part of the station. It was lovely, with its dark marble and its dark woodwork and its Art Deco tiles, but they'd seen it all before, since they were tiny kids; they were inured to the beauty. They sat without speaking for a few moments, lost in their own miserable thoughts until Aiden decided to provide some comic relief.

"Look, look Aidie!" said Aiden at one point, proudly blowing streams of apple juice out of his nose and down the front of his shirt.

Alice and James laughed in spite of themselves, scrubbing Aiden's damp shirt with napkins. "Again!" laughed Aiden, reaching for the juice.

"No," said Alice. "No more, Aidie." She put the bottle out of his reach.

James went to a nearby trash can to toss the napkins.

As he walked back to the table, he saw it: a neon-blue sheet of paper affixed to a post on the far wall. He paused, staring. Alice followed his gaze.

"What the *heck*," she said. "Don't tell me that's the *Magickal History Hunt* flier? The one the weird guy on the train showed us."

"I think so," James said.

They were sitting across from the station's old ticket-selling area. It had been blocked off years before by a low, wooden barrier. The general public wasn't allowed in, but passers-by could see over the barrier, could see the beautiful high ceilings and the marble-and-wood counters where in the olden days travelers bought their train tickets.

The way the light fell through the tall, narrow windows and the way the dust floated in the shafts of light, giving the air texture, had always struck James as a bit magical. When he was a kid, of course, when he was little and believed in magic.

Without thinking about it, Alice stood, and Aiden stood too, copying her. The three children walked slowly toward the abandoned wing and paused at the blue flier affixed to the post. It was indeed the same announcement the stranger had showed them on the train. *L.A. Magickal History Hunt*.

"What does this *mean*?" asked Alice. She loved puzzles, but it annoyed her when she couldn't solve them. "Could this day get any weirder? This is the contest the hypnotist guy on the train told us *not* to enter."

"Yeah." James reached out hesitantly and touched the flier. It was real. It felt like normal paper under his fingertips. Alice reached up and tore it down, shoved it into her pocket.

"I'm keeping this," she said. "Whatever happens, this is proof *something* weird happened today."

"Of course something weird happened," said James. "Who says it didn't?"

He moved closer to the barrier that separated them from the deserted wing.

Over the low wooden wall he could see, in the dim, glittering shafts of evening light, that there was a booth of some kind against the far wall, a booth like those at a school carnival. Two women in garish dresses stood behind it.

"I think we're supposed to go in there," James said.

Alice took a deep breath, ready to argue. *The guy on the train told us not to. He told us this Magickal History Hunt contest is life-or-death.*

But Alice closed her mouth without saying a word. She could sense it too, what her cousin was sensing. It was almost like a magnet drawing her into the abandoned wing. For just a moment, she thought she saw, in the shafts of evening light, some kind of glowing sparks, like the bits of fire that flew off sparklers on the Fourth of July, bright little flashes that faded under a flow of murky shadows.

She shook her head. *Great. On top of everything else, I'm getting a detached retina!*

Aiden seemed to sense something too. He looked up at James and Alice and then pointed toward the booth.

"There," Aiden said firmly.

There was a gate in the barrier, with frosted glass, and brass hinges.

"Probably locked," said James, but he pushed it anyway, and it swung open smoothly.

They passed through the gate, and it closed soundlessly behind them. They walked toward the booth, the heels of their sneakers silent on the marble floor.

James glanced back over his shoulder. *Why isn't anyone stopping us? We're not supposed to be in here.* But none of the passers-by on the proper side of the barrier seemed to notice the children …

When they reached the booth they could see that it was a homespun thing, made of plywood and cardboard and poster paint. It looked like something kids would build to sell lemonade or ice tea on their front lawn.

L.A. MAGICKAL HISTORY HUNT was painted on the front of the booth in large, slightly crooked, rainbow-colored letters. *Kids 4 to 16 yrs. Entry Deadline: TODAY!!*

On the wall behind the booth hung a strange clock. Its numbers were reversed, noted Alice, the six at the top and the twelve at the bottom. Not only were the numbers switched, the hands of the clock moved backward, counterclockwise instead of clockwise.

"Hello, duckies," said the blonde woman behind the counter. Her accent was British, not refined, but rather, as Alice knew from watching a lot of PBS, a cockney accent. It sounded phony, theatrical. *I don't like her,* Alice realized instantly.

With carefully masked disapproval Alice took in the woman's strange ensemble, a purple plaid dress, mustard-yellow leggings and crazy hat, a bizarre combination of green top hat on the right side and pink pirate hat on the left. *Fashion disaster*, Alice thought.

The other woman behind the booth was a red-head, and she was no less strangely dressed in a purple paisley dress and bright yellow leggings, with a combined green top hat and royal blue pirate hat.

"You're just in time," said the blonde, pointing up at the backward clock. "Let's see, now. Contestants must be aged four to sixteen. You little lambs *look* ages four to sixteen."

"We are," said James. "We're exactly ages four to sixteen."

"Now, then, that's perfect, an't it? An't it, perfect, Flo?"

"Perfect," agreed the red-head. "Lovely."

The women appeared to be in their mid-twenties, plain rather than pretty, but it was hard to tell under their heavy layer of makeup, the foundation, powder, eye shadow, rouge and lipstick.

Theater troops had visited Alice's gifted-and-talented camp in past years, performing for the campers and giving them acting lessons. They had been heavily made-up, like these women; stage makeup, it was called. It had to be thick and exaggerated to be visible to the audience in the back rows.

"Now, it's free to enter the contest," said the blonde, "but if you win, the prize is enormous."

"What is the prize?" asked James.

"The prize? What's the *contest*?" asked Alice.

Both the blonde and red-head darted shrewd glances at Alice. The women smiled, but the smile didn't touch their eyes.

"You'll be the smart one, eh?" said the blonde. "She's the smart one, Flo."

"So I gather, Lou" said the red-head.

"The contest," said the blonde, "is an h'exploration o' historical Los Angeles. Children have fun while learning L.A. history. Contestants ages four to sixteen visit historical-like locations around the city and its entrails – "

"Environs," corrected Flo, the red-head.

"Sorry, environs," said the Lou the blonde. "Contestants travel around the city and its *environs* solving puzzles and completing challenges. There is, you see, a special little prize at each location, and you have to find it. The first team to complete *every* challenge satisfactorily and turn in *all* the little prizes wins the grand prize."

"What about the runners-up?" asked Alice.

"They lose," said the blonde, with an unpleasant smile.

"Well, that sounds interesting," said James politely, "but we're not going to have time for a contest this summer. I have to watch these little monsters, and somehow find time to be in the Mortal Quest competition. So thanks anyway, but we – "

"Just sign here," said the blonde, pushing a gleaming silver fountain pen and a sheet of parchment across the counter toward James.

"Sure thing," he said, and, as if hypnotized, he found himself picking up the pen and signing what appeared to be a one-page contract.

"Mortal Quest," chuckled the blonde, "*we'll* give you a Mortal Quest, dearie!"

"Oh, my, yes," grinned the red-head.

"You next," said the blonde, and Alice found herself reaching for the pen and signing too.

"Very good," said the blonde and red-head together, nodding at each other with satisfaction.

"Aidie pen!" called Aiden, reaching upwards. "Aidie pen!"

"There's no need for him to sign," said the blonde. "You don't have to sign, duckling."

"Aidie pen!!!" shouted Aiden.

Aiden grabbed one of James' arms, and swung himself up onto the counter. He grabbed the pen from Alice and scribbled a crooked line at the bottom of the paper – Aiden's version of his signature. Then his face lost its storm cloud expression; he handed the pen to Alice, and gave the women his most angelic and winning smile.

"Well, well," said the blonde, "*you* must be the tricky one."

James didn't like the way the women were looking at Aiden.

He didn't like *anything* about the whole situation. James gently picked up Aiden and held the child against his shoulder, turning away from the booth and the strange women.

"Ah," said the red-head, "the protector."

"And so the chosen are complete," said the blonde.

And so the chosen are complete. The words seemed familiar to James. He had heard them before ... But it had been a man's voice saying them.

"Who *are* you?" Alice asked the women.

"We an't anybody special," sniffed Lou, the blonde. "Functionaries, duckie. We an't important like you three."

The red-head, Flo, sneered at Alice with open dislike.

"And what document did we just sign?" asked Alice. Her head seemed to be clearing now; logic was returning.

"The paper? Just the contest agreement," said Lou. She reached for the paper but Alice was too quick for her, whisking the paper off the counter and reading it.

"We the undersigned," Alice read aloud, "do hereby agree to follow all rules of *L.A. Magickal History Hunt*, and we shall relinquish all magickal objects obtained, at the conclusion of the contest, upon pain of – "

"Give me that," hissed the blonde, snatching the paper from Alice's hand.

"Since we signed it, we need copies of it," said Alice. "That's the law."

"Yes, owlet, we'll see you get copies," Lou said unpleasantly.

"When?"

"Soon. Soon, pet. My, an't you the smart one, though? Even more so than less so, if you follows me meanin'. Now," Lou began rummaging around under the booth, "all contestants get a little kit, like, you know, trinkets what'll help you along your way. This is for you," she handed a small, black leather pouch to James, "and this is for you," a small, blood-red beaded pouch to Alice, "and this is for *you*, my likely lad," a small, sky-blue felt pouch to Aiden. "Please be advised that you should keep these kits with you at *all* times, and we the facilitators of the *Magickal History Hunt* competition shall not be held liable for no mayhem nor morbid outcomes which results from any of you *not* havin' your kits handy."

"Was that in the contract?" Alice asked skeptically.

"Section two, para three," Flo said smoothly. "Now, on account of we've concluded our business, and these darn shoes is killin' me feet, I declare our business concluded." She rummaged under the counter again, and retrieved what appeared to be a handful of glittering silver powder.

"What's that?" asked Alice.

Instead of answering, Flo dashed the handful of powder to the floor.

It swirled and billowed and expanded into a glittering cloud that covered the entire booth and blinded the children. They hacked and coughed and rubbed their watering eyes.

When the shimmering cloud finally cleared, the booth was gone. The children were alone.

Chapter Four – The Sircus of Impossible Magicks
June 24th – Los Angeles

When James woke, it was still dark outside. He felt exhausted; he had slipped in and out of sleep all night long, having nightmares about the strange man on the train and the strange women at the train station.

What had happened at Union Station yesterday was bizarre, but it had happened to all three of them. He and Alice had discussed it quietly before rejoining their mothers, deciding that either all three of the children had lost their minds at the same time, or they had been the victims of some truly weird hypnotists.

Half-asleep, lost in thought, James got dressed, combed his hair, and brushed his teeth.

He went down the hall and peeked into Aiden's room. Aiden was sprawled across his small bed, sleeping the deep, perfect sleep of the very young.

James went down to the second floor, down a side corridor, and looked into his mother and dad's room. His mom was, as he expected, already gone. She was on a new schedule, effective immediately, working an early shift at her first job so she could get to her second job, the night job, on time. *Mom's at work ... Dad's in New Mexico.* James felt small and lonely.

He padded down the stairs to the kitchen in his bare feet. He smelled fresh-brewed coffee.

There was a note taped to the coffee maker. "James, have a cup. You'll need it. Mother." He smiled wryly. Yeah, he was gonna need it all right, if today was even *half* as crazy as yesterday.

From the street there was the chug-and-cough of a small engine idling, the slam of a car door, the slap of footsteps running up the walk. The front door knob rattled, and then there was a pounding on the door panels.

James unlocked the door, and was almost flattened as Alice pushed it open and stormed past him. He caught a glimpse of Aunt Peggy's microscopic VW bug in the driveway, and Aunt Peggy compressed behind the wheel. She waved to him as she drove away.

"Where's Aiden?" asked Alice, tossing her red messenger bag and her red-and-black sweater on the couch.

"Aiden's still sleeping."

"Coffee smells good," said Alice.

She swept into the kitchen and poured out a cup of coffee.

"Make yourself at home," James called sarcastically. "I take milk, no sugar."

"This coffee is for *me*, dork. Brain fuel. Get your own." Alice rummaged around the refrigerator. "Ew! What is this? Everything's all gross in here!"

"My mother hasn't had time to go to the store lately," James said defensively. "Who asked you to stick your head in our refrigerator?"

Alice pulled a quart of Pasadena Farms milk from the fridge. She shook it, heard a faint sloshing. She checked the expiration date, opened the carton and sniffed cautiously.

"There's barely any left, but it seems OK," she said dubiously. She poured a healthy dollop into the coffee cup, then stirred in four packets of sugar and a dash of cinnamon sugar.

"You're totally going to get diabetes," said James, pouring his own cup of coffee. He grabbed the milk from Alice, added it to his cup, and tossed the empty milk carton in the trash. He inhaled the coffee fragrance deeply before taking a sip. "That's the stuff," he said.

"Amen," agreed Alice, downing half her cup of coffee in one deep draught.

"You're going to get diabetes from all that sugar," James predicted, "*and* you're going to stunt your growth from the coffee."

"My parents let me have coffee sometimes," said Alice. "It's perfectly safe. Besides, I like being petite. We don't *all* want to be gangly, lumbering dorks." She smiled sweetly. "Now, on to something that r*eally* matters – what are we going to do about those weirdos?"

James took another sip of coffee, slowly, thoughtfully.

"Earth to dorko, earth to dorko – can you hear me, mister dorko? Who *were* those people?"

"I don't know," said James. "We shouldn't rush to any conclusions. I think we're agreed they're some kind of circus freaks. Or carnival freaks. Some type of freaky entertainers."

"Duh, of course."

"And they were messing with our minds."

"Again: 'Duh'."

"But the question is, 'Why'?"

Alice downed the rest of her coffee. "I don't like that they got us to sign something. Who knows what it was? Not that it matters, technically, since we're minors, but you really don't want your signature floating around on something you didn't get a chance to read. We need to find out who they are and report them."

"To who?"

"To whom. And, to the police, of course. You can't just scare little kids and get them to sign things and then disappear. That's all totally illegal."

"What really bugs me," said James, "is that they seemed to *know* us. Like, they weren't just randomly messing with random kids."

"True. And, very disturbing. Could, I mean …"

"Could what?"

"Could someone be mad at our parents or something? Is this some kind of prank to get at them?"

James shrugged, sipped more coffee. "I don't think so," he said. "I mean, our parents are great, and we love them and all, but it's not like they're, like-"

"Like they're anybody," Alice agreed, finishing his thought. "Just regular, nice people."

"Yeah."

Alice snapped her fingers. "Got it!" she said.

She dashed out of the kitchen and down the hallway, opened the front door and grabbed the *Los Angeles Telegraph* off the door mat. She returned to the kitchen, already unfolding the pages and skimming headlines.

"We're on the same wavelength," James said approvingly. "Check the entertainment section. See if there's a circus or a carnival in town."

"I know, I know. That's what I'm doing. I'm miles ahead of you, as usual." Alice thumbed through the newspaper, shedding irrelevant pages until the kitchen counter was adrift with them. "OK, here we go. Concert at LA Live … Disneyland discounts … movie reviews … THERE!"

"What?"

James craned his neck so he could read over her shoulder.

The headline read "*Sircus of Impossible Magicks* Stuns Seniors at Sony Stadium". Above the article was a smudgy black-and-white photo of a woman in a sparkling dress doing a handstand on a galloping pony. Behind her were tiers of seats filled with gaping senior citizens.

The woman in the sparkly dress looked like Lou, the blonde from Union Station.

"'Yesterday,'" James read aloud, "'a troupe from London's famous *Sircus of Impossible Magicks* gave a free performance at Sony Stadium for local senior citizens. Residents of Sunnybreeze Rest Home, Cathedral Retirement Home, and Pasadena Palm Acres were bused to the stadium and given free popcorn and candy apples.'"

"That sounds really bad for their teeth," interjected Alice.

"Shh."

"Don't shush me! Old people have really bad teeth. Or false teeth. You can't give them things like popcorn. And candy apples. Remember when old Tia Rosa-"

"'For two hours,'" James interrupted loudly, "the seniors sat in stunned amazement as the *Sircus of Impossible Magick*'s seasoned troupe performed a broad range of death-defying, seemingly magical stunts, from acrobatics on horseback to daring flame-juggling dances on a high wire one-hundred feet above the stadium floor.'"

"Blah, blah, don't read the whole stupid thing," said Alice. "Do you see anything about our weirdos? Or the *Magickal History Hunt* contest? Although it's significant enough," she said, "that they misspell 'magic' the same way."

James continued reading. "The *Sircus of Impossible Magicks* claims to have been founded in AD 576 by the wizard later fictionalized as Merlin, advisor to the legendary King Arthur. The original troupe was organized to preserve and perform Merlin's most astonishing magical feats, as well as feats developed by the great magicians of every era.'"

"'Impossible Magicks'?" snorted Alice. "A little hypnotism, some flash powder, some circus tricks – not *that* impressive."

James turned the page at the jump, found the rest of the article and kept reading. "'Millie Von Berger, 84, of Pasadena Palm Acres said "It was the best circus I ever saw! Even when I was a little girl, I never saw anything as amazing as this."'"

Alice glanced at the smudgy black-and-white photo of Millie Von Berger. "Jeesh," said Alice, "she looks like she could've seen the building of the pyramids."

James continued. "'Francisco Alberto Ramon Rios, 92, of Sunnybreeze Rest Home said "The best part was the fire juggling. They didn't even use a net. It looked like they slipped at one point but somehow they didn't fall! It was like magic!" The *Sircus of Impossible Magicks* will be performing at Sony Stadium through the first week of July. Call Ticketseller or visit www.ticketseller.com for tickets and information.'"

James dropped the paper onto the counter.

"So, it has to be them," he said. "The *Sircus of Impossible Magicks*."

"Agreed," said Alice. "But why are they bothering *us*? They're from London. Do we have any connection to London?"

"Not since, like, 1676," said James, "when one of our ancestors left England and sailed to Massachusetts."

"How would you possibly know *that*?"

"Had to do a report last semester. American history. When did our ancestors settle here, etc. The Myrddins got here in 1676, and then the Irish side came over with the potato famines, and then the Iztali family moved to Los Angeles in 1955 – that's where the Mayan comes from."

"So no London connection since 1676? That doesn't help us at all," complained Alice. "Unless … what was the guy's name, the guy from England?"

"Jonathan Myrddin."

"Maybe Jonathan Myr – what is it again?"

"Myrddin. M – y – r – d – d – i – n."

"Maybe Jonathan Myrddin was a member of the old *Sircus of Impossible Magicks*."

James made a skeptical grimace. "Do you really think there *was* a *Sircus of Impossible Magicks*?"

"Why not?" asked Alice. "There were all kind of weird groups in the old days. People really believed in magic, you know? There were the alchemists, who were trying to turn lead into gold – that goes back to ancient Egypt. And there have been con artists forever. Don't you *ever* read any history?" she finished with supreme disdain.

"Hey, at least I know our family history, genius."

"But do you know anything *useful*? What did this ancestor of ours, this, this – "

"Jonathan *Myrddin*," James said smugly.

"Yeah, what did this Jonathan Myrddin do?"

"Hang on a second," said James. He left the kitchen. Alice heard his feet padding down the long hall, heard him climbing stairs, heard a door open. Very distantly there was a thud, a muttered imprecation, and then his footsteps approaching.

"OK," James said, "I *knew* I saved this. In case I ever have to do family history report for another class, I can just change the date on it."

"You are, like, the laziest student ever."

"It's called efficiency, Alice. No need to reinvent the wheel." James flicked through the school report. "OK … OK … here." He held the page out so that Alice could read it with him. "Second paragraph. 'In 1676 Jonathan Myrddin, a Dean of Divinity at Oxford University, packed up his worldly goods and his wife Sarah and set off for the new world.'"

"He wouldn't 'pack up' his wife," objected Alice, "and 'the new world' is too, too trite, but who knew that we were related to a Dean of Oxford University? Cool! That must be partly where I get my dazzling intelligence."

"A Dean," said James. "That means … he ran the school?"

Alice rolled her eyes. "Not the school, the Divinity program. You know, becoming a professor of religion, becoming a minister of the church. I mean, it's not running the place but it's still totally cool."

"And you call *me* a dork! How do you know all that useless junk?" James shook his head.

Alice ignored him grandly. "Soooooo … if Jonathan Myrddin was the Dean of Divinity, he was dealing with God, religion, the supernatural … It's not such a giant step to say he *might've* been involved with the *Sircus of Impossible Magicks*."

"If they existed then."

"Which they probably did. Where's your computer? Let's Google the *Sircus*."

The sound of pattering feet filled the hallway, and Aiden appeared, leaping down the steps into Alice's arms like the crazy little wild boy he was. Alice caught him and staggered back, almost dropping him.

"Allie!!!" shouted Aiden gleefully. "Allie! Allie's here!!"

Alice gave him a bear hug.

"Allie is very happy to see Aidie," she said.

"Allie!!" He gave her another hug, and then slipped to the floor. He dashed over to James and hugged his brother's leg, and then stood back nodded at the microwave. "Oatmeal," he commanded regally.

"Aye, aye," said James. He rummaged around the shelves for a packet of oatmeal and a bowl.

"While you're doing that, I'll research the *Sircus*," said Alice. "Where's your computer again?"

"I didn't tell you," said James, popping a bowl of oatmeal and water into the microwave.

"Please, you think I'm going to break your stupid, lame computer?" demanded Alice.

"Not at all. Because you're not going to touch it." James thumbed the "Start" button, and the bowl of oatmeal began spinning in the microwave.

"I'm not a baby," said Alice. "I know how to use a computer. Probably better than you do."

"Yeah," said Aiden, "Allie not baby!" He put his tiny hands on his hips and glowered up at James.

"It's so wonderful," said James, "how you've totally turned my baby brother – *my* baby brother – against me."

Alice shrugged. "What can I say? He knows a winner when he sees one."

The microwave began to beep insistently. James took out the bowl of oatmeal, stirred it and set it on the counter to cool.

"Don't let him touch it for a minute," said James. "It's really hot. I'll be right back." He disappeared into the depths of the massive Victorian.

Alice scooped up Aiden and held him on her lap while the oatmeal cooled. "Did you have a good sleep, Aidie?"

Aiden shook his head darkly. He snuggled against Alice. "Bad sleep," he said. "Bad guys. Mean girls."

"That's just a dream, Aidie," Alice said comfortingly. "No one can hurt you. Me and James watch you really good, right?" Aiden nodded against her shoulder. "What kind of bad guys were in your dream," Alice asked. "What kind of mean girls?"

Aiden shuddered and burrowed into her shoulder.

"Monsters," said Aiden.

Alice felt an icy finger on her spine when he said it. *Monsters.* After the day they'd had yesterday, the word "monsters" had a new gravitas – especially since her sleep had been broken by nightmares of dark caverns, dark corridors, and shadowy, menacing figures.

"Dreams are pretend," she told Aiden, but she was talking to herself, too. "Remember, you watched that scary movie yesterday, when Allie took her nap."

Alice stirred the oatmeal. A fragrant steam of maple and brown sugar rose from the bowl. She took a tentative bite.

"Hey, *Aidie's* oatmeal!" said Aiden, outraged.

"Yes, yes, it's Aidie's oatmeal. Allie has to make sure it's not going to burn Aidie."

"Oh." Aidie tilted his head. "Oatmeal OK?"

"Yeah. Go ahead." Alice handed him the spoon. Aiden began gobbling his breakfast.

James returned, opening his laptop computer and plugging the power cord into the counter outlet. In a couple of minutes he had it up and running and was on the Internet.

Finishing his oatmeal, Aiden demanded another bowl. Alice prepared it while James read aloud from the computer screen.

"OK, Google directs us to a *Sircus of Impossible Magicks* Wikipedia site. Wikipedia is- "

"I know, I know," said Alice. "*Everyone* knows what Wikipedia is. What does it say about the *Sircus*?"

"Well, it says pretty much … Yeah, supposedly founded in 576 AD – by the wizard Merlin and his followers. They had discovered 'many impossible magical secrets of the universe, and pledged to safeguard them from evil sorcerers and preserve them for the cause of good, until the world's heart shall cease to beat.'"

"Sounds noble," said Alice. "Crazy, but noble. Whereas our friends on the train and at the station didn't seem all that noble."

"But plenty crazy."

"Is there more?"

"Yeah," said James. "It goes on … 'It seems likely that the ancient *Sircus of Impossible Magicks* is a fictional invention of the modern *Sircus of Impossible Magicks*. In the first place, there is no historical evidence to support the existence of King Arthur or Merlin the magician. In the second place, if Merlin did exist, it was likely during the late 5th and early 6th centuries – many decades *before* the *Sircus* was supposedly founded."

Alice waved her hand impatiently. "The records at that time were all primitive and muddled. Who's to say, if they were real, Arthur and Merlin didn't live around 576?"

"You'll be a great lawyer," James said.

Alice acknowledged the compliment as her mere due with another impatient wave. "What else, what else? Something that helps us. Skip ahead."

"I hate skipping ahead," said James. "That's not logical. We might miss something."

Alice sighed.

"OK," he continued, "Hmm …"

"For crying out loud," said Alice, handing Aiden his fresh bowl of oatmeal. "*I'm* going to be 576 before you find something!"

"Wait, this is interesting," said James. "'For its first thousand years, the *Sircus of Impossible Magicks* operated under conditions of almost total secrecy. Members recognized each other by a special tattoo that designated their animal totem.'"

"If it was such a big secret, how come it didn't die out? How did they get new members?"

"Don't be so impatient," said James, "it's the next sentence. 'Members were rarely recruited from outside, but rather recruited from within the families of existing members. Children that passed the 'Tests of Magick' were inducted into the *Sircus* and followed in their parents' footsteps. On rare occasions, talented outsiders were invited into the troupe, but if they failed the tests they had to be eliminated to keep the *Sircus*' existence secret.'"

"Harsh!"

"No kidding! 'Because of this secrecy, little is known of the *Sircus*' first thousand years. However, after the Great Fire of London in 1666, a cache of documents was found in a strongbox in the charred residence of Sir Dennis Arthur, documents that listed many of the contemporary members of the *Sircus of Impossible Magicks*. While condemned as a hoax or the ravings of a madman – for Sir Arthur was generally considered to be addled – the list caused a brief scandal, mentioning as it did the names of many prominent Englishmen, including nobles and *respected deans of university*.'"

"Jeez!" said Alice.

"'This caused a great hue and cry for some days, and many of the gentlemen and ladies named in the documents as members of the *Sircus* fled England for the new world and points unknown. However, few citizens wanted to believe that pillars of society could possibly belong to a secret magical society, and in the aftermath of the great blaze, the focus shifted to the much more pressing matter of rebuilding the great city of London.'"

"That ... is ... *incredible*!" said Alice. "If our ancestor, ye olde Dean of Divinity, was named as a member of the *Sircus*, no wonder he fled to America. How could you be a Dean of religion and belong to a secret magic troupe?"

James continued to skim the Wikipedia entry, eyes flickering doggedly across the text onscreen. "OK," he said, "that's all that can really help us."

"They don't have the names? *Any* names from the list?" Alice was disappointed.

"No," James said, "but you're right; it seems too much of a coincidence that the *Sircus* membership list goes public and our good old ancestor hopped on a boat for Massachusetts."

"When was the great fire?"

"September 1666. And Jonathan Myrddin emigrated in *October* 1666, even though you'd think that'd be a pretty crummy time of year to cross the Atlantic in one of those old wooden boats."

"Ships," Alice corrected absently. She shook her head, feeling dazed. "This is … this is pretty crazy, James."

"I know."

"I mean, it's pretty crazy because it seems to fit together."

"Yeah. I know."

"So we had an ancestor who belonged to the *Sircus* magic troupe back in the 1600's, and now we're being hypnotized to enter a crazy contest sponsored by the modern-day *Sircus*. What does it *mean*?"

"More oatmeal!" said Aiden, absolutely disinterested in family research and weird magic troupes. "Aidie hungry." He grinned winningly at each of them, knowing he could charm one of them into preparing a third bowl of oatmeal.

"I've got it," said James. He emptied another pack of oatmeal into the bowl, added some water, popped it into the microwave, pushed the buttons. He ruffled Aiden's hair. "OK, Aidie, just a minute. But this is the *last* bowl for today."

Aiden patted his brother on the back approvingly. "Last bowl," Aiden promised.

When the oatmeal was ready, James placed it on the dining room table and Alice gently sat Aiden in one of the chairs. "Here you go," she said, "Aidie eats like a big boy."

As Aiden happily dug into the oatmeal. James and Alice stepped back into the kitchen.

"What I don't understand," said James, "is why they spell 'circus' like 'sircus'."

Alice waved aside that concern. "Standardized spelling is fairly recent," she said. "For most of history, people just spelled words however they wanted to. They just sounded it out and did their best. You know – like you do."

James was too preoccupied to be drawn by the insult.

"So, the way it stands," James said quietly, "Jonathan Myrddin, our great-great-whatever, was probably a member of the *Sircus of Impossible Magicks*. Or at least people thought he was. And he fled England for the U.S."

"Which means," said Alice, "that *we're* somehow related to those nuts!"

"And they gave their kids tests," James said thoughtfully, "magical tests, to see if they were worthy to join the troupe."

"Magical tests – like this goofy *Magickal History Hunt*. James," Alice said, "those crazy people want *us* to join the *Sircus*."

"Yeah," said James. "Seems like."

Chapter Five – The First Companion
June 24th – Los Angeles

"Tell me again why we're here," said Alice.

It was raining softly. When Alice was in second grade everyone in her class got pen pals in Japan. Her pen pal had written her how wonderful it was Alice lived in Los Angeles, "where it never rains". In her next letter, Alice had set her new friend straight. Not only did it rain in Los Angeles, but the city had an entire rainy season. Some years, it felt like it rained almost every day in January, February and March, cold rains that winds whipped against windows and swooped up under umbrellas.

But this was soft, warm, June rain. James had bundled Aiden into a light jacket and put a Dodgers baseball cap on his head. Alice and James had pulled up their hoods. They had waited for the train under the South Pasadena station's shelter, jammed against everyone else who was trying to keep dry …

"Tell me again why we're here," Alice repeated. She was holding Aiden. James was repeatedly dialing someone on his cell phone, and not getting through. They had exited the Gold Line train in one of L.A.'s less scenic neighborhoods; Alice hated taking the train *through* this area, let alone getting out at its graffiti-tagged station platform and walking down one of the streets …

They stood in front of a spike-topped iron fence, behind which two enormous black German shepherds dozed, snoring almost as loudly as Alice's father Roberto snored, and seeming very contented, despite the rain.

Beyond the fence – and the dogs – two giant black SUVs were parked in front of a one-story bungalow with peeling green-grey paint.

"I told you," said James, "we need help ."

Alice looked around the street, the crazy quilt of decaying little bungalows, spike-topped fences, dozing dogs and fortress-like SUV's. Despite the flashes of color provided by tiny gardens and flower beds, there was something harsh, bleak, lost about the neighborhood.

"Yeah," she said darkly, "we need help all right."

The fence they were standing in front of was the tallest on the street, with the sharpest spikes, and behind it were the biggest dogs, the biggest SUV's, the bleakest bungalow.

James sighed and dialed his phone again. This time, someone picked up.

"Finally!" said James. "What the heck is going on?"

"Sorry dude!" Tariq's deep, loud voice boomed out of the receiver of James' cell phone. "Middle of a practice round. I *never* answer the phone during a practice round. Gotta stay in the Zen zone, capeesh? You got here faster than I expected."

One of the curtains in the bungalow was pulled aside, and a hulking, shadowy figure was visible against a square of ruddy light.

"Whatever," said James, "just let us in."

"Come on in, why dontcha?"

"Uh, because I don't want us to be devoured by your gigantic, evil dogs?"

"Oh, sorry. Mom must've let 'em out when she left, dude. They won't *really* devour you, well, probably not. But I'll call 'em in. Hang tight."

The figure disappeared and the curtain closed.

James snapped his cell phone shut and put it in his hoodie pocket.

The front door swung open. The shadowy figure appeared in the doorway, a burly silhouette against the ruddy light.

"*Fred!*" boomed Tariq's impossibly deep, resonant voice. It was like thunder. "*Ginger!*" it boomed.

The dogs woke instantly, leaping up and barking like ravenously hungry beasts. Spittle flew from their muzzles, blending with the rain.

Aiden covered his ears against the barking.

"Get up here, dudes! *NOW!!*" Tariq shouted to the canines. Fred and Ginger dashed up onto the porch, their claws clicking on the wooden floorboards. They both leaped up at Tariq at the same time. It looked like they were going to tear his throat out, but instead they began licking his face.

"Ha, ha, ha!!" Tariq's laughter rumbled out like thunderclaps. He caught each of the dogs in a rough bear hug, and then shoved them into the house. "Go on, dudes. Go on!" He disappeared after them, and a moment later there was the sound of a door slamming. The dogs began barking wildly. "No!" Tariq shouted, "Cut it out, dudes! Quiet down in there!"

Tariq reappeared in the doorway. He waved toward the house.

"Come on, whaddya want, an engraved invitation or something?"

James pushed open the iron gate.

Not without some reluctance, Alice followed him into the yard, which was overgrown with weeds and wild flowers and littered with giant chew toys for Tariq's giant dogs. She held Aiden close to her, prepared to run for the sidewalk at the first sign of the massive dogs.

Aiden was staring wide-eyed at Tariq. "Giant?" he asked Alice in an awed whisper.

"No giant," she whispered back, hiding a smile. "This is one of James' friends."

"Oh."

"Come on, you're gonna melt, dudes," laughed Tariq. James hurried up onto the porch, Alice following him warily.

"Hail the conquering Night!" bellowed Tariq, clapping James on the shoulder so heartily that James almost toppled down the porch steps. James was strong, but it was a lean, wiry strength. Compared to Tariq he was practically a midget. Tariq was six feet tall, with flowing dark hair, strapping as a baby giant. He had biceps on his biceps and triceps on his triceps and looked like he could bench press James with one hand and Alice and Aiden with the other.

Alice didn't like visiting strangers' houses. It was, as James would have put it, one of her things, like being picky about what she ate. It was part of what James considered her overall finicky attitude.

Tariq's house had low ceilings and narrow halls and smelt strongly of dog (not pleasant) and kerosene (surprisingly pleasant). Either there was no electricity or Tariq's family just preferred not to use it, because there were no electric lights on. In the rooms that Alice saw, there were kerosene lamps – real old-fashioned kerosene lamps – burning on table tops and giving the only light in the place.

They followed Tariq to the furthest room on the left, at the very end of the hall. He pushed open the door as if he were knocking over an enemy. It was messy inside, cluttered with fast-food wrappers, pizza boxes, cushions that seemed to have been scavenged from many different sofas with many different patterns, and tottering stacks of video game cases. The walls were hung with posters of foreign heavy metal bands that Alice had never heard of.

Tariq's room was lit with a kerosene lamp on his bedside table, but somehow *he* had electricity. His single electrical outlet was connected to multiple power strips and they were all connected to computers, laptops, video game systems and television monitors. Aiden was glancing all about with wide-eyed approval. "Cool!" he breathed.

It's like command central at video-game geek heaven, thought Alice. But she didn't say it. Tariq could snap her like a bread stick. Not that he would. But … still. He could.

"Sit down, dudes, sit down!" said Tariq cheerfully, waving to the sofa cushions. *"Mi casa es sus casa.* My house is your house. Take a load off. Sit a spell."

James sat down, looking instantly comfortable on a discarded red sofa cushion. Alice hesitated. On the one hand she didn't want to be rude. On the other hand, another one of her things was not sitting down on strange cushions that appeared not to have been washed for several hundred years.

She spotted a lime-green cushion that looked comfortable and relatively clean. Still clutching Aiden, she gingerly sat down. Aiden squirmed out of her arms and sat on a blue cushion near James.

"So," Tariq said genially, "to what do I owe this visit? Of what service can I be?"

Alice had heard about Tariq when James babbled on about his video game competitions, and she had heard Tariq's voice bellowing over James' phone, but she had never met him in person. He really was like a giant, but a friendly giant, with kind, shining eyes.

"We need help, buddy," said James. "We're in kind of … a weird situation."

"I *love* weird situations!" cried Tariq. "What have you got yourselves into, dudes?"

Alice cleared her throat delicately.

"Oh, sorry," said James. "Guess I should introduce you guys. Tariq, this is my cousin Alice and my brother Aiden. Guys, this is Tariq."

"Welcome," said Tariq, sweeping his arms out expansively. "I'm also known as *thadude1055*. And any kin of Night is kin to me. Night and I have shared bread and salt."

"Tariq is very dramatic," said James.

"At least he's polite," said Alice. "Some people might learn something from him."

"So, can I get you dudes, anything?" asked Tariq. "We've got ice tea, we've got lemonade – though it's not really an ice tea or lemonade kind of day, with this rain. What about some cocoa?"

"Cocoa for Aidie!" shouted Aiden. Tariq laughed and gave him a high-five. "Cocoa for Aidie!" Aiden shouted again, and hopped up and started running around the room.

"I like him," said Tariq. "He's kind of crazy."

"Aidie crazy!" shouted Aiden, jumping up and down.

"Yeah, he *really* needs more sugar," said Alice. She hooked Aiden with one arm when he ran past her, tried to settle him on the cushion but he squirmed out of her grasp and kept running around in circles. "Aidie, come to Allie" she said. "Be a good boy. Aidie doesn't need any cocoa right now."

"Aidie want cocoa, Aidie want cocoa!!!" the little boy chanted. Alice rolled her eyes. The Lord-of-the-Flies-slash-Lost-Boy vibe of Tariq's room had put Aiden on his worst behavior.

"Let him be," James told her. "He's fine."

"Cocoa, cocoa," Aiden sang.

"What do you want?" Tariq asked Alice.

"Nothing," she said, "but thank you."

"She wants lemonade," said James.

"Then lemonade it is!" Tariq lumbered out of the room. As soon as he was gone, Alice elbowed James in the side.

"Ow!"

"I *said* I didn't want anything," Alice complained.

"You know you want a lemonade, Alice. It's not going to poison you to drink out of someone else's glass just once. And that really hurt, by the way."

"Good."

Aiden finally stopped running around and collapsed in a heap on the blue cushion. He clutched the sides of his head. "Aidie feel bad," he said.

"That's because Aidie is dizzy," said Alice. "That's what happens when Aidie runs around like a crazy nut."

Aiden laughed. "Yeah," he said, "Aidie is crazy! Ha, ha, ha!"

Alice shook her head. Her first impulse was to explain to him that it wasn't polite to run around stranger's houses like a nut, but she just ruffled his curly hair and said nothing.

"So," she said, turning to James, "*why* are we here?"

James stretched and yawned. He seemed thoroughly at ease, and had clearly been here before. "Tariq is a really cool guy," he said. "Eccentric, you know – "

"Oh, gee, I hadn't noticed."

"Eccentric, but very smart, and very loyal. Whatever is up with the whole *Sircus of Impossible Magicks* thing, Tariq is a good person for us to have in our corner."

Alice held up her hands. "Wait, wait, wait, wait, wait. You're not saying we're taking him into our confidence?"

"That's exactly what I'm saying, cousin."

"You know, just when I think you can't get any dumber ... I am in awe of your new level of dumbosity. What is Tariq supposed to *do* to help us? On the off chance that he doesn't just think we're total goofballs?"

"Tariq doesn't think anyone is a goofball. He is totally open to the universe."

"Meaning he's so crazy that our crazy will seem normal to him?"

"That's a mean way to put it," said James. "But, yeah."

Tariq strode in, grinning his enormous grin, somehow clutching three glasses full of lemonade in one large hand and holding a mug of cocoa in the other. He stooped down and gave the mug to Aiden. "I put a lot of milk in it, but that's really hot, little dude, so be careful. 'Kay?"

Aiden smiled at him and nodded.

"What a great little dude," said Tariq. "I wish I had a little brother." He handed one lemonade to Alice, one to James, and then kept the third for himself. He sat down easily, his bulk reclining over three cushions, and leaned back against a fourth. "I've got a bunch of older sisters, and they're great, you know, they're salt of the earth and all that, but it would've been cool to *have* a baby bro', instead of just *being* a baby bro'. Now," he looked directly at James, "what is this weird situation that you got yourself into?"

James took a deep draught of lemonade, and wiped his mouth on his sleeve.

"Grow some manners," murmured Alice under her breath.

"Go mute," muttered James. He took another sip of the lemonade. "It's kind of hard to know where to start," he said to Tariq.

"Only if you're a lack wit," said Alice. She turned to Tariq. "We met some very odd people yesterday. One on the Gold Line train to Union Station. Two at Union Station. One man, two women, all with English accents. The man told us not to enter a contest called *L.A. Magickal History Hunt*. The women somehow got us to enter that exact contest, even to sign a contract. We think they're hypnotists. They seem to be circus performers from the *Sircus of Impossible Magicks*, which our ancestor Jonathan Myrddin belonged to before he fled to the United States. We don't know what it all means, but we seem to be somehow related to these weird people and we suddenly seem to be the focus of their interest."

Tariq nodded thoughtfully during her speech. "Uh-huh. Uh-huh. *Very* interesting. Good Cliffs Notes version. You, I can tell, are *all* about efficiency, Ellis."

"Alice," she said waspishly.

"Right. Now," Tariq turned to James, "let's have the *detailed* version."

James nodded. He drank some lemonade. "It really started," he said slowly, "when I woke up yesterday morning after these strange dreams …"

* * *

When James had finished, Tariq was silent for a moment, eyes closed. It almost looked like he had gone to sleep. Then he opened them and looked from James to Aiden to Alice, and back to James, beaming at them with his warm smile.

"We're not imagining it," Alice said defensively.

Tariq was startled. "I know."

"It's just, your smile. It looks … indulgent."

"Hey, it's just a smile, dudette. You've got to chill, OK? I'm just thinking how lucky I am to know three amazing heroes. 'Cause that's what this sounds like, a hero quest. But, I mean, for real instead of for play. This is heavy, very heavy, in the coolest possible way."

"So you believe us?" asked Alice, surprised.

"He just *said* that," complained James. "*Now* who's the lack wit?"

"You," she said sweetly. "Always you." She turned back to Tariq. "But you *do* believe us?"

"Absolutely," said Tariq. "I'm even a little jealous, maybe. I'd *love* to find out I was descended from Merlin. I'd *love* to be given a magic quest to be inducted into a magic troupe! I happen, you know, to know a bit about the Arthur legends. Kind of a hobby of mine. Merlin was a total dude. It would be totally like him to live for hundreds of years and start some totally awesome secret magic group. And you guys seem to be related to one, well, *at least* one of the members, this Jonathan Myrddin dude. It might interest you to know that 'Myrddin' is Welsh for 'Merlin'."

"No way!" James and Alice said at the same time.

"Way!" said Tariq.

"Way!" shouted Aiden, not following the conversation, but not wanting to be left out.

"'Myrddin' is Welsh for 'Merlin'?" asked James excitedly.

"Yeah."

"Really?" asked Alice.

"Yeah, really. So that means that either your great-great-great-grand-dude took a form of Merlin's name, like, as a tribute or something, or it means-"

"We're descended from Merlin," Alice said. "*If* he was a real historical personage."

"Yeah. And the way those weirdos talked to you and are taking all this trouble about you, I would vote for the descended-from-Merlin theory. You guys gotta have *beaucoup, beaucoup de mojo* among the three of you."

"But, I mean … I hate to admit this," said Alice, "but we're pretty ordinary. Besides which, magic isn't real."

"You *seem* ordinary," Tariq corrected. "On the surface. That's part of the hero's journey. When heroes are kids they *seem* pretty ordinary and they're usually hidden with families or guardians that seem ordinary."

"Of course," said Alice, calling to mind her advanced English seminar from the year before. They had studied the archetypical hero's journey. "The ordinary environment protects the heroes from their evil adversaries until they're ready to confront them."

"And then when the time is right," said James, "the heroes are called to go on a quest."

Tariq and Alice both stared at him.

"Hey, just because I don't like school doesn't mean I don't know things," said James. "The hero's early life, his back story – it's Video Game 101. The hero is either contacted or attacked, or both, and he learns a little bit about his real heritage, and he gathers some loyal companions and goes on a quest."

Tariq grinned broadly. "And I'm loyal companion number one," he said. "At your service, dudes! Let's get to the questing!"

Alice shook her head. "I've got to absorb this," she said. "Give me a few minutes."

"Aidie is hero," shouted Aidie. "Pow, pow!" He punched the air with his tiny fists.

The three older kids laughed. "If anyone's a natural hero," said James, "it's this little wild guy."

"No kidding," said Alice.

"But for real," said Tariq, "what is the next step? When are the weirdos going to contact you again? Or should you try to contact them? And are we sure, dudes, that they're part of the *Sircus* troupe, which, we assume, is the good-guy team? Or could they be part of an opposition, trying to mess with you before the *Sircus* folks connect with you?"

"Hey, one question at a time," said James. "My head's already swimming."

Alice gave him a patronizing smile. "I wonder," she said, "if we're *all* heroes. I mean, Aidie is a natural athlete and one-hundred percent fearless, and I'm a genius, but you, what is *your* amazing talent supposed to be?"

James pantomimed holding up a remote control, pointing it at Alice, and clicking a button.

"Why … won't … this … 'Mute' button … work?" he asked the universe.

"She *does* raise an interesting question," said Tariq.

James shook his head. "*Et tu*, Tariq?"

"For real, dude," said Tariq. "I mean, the little guy does seem like a natural hero, and even though the girl is annoying – sorry, but you are, Alice – she *is* a freaky-smart genius kid."

"Thanks," she said drily.

"You're welcome," Tariq said sincerely. He snapped his fingers. "I'll tell you what it is, James. It's your battle smarts. Your tactical abilities, your brilliant strategies. You're, like, a military prodigy!"

"Do you think?" asked James skeptically. "I mean, I know I'm pretty good at gaming – "

"Pretty good?" laughed Tariq. "Dude, I don't want to turn you into a conceited jerk, but there's a reason we're going to win that Mortal Quest competition. I'm good muscle and Hisoka is a terrific stealth guy but you're the brains, dude, and you're the heart."

"Really?" asked James.

"Totally, dude."

"This is all very sweet," said Alice, "but whatever our talents are, we still need to figure out what our next step will be. Do we wait to hear from the weirdos? Do we do more research? Do we actually go through with the contest and try to solve puzzles and find magical whats-its?"

"Hey, you said they gave you some pouches. For the contest. What was in those pouches, anyway?" asked Tariq. "Maybe there's some clue there."

"Yeeessss," James said slowly. "The … the pouches."

He and Alice exchanged a look.

"What was in them?" asked Tariq.

"Weeelll …" said Alice. "I didn't exactly – "

"Neither did I," said James.

Aiden pulled on a little cord around his neck and pulled his sky-blue felt pouch from beneath his shirt. He held it up. "Pouch," he said helpfully.

James and Alice each pulled on cords around their necks and revealed their pouches.

"Cool," said Tariq. "So what's in them?"

"Weeelll …" said Alice.

"Oh, please tell me you're kidding," said Tariq. *"You guys haven't opened them?"*

"I know, it's crazy," said James. "I remember we all put them around our necks before we said goodbye yesterday, and then …"

"I just sort of forgot about it," said Alice.

"Yeah," said James.

"Pouch," Aiden said helpfully, smiling.

"Hmm," said Tariq. "Sounds like a 'spell of inattention'. You know, if you don't want someone to notice something, or think about something, you put a spell of inattention on it. Like when we played 'Kingdom of the Elves'."

"Oh, yeah, I remember," said James. "We put that spell on our bags of gold, so no one would see how rich we were and try to rob us."

"Exactly."

"So they give us the pouches but they don't want us to open them?" asked Alice. "Kind of pointless."

"There'd be a lock on it," said Tariq. "On the spell. Like, at a certain time or under a certain circumstance, the lock will open and you'll notice the pouches and look in them."

"No time like the present," said Alice. "I want to see what's in here before I forget about it again!"

She kept the blood-red-and-black beaded bag around her neck, but extended the cord so that she could hold the pouch out in front of her. She wrinkled her nose. "Not exactly Prada," she said. "Kinda cheap – a little girl's bag."

"And why, oh why, would they give *you* a little girl's bag?" asked James in mock bewilderment.

"What I mean," she glared, "is that it seems a little cheap and childish for a hero's bag." She tugged at the black strings that held the pouch shut. They slackened easily. She peered inside the bag, but the light of the kerosene lamp and the computer monitors was too dim to touch the contents of the pouch. Gingerly she tipped them into her hand.

Tariq, James and Aiden craned their necks to see the items that tumbled onto her palm.

The four of them stared for a moment. Then, "Is that *it*?" they all asked.

Chapter Six – Magic Bags
June 24th – Los Angeles

"There's got to be something else in there," said James.

"And yet, there's not," said Alice. She shook the pouch hard and squeezed it to see if she could feel anything else inside. "Empty," she said.

They all looked at the small objects on Alice's palm: a postage-stamp-sized temporary tattoo, a clear plastic vial of what appeared to be water, a clear plastic vial of sand, and a red-and-black plastic ring. The temporary tattoo was a black cartoon snake with red bands, inexpertly drawn. The plastic ring was a red band decorated with a black-and-red-striped cartoon snake.

"So, I'm going to go out on a limb and say this is a gift from the *bad* dudes," said Tariq. "Whoever they are. Because I don't know exactly what good that stuff is supposed to be in a fight."

"I don't know," said James, "I think Alice would look scary, I mean, scarier, with that tattoo."

Alice whomped him on the shoulder.

"See," said James, "it's already making her warlike."

"No hit James!" said Aiden, whomping Alice on the shoulder. "No hit, hit is bad!"

"Sorry, Aidie," said Alice. "You're right. Hitting is bad. I won't hit James, and Aidie doesn't hit me. OK?"

Aiden nodded and hugged her.

"So," Tariq said to James, "how are *you* armed?"

James unfastened the drawstring of his black leather pouch and tipped the contents into his hand.

"Son of a gun," he said softly, disappointed. Like Alice, he had a temporary tattoo, a vial of some clear liquid, a vial of sand, and a plastic ring. His tattoo was a black cartoon panther, his ring a black band with a panther emblem.

"What am I supposed to do with this?" he asked no one in particular. Alice considered a snide response, but bit her tongue.

"Here," she said to Aiden, "it's Aidie's turn now. What's in your pouch, Aiden?"

Aiden untangled the drawstrings of his sky-blue felt pouch with some difficulty and much dignity. Alice's first instinct was to help him, but something about his grave self-importance stayed her hand; this was something Aiden wanted, and needed, to do himself.

When the bag was open, Aiden spilled the contents into Alice's hand. "Allie hand bigger," he said. His kit contained essentially the same items as Alice's and James', but his temporary tattoo portrayed a sky-blue cartoon monkey, and his sky-blue plastic ring had a cartoon monkey emblem.

"So … where are we?" asked James. "Do we try to do something with these, or what?"

"No," Alice said instantly. She put a hand to her mouth. "Wow. I don't know why I said that. It just came out."

Tariq nodded. "When that happens, when some dude suddenly has involuntary speech, that's the hero instinct guiding you."

"Really?"

"Either that, or it's an evil influence trying to trick you. But let's go with hero's instinct."

"Yeah, let's," she said. She rubbed her forehead. "I don't know why, but I'm feeling we should put on these tattoos."

"You're kidding," said James.

"No. We need to put these on."

"Like, on our arms?"

"Shoulders," she said instantly. She covered her mouth. "OK, this is really weird," she said. "It's like, it's me speaking and as soon as I say it I know it's right, but I'm not thinking about it before I speak."

"Alice speaking without thinking," mused James, "how bizarre."

She almost whomped him on the arm, but remembered just in time to set a good example for Aiden. "We have to put these on our shoulders," she said. "Our left shoulders."

"Why not?" said James.

They all pushed their sleeves up over their shoulders, including Aiden. Tariq ran out of the room and returned with a cup of water for wetting the paper. They pressed the damp tattoos against their left shoulders and waited for several minutes, not speaking, each lost in their own thoughts. Tariq kept time watching the seconds tick away on his cell phone clock.

"Time," he said finally. "Three minutes is usually good for temporary tattoos. And if these are actually magic …"

James, Alice and Aiden peeled the papers off and regarded their shoulders, which now bore colorful cartoons, the black panther for James, the red-and-black snake for Alice, and the sky-blue monkey for Aiden.

"Well," said James, "I don't *feel* any different." He looked at Alice. "Did we do it right?"

"Why are you asking me?"

"Because you're doing that weird automatic speech thing," he said. "You suddenly are channeling mystical instructions or something."

"I don't know," she said helplessly. Alice hated to feel helpless. And clueless. "It feels … it felt like that's what we were supposed to do. Now, I don't feel much of anything."

"At least she doesn't feel something went wrong," said Tariq encouragingly. "What next, dudes?"

"We go to the circus," she said without hesitation. She started to clap her hand over her mouth, but James stopped her. He shook his head.

"That's getting old," James said. "You are now freaky channeling girl. Stop being shocked. Just deal with it."

"Where is the circus playing?" asked Tariq.

"Sony Stadium," said James. "And wherever the idea came from, I like it. We need to scope out these *Sircus* people, see what's what. The best defense is a good offense."

"Rah, rah," said Alice. "And how are we paying for tickets? Mom gave me five dollars for snacks in case you took us somewhere fun – ha, ha, ha, by the way, does she ever *not* know you! And I'm guessing *you're* dead broke, being a bone-idle video-game addict, and all."

"I spent my birthday money on that new game console."

"As long as you spent it on something totally stupid, dork."

"Whoa," said Tariq, "you two are brutal! Have you always been like this?"

"Only since birth," said Alice.

"Well it's less than helpful," said Tariq. "How are you supposed to go on a magical quest busting each other's chops all the time? You gotta work together, dudes. You gotta be nice to each other."

"Nice," agreed Aiden, demonstrating by patting James on the head and Alice on the shoulder.

"See, the little dude totally grasps the concept," said Tariq.

"No offense," said James, "and you are totally my best friend, but butt out, Tariq."

"Ow! OK, OK, maybe it's not exactly my business, but if I'm going to be a loyal sidekick-type on this quest, it's part of my job to make suggestions that are really common sense but the heroes are too distracted or stubborn or whatever to see it for themselves."

"Butt out, Tariq," James and Alice said together.

"There we go," smiled Tariq. "I've already got you working together." He leaned forward and ruffled Aiden's hair. "*You're* my friend, right, little dude?"

"Butt out, Treek," said Aiden. James and Alice laughed. Aiden wasn't exactly sure what he'd said that was so funny – he was just copying his brother and cousin – but he loved getting a laugh. "Butt out, Treek!" he said again.

"That's enough, Aidie," said Alice.

"If comedy time is over," said Tariq, "it *is* a good question how we're supposed to get into the show." He picked up one of his computer keyboards, began tapping at the keys and skimming one finger over the touch screen.

One of the computer screens was filled with a photo of Sony Stadium and an inset photo of a blonde in a sparkling costume doing a handstand on a galloping pony. The caption read *Sircus of Impossible Magicks*.

"That's one of the girls from Union Station," said Alice. "That's Lou."

"How much is the show?" James asked.

"Oh, yeah." Tariq scrolled down the screen, dark eyes skimming the text. "The matinees are twenty-five dollars each for kids – "

"For *kids*?" James asked, outraged.

"Yeah, for kids, and forty dollars for adults, which, according to *Sircus of the Surreal*, is anyone over fifteen, bummer. And the evening shows are forty dollars for kids and fifty-five dollars for adults."

"That's crazy," said James. "What do they do, give you a lump of pure gold as a souvenir?"

"I guess they're a really big deal. It says the *Sircus of Impossible Magicks* has performed for royalty around the world."

"So you've got to be a king or queen to afford the tickets!"

Alice smoothed back a lock of Aiden's curly hair. She shook her head slightly. "OK," she said, "I'm starting to get used to this."

"Incoming message?" asked James.

"Yeah. It just popped into my head: The money doesn't matter."

"So how do we get in to the show?"

"I don't know. But the money doesn't matter. We just need to go. Like, now."

"Now?" asked James.

"Now," she said. She stood up, carrying Aiden, staggered a little bit under the small boy's weight.

"Here," said Tariq, "I'll take him."

She hesitated. She still didn't really know Tariq. He seemed cool, but he was essentially a stranger. Aiden was her cousin, but more than that, he was as close to a little brother as she'd ever had.

"I'll carry him like he's breakable," Tariq promised.

Alice nodded. "OK," she said. "Good. Because he is." She handed Aiden over. Tariq held the boy in one arm, as if Aiden weighed roughly the same amount as a cube of sugar.

Alice gingerly put Aiden's sky-blue pouch back inside his sweatshirt, then did the same with hers. James silently followed suit.

"If we're going to make the matinee, we have to hurry," said Tariq.

"The Gold Line runs every fifteen minutes this time of day," said Alice, "so if we – "

"Nah, forget that," said Tariq, "I'm driving."

Chapter Seven – Impossible Magicks
June 24th – Los Angeles

Alice shuddered and squeezed her eyes shut for the hundredth time.

Driving? she thought. *He calls this driving?*

Flying was more like it! Tariq was a couple of years older than James, so Tariq had his license and Tariq had keys to one of the family SUVs. He drove the big black SUV at breakneck speed along the rain-slick 110 freeway, weaving in and out of traffic with wild abandon, making sudden swerves that seemed guaranteed to smash them into either the nearest car or the concrete freeway divider.

James rode shotgun next to Tariq. Alice was in back, her seat belt securely fastened, her fingernails digging into her palms as she mentally recited every prayer she'd ever learned. Aiden was strapped into the car seat next to her. The car seat belonged to one of Tariq's sisters; Tariq buckled his nephew in it when he babysat.

"Do we," Alice began in a faint, high-pitched voice, "do we *really* need to go this fast?"

"Fast?" shouted Tariq. "We're not going fast. I never drive fast when there's a kid on board."

"Oh," Alice said faintly. She closed her eyes as the back end of a bus suddenly filled the windshield. She kept her eyes closed for the rest of the journey, which was the fastest ride she'd ever taken, and yet, paradoxically, seemed to last for a terrifying eternity.

When they pulled into Sony Stadium's underground parking garage, Tariq jammed on the brakes and took a ticket out of the dispenser. "Yow," he said, reading the ticket, "the parking's going to be more expensive than the show."

"Well, we can't afford either, so don't sweat it," said James.

"In for a penny, in for a pound, right, bro'?" said Tariq. "Onward!" He stepped on the gas pedal and Alice closed her eyes again. Tariq roared up and down the garage ramps at what felt like one-hundred miles per hour, carving such tight turns that she felt like she was on a roller coaster.

"Wheeeeee!" Aiden cried gleefully, delighted with the exciting ride. "Go Treek! Go Treek!"

"You are *awesome*, little dude!" shouted Tariq, laughing. He darted into an empty space, jammed on the brakes and cut the engine.

"Aidie awesome! Aidie awesome!" shouted Aiden.

"That kid's just got two speeds, huh?" said Tariq. "He's either dead asleep or roaring full speed ahead."

"Pretty much," agreed James.

They exited the SUV, Alice a bit wobbly-legged, still twitchy with adrenalin from the terrifying drive. She took a deep breath.

"You OK?" asked Tariq.

"Just great," she muttered.

* * *

Signs led them to a series of escalators that carried them up, up, up to the vast lobby of Sony Stadium. Crowds of people, mostly families, were milling about, most standing in impossibly long lines for the ticket windows.

"In this age of the Internet," said Tariq, "why do all these dudes waste their time standing in ticket lines? Download and print, peoples, download and print."

"At least they're going to *have* tickets," said James. He glanced pointedly at Alice. "Well, psychic girl? There's the entrance. How are we getting in without tickets?"

"Backstage," Alice said without hesitation.

"Backstage?"

"Backstage."

"And how exactly will that work?"

"No idea."

"Great."

"I can't control when I get the information," she said. "And I can't control what information I get. It's not, I don't know where it's coming from, but it's not something I can turn on and off like a faucet!"

"OK, calm down."

"I'm perfectly calm," she hissed.

Tariq looked around. "Where's the backstage entrance?" he wondered.

"Left," Alice said immediately. She pointed to a pair of nondescript doors, painted the same pale grey color as the wall in which they were set.

"So, let's go already," said Tariq. He led the way with long strides, James behind him, Alice next and then Aiden, holding Alice's hand.

Clusters of people were gathered near the backstage doors, chatting with each other, laughing loudly and leafing through colorful programs. They were keyed up, especially the kids, waiting for the show to start. Everyone kept looking toward the bank of entrance doors in the distance. No one seemed to notice James, Alice or Aiden as they passed, although Tariq attracted some quick glances.

Tariq didn't even stop at the backstage doors, he just boldly pushed them open. James, Alice and Aiden followed him into a dim hallway. The door was weighted and slammed shut instantly behind them, just missing Alice and Aiden by millimeters. Aiden laughed.

"Door go 'Bam'!" shouted Aiden.

"Yes, Aidie, and we almost go 'Bam' too," said Alice.

She looked around. The hallway was long; it seemed to stretch on forever, lit at infrequent intervals by dim lights that flickered off and on. It ended in a darkness that her eyes couldn't penetrate. There were streaks of rust on the wall, where water had leaked, and puddles of oily water here and there along the floor.

"You know those movies," said Alice, "where the teenagers go into the abandoned theater and get attacked by the monster?"

"Which one?" asked James.

"*Any* of them. This is what the hallway always looks like."

"Aidie no like monsters," said Aiden thoughtfully, trying to put a brave face on it but clearly worried.

"Don't upset Aiden," said James, annoyed. "Aidie, pal, there's no such thing as monsters."

"No monster?"

"Nope, no monster. Everything is fine."

Aiden smiled and gave his brother a thumbs-up. He scowled at Alice. "Allie scare Aidie. Bad Alice."

"Which way do we go?" James asked.

"Forward," said Alice. *"Ow!"*

"What's the – *Ow!*" said James.

"Ouch!" said Aiden.

"What the heck's wrong with you guys?" asked Tariq. James, Alice and Aiden were scratching their left shoulders, faces contorted in pain. "Are you OK? What's wrong?"

"My shoulder," said Alice. She pushed up her left sleeve. "Probably the cheap ink in those stupid, cheap temporary tattoos. It's – *WHAT?*"

She goggled at the tattoo on her arm.

It was no longer a cartoon snake, but an elaborately etched serpent, so detailed that she could distinguish every scale.

"What the heck?" murmured James. He pushed up his left sleeve. His cartoon feline was now a beautifully rendered panther, so well-crafted that you could see each hair of its fur.

"What happen Aidie tutu?" asked Aiden. He had pulled up his sleeve, and his cartoon monkey was now a photo-realistic tattoo of a blue capuchin monkey. Aiden rubbed the tattoo with his tiny fingers. "Wow," he breathed.

"OK … It stopped hurting," said James.

"Mine too," said Alice. "Are you OK, Aiden?"

Aiden gave her a thumbs-up.

"Well, this is … interesting," said James.

"Interesting? It's totally freakin' AWESOME!" said Tariq. "Dudes, I am soooo jealous. I want one of those."

"Believe me, if I could give mine to you, I would," said Alice. "That *hurt*!"

"Why did they change?" mused James.

"I have a theory," said Tariq. "Didn't you say that back in the day that was how *Sircus* members recognized each other? Back when it was a big, bad secret to belong to the *Sircus*? They had tattoos of their animal totems – right?"

"Right," James agreed. *Huh. A panther … that's a pretty cool animal totem,* he thought.

"Why do I have to be a snake?" complained Alice.

James opened his mouth to answer, but –

"Don't you dare," warned Alice.

James shrugged innocently.

They walked down the seemingly endless hallway, moving quickly but quietly. The few lights continued to flicker and buzz erratically, as if powered by a dying generator that could seize up at any moment and leave them in total darkness.

It was eerie, Alice thought, in the shadows between the narrow islands of light. The further they walked, the more rusty water dripped down the walls.

"So, here's the thing," said Tariq in an uncharacteristically soft voice. "When you talked about how things got weird on the train yesterday, and then things got weird at the station, but then everything went back to normal? That gets me thinking about faery realms."

James snapped his fingers. "Of course!"

"For those of us who are *not* dorks – explain, please," said Alice.

"Faery realms are mythical places where faeries live," said James. "They're sort of, they're not part of our world. They're in the spaces *between* worlds. So weird things can happen. Time gets weird, and physics get weird."

"James," said Alice carefully, "you're not starting to think this is *real*, are you?"

He gestured to his panther tattoo. "How do you explain this?"

"The way we explained the rest of it. Hypnotism. Tricks. Stage magician stuff, by professional circus freaks."

"How could they do *this*?" James touched the panther tattoo gingerly, with a kind of reverence.

"Off the top of my head, some kind of chemical reaction," said Alice. "The *real* design was on the paper in some kind of clear chemical, sensitive to our chemistry – to sweat, maybe. It appears after it absorbs enough of our sweat."

"Come on," James said skeptically.

"That's why it burned us," Alice said. "That's why it hurt our shoulders. It was a chemical reaction – those always absorb or release heat. James, you can't honestly think it was, like, actual *magic*? Because that's just not possible."

"Hence the name," said James. "You know: *Sircus of* Impossible *Magicks*."

His cousin sighed. "James, in the old days, a lot of people thought science was magic. Could you please *try* to evolve into a modern human?"

"I don't know, dudette," said Tariq, "I think maybe *you're* the one that needs to evolve. You gotta open your mind to the mysteries of the universe."

"I'm very open to the mysteries of the universe," said Alice. "They can all be explained by science."

Tariq shook his head.

"I don't like this hallway," said James. "There are no doors in it, no cross-passages, and it doesn't seem to have an end."

"That's because it's a maaaagical hallway, ooooh-ooooooh," said Alice, making spooky ghost noises.

"Do we stop?" wondered Tariq.

"No," said Alice instantly. She put her hand to her forehead. "Still getting used to this," she muttered.

"Ah-ha!" said James. "How are you doing *that*? How are you channeling what we should do, if it's not something mystical?"

"Duh. Post-hypnotic suggestion. The weirdos put instructions in my head, and I recall them as needed. That's why it happens without any effort on my part."

"So it's like they hacked into your brain and planted a hidden sub-program."

"I guess. I don't speak techno-geek."

"Well I do," Tariq said cheerfully. "Hmm. You both have very persuasive arguments. Are we on a mystical quest? Or a real-world quest with freaky but explainable elements?"

"*STOP!*" Alice shouted.

They all stopped instantly, Tariq pin wheeling his massive arms to keep from pitching into the deep crevice in the floor.

"Yow, that was close," he said. "Thanks, Alice."

They peered into the crevice. It was seven feet across – too wide to leap across. It was pitch-black and seemed impossibly deep.

"Cool!" said Aiden.

He leaned over the blackness, overbalanced, and would have fallen in if James hadn't grabbed the back of his sweatshirt. The material bunched in James' fist as he lifted Aiden into the air and swung him next to Alice.

"You're supposed to be *watching* him," James yelled at her.

"I am!"

"Then *do* it!" he yelled.

Alice picked up Aiden and held him close to her. Her heart was pounding in her chest. Aiden had almost fallen. Aiden had almost fallen into a bottomless pit!

Suddenly it wasn't just an interesting adventure.

"How do we get across the chasm?" asked Tariq.

"And why is it here?" asked James.

"Definitely doesn't look like it's up to code," said Tariq. "Really big termites, maybe? Or it's a mystical trap. Or maybe it's not even here – maybe it's all in our heads. Dang. Heavy."

"Wherever it came from, somehow we have to cross it," said James.

"No – We don't," Alice said decisively. "There's," she turned to the left, "there's a secret door."

James looked at the wall on their left. "I don't see it."

"A *secret* door," Alice repeated. She narrowed her eyes. It was the oddest thing, but part of the wall seemed to be shimmering with thousands of tiny, undulating pinpricks of light. "Can you see that?" she asked, pointing.

"What?" asked Tariq.

"Little lights," said Alice.

"I don't see anything," said James. "Do you see a door?"

"I think so." Alice handed Aiden to James, slowly approached the shimmering rectangle that only she could see. The lights formed a pattern the size and shape of a door. She pressed her hand against the twinkling wall – and her hand went right through it. She shivered. Her hand felt cold, as if she'd plunged it into a snow bank.

"That ... is ... so ... *COOL!*" shouted Tariq. "What do you feel?"

"What do you see?" asked Alice.

"Dudette, your hand just *totally* disappeared into the wall. It didn't get cut off or anything, did it?"

"No. It's cold but it's still attached."

"How are you *doing* that?"

"It's a portal," said James.

Alice swallowed. "It's not a portal," she said, trying to sound disdainful, but sounding querulous and childish instead. "Just more post-hypnotic suggestion. It's just a regular open doorway, I'm sure, but *you're* seeing it as a part of the wall and *I'm* seeing it as a shimmer."

She pulled her hand back. They all looked at it as she flexed her fingers.

"Looks normal," said Tariq. "Are you OK?"

"Sure," she said.

"So, that's where we go?"

"Yes," she said without hesitation.

"Let me ask you this," said James, grinning suddenly, "when was *Tariq* hypnotized?"

"What do you mean?"

"I mean, when was Tariq hypnotized? You're saying he can't see the doorway because he was given this hypnotic – "

"Post-hypnotic," she corrected.

"OK, post-hypnotic suggestion. But *when*? Tariq wasn't on the train with us. He wasn't at Union Station with us, either."

Alice frowned. "That's a not *completely* stupid question," she said. "But I'm sure there's some explanation."

"Of course there is."

"There *is*," she said defiantly. "Now come on; we don't have much time."

"Much time before what?"

"I don't know!" She shrugged helplessly. "This is very frustrating. I'm starting to feel like a puppet."

"Not a puppet," James disagreed. "A computer. Like you said, whether it's magical or hypnotic or whatever, you've got instructions programmed into you. In fact, we should be asking you questions.

"Dude, it's like she's a terminal," Tariq said excitedly. "She's got access to all kinds of answers!"

"What's through that door?" James asked Alice.

"Friends," she said immediately. "Danger."

"Interesting combination," laughed Tariq.

"What kind of danger?" asked James.

"Mortal danger."

"What kind of friends?"

"Old friends." Alice put her hands over her ears. "Stop it!" she told James. "I'm not a computer terminal; I'm your cousin. Anyway, *they* planted the instructions, they only tell us what *they* want us to think. 'Old friends'. Says who? We won't really know *anything* until we go through."

"Then I say, let's go through!" said Tariq.

"Go through wall, go through wall!" shouted Aiden.

James bowed to Alice. "Ladies first," he said.

Tariq stepped in front of all of them. "I go first. Just like in the games, bro. I'm the bodyguard."

"Then I follow you," said James. "Like in the games."

He handed Aiden to Alice. "Keep a good grip on him, OK? And if anything crazy happens, take him and run. Don't let anything happen to Aiden. It doesn't matter if anything happens to me."

Alice was ready with a snide comment, but somehow it didn't feel right.

"We ready?" asked Tariq.

"Yeah," James and Alice said together.

Tariq stepped through the wall.

Chapter Eight – First Blood
June 24th – Aelwyd

It's so cold, thought Alice.

She shivered, and she heard Aiden's teeth chattering as her burrowed against her.

It felt like they'd been walking for an hour, through a dense grey mist.

Tariq and James saw it merely as a mist, but Alice saw it as a glimmering, sparkling cloud of tiny lights. It was the most beautiful thing she'd ever seen, even if it was icy cold.

"Turn right," Alice called. Tariq turned to the right. "Not so far," she called. He adjusted his course.

The mist was so thick, it was impossible to distinguish anything beyond it, no walls, no objects, no landscape. But somehow Alice knew when it was time to turn. The points of light seemed to coalesce in a certain spot, just for a moment, and she knew that was where they had to go next. It was an unsettling way to navigate, but strangely beautiful.

No one spoke aside from Alice.

Tariq's mind was clean as a freshly polished lens, free of thought until an occasion demanded one.

James was wondering what the heck was on the other side of the mist, and worrying about Alice and Aiden. What had they gotten themselves into? What did it all mean?

"Left," called Alice. Tariq turned left …

* * *

It seemed like an hour before Alice finally saw the points of light gather together in the shape of a bright, shining archway. They pulsed, changing colors from silver to gold to white and back again.

"There!" she said.

"Uh, where?" asked James.

"Sorry, to the left. A little more, Tariq. Yes. It's the way out."

"I don't see anything," said Tariq, "but you're the boss."

"God help us all," said James.

"I heard that," said Alice.

"You were meant to."

Aiden had fallen asleep in Alice's arms. He was sleeping a lot lately, probably all of the weirdness and excitement taking its toll. He was so heavy when he slept. She shifted him from the crook of her left arm to her right.

"Wake up, Aidie," she said gently. "Come on, little guy." He stirred, and then snapped to attention as if zapped by an electric current.

Tariq put his hands out in front of him. Alice saw the motes of light scatter wherever his hands touched, then return when his hands moved. "Is it here?" Tariq asked.

"Yes, exactly," she confirmed.

"Are we ready to meet some old friends?" asked Tariq.

"Or new enemies?" asked James.

"Pessimist!" Tariq laughed. "But, for real, dudes, are we ready?"

"Yes," said Alice.

"We go on three," said James. "One … two … three."

Tariq stepped through the twinkling archway. One moment Alice saw his enormous bulk silhouetted against the lights; the next moment he was gone.

"Do you want to live forever?" shouted James, stepping through the archway. It was a warrior's rallying cry; his character Night said it when he gamed; James had always wanted to say it in real life.

"Weeehooooo!" shouted Aiden as he and Alice stepped through the arch.

It was like stepping into warm pitch, completely dark, damp, smothering.

Alice panicked, and almost froze, but she felt Aiden nestled against her. She couldn't let anything happen to her small cousin. They had to get out of here!

She walked, holding Aiden tight. The viscous air seemed to restrain them, to pull at them. And then they were free, eyes dazzled by a bright light.

Alice put a hand over her eyes. Aiden buried his face in her hair.

But the light-blindness was temporary. Within a few seconds she could see her surroundings: a green hillside above a babbling brook.

On the other side of the brook was a forest of birch and evergreens, impossible deep and tall and lovely. Tariq and James stood a few paces away, at the crest of the hill, looking in every direction.

"Nice of you to join us, dudette," called Tariq, grinning.

Alice gently set Aiden on the ground, but kept hold of his hand. They joined the James and Tariq on the crest of the hill.

The hillside spilled down into a deep wooded ravine tangled with briars. Alice breathed deeply. The air was heavy with the scent of roses. Among the briars, golden butterflies flitted here and there, now in shadow, now in light. They seemed to hum as they flew, and the hum rose from the ravine to the children like a song.

"Pretty good hypnotic illusion," James said drily.

"I gotta say," said Tariq, "this is looking more and more like actual magic to me."

"Aidie go to park!" Aiden said excitedly. "Aidie like park!" He began running in circles around the older children, head thrown back, pumping his tiny fists in the air.

"Watch out for the edge, Aidie," Alice said a little sharply. She stepped closer to the ravine, positioning herself between the little boy and the drop.

Tariq rubbed his massive hands together, eyes gleaming like the eyes of the proverbial kid in the candy store. "Gotta say, this adventure is *not* disappointing me. Especially the part where we're still alive. So, where do we go now?"

He and James looked expectantly at Alice. She frowned.

"Our choice," she said.

"What does that mean?" asked James.

"That it's our choice, dork."

"I get that, but why do we suddenly get to choose? No, never mind. This must be level one."

"Translation for us non-geeks?" Alice requested.

"We're in a quest game now," said Tariq. "Metaphorically speaking. When you start a game, there are instructions, and some kind of back story. But once you hit level one and start playing, you have to start making choices."

"I wouldn't mind *more* instructions," mused James. "And more back story. This is pretty free-range." He turned to Alice. "Can you see *anything*? Is anything, like, glowing or whatever?"

Alice made a 360-degree turn, slowly, scanning the horizon. "Nothing."

Tariq clapped James on the shoulder. James staggered.

"Be careful, he's breakable," said Alice.

"Dude," said Tariq, "it's your show now. Brainy little dudette got us here, now *you* gotta figure out which way we go."

James turned slowly in a complete circle. His face was expressionless, flat calm. But there was something in his eyes, a fierce concentration that Alice had never seen before.

"That's it, dude," Tariq said encouragingly. "You're all over this, Night!" He leaned conspiratorially toward Alice. "That's Night's game face."

"Well, it's better than his regular face," Alice deadpanned.

"Hey, no insults, no distractions. He's in his zone, dudette."

James made several more slow turns, thinking, coolly calculating. As a game environment, it wasn't as wide open as it first appeared. There was the forest – too lovely for James' taste. The really nasty monsters were often hidden in the loveliest places. There was the ravine – more to James' taste. It looked difficult to descend, especially with the briars, but that might be deceptive. Often the best route was camouflaged with apparent obstacles, to discourage gamers from taking it.

Then of course –

"We follow the brook," James said decisively.

"What?" asked Alice.

"Brilliant, dude!" said Tariq.

"Come on," said James, descending the hillside. Tariq followed, Alice and Aiden bringing up the rear. The brook originated from a stony spring at the hill's base, rolling merrily along a narrow, pebbly channel that cut between the forest and the ravine. "Watch your step," said James, gesturing to the slippery moss that lined the banks of the brook.

"I take lead," said Tariq, passing James. "You know the drill." James nodded.

"Why are we following the brook?" asked Alice.

She kept a tight grip on Aiden's hand; he was looking longingly at the water, and she knew him well enough to realize he was considering leaping into the charming little stream for a swim.

"It's the unexpected thing," said James. "Most people would pick either the woods or the ravine."

"So, 'unexpected' is good?"

"In a campaign environment? Always. Besides which, streams always lead to settlements, and settlements mean people, and we can ask them where the heck we are and get more instructions."

Alice nodded with a grudging admiration. "Interesting. Your embarrassing über-geekness actually serves some purpose."

James shrugged. He was only paying partial attention to his cousin. The rest of his attention was spread out in a sphere, in every direction around, above and below them.

It was so comfortable, so amazingly comfortable for him. For the first time he was doing in a real-world setting (*If you can call this a real world*, he thought) what he had been doing in game settings since he was four years old. Slipping into a virtual world where you could be attacked at any moment was second nature to him. It was like putting on a comfortable old flannel shirt.

Tariq moved steadily ahead of him, astonishingly silent for such a huge guy. He never stepped on a twig, never snapped a branch in passing. His footsteps didn't make a sound.

Just like in a game, James thought. *This is so wild!*

Something was missing, of course – Hisoka's stealthy rear guard, bringing up the back of the group almost invisibly, picking off any enemies foolish enough to try to attack them from behind. Instead ...

Alice huffed and puffed behind them, trying to keep up, not only with Tariq and James but with Aiden, who was pulling hard on her hand. She and Aiden were snapping twigs and scattering pebbles with every step.

James whistled, the signal for a quick stop. Tariq halted instantly. Alice and Aiden stopped, confused.

"What's the problem?"

"You need to quiet down," said James. "You sound like a couple of elephants. Well, one elephant and one baby elephant."

"Are you calling me an elephant?" Alice asked with dangerous calm.

"Aidie not baby!" said Aiden.

"You *sound* like elephants," James said.

"Aidie not baby!" Aiden kicked James' shin. Hard.

"All I'm trying to say," said James through gritted teeth "is that if there's anything lying in wait along the brook, it's going to hear you. And it's going to get you. Because it won't hear Tariq, or me, and we'll already be waaaay up the trail when *you* get chomped."

Alice shivered. Her post-hypnotic instructions or channeling or whatever it was didn't seem to be working any more. She had no idea what was lurking in the ravine to their right, or the dense green woods to their left. But, pretty as they were, *both* areas looked like prime places for monsters to hide.

"I don't want to scare you," James said more gently, noticing Alice's wary glances, "but it's just campaign protocol. Don't step on anything or kick anything. Be as quiet as you can." He squatted so he was at eye-level with Aiden. "Aidie must be very quiet," James said. "Like the good little mouse."

Aidie hugged him back. "Aidie be good mouse," he agreed.

"I don't have anything against sweet family moments," called Tariq, "but I think *they* might."

"Who?" asked James.

"Them!" Tariq pointed toward the ravine, from which a seemingly endless cloud of golden butterflies was boiling with a menacing hum.

"Are they, are they *attacking* us?" Alice demanded, wondering why her voice sounded so high-pitched. It sounded like she was five. Without thinking about it, she stood between Aiden and the cloud of butterflies, protecting her small cousin. Without thinking about it, James stepped in front of her.

The butterfly cloud swelled, spreading out further and further until it rose a good twenty feet in the air and blocked their path along the brook.

The butterflies' humming swelled and deepened into a menacing growl. The cloud flew closer; close enough for Alice to see the small black flecks among the butterflies' golden scales.

Tariq stepped in front of James.

"Got this, bro'" he said.

"Let me – "

"Got this." Tariq reached into the pocket of his jacket and pulled out a tiny, black plastic bottle. He aimed it toward the cloud of butterflies.

"Wait," called Alice. "What are you going to do? We aren't sure they want to hurt us."

"Do we wait and see if one of us gets chomped?" Tariq asked, looking over his shoulder at James.

Before James could answer, a flock of butterflies broke off from the main cloud, skimming toward Tariq and encircling his right arm. Tariq shouted as each butterfly pierced his arm with a sharp stinger.

"*Man*, that hurts!" Tariq yelled. He slapped at the butterflies, but they were attached to his arms by their stingers, through which they were drawing forth streams of blood, as if their stingers were straws and Tariq's arm was a protein shake.

"Treek! Treek!" shouted Aiden. He broke free from Alice and ran toward Tariq, and would have leaped into the fray if James hadn't grabbed his little brother by the shoulders.

"Tariq is fine, little dude!" called Tariq. "A-OK!" He lifted the small black bottle and sprayed it at the butterflies on his arm. Their wings drooped instantly; their stingers detached, and they wafted lifelessly to the mossy ground.

"Take this, blooderflies!!" shouted Tariq, aiming the nozzle at the massive butterfly cloud. He sprayed in a wild, berserk pattern, up, down, left and right. The cloud retreated immediately, its growl fading to a hum.

Some of the butterflies fell to the ground in a dreamlike, see-saw motion dead or stunned; most broke away from their peers and flew rapidly down into the ravine.

In a few seconds the cloud had disappeared. It was as if nothing had happened – except for the vicious red dots on Tariq's right arm.

"What the *heck* was that?" James asked. "What did you spray them with?"

Tariq flipped the bottle around a couple of times like an old-time sheriff twirling a six-shooter, then dropped the bottle into his pocket.

"Body-spray. Gift from my girlfriend. *Ex*-girlfriend. This stuff can knock out a rhino at twenty paces, dude."

"Are you OK?" asked Alice.

"As you can see, dudette, not exactly. Who has a first aid kit? All right, I can see by your blank stares that no one thought to bring a first-aid kit on this perilous, magical adventure – an oversight we will fix if we survive to fight another boo-yah day." Tariq calmly tore a strip of cloth from the sleeve of his T-shirt, and began dabbing at the bloody red dots. "Hmm. Wounds seem to be closing up already." He wrapped the strip of cloth around his arm a couple of times, "Just in case."

James clapped him on the shoulder. "Thank you," he said simply. *Thank God Tariq drove that cloud away. If those butterflies had hurt little Aiden with their stingers ...*

"What I'm here for, dude," Tariq shrugged. "Nothing epic."

"Why did those things attack us?" asked Alice. "We saw some way back where we started – why did they attack us *now*?"

"When you get attacked, that's usually a good thing," James said. "I mean, *if* you survive it. You only get attacked if you're getting close to something that matters."

Alice peered into the distance, following the line of the burbling brook. "I don't … see anything," she said. Although … She shifted her attention from the brook to the forest running alongside it. There was a faint shimmering of the air among the trees. But it wasn't like the lights she'd seen earlier. It was –

"Smoke!" she said, pointing. Tariq and James followed her gaze.

"White smoke," observed Tariq.

"Cooking fires," said James. "We found a settlement."

"Great," said Alice. "I hope they want to be found."

Chapter Nine – Teulu
June 24th – Aelwyd

Tariq and James had a subdued but lengthy disagreement about which one of them would take the lead in approaching the settlement. They were muttering quietly, so Alice didn't catch most of it, but she got the gist, which was that Tariq wanted to go first, as the bodyguard, and James wanted him to hang back because his arm was wounded.

"I respect you, bro," Tariq said finally, "but if you don't shut up and let me go, James, I'm going to have to stomp you into a pancake."

"Well argued," James said drily. "Proceed."

Alice was amazed by how gracefully Tariq ghosted through the dense trees and ferns.

James followed silently about ten paces behind Tariq; when he got about ten paces into the forest, he lifted his hand, the signal for Alice and Aiden to join them.

Aiden clung to Alice's back; he had been told about fifty times not to make a sound.

How do they do it? wondered Alice. *How are they so quiet?* Her very first step into the woods, she stepped on a dry stick and it snapped like a rifle shot. Ahead of her James twisted around (noiselessly, of course!) and glared at her.

Her next step was more tentative; she skimmed the ground below her before putting her foot down. It was, she realized, as she moved deeper into the forest, a matter of being careful, of thinking through each movement, and slowly easing her weight onto her foot with every step.

The pale smoke grew thicker as they walked, and Alice realized it had a scent to it. It wasn't coffee but on the other hand it was like coffee. Her stomach growled, and she realized how hungry and thirsty she was. They hadn't had anything to drink since Tariq's house and nothing to eat since the morning.

James' fist suddenly shot up, a stop signal. Alice froze in her tracks. She watched James creep slowly, silently through the heavy ferns, and then he slipped behind one of the trees, and was gone.

The trees were beautiful; the pale birch bark glowed, as if the tree had an inner fire; the needles of the evergreens glistened, and the green moss and ivy clinging to their trunks seemed to burn with a green fire. But notwithstanding the strange loveliness of the landscape, Alice felt suddenly alone, very alone, even with Aiden clinging to her back.

Imagine, she thought, *if they never came back. If something happened, and it was just me and Aiden here ...*

A hysterical laugh formed itself in her throat, almost bubbling out of her mouth but she bit it back. *Holy cow*, she thought, *keep it together, Alice. You've got Aiden to think about.*

There was a faint movement in the ferns ahead of her; it was James waving her forward.

"Come on," called James. "It's OK."

Alice walked toward him quickly, abandoning her attempt at a stealthy pace. He turned and walked away from her at a rapid clip. In a moment they were in a clearing among the thick evergreens and birch.

Flames danced in a fire pit in the center of the clearing. Over the fire hung a kettle of some bubbling liquid. *That's what I smelled*, thought Alice, *some sort of backwoods coffee a-brewin'.*

Tariq stood in front of the fire, talking to someone even taller than he was.

Aiden yawned hugely and slumped against Alice's back, instantly asleep.

"Not now, Aidie," said Alice, but he was out like a light. His arms were still wrapped loosely around her neck, but they were beginning to slip.

"James!" she called, "Get Aiden before I drop him."

James darted to her and lifted Aiden, cradling the sleeping boy in his arms.

"Wow, are you giving him sleeping pills or something?" asked James.

"*I* can't control when he sleeps," said Alice. "Who's Tariq talking to?"

"The village chieftain."

"What village?"

"This village. It's called Teulu."

"Teulu?"

"Teulu." James gestured broadly.

"Where are the houses?" asked Alice. It didn't seem to be much of a settlement.

"Look closer," said James.

Alice squinted and looked around the clearing – *really* looked, this time. It took her a moment to see that there were subtle windows and doors carved into the massive tree trunks, and the branches seemed to form a roof here, a staircase there …

"Wow," she said, impressed. It was like an optical illusion; what looked simply like trees were a circle of elaborate village dwellings.

"The villagers are peaceful," said James. "So they need the camouflage. Pretty much anybody will walk right through and not notice them."

"Except, their fire and smoke is like a big neon sign," Alice pointed out. "'Here we are! Come kill us and steal our coffee!'"

"Usually they'd have a camouflaged structure around the fire pit. But they dismantled it today. Their chief told them the Chosen Ones were coming, and they wanted to be sure the Chosen Ones found Teulu."

"Lucky for us," said Alice. "When are the Chosen Ones supposed to arrive?"

James shook his head. "You are so smart, you're dumb," he said.

"I'm just asking," she said, stung.

"*We're* the Chosen Ones, cousin. Me, you, Aiden. "

"Oh." Alice *did* feel a little stupid. *Of course* they were the Chosen Ones. This whole crazy thing had been set up for them. A test of "magic". A test to see whether they were worthy to take their place in the *Sircus* troupe their ancestors had belonged to …

She peered past Tariq, to get a better view of the village chief. The man had close-shorn, curly dark hair, appeared to be seven feet tall as opposed to Tariq's six feet, and was wrapped in a long black cloak. He had a nasty-looking scar on his right cheek.

"But, *that's* the weird guy from the train!" Alice whispered to James.

"Yup."

"He's the village chieftain?" she asked in disbelief.

"So he says."

"Do we believe him? He didn't *sound* like the chieftain of some little nowhere village."

James laughed.

"I'm not putting down their, this little society, or whatever it is," Alice said defensively, "but he just didn't sound like someone who lives in a tree."

"Oh, OK. As long as you're not putting down their little society."

"You know what I'm trying to say."

"The problem with you," said James, "is you don't know anything about elves."

"Believe me," said Alice, "whatever problems I might have, that's not one of them."

"Elves are a highly advanced race," said James.

"And, by the way, totally fictional."

"They're a metaphor," said James, "for living simply. You can be extremely sophisticated and intelligent but still run your society on principles of simplicity and respect for nature."

Alice yawned. "I'm sorry," she deadpanned, "pardon me while I faint from complete boredom."

"You are such a brat," said James. "Nice to know our adventures aren't expanding your perspective in the least bit."

"Where are the rest of the villagers?" asked Alice.

"Look closer."

She glanced around the clearing again.

As far as she could see, the place was deserted except for the chieftain. Although ... She finally saw them, the glint of dim forest light on human eyes. There were dozens of them, no, hundreds, in the shadowy doorways and windows, most staring at Tariq and the chief, some staring at her and James.

"Are they ... do you think they heard me?" she whispered to James.

"Some of them, sure," he said.

"Maybe they don't speak English."

"They do. Very good English, since they're partly descended from the English."

"Well, that's just ... awesome," Alice said ironically.

"Relax," said James, "you're one of the Chosen Ones. They can't kill you for being a snob until we complete our quests."

Alice looked into the shadows again. The villagers all appeared to be tall, like the chief, with dark curls and enormous dark eyes, all wearing dark cloaks fastened with wooden pegs. As her gaze swept one of the shadowy windows, she saw that one of the women was staring directly at her. Alice shivered.

"I'm just kidding," said James. "There isn't anything to worry about. They didn't hear you. I don't think our voices carry that far."

"You're really OK with this, aren't you?" Alice asked curiously.

"Well … yeah, I guess," said James.

"Because this is part of your normal dork routine, pretending to be an elf or something and running around inside a fantasy world."

"I'm rarely an elf," said James, "I'm usually a warrior."

"Whatever. Not the point, cousin. You feel comfortable here."

"I really kind of do."

"Well, I *don't*."

"Sure you do," he said. "How about when you were channeling all that stuff? You felt OK then, didn't you?"

"Better than now," she said. "And … those lights that led us, they really were beautiful. I felt very connected."

"Sure, that was your turf. But now, I guess this is my turf. We followed you through the mist. We knew you'd get us through. So now, you've got to trust I'll get you through this."

"But I'm awesome," Alice objected, "and you're a dork."

"I totally give up," James said to the universe.

Tariq wrapped up his conversation with the chieftain, shook the massive man's hand, turned and strode over to the cousins.

"OK," said Tariq, "I don't know why, but the chieftain says he can't have any contact with you at this moment. So he told me what we need to know, and now he's going. But we're supposed to take refreshment here with the villagers before we go any further. They're very excited to meet us."

"I can tell," said Alice, regarding the villagers hidden among the trees.

"That's just their way," said Tariq. "Whenever strangers approach, they hang back until Fuego tells them it's OK to come out."

"Fuego's the chieftain?" asked James. Tariq nodded. "*Fuego*, 'fire'. Cool name."

"Cool dude," Tariq said admiringly. "You can tell, he's like, a fearsome, head-busting warrior."

"So what *are* our instructions?" Alice asked impatiently.

"She's feeling brain-blind," James told Tariq. "Since her channeling thing stopped. It's freaking her out a little bit not to know what's going on."

"I'm *not* freaked out," said Alice. "Is it weird to want to know what we're supposed to do next?"

"Not at all," said Tariq. "Fuego's going on ahead to the fortress. After we kick it here with the village dudes, we're joining him."

"Fortress?" Alice and James asked together.

"All will be explained. Or so Fuego promised. He *seems* like a dude that keeps his word."

There was the faintest of rustling sounds, as if a delicate breeze were stirring the birch leaves.

Suddenly the clearing was full of villagers, hundreds of them, children and youths and the middle-aged and the elderly. Some peered down from the camouflaged windows, branches, balconies. Most gathered in a ring around the fire pit. Their body language was wary. They were still hanging back from the Chosen Ones.

Like they're afraid of us, thought Alice.

Like they don't want to frighten us, thought James.

Alice could perceive, very faintly, tiny pinpoints of light around the villagers. But even beyond that, their very appearance was otherworldly. Their beautiful dark eyes were so large, much bigger than human eyes – more like the eyes of the characters in Japanese Manga books.

They were extraordinarily tall, even the children and the women, proportionally about a foot taller than a typical human. They all wore long black cloaks, and their movements betrayed a combination of impressive strength and grace; it was like all the villagers, even the children and the elderly, were trained warriors.

Everyone had long hair, wavy or curly, and dark. Some wore it loose. Others had caught their hair in braids secured with clasps of wood and stone. Their skin was tan, bespeaking a life spent largely outdoors under the sun.

Their faces were uniformly beautiful, gaunt and chiseled, like Fuego's when they'd seen him on the train. It was a peculiarly grave beauty, with frown lines etched on the brow of even the youngest child, as if they rarely found anything to smile about and rarely found anything amusing.

The woman that had been looking so intently at Alice stepped forward and bowed hesitantly. She was one of the tallest villagers, and she wore one of the most elaborate hair clasps, a riot of colorful, polished pebbles, red, blue, green and purple. Whereas some of the villagers were surrounded by a few motes of light, this woman was almost cloaked by them.

Alice found herself returning the bow automatically. James and Tariq followed her lead.

"You are most welcome in Aelwyd," said the woman. "I am Fuego's wife, Tanwen." The accent was British, but with a liquid lilt.

"Thank you, Tanwen," said Alice, knowing she was butchering the pronunciation of the woman's name. "I am Alice. This is my cousin Aiden," she pressed her cheek against her sleeping cousin's curls, "my cousin James," she nodded toward her older cousin, "and his friend Tariq," with a nod toward the hulking teen.

"Aelwyd welcomes you," said Tanwen, bowing again. "At least, our village Teulu welcomes you. Not all in the land will be pleased to see you. Even as we speak, the Ilwgyld's spies are no doubt informing them of your arrival. It is only safe for you to stay here a brief time, and then you must repair to the fortress, where you will be safe until you return to your world."

"And who are the ... the Ill-wig-ild?" Alice asked, stumbling over the strange word.

"You would call them 'the hungry'. They are the Hungry Ones who have drawn you into this world before your time."

"The ladies at the train station," Alice guessed.

"Not ladies," Tanwen said darkly. "Far from ladies. But yes, those are two of the ... creatures." She turned to the villagers, said something in a sprightly, liquid language that Alice couldn't begin to identify. The villagers hurried off into the trees.

"Please, sit," Tanwen said graciously gesturing to the area around the fire pit.

On the ground? wondered Alice, appalled.

James and Tariq dropped easily to the ground and sat cross-legged, as if it was nothing new to flop down in the dirt. *Boys!* thought Alice.

Tanwen smiled faintly, as if reading Alice's expression. She whispered something to the elderly woman next to her; the woman disappeared into one of the doorways. "Nain will fetch you a cushion," said Tanwen.

Alice blushed. "I'm sorry," she told Tanwen, "I don't mean to be all HM."

"And yet you are," said James.

"Aych Em?" asked Tanwen. "I am not familiar with this word."

"Acronym," James said helpfully, "for 'high-maintenance'. It means she needs a lot of attention and special treatment."

Alice glared at him. She wasn't going to pitch a fit here and now, not in front of these graceful and gracious people, but James was going to pay later for insulting her in front of the whole village!

"Ah," said Tanwen, "you mean she's a lot of work. Yes. We were advised of that. We have known all about you, the three of you, for some time now. We have been preparing for the Chosen Ones for generations." Tanwen bowed again, and sat on the ground across from Alice as gracefully as if she were sitting on a throne.

Nain, the elderly woman, returned with a beautifully woven red-and-black cloth. She placed it carefully on the mossy ground next to James. She said nothing, but smiled brightly and nodded at Alice to take a seat.

"Thank you," said Alice, sitting slowly, careful not to drop her dozing cousin. The cloth was surprisingly soft and comfortable.

The villagers Tanwen had dispatched moments before returned with bowls and hollow gourds. They filled the vessels with the fragrant brew in the cook pot over the fire. At a simple nod from Tanwen, they gave a bowl and a gourd to each of the visitors.

"Drink," said Tanwen. "It will give you strength for your return journey."

Tariq shrugged and took a deep draught from his bowl.

James and Alice took polite but shallow sips.

It looks gross! thought Alice.

I hope it's not poisoned, thought James.

Tariq, James and Alice exchanged startled looks and then grinned at each other. The drink was delicious! It was like coffee blended with chocolate seasoned with vanilla and gingerbread and cinnamon. James and Alice drank deeply from their bowls.

"Wow," said Tariq, "village dudes, you need to sell this recipe to Starbucks! You'll be living in solid gold pine trees! Truly, hats off. This is magical."

Tanwen nodded absently. Her attention was on James, Alice and the sleeping Aiden.

"I am sorry," she said, "that you find us less than fully prepared to welcome you and defend you. As I said, the Ilwgyld have tricked you into visiting us rather sooner than expected. You are still too young, but the quest, once begun, must be completed. So you must do your best. And we will help you as much as lies within our power."

Tariq emptied his bowl and wiped his mouth on his sleeve. "This stuff is a great start!" he said. "Might I have some more?"

A villager took his bowl, refilled it, returned it, with the dexterity of a magician.

Tariq lifted his bowl in a toast to the entire company. "Mud in your eyes, dudes!" He drank.

"Tanwen," said James quietly, "what exactly *is* our quest?"

She started to speak, but hesitated.

"It's too much," she said, "to explain in mere moments. And were I to explain the entire quest, it might be too terrifying for you to take in."

"Hey, we don't even have 'terror' in our vocabulary," said Tariq.

"It's like a game," said James thoughtfully, almost to himself. "We're on an early level. The challenges get doled out level by level, not all at once."

"I assure you, this is no game," said Tanwen, "although when you return to your world, it will feel as if none of this were real."

Alice finished the delicious drink. The bowl in her hands was rough-hewn, carved from a tree bole. She could feel the discomfort of the pine needles and pebbles beneath the cloth on which she sat digging into her legs. A faint breeze made the flames in the fire pit dance.

So much detail. Such texture. It was crazy, but this place *felt* real. How could all of it, all of this, be a hypnotism-induced hallucination?

"You called this village Teulu," said Alice. "Are you related to the faeries of English folklore?"

Tanwen nodded appreciatively. "You are nimble-minded as your reputation promises. We are descended of the faeries of the British Isles, and the faeries of other nations – but they are not folklore."

"And what is your relationship to the *Sircus of Impossible Magicks*?"

"We are …" she hesitated. "We are the children of Myrddin's tribe, and we are the children of the faeries. Merlin and the magicians in his circle had a great affection for the faery clans. There were marriages. From this great magic, the *Sircus* was born. But as will happen in any community, differences arose over the centuries. Our ancestors parted ways from the *Sircus* troupe because we did not agree with their darker rituals and customs. We sought a life of greater simplicity, of deeper light. In this realm, we found like-minded faeries from many different clans."

"Cool," said Tariq. "Sounds very multi-cultural. You guys could totally settle in L.A."

"We *are* in L.A.," said Tanwen, "but in a different L.A. This is another … it's so difficult to find the precise words. We are in Rath L.A."

"Huhn. I've heard of East L.A., South L.A. and West L.A., but I never heard of Rath L.A."

"We exist at a different, I don't know how to put it, a different pitch, a different frequency. We are here, but no one in your L.A. notices us, and vice-versa. Unless you are descended from the children of Myrddin and the children of the faeries. And, of course, unless you find the portals where the barriers between the two worlds have worn thin."

"So, Sony Stadium, that's a place where the barrier's worn thin?"

"Yes."

"We have an ancestor," James said, "Jonathan Myrddin."

"Yes." Tanwen nodded.

"He belonged to the *Sircus of Impossible Magicks*?"

"Yes. He was born into it, as are all descendants of Myrddin and the faeries. But he never accepted its … darker aspects. When his association with the *Sircus* was exposed after London's Great Fire, he left England, determined to create a branch of the *Sircus* that was devoted purely to good. And for a long time … a very long time, more than you can imagine … that is what we have been."

"But the bad *Sircus* folks, the, the-"

"Ilwgyld," said Tanwen.

"The Ill-wig-ild," said James, "want to wipe you out."

"Yes. They have always wanted to destroy us."

"Why?" asked Alice.

Tanwen shrugged eloquently, and smiled at Alice a little sadly, as if the girl had just asked an impossible and grave question, like "Why is there death?"

"Evil cannot abide good," Tanwen said softly. "It has been thus for all time."

"Dude! It's dang sure a rule in every quest video game!" said Tariq.

He clapped James on the shoulder, almost knocking the bowl out of James' hands. "At least we know we're on the good side, heh? Those evil dudes aren't even gonna know what hit 'em!"

Alice was frowning, brow knit in thought. "But, what are we supposed to *do*?" she asked Tanwen. "You said we were supposed to follow this quest thing when we were older. What are we supposed to do since we've been pushed into it now?"

"The best you can, child," Tanwen said kindly. She dipped her head in an almost reverential gesture. "We have the deepest faith in the Chosen Ones: in the panther's heart, the serpent's wisdom, and the monkey's chaos. Your victory has been foretold among our people for … a very long time indeed."

James pushed up his sleeve, regarded his panther tattoo. A murmur ran through the villagers like an electric current.

Alice pushed up her sleeve, revealing her intricately scaled serpent tattoo. A louder murmur flowed through the crowd.

Tanwen closed her eyes, as if suddenly gripped by a great pain. She slumped forward, and then sat up straight, opening eyes that flashed with anger.

"The Ilwgyld – they gave you quest kits," she said bitterly. "Show me. Now, please."

Wordlessly, Alice pulled her red-and-black beaded pouch from within her hoodie, and removed Aiden's sky-blue felt pouch. Aiden mumbled something but didn't wake. James pulled the black leather bag from within his sweatshirt.

"Open them, quickly!" said Tanwen. There was no mistaking the urgency in her voice. Alice and James obeyed without question, tipping the contents of their bags onto the ground. They gasped.

The plastic vials of "water" were silvery flasks. The plastic vials of "sand" were silver boxes. The "plastic" rings were heavy silver rings, encrusted with minute jewels. Aiden's ring bore an elaborately carved capuchin monkey with sapphire eyes, James' a panther with jade eyes, and Alice's a serpent with eyes formed by rubies.

"May their eyes never see light!" groaned Tanwen. "May their ears never hear music!"

"What's the matter?" asked James. "I think it's just the faery magic."

"Sure," said Alice. "In our L.A., all this stuff looks like cheap little toys. And the pouches have a spell of inattention on them. So no one notices them, and if they do they'll think it's all just junk. But here in Aelwyd, their true forms are revealed."

"The clever, awful cunning of it!" groaned Tanwen. "We were to present you with your quest kits. Along with our blessing. But they forestalled us. They gave you your quest packs first."

"Not to be a moron, or whatever," said Tariq, "but as long as the Chosen Ones got their magic bags, who cares who gave it to them?"

"Is there something wrong with these things?" James hazarded.

"Yes," said Tanwen. "And no. These *are* the elements with which you were to begin the quest. I can feel their magic. They are untainted. But the tattoos – those are *not* part of the kit. Those are Ilwgyld markers. You are branded now. They will sense you wherever you are. And they will know you by your marks – the warrior, the seer and the trickster."

"What?" Alice demanded. "You mean these are like, like GPS trackers or something? They can find us wherever we are?"

"I am afraid so."

"Then we'll get rid of them," James said decisively. "When we get back to our L.A., we'll wash them off first thing. In our L.A., they're just temporary tattoos."

"Sure," said Tariq. "A little rubbing alcohol and they go bye-bye."

Tanwen shook her head. "You cannot remove them now," she said, "not in your world or any world. They are Ilwgyld brands, and the curse of the marks is that they are eternal."

Alice got a queasy look. "We're not going to … we're not going to be *possessed* or something, are we? We're not going to go all evil, are we?"

"It wouldn't be anything new for you," said James wryly. She stuck her tongue out at him.

"The marks cannot make *you* evil," said Tanwen. "But they call out to evil things."

"What does that *mean*?" demanded Alice. Her mind swam with images of monsters swarming into her room at night. "Oh my gosh!" She pushed up Aiden's sleeve. "How could we be so stupid? *So stupid*! What if something comes after Aidie?"

Tanwen's face drained of blood, until it was chalk white. "You … you put a tattoo on … *him*? On the child?"

Alice hugged Aiden tightly to her chest, James leaning over both of them, grim-faced. The sleeping child looked angelic.

"Don't worry," James said to Alice, "I won't let anything hurt you guys."

"Me neither," Tariq said stoutly.

Alice shook James' hand away, turning on him angrily. "What are you supposed to *do*, dork? If these crazy things are *really* real, what can you do about it?"

"I don't know!" he shouted. "But I'll do something!"

"Enough!" Tanwen said. Her voice crackled like lightning. "Enough of this bickering. You are all in grave danger, most especially the child. You go to the fortress now."

She gestured curtly to the villagers standing closest to them. They were the tallest of the villagers, and had unobtrusively formed a ring around Tanwen and the visitors. James noticed they all had longbows slung across their backs.

"Fuego's personal guard," said Tanwen, "our finest warriors. They will transport you safely."

Tanwen stood. James, Alice and Tariq followed suit. James' knees felt a little wobbly.

They're in danger! It was all he could think of, over and over. *Aiden and Alice are in danger!*

Tanwen surprised Alice by suddenly ruffling Aiden's curls. He mumbled something and stirred in Alice's arms. "Nothing must happen to him," Tanwen said intensely.

"Nothing will," said James. Alice looked at him in surprise. Except for her, nothing every made James lose his temper, but he looked plenty mad now. "Listen, lady," he said to Tanwen, "we're flying blind here. We didn't ask for any of this, and we don't know what we're doing."

"I know," Tanwen said coolly. "That is abundantly clear." She touched Aiden's curls again, but Alice turned, moving Aiden away from her. Tanwen smiled a bitter little smile. "You don't understand," she said to Alice. "That is your great blind spot, seer. You think you know things that you do not understand. And you understand things that you do not realize."

James put an arm around Alice's shoulders, drew her and Aiden to his side.

"Aren't we supposed to be making a getaway?" he said pointedly.

Tanwen snapped her fingers. Fuego's personal guard swarmed around the visitors.

"Fare thee well," said Tanwen. She turned away from them.

"Onward," called the lead guard, and they set off at a quick pace into the trees.

Tariq took the lead within the circle of guards. James took Aiden from Alice. James nudged Alice so that she was walking ahead of him, just behind Tariq. "You'll be all right," James told her.

"Oh, of course I will," she said sarcastically. "Sounds like we're all gonna be just fine!"

None of them bothered to muffle their footsteps, they just trotted like mad through the forest. Clearly speed, not stealth, was of the essence.

Alice turned, just once, before they drew out of sight of the village. She saw Tanwen, her back still turned to them. Tanwen slumped, suddenly, against the old woman called Nain. Tanwen's shoulders trembled as if she were crying.

Chapter Ten – The Fortress
June 24th – Aelwyd

Alice had never been so frightened in her life.

She barely noticed her surroundings. Trees flicking past as they jogged through the forest. Moss and leaves and pine needles under foot, stones and pebbles and tree roots, any manner of hazards but somehow they all raced along without stumbling or pausing.

The gold-green forest light began to darken into a cool green-blue, and shadows pooled among the trees. As Alice ran – she had never run so far in her life – her eyes darted now and again to the shadowy places where … what? Something, *anything* could be lurking.

What were the Ilwgyld like? "The Hungry Ones." That was a foreboding name. Alice imagined the gleam of very sharp claws and very sharp teeth and very pointy horns. As they passed a fallen tree, it seemed to her as if it moved slightly, as if it were not a tree at all, but a crouching monster. Lou and Flo had had a dark air about them at Union Station, an unpleasant, hungry manner. What would they look like, here in this realm, where their true appearance would be revealed?

"There!" said the lead guard, not slowing down, but pointing to a gap in the trees.

This edge of the forest dead-ended at a rocky hillside. Alice could see the hidden door in the stone, its edges lined with shimmering sparks of light.

James slowed a bit behind Alice.

"It's OK," she called back to James, guessing his concern. James wouldn't carry Aiden full-tilt into a rock wall unless he knew it would be OK. "There's a door in the rock," Alice assured him. "I can see it."

They barreled through the secret door, the lead guards first, then Tariq, then Alice, James and Aiden, and, finally, the rear guard.

They found themselves in a tunnel lit by luminous flowers that grew at intervals along the damp stone wall.

The flowers were pale blue, and pale green, and cast a lovely glow, accompanied by a crisp fragrance, like the smell of the ocean.

No one slowed their pace. They all trotted down the hall as if a pack of Ilwgyld were right on their heels.

The tunnel had numerous cross-channels, smaller tunnels that cut away to the left and right, but the guards kept jogging dead ahead. Finally they made an abrupt turn to the left.

Alice stumbled and almost took a spill, but James steadied her elbow. She shook his hand away, embarrassed that she'd almost fallen.

A ruddy light smudged the narrow slice of horizon; it looked like they were about to enter a chamber. In a moment they stepped into enormous stone chamber, with vaulted ceilings, where a fire burned in a hearth twice as tall as Tariq.

Alice gasped.

The walls were at least a hundred feet high, and lined with shelf after shelf of books.

There have to be thousands of books here … Maybe hundreds of thousands …

The bindings were leather, well-worn, stamped with golden lettering and symbols.

A long wooden table dominated the center of the room. It looked like it could have comfortably seated the whole village, but the only person sitting at it was Fuego.

He had shed his dark cloak, draping it over his chair. He wore black trousers, black boots, and a white hooded tunic. Fuego sat comfortably, fingers stitched behind his closely shaved head, leaning back and balanced the chair on two legs.

"Astonishing," Fuego said, grinning, "I had no idea anyone but me could place Tanwen in so foul a mood!"

"How did you – " Alice began, but Fuego cut her off.

"A little bird told me, child," he said. "So – Tanwen is having fits because you adorned yourselves with tattoos of evil. And, who can blame her. It was not *precisely* the best first move you could have made in the campaign."

"We didn't *know*," Alice said.

"Too right," Fuego agreed. "We'll find a way to work around it. Please." He gestured to the chairs nearest him. James sat on Fuego's left, cradling Aiden. Alice sat on Fuego's right.

Tariq stood behind Fuego's chair, acting as look out for James, Alice and Aiden, just as Fuego's personal guard had fanned out around the room to protect their leader.

"And so," Fuego said quietly, "the quest company is nearly complete."

"Who's missing?" asked James.

Fuego waved a dismissive hand. "No time to go into details at present. More pressing matters. Such as returning you home in one piece. I have time only to share the essence of your situation: Ilwgyld are bad, my people are good. You are descended from the good tribe. You were *supposed* to begin a quest several years from now, when you were ready, and I was going to help prepare you. The Ilwgyld have accelerated the time table, forcing you to follow the quest as mere children."

"Hey," said James. "I'm sixteen."

"Sorry. I should say, rather, when you're still *young*. And, anticipating your questions, no, we cannot halt the quest now that it's in motion. *That* is why I warned you not to enter the *L.A. Magickal History Hunt*. And before you protest, yes, I quite realize the Ilwgyld mesmerized you into signing that contract. I do not criticize. I merely wish ... that you did not have to quest four years before the appointed time."

"Isn't there any way to remove the tattoos?" asked Alice. "It's awful," she shuddered, "to think the Hungry Ones can track us with these things."

"Unfortunately," said Fuego, "there is no way that *I* know of to remove your tattoos. But my people will work on that. And yes, you *are* in danger, because the Ilwgyld can track you – but you are in less danger than you or Tanwen fear. It is my surmise that the Ilwgyld would rather win you over to their side than eliminate you. At any rate, they would be mad to destroy you before you obtained all of the touchstones, which they wish to obtain as fervently as we."

"And, just out of curiosity," said Alice, "what *is* their side?"

Fuego considered the question, tilting back and forth on two legs of his chair. "Greed, lass. Envy. Hatred. Destruction. That is why our people broke with the *Sircus* hundreds of years ago. Their methods ... If they encountered mortal children who seemed gifted, they stole the children from the parents."

"That's terrible," said Alice. James instinctively held Aiden closer. Aiden stirred restlessly in his sleep.

"Aye," agreed Fuego. "Quite terrible. And, if *Sircus* children did not pass the magickal initiation tests, they were ... disposed of. And anyone who tried to leave the *Sircus*, or challenged its methods, well, those persons were disposed of, as well." Fuego drew a forefinger across his throat. "Does that answer your question?" he asked Alice.

"Yeah," she said. She felt queasy.

"The Ilwgyld are the epitome of ravenous discontent."

"That's why you call them 'the Hungry Ones'."

"Precisely," Fuego said. "Although, there is *second* reason we call them the hungry. But that is a tale for another time."

"What do we – " James began, but Fuego held up a huge hand, signaling him to be silent.

"No time for exposition, James. We'll talk at length, another time, I promise. You have been through much for one day, and you have yet to complete the first task of your quest. We need to send you home, for now; and you must retrieve the first touchstone."

James was studying Fuego. Teulu's chieftain certainly *seemed* like one of the good guys – heroic, intelligent, a leader, a warrior. Fuego was the chieftain of Teulu village, and Tanwen's husband, but he didn't appear to be of pure faery descent. His eyes were human, and his accent, at times seemed more American than British ...

"Who *are* you?" James asked.

"There is no way to answer that, at present," laughed Fuego. "In the first place, you wouldn't believe me, and it would create unnecessary arguments and distractions. In the second place, if you *did* believe me, it would, in the idiom of your world, 'mess with your heads' – again, creating a distraction. So let us simply say I'm a gent from your world, who went over the wall, and settled in Aelwyd."

"More than settled," James said. "You seem to run the place."

"It's a rather large place," Fuego said, shrugging, "and you've only seen a sliver of it. Now, no more time for conversation. You will see me again soon. In the meantime, you must recover the first touchstone, and you must be on your guard. The Ilwgyld will track you via the tattoos, and they will send you on quests and you will retrieve the magical objects at each site. But you *must* wait for my signal before you begin each task. And you must deliver to me, and *only* me, the magical objects you recover."

"Yeah, I don't see the Hungry Ones being too happy about that," said Alice, picturing Lou and Flo.

"Don't tell them, of course," said Fuego. "Tell them that you are hiding the touchstones as you find them, that you will deliver the magickal objects in one fell swoop, when the quest is complete. If you were to deliver the touchstones to the Ilwgyld ... It does not bear thinking about. The destruction they could cause to my clan, to this land ..."

He snapped his fingers and the four tallest and fiercest looking of his guards snapped to attention, two men and two women. Their hair was banded with elaborately carved wooden rings gleaming with sky-blue stones.

"Escort them to the tower portal," said Fuego.

"It shall be done," the guards replied in unison.

Fuego put one hand on James' shoulder, and one hand on Alice's shoulder, and looked earnestly from one to the other.

"Once you have retrieved the first touchstone, rest long and well. The fate of my clan, of this land, is riding on your young shoulders."

Fuego gripped Tariq's wrist, a warrior's hand-shake.

"Take good care of them," he said, "and yourself."

Tariq nodded with unusual gravity. "I will, chieftain dude," he said.

Fuego snapped his fingers.

The four elite guards surrounded the four visitors and marched them down the length of the massive library.

Alice glanced back at Fuego, who looked very small in that gargantuan chamber. He was paging through a massive tome, rubbing his temple thoughtfully.

The guards halted in front of a blank wall. "Is this – " James began to ask.

"Yes," said Alice, "it's a door." She could see the door's edges limned with particles of light. *Weird … I'm already getting used to this … seeing things others can't see …*

This time when they passed through the wall, it wasn't into a tunnel or a chamber, but rather the same cold, black morass they'd passed through when they entered the faery realm of Aelwyd.

Mercifully, they passed through it quickly, the dense darkness, and in mere seconds were strolling through the chill, grey mist that separated the mortal world from the faery realm.

The guards and the children walked … and walked … and walked some more. Alice and the faery guards could see the path, which was picked out by flickering flecks of light. Tariq and James simply followed the guards, Alice once again walking between them …

They couldn't see the ground, but they could feel it sloping steeply downward as they traveled.

"What *is* this place?" Alice wondered aloud, and then immediately answered her own question. "This place is a neutral valence," she said, the words filling her mind, "a non-place *between* places that is, literally, neither here nor there."

"Wow, that is *so* freaky, dudette," Tariq said admiringly.

"A non-place," mused James.

"I don't even understand what I just said," Alice complained.

"A valence is a zone," James explained. "Basically, this is the void zone between the real world, well, our world, and Aelwyd. It's no place."

"That's why it's so scenic," laughed Tariq.

"With all due respect, Chosen Ones and Companion," said a guard, "how about being quiet so we are not attacked?"

"There's no violence permitted in the valence," Alice said.

"True. The Ilwgyld, however, have been known to break rules. Let us all quieten down," said the guard, "lest we be slain."

They walked in silence for what felt like another ten minutes. Aiden never woke. The down slope continued but it was less steep, more gradual.

At last, Alice saw the luminous outline of a door ahead. She almost shouted "Finally!" in sheer relief, but stopped herself. If the Ilwgyld were going to set a trap, setting it right at the valence exit would be a clever move.

They followed the guards through the invisible door, back into their world.

It was pitch black on the other side.

There was a scrape of stone against metal, a splash of flame, and then one of the guards lit a torch. The faery warrior woman lifted the torch high and moved it from side to side, inspecting the surroundings.

James and Alice could see that they were within what appeared to be a small pyramid, about fifty feet tall at the center point. It appeared to be empty.

"All is clear," the guard announced to her comrades. "We may leave the Chosen Ones here in good conscience."

"Where is 'here'?" James asked, looking around the empty pyramid.

The warriors ignored the question. By torchlight, they led the Chosen Ones to a door – an actual, physical door, not a magical door – and then halted.

"Here we leave the Chosen Ones," the guards said in unison, "hale and well."

"I don't know if I feel *completely* well," said Alice. "I have kind of a stomach ache."

James rolled his eyes.

"I don't feel completely well either," said Tariq, looking at the angry red welts on his arm where the golden butterflies had attacked him.

"Yes – hale and well," the guards repeated emphatically.

They bowed deeply, handed the blazing torch to Tariq, and then, at an impossibly fast speed, and with a sound like the faint ringing of bells, dashed back through the magic door into the valence.

"Well *that* was rude," Alice said peevishly. "I'm going to complain to Fuego when we see him again."

"Maybe he has, like, a customer service hot line," laughed Tariq.

"Well, it *was* rude," Alice insisted. "Are they supposed to treat the Chosen Ones this way? I mean, where *are* we? *Why* are we here?"

"Let's find out," James said reasonably. He stepped toward the door, but Tariq cut him off.

"I go first. It's what I do, bro."

"Right," said James. "I don't know why I keep forgetting that. It's second nature in the game."

Chapter Eleven – The Tower
June 24th – Los Angeles

Tariq slowly pushed the door open, and then stepped noiselessly into a long corridor. It looked like an ordinary, windowless hallway, tiled with inexpensive linoleum squares, the kind you'd find in just about any large building, but the flickering red torchlight gave it a sinister cast. The corridor seemed to wrap around the pyramid room they'd just vacated.

"Looks OK," Tariq said quietly, waving Alice and James forward.

Their sneaker soles were silent on the linoleum.

"I don't see any doors or windows," Alice whispered.

"Magical or normal?" asked James.

"Either," she said.

"Are you getting any incoming transmissions?"

"Nope."

"So ... I guess we just explore 'till we know what we're supposed to do," said James.

They followed the corridor all the way around the exterior of the pyramid. There found no doors or windows.

There was, however, an alcove containing a freight elevator. The doors were heavily scratched and scraped, and their dark green paint was peeling off in narrow strips.

"Looks like one of those elevators in a horror movie," Tariq whispered cheerfully, "where you get in and something pops out at you and the elevator starts zooming up and down – "

"That is *not* helpful," said James. As his eyes adjusted to the torch light, he noticed a very narrow wooden door adjacent to the elevator. "Stairs, maybe," James said nodding toward the door.

"Allow me, Chosen Dude."

Tariq tried the doorknob – unlocked. He opened the door slowly; rusty hinges squealed. Tariq thrust the torch inside, revealing nothing more than an ancient mop and bucket, a broom that had shed most of its bristles, and a plastic jug of floor cleaner. "Janitor's closet," he said, disappointed.

"Better than a bloodthirsty Ilwgyld," said James.

"I guess." Tariq sounded unconvinced. "Well, come on dudes – hop aboard the cursed elevator!" He pushed the "down" button – the only button – and it lit. The elevator doors slid open with a rusty groan. "This way to the inferno!" said Tariq, grinning.

Alice shivered.

"*Really* not helpful," James told Tariq. "Alice is already totally claustrophobic. And afraid of heights."

"I am not!" Alice said indignantly. "I just don't like tiny spaces. Or being too high up."

"Yeah," said James. "Claustrophobic. And afraid of heights."

"It's not *that* cramped in here, actually," said Tariq, bounding into the elevator, panning the torch left and right. "Pretty big, you know, so they can fit equipment and furniture and stuff in here."

"It'll be OK, Alice," James said encouragingly.

"Do *not* patronize me," Alice complained.

Heart starting to pound, she stepped into the elevator as calmly as she could manage.

James followed her. He shifted Aiden from one arm to the other. Aiden was beginning to stir.

"Not a lot of choice here," said Tariq, holding the torch under the elevator's single button. The button read "27" in white numerals against a black background. "Gang, I guess we're going to floor 27." He pressed the button, and the doors groaned shut.

Aiden lifted his head, rubbing his eyes. "Where Aidie?" he asked.

The elevator gave a sudden lurch and dropped what felt like several feet.

Alice screamed.

"*Weehooo!*" shouted Aiden, pumping his small fists. "Tower Terror!"

The elevator lurched again and dropped what felt like close to ten feet.

Alice screamed again. She grabbed one of James' hands and one of Aiden's hands.

"No scared, Allie" said Aiden. "Tower Terror! Go again, go again!"

"If we die," said Tariq, "it was totally an honor protecting you guys."

"And if we die," hissed Alice, "I hope you know you did a terrible job."

Tariq pressed the "27" button repeatedly. The elevator made a third, stomach-flipping drop of about fifteen feet.

Alice screamed and hid her face against Aiden's small shoulder. He patted her head.

"Allie, no scared," he said comfortingly.

The doors slid open with a horrific grinding of metal against metal.

Alice leaped through the open doors.

She found herself in a dimly lit, columned chamber with floor-to-ceiling windows flanked by floor-to-ceiling drapes. She could barely discern, high above, words written along the edges of the ceiling …

Alice slumped to the floor. She wrapped her arms around her knees and began to rock back and forth.

"Wow," said Tariq, "she's like, totally traumatized."

"She'll be OK in a minute," said James. "It's just the claustrophobia. And the fear of heights."

"What a combination!"

"I don't have claustrophobia," Alice objected querulously. "And I'm *fine*!"

"Dudette, trust me," said Tariq, "you are totally, completely messed up. But that's OK, because we are now out of the elevator."

"Out of the elevator, but where," wondered James, looking around. "A museum?"

"It's a reception room. A place for ceremonies and celebrations," Alice said, reciting the information that flowed into her mind. "Ceremonies, celebrations, and press conferences."

"How do you know – oh," said James. "Channeling."

"The fun that never stops," Alice said drily.

"Well, this place has a totally creepy vibe," Tariq said approvingly. "In a kind of cool way. Hey, there's a bunch of windows," he said excitedly, swinging the torch around. "The outer walls, they're practically all windows. So this is like some kind of observation place, right?"

Alice sat up, feeling steadier already.

"City Hall," she said. "We're at City Hall."

"What city?" asked Tariq.

"Los Angeles. The pyramid on top. An observation deck on the 27th floor."

"Cool!" Tariq strode up and down the line of windows. "We're on top of City Hall! Is there a door? There must – there we go!" He pushed open a swinging glass door and rushed outside. "God, this is gorgeous!" he shouted. "Hello, Los Angeles!"

"Aidie go too, Aidie go too!" shouted Aiden.

Alice shook her head.

"Come on, Allie," coaxed Aiden.

"Allie is scared, Aidie."

"But it's Tower Terror!"

"No, it's *not* the Tower of Terror," said Alice. "It's City Hall. It's *very* tall, Aidie."

"Aidie want see!" shouted Aiden.

He jumped out of her arms and raced out the door.

"Aiden!" she yelled.

Alice was on her feet and out the door without thinking about it.

It was dark outside on the narrow walkway. The cool summer night air enveloped her.

She could see torchlight flickering way down the walkway, maybe a hundred feet away. She heard Aiden's light, quick footsteps running away from her, toward the light.

Her first instinct was to run after Aiden, but she hesitated for a moment. The observation deck had a waist-level stone wall along its perimeter – but that was it. There was no screen; it wasn't caged floor-to-ceiling like the Empire State Building, or glassed-in like Chicago's Sears Tower.

If she tripped, if she fell – it was twenty-seven stories down. Alice almost swooned just thinking about it – *falling, falling, all that way* – but she steeled herself and ran after Aiden.

Don't trip, don't trip, don't trip, she thought desperately.

The torchlight grew closer. To her right, the million lights of Los Angeles gleamed like incandescent jewels. It was beautiful, she had to admit, but –

Don't trip, don't trip! was all she could manage to process at the moment.

She skidded to a stop just before she cannoned into James, who had picked up Aiden.

"Pretty good view, eh, kid?" James asked his brother.

Alice pressed her back against the observation room wall. Feeling the solidity of the building helped ... a little bit.

"City Hall," said Aiden, nodding wisely, as if he knew all about it. He pointed at the city. "Lights!"

"Be careful with him," Alice told James in a small voice. "Don't drop him."

"Don't worry," James said. "I'm not too close to the edge."

Tariq waved the torch high above his head. "Wheeeeee-ha!!!" he yelled. "Top of the world, ma! Top of the world!!"

"Come on guys," Alice said. "Let's get out of here. What if that door had a silent alarm? Or what if someone hears Tariq? Security will be coming up here any minute."

"Yeah," James agreed. "It's just ..." He gestured to the glimmering lights of the city. "I've never been up here. Kind of amazing. Wonder how high up we are?"

"138.38 meters, or 454 feet," Alice said promptly.

James laughed. "When did City Hall open?" he asked.

"In 1928. Hey – cut it out!"

"I wonder why City Hall has a pyramid on top of it?" James asked innocently, rubbing his chin.

"The pyramid atop the Los Angeles City Hall was designed to resemble the Mausoleum at Halicarnassus, which was 148 feet tall and considered one of the Seven Wonders of the Ancient World." Alice clapped her hands over her mouth. "Stop it!" she said in a muffled voice.

James laughed again. Aiden laughed too, not because he understood what was happening, but because his brother was laughing and Aiden liked to be included in things.

Tariq joined them. "What's the joke?" he asked.

"Alice is channeling again," said James. "This never gets old."

"Handy, too," said Tariq. "OK, dudette, serious question: How do we get out of here?"

"We take the marble staircase to the 26th floor," Alice said immediately, "where the Mayors' portraits are hung. Then we take the elevator to the 22nd floor, and then another elevator to the ground floor."

"Sounds nice and complicated," said Tariq.

"Hello – it's L.A.," said Alice.

James set Aiden down on the floor. "I need to rest a minute, Aiden."

Aiden went to Alice and held out his arms. "Pick up Aidie," he commanded cheerfully.

Alice stood up, keeping her back against the solid wall, and then lifted Aiden into her arms. She walked slowly and very carefully toward the door into the tower, keeping an iron grip on the little boy while keeping one of her shoulders firmly against the wall.

"You're not going to fall off City Hall," James told her.

"How do you know?" she asked. "What if an earthquake hits, right now? Like, a 7.8 or an 8.1? We'd be thrown off this catwalk like little dolls!"

"How likely *is* that?" James asked skeptically. "An 8.1? Right now?"

"You never know," said Alice. "Better safe than sorry."

"Wow, you sound like old Tia Rosa."

"Tia Rosa has a lot of wisdom."

Before Alice could enter the building, something caught her eye. There was a large bell hanging between two of the walkway's massive columns. The great bell was a silhouette against the night sky. And on the bell's dark surface … something glowed with the twinkle of faery lights.

"What is it?" asked James, noticing that Alice had paused. He followed her glance. "Is the bell glowing? Is it magical or something?"

"Not the bell," said Alice. "That's just the Friendship Bell. It was given to the city in 1964. What I'm seeing is, there's something stuck to it. Something magic, judging by how bright it is."

"Must be the first touchstone," said James.

"I'll get it," volunteered Tariq, stretching his long arms toward the bell. He couldn't reach the bell, however, so he leaped gracefully onto the rail.

Alice gasped.

"Tariq!" she cried. "Be careful!"

"No worries, I'm fine," he said nonchalantly.

Tariq reached toward the bell again. "So, where's the magical whatchamacallit? Give me directions, Alice, and I'll grab it."

"It's near the top of the bell," she said, voice faint with fear for Tariq. She had an image of the boy toppling off the rail, falling 27 stories, down, down, down. The thought made her light-headed. She set Aiden down on the floor, in case she fainted.

"Huhn, I don't see it," said Tariq. He leaned precariously, stretching higher, running his hands along the bell. "Dudes, I still don't see anything. Can't feel anything, either. Course, I can't see magic stuff like you can, Alice."

"Higher," Alice said. "You're not reaching high enough, but, Tariq, please, *please* be careful."

"Piece of cake," he said confidently, stretching higher, and leaning further out over the city.

In a moment, Tariq's hand finally reached the glowing object; Alice watched in dismay as his fingers passed through it.

She sighed.

OK, thought Alice. *I think I get this. I don't like it ... but I get it.*

"Tariq, climb down," she said.

"But you need the magic thing," he objected. "You have to give it to Fuego."

"Exactly," Alice said. "But *I've* got to get it. *I'm* the only one who can see it; *I'm* supposed to get it."

"You'd never reach it," he scoffed.

"You have to help me. You have to hold me up so I can reach it."

"Dudette, that's a bad idea. You can't even watch *me* standing up here without turning green."

"I'll get it," said James. "I'm not afraid of heights, and I'm taller than you, and Tariq can keep a good grip on my legs so I don't – "

"It *has* to be me," Alice insisted. "Trust me. This is one of those things I just know."

"But you – "

"Get out of my way, dork," Alice muttered, pushing past James. She hated feeling scared; it felt better to be angry. "Take care of Aiden. Tariq won't let me fall."

"I don't know about this," Tariq said dubiously. "But if you're sure – "

"I am," she said.

Alice walked slowly to the rail. She didn't allow herself look down.

"Here." Tariq handed the torch to James, then helped Alice climb onto the rail.

Alice took a deep breath. She felt shivery and ill. Her hands were damp.

She looked straight ahead, at the dark sky and the constellation of lights across the distant hillsides. She did not look down. *There's a floor down there,* Alice told herself sternly. *It's not a 27-story drop. There's a floor ... If I fall, I'll just land on a floor ...*

Tariq circled Alice's ankles with one massive arm, her knees with the other.

"I'll try not to let you fall," he told Alice.

"You better do better than try," said James. "Don't drop my cousin!"

"I won't let you fall, dudette," Tariq amended, "but don't make any sudden movements – OK?"

The little girl nodded.

She reached upward, toward the glowing object.

She could see it so clearly, glowing brightly near the top of the bell, but it was much too high for her to reach. It was maddening. She stretched as high as she could ...

"Tariq," she said tensely, "you're going to have to lift me."

"Whatever you say. You're the Chosen One. But, please, kid, please –"

"I know, I know – 'No sudden movements'."

Tariq lifted Alice off the rail, held her up higher, closer and closer to the bell.

"Allie fly?" Aiden asked his brother.

"No," said James. "We hope not."

Alice stretched her arms as she drew closer to the bell. She could almost touch the object, whatever it was ... almost ... almost .... she reached forward, heart pounding ...

"Got it!" she said triumphantly, palm closing around the glowing metal object.

It was heavy. It glinted in the dim light. *Gold. A golden amulet.*

Tariq carefully lowered Alice until she was standing on the walkway.

"That was *crazy* brave!" he said admiringly.

"Just crazy," Alice said, voice shaky. "But we did it. We got it."

She opened her hand, displayed the amulet.

James tilted the torch so the flickering light shone on the touchstone. It was gold, forged in the shape of a heart, engraved with the noble head of a panther, ringed with hieroglyphics.

"Wonder what it says?" mused James. "Is that Egyptian?"

"Mayan," said Alice.

"Yeah?"

Alice nodded. "Penny and I wrote a report on the Maya last year."

James tilted his head. The hieroglyphics were all Greek – or, rather, Mayan – to him.

"What does it say?" he asked.

"Don't know," Alice admitted. "I can recognize Mayan, but I can't translate it." She hefted the amulet. "I think it's solid gold. And I think it's yours, James. See the panther? Like your tattoo, and the ring in your quest kit."

"Yeah," said James. Alice was right; the panther on the amulet was rendered in the same style as the panther on his tattoo and ring. *What does it mean? Not that it matters …*

"Whatever it is, it's Fuego's," James said. "We promised to give the touchstones to him when we see him again."

"Whenever that will be," Alice said wryly.

James ignored her. "The Ilwgyld are gonna want this amulet. For all we know, they can already sense we found it."

"Well, good luck," said Alice, dropping the amulet into his hand.

"What are you doing?"

"It's got a panther. It's yours, cousin. *You* can keep it safe from the bad guys."

"Dudette, you are really cold," said Tariq, shaking his head.

"I'm just practical," she said. "Look, I risked my life to get this thing. But it clearly belongs to James, so it's his problem now."

James traced the panther design, and the wreath of tiny hieroglyphics. "Wish we knew what it says. Anyhow," he looked at his cousin, "you're wrong about me carrying it. It *does* look like it's mine – so the Ilwgyld will expect me to have it. We've got to outsmart them."

"Well, I'm not keeping it," Alice said firmly. "I'm not bringing that thing into my house, with my mom. What kind of jerk are you, trying to put me and my mom in danger?"

"I'll protect it," offered Tariq. "No bad guys are gonna get past good old Fred and Ginger. And if they did, my sisters and I can take care of 'em just fine." He cracked his knuckles. "I *dare* those Hungry Ones," he grinned. "I *double* dare 'em!"

"I'm sure you and your sisters could protect the amulet," said James. He had met a couple of Tariq's sisters. They were even more intimidating than their baby brother. "But it's not your duty. It's mine and Alice's."

"I am *not* putting my mom in danger," Alice repeated. It made her shiver just thinking about her sweet, vulnerable mother being confronted by Lou and Flo.

"They won't even look for it at your house," said James. "They'll come to me. But I won't have it."

"Exactly – so *then* they'll come to me," said Alice.

"No, they won't. Because I'll tell them I hid the touchstone. I'll tell them they'll get all the touchstones at the end of the quest."

Alice rolled her eyes. "And, of course, they'll just say, 'OK' and leave us alone. Because that's how nice and civilized they are. It's not like they're, you know, greedy, evil magicians or anything!"

"Do you always have to be sarcastic?" asked James. *But she's right,* he admitted to himself. *She's totally right …*

"When they see you don't have the amulet, they'll go to me," said Alice. "James, think about it: they could probably hypnotize you into telling them where the amulet is. Like they hypnotized us into signing those contracts."

"All right. You have a point," he said grudgingly.

"The only solution," said Alice, "is for us to hide it somewhere so we *really* don't know where it is. That way if the Ilwgyld hypnotize us, we can honestly say we don't know."

"I'll hide it," offered Tariq.

"No," said Alice. "James and I need to be able to find it at a moment's notice when Fuego comes for it."

"So, call me a little dense, dudette, but how are you gonna hide it somewhere you don't know where it is, *but* you know where to find it at a moment's notice?"

Alice looked at Aiden.

"No," James said instantly. "No way."

"They'll *never* think to ask Aidie," Alice said reasonably. "They don't consider him a threat; they didn't even care if he signed the contract. To them, he's just an annoying little kid – even if he is a Chosen One."

"No," James repeated.

"You take the amulet home," said Alice. "You give it to Aidie and tell him to hide it somewhere, and to remember where he hid it. When we see Fuego, *then* Aiden can tell us all where he hid it."

Aiden put a hand on his brother's arm. "Aidie help," the boy said simply. He smiled.

James frowned.

"They're *not* going to ask him," Alice insisted. "It won't cross their mind. He won't be in any danger."

"We'll talk about this later," said James. He slipped the amulet into his hoodie pocket.

"I think we should – "

"Later," James said sharply. *There's no right answer,* he thought. *Whatever we do, we're gonna be in danger … all of us …*

Alice let it go for the moment.

She followed James and Aiden into the reception room, breathing a sigh of relief as she left the walkway behind. It felt better, *much* better, not standing next to a 27-story drop.

She looked around the chamber. Faintly, very faintly, she could perceive tiny flecks of light floating throughout the chamber, pale little particles of faery luminosity. *This is a place of power,* she thought. *The top of City Hall. A place where the border between worlds is worn thin …*

"That government is the strongest," read one of the inscriptions in the room, "of which every man feels himself a part." She turned to another inscription. "The City came into being to preserve life," it read, "it came for the good life …"

Tariq hung back, remaining on the observation deck for another moment. He peered down into the glimmering heart of Los Angeles.

"You know what'd be awesome?" he called to the children. "Bungee jumping. Right from here. Dang, that'd be awesome!!"

"Get in here, pal," James called. "We need you in one piece."

* * *

In the dim light, they found the grand marble staircase that swept down to the next level.

Alice found this floor eerie, ringed with portraits of almost all L.A.'s past mayors. She sensed a current of power flowing through the corridor, and it was a current of light, and a current of shadows.

She regarded several portraits intently, until James tugged at her sleeve.

"This isn't a field trip," he said. "Be a history nerd on your own time …"

They took an elevator to the 22nd floor, and then a separate elevator to the ground floor.

Alice was nervous in both elevators, chewing the red-and-black nail polish off her finger nails. But the elevator rides were uneventful; there was no repeat of the lurching drops they'd experienced in the freight elevator.

"Great craftsmanship," Tariq said, tapping the beautifully designed vintage interior of the elevator car.

"It's a box," said Alice, shuddering. "It's a box that goes up and down twenty-two stories …"

When they reached the ground floor and stepped out into the lobby, Tariq cursed under his breath.

"Hey – kids present," James admonished his friend.

"Sorry. But, look." Tariq gestured toward the exit, just beyond a bank of metal detectors, where a single electric light burned above a security station.

A *manned* security station; a guard in a blue uniform sat in a chair, regarding an electronic tablet. There were faint, high-pitched, electronic noises; the guard was playing a video game to pass the time.

James swept the lobby with a slow, searching glance, taking in the location of any video cameras. There were three, and their blinking red lights meant they were probably operational.

"This is going to be a little tricky," James said quietly. *I don't even know how we could explain it to Mom if we got caught by security at City Hall.* And Roz wasn't exactly the kind of mother who would believe in faeries and magic and weird circus folk and heroic quests. "Tariq, I need to take the lead this time. Alice, you're behind me. Hold Aiden – tight. Tariq, take point like Hisoka would."

"Aye-aye." Tariq twirled his fingers in a little salute.

"If anything goes crazy, we make sure Alice and Aiden get away," James told Tariq. "You got that, Alice? Whatever happens, just get out of here with Aidie. If the guard gets into the mix, I'll run one way and make a lot of noise, and Tariq will run the other way and make a lot of noise. If one of us gets caught, we call Alice, and she bails us out."

"I do? With what?" Alice asked skeptically.

"My mother keeps a bunch of emergency money in a shoe box in the freezer."

"Wait a minute," said Alice, "let's discuss this."

"No time." James crouched down and zig-zagged toward a marble column.

Alice held Aiden closer to her. "Aidie," she whispered, "this is very, very serious."

"Serious," Aiden said gravely.

"You have to be quiet. Shh. *Very* quiet. Right?"

"Quiet," he said obediently.

Alice hunched over and followed the zigzag path James had taken. When she reached her cousin, she crouched next to him behind the pillar.

For the next several minutes, the children enacted a stealthy ballet, creeping from pillar to planter to shadowy nook, circumventing the metal detectors and at all costs avoiding the three video cameras. Finally they were next to the exit door. James examined it in the dim light. No chains, no padlock … Please, let it be unlocked, he prayed silently.

He crept to the door. There was a slender metal rod on the bottom of the door, driven into a floor slot. James knew that if he pushed against the door right now, it wouldn't open – the metal rod would hold it in place. The door wouldn't open, but it would rattle, and the guard would hear it, and they'd all be caught.

James touched the metal bar gingerly, sliding it up out of the floor.

"What's the problem?" Alice hissed impatiently.

He had never wanted to strangle her so much, but he couldn't say or do anything – it was too risky. The guard was only a few yards away, tapping at the tablet as he played his video game. It sounded like Tetris, James thought. Old school …

James slowly lifted the metal bar, then fastened it in the "open" position.

He held his breath, and stealthily pushed against the door. It swung forward. He pushed it open gently, silently, inch by inch.

When the door was ajar enough for them to squeeze through, he turned and looked hard at Alice.

"Go!" he mouthed.

She crept past him. It was a tight squeeze, holding Aiden, but she made it outside.

They were on the broad top landing not of City Hall's famous grand steps, but the more modest steps on the east side of the building. Alice remained hunched over, hardly daring to breathe.

"Aidie talk now?" whispered Aiden hopefully. Alice shook her head.

"Move your caboose," whispered James. He was halfway out of the door, but Alice and Aiden were blocking him.

Alice scooted forward and James crept clear of the building with a sigh of relief. Tariq joined them a few seconds later. He had had to shove the door open further to fit through, but had done so with an amazing stealth.

Still hunched over, the children crept down the shallow steps, not daring to stand until they reached the sidewalk. In silence they ghosted south and then west, until they stood on Spring Street.

It was eerie, thought Alice, how deserted Downtown LA was at night. This was the civic district, and all of the civic workers, except security guards, had long since finished working and headed home.

Although the rain had stopped, the streets were still damp. The neon "Times" sign glowed a block to their left, its light reflected on the damp pavement. The dark windows of the Criminal Court building glowered down at them across Spring Street.

Spring Street was deserted. No pedestrians, no vehicles. Although –

Suddenly they heard loud, slurred singing coming toward them, accompanied by clanking and rattling sounds.

The street lamps shone feebly on a tall man in ragged clothes who pushed a shopping cart along the sidewalk on the other side of Spring. As he pushed the cart he danced, and he sang at the top of his lungs.

"I'm dreaming of a whiiiiite Christmaaaas, just like the ones I used to knooooow …"

Alice drew closer to James and Tariq.

"This isn't the greatest neighborhood after dark," said James.

"Where the treeee tops glisssten," sang the man, "and children lisssten …"

"Dudes, my SUV is back at Sony Stadium" said Tariq. "That's, like, a lot of blocks away. Don't think we should walk it."

"There's a Red Line stop one block up," said James. "Near the Cathedral."

"The subway?" asked Alice, less than thrilled.

"Hey," said James, "it's better than the streets."

They waited until the singing man and his shopping cart and his Christmas song had passed them on the other side of the street. The song, and the clanking and rattling of the cart, faded into the distance.

The children crossed Spring, dashed up Temple, and hung a hard left onto Hill. James took the lead, with Alice carrying Aiden and Tariq guarding the rear.

"There it is!" said James, pointing to the "Metro" sign.

A staircase flanked by two escalators plunged deep underground.

Two raggedly dressed men sat on a concrete bench near the escalators, laughing and passing something in a paper bag back and forth between them.

"Come on," James said. He ignored the two men and stepped onto the down escalator. It carried him away from Alice and Aiden at a surprisingly fast speed; it made Alice think of an ocean wave, grabbing someone and dragging them down, deep under the water ...

Before Alice, with Aiden in her arms, could step onto the escalator, one of the ragged men leaped up and blocked her path.

Although her mom had always cautioned Alice against strangers, Peggy had also taught Alice to be kind to anyone unfortunate, to give them a coin, or even just a smile – to treat the homeless with compassion.

But this man, smelling strongly like her Tio Egberto's liquor cabinet, was no harmless unfortunate. This man glared at Alice with bloodshot eyes and an ugly grin twisting his face.

"Hello, sunshine," he said gruffly. "Escalator costs a dollar. Dollar for you, dollar for the little one."

"Here you go," Tariq cheerfully, pushing past Alice and punching the man in the gut.

"Oomph," said the thug, stumbling backward. He doubled over and clutched his stomach.

"And here's a tip, too, dude" said Tariq, giving the man a right-hook to the jaw.

The man fell.

The other man glanced quickly from Tariq to the fallen thug, and then ran off along Hill Street.

"Have a great night!" Tariq called after him. "You OK?" he asked Alice.

She nodded.

Tariq gestured to the escalator. "Come on, then. Before that guy comes back with some friends."

"Thank you," said Alice.

"What I'm here for."

The escalator seemed to take forever to carry them down to the subway station. James had already bought train passes from one of the ticket machines. He pressed the little rectangles of plastic into their hands.

"You guys sure took your time," James complained. "We're not on a sightseeing trip."

"Sightseeing!" demanded Alice. "*Sightseeing*? Aiden and I were almost *attacked* by two of those weirdos up there, and if it wasn't for Tariq, you'd probably never see us again!"

James looked at Tariq, who nodded.

"Thank you," James said sincerely.

"No big deal," Tariq said. "Just my sacred duty to defend the Chosen Ones. C'mon, dudes, let's get to my SUV. I'm starting to get separation anxiety. It's my graduation present, you know? It's, like, my baby. What if someone dinged the bumper, what if someone scratched the door?"

Sony Stadium was only a couple of subway stops along the line. When they exited at 7th and Figueroa, the children had to walk several blocks to Sony Stadium, but this was LA's Financial District, lined with well-lit skyscrapers and battalions of streetlamps. Taxi cabs and security guards were everywhere. With Tariq taking the lead now and James guarding the rear, Alice felt reasonably safe.

"What time is it?" she asked.

James checked his cell phone. "Nine-ten," he said.

"That's crazy. We weren't gone *that* long."

"Faery time," said James. "Classic world-hopping stuff. Time moves differently in different realms. Faster, slower, it all depends. Shoot!" He was scrolling through his "Missed Calls" screen. "My mother tried to call me, like, *five* times."

"I guess Aelwyd doesn't have cell reception," said Tariq.

"Shoot," muttered James. "Shoot, shoot, shoot."

Roz had left him voicemail messages; James played the messages as they walked, listening intently.

"Nothing's wrong," he reported finally, "she just left me a bunch of instructions. She kept calling back when she thought of something new to tell me. I was supposed to make sure Aidie took a bath today, and I was supposed to make sure you both ate lunch, and supper, and that you had a fun day."

"Well, you totally struck out on all of those," said Alice.

"Kind of had other things to worry about," James said. He sighed, closed the phone and put it back in his pocket. "Mom's always like that. She's so amazing, and everything, but she's not … I just wish sometimes she'd …"

"You are so dumb," said Alice. "Your mother totally *adores* you. Just because she's not a sap and doesn't say it every two seconds – "

"How about *ever*," said James.

"She says it constantly. She just doesn't say it the way you expect it. All those messages she left you? That's what they mean. She loves you. She misses you."

"No, she just thinks I'm incompetent ..."

The Sony Stadium parking garage was full of vehicles but not people. Everyone was in the stadium, watching the circus.

Tariq's SUV was fine, not a single scratch. He patted the hood as if he was patting the muzzle of a prized horse. "Good girl," he said.

"I worry about you," James told his friend as he climbed into the SUV.

"Never mind about Tariq," said Alice, as she buckled Aiden into the car seat. "We've got to talk about hiding this amulet ..."

Chapter Twelve – Monsters in the Closet
June 24th – Los Angeles

Tariq drove them to James' house, the majestic Victorian on Orange Grove.

Tariq and James kept glancing at the side-view mirrors as if expecting to see a tribe of wild-eyed Ilwgyld racing after them with swords, or longbows, or whatever their weapons of choice might be. But except for a brief tactical discussion, the drive was uneventful.

They had all agreed that in the short term, they wouldn't attempt to contact the *Sircus* or venture into Aelwyd. "We'll wait for Fuego to come to us."

James, Alice and Aiden would stick together like glue. They'd keep their quest packs with them at all times, but wouldn't use any of the contents. They would hide the golden amulet as decided during the drive.

Before he pulled away in the big black SUV, Tariq gave James a hearty handshake and crushed Alice and Aiden in a bear hug.

"I'm just a text message away," Tariq said. "Anything weird – I'm here in five minutes."

"You live fifteen minutes away," said Alice.

"And I'll be here in five minutes," Tariq repeated. "Mahalo, dudes and dudette!"

He honked the horn loudly, several times, and tore away from the curb at top speed.

The house was dark. Their mothers wouldn't be finished with their second jobs until eleven, not home until eleven-thirty.

James unlocked the door, flicked on the living room light, and flung himself down on the couch. He had never felt so exhausted, physically and mentally, in his life.

Alice set down Aiden next to his brother, then closed and locked the front door.

"Aidie hungry," announced Aiden.

"Me too," Alice agreed. She kicked James' foot. "What do we order? I vote for Thai."

"Thai gives Aiden a rash," James objected.

"Indian?"

"That gives *me* a rash."

"You *are* a rash," said Alice.

"Har-har-har," he laughed simple-mindedly.

"Well we have to eat something," she said. "What do you want?"

"I want, like, a giant burger with gooey cheese," said James.

That *did* sound pretty awesome, Alice thought, but she wrinkled her nose.

"How boring," she complained.

"Chicken?" he suggested.

"Even more boring. Go back to the burger. Who delivers burgers around here?"

"Papa Juanito's. They deliver burgers, pizzas, pastas. There's a menu on the fridge."

In the end, they all ordered burgers, plus chicken wedges for James, French fries for Aiden and a side of Fettuccini Alfredo for Alice.

They sat on the floor in front of the flat screen television and watched a mindless summer reality program while they pigged out.

"I hope they eliminate that guy next," said Alice, chomping on a forkful of pasta.

"Why?" asked James around a giant bite of burger.

"He just bugs me."

"Well, as long as you have a logical reason."

"Everything's not always logical. Don't you ever have a gut instinct?"

"Sure. But it's usually rooted in some kind of logic."

"Then it's not a gut instinct, duh."

"Gut instinct is just subconscious logic," argued James.

Alice downed another huge forkful of pasta. "You know, despite the fact that you are one-thousand–billion percent wrong, I'm too tired to argue. You can have this one, dork."

"Real generous of you," said James around a mouthful of burger and cheese.

"Look!" said Aiden.

His brother and cousin glanced over at the little boy. Aiden opened his mouth, which was full of mushed-up French fries. "Blaaaaaaaaah!" he said.

James and Alice laughed so hard they got tears in their eyes.

Aiden laughed too, big belly laughs, and some of the French fry-mush sprayed out of his nose.

"Aidie!" chided Alice, trying to keep order – but she and James just laughed harder.

"I got it," said James, going to the kitchen and coming back with a cloth. "C'mere, Aidie. Let's get that off your face. And your shirt. And, for some reason, your toes." Aiden obligingly let his brother clean him.

Aiden dozed off a short while later and James put him to bed.

"He's been sleeping all the time," Alice said. "Have you noticed that?"

"Yeah. I think this whole alternate universe thing is sapping his energy."

"Or maybe it's a protective thing. He seems to doze off anytime anything weird happens. It's maybe, some kind of programming, or spell, like if anything weird goes down, he's out like a light."

"He wasn't out at Union Station," James said thoughtfully. "He was completely alert then. Remember how he leaped up on the booth?"

Alice laughed. "Did you *see* their faces? They didn't expect that!"

"Chaos," James said thoughtfully. "I'm the protector, you're the seer, and Aidie is the unexpected."

"He sure is!"

There was a rattling of the doorknob, a jangle of keys and the front door swung open. Roz and Peggy entered the living room.

Roz looked bone-tired, dark circles under her eyes. Peggy's shoulders drooped, but her face was beaming.

"Alice!" Peggy said, sweeping her daughter into a hug. "I missed you sweetie! How was your day?"

Roz dropped her purse and keys on the table by the door. She looked around the living room and into the kitchen.

"Well, the place is still standing," Roz said. "Although … why am I seeing mashed potatoes on the throw rug?"

"That's actually mushed-up French fries," said James. "I'll take care of it."

He went quickly to the kitchen, grabbed a handful of paper towels, held them under the cold water faucet for a second then returned to the living room. He began dabbing at the throw rug. "See, it's coming right out."

"That's why I want you kids to eat at the counter," said Roz. "Or at the table. What if that was soda?"

"Got it," said James.

"Thank you for watching Alice," Aunt Peggy told her nephew. "I don't know what I would do if you, if you weren't able to – "

Aunt Peggy's eyes welled up with tears of gratitude.

James smiled at her, the same sweet, lopsided smile she remembered from when he was a toddler.

"It's OK, Aunt Peggy, I'm happy to do it," he said politely. "Even though your daughter is a demon child."

Alice snorted.

Aunt Peggy gave her daughter an anxious look. "Alice, I hope you're behaving for James. We're very lucky he's watching you."

"You know me," said Alice.

"Yes. She does," said James. "That's why she asked."

Alice stuck her tongue out at him. She was trying not to do that so often; it was beneath her dignity as a twelve-year old; but sometimes, it seemed like the only response that was appropriate.

"Alice!" said Aunt Peggy.

"She's actually been great," James told his aunt. "She's great with Aiden. She's actually been, like, a big help."

"Well, I hope so," Aunt Peggy said. "Come on, Alice, let's get home. Did you eat?"

"Yeah, I'm fine."

"Well I'm starving. We're stopping at Burger King on the way home." Peggy waved to Roz, who was sitting at the kitchen counter opening bills with a sharp little letter opener. "Bye, Roz, see you tomorrow!"

"See you, Peggy!" Roz lifted her head to give Peggy a brief smile, and then went back to the bills.

"See you tomorrow, dork," Alice said to James.

"See you tomorrow, evil brat."

* * *

Peggy was chatty during the drive home, talking about her new evening job, her new coworkers, her new boss. Alice only paid partial attention, nodding and saying "Oh, wow," at the right moments.

The great thing about her mom liking to talk, Alice thought, was that Alice didn't have to say much. Because how could Alice *possibly* describe the events of the day?

But as they pulled into the driveway, Peggy turned to her daughter and asked "So – what did you guys do today?"

Alice shrugged. She didn't like to lie. It always gave her a sick feeling in the pit of her stomach even to contemplate it. She had been known to creatively – *very* creatively – twist a few truths, with the skill of a $400-per-hour attorney. But nothing she said was ever an outright lie.

"Well, you must've done something," Peggy said encouragingly, turning off the engine.

Alice shrugged again. "You know, mom. Stuff." And she got out of the car quickly, hoping that would be the end of the questions.

But her mom was in one of her ultra-nurturing modes. *She feels guilty about the second job*, Alice thought. *She wants to be sure I know she loves me.*

"I know it's late," said Peggy, smiling sweetly as she set her purse on the kitchen table, "but I'm making us hot fudge sundaes. We'll talk all about your day. How does that sound?"

"Great!" said Alice, but her stomach suddenly hurt. What could she say that was *remotely* true?

Alice considered going to her room and pretending to fall asleep, but she didn't want to disappoint her mother. Peggy looked so excited about the sundaes and the gab session.

Alice sighed inwardly. "I'll help with the sundaes," she volunteered.

Peggy took two chilled, glass ice cream dishes out of the refrigerator. "For once I was thinking ahead," she said happily.

Alice scooped vanilla ice cream into the chilled glasses, while Peggy popped the hot fudge into the microwave.

"This is delicious!" Alice said when they were sitting at the counter, pigging out.

The little black-and-white kitchen television was tuned to an old episode of "CSI". Alice and her mom both loved mysteries. "This was a *way* great idea, mom!"

"Oh, it's no big deal," Peggy said modestly, but Alice could tell her mom was pleased that Alice was pleased. "Things are going to have to be really simple around here for awhile, but they can still be fun." Peggy took another bite of hot fudge. "So tell me," said Peggy, "what *did* you guys do today?"

Alice had had some time to think while she helped make the sundaes.

"It was kind of a weird day," Alice said carefully. "I'm not used to spending so much time with James and Aiden."

"Oh, sweetie," her mom's eyes filled with tears, "I'm so sorry we have to do this. It's just, right now, to get through – "

"No, no," Alice said quickly, "I didn't say it was bad. Just weird. But I'm sure I'll totally get used to it. And, as much as I hate to admit it, James took really good care of me and Aiden." *Considering the crazy circumstances*, she added mentally. She hated to admit it, but the dork really *was* protective. "I actually think it's going to be a very interesting summer," she said.

"Really?" Peggy brightened. "So, you had fun?"

"Fun was definitely had," said Alice vaguely. She *had* liked the unusual beverage at the Aelwyd village of Teulu. And she *had* liked Fuego's massive library. And it *had* been kind of fun, scary fun, to creep past the security guard and escape from City Hall.

"Did you go anywhere?" asked Peggy.

Alice had to hold back a semi-hysterical laugh. *We sure did!* she thought.

"I got to meet James' friend Tariq," Alice answered. "And we all visited City Hall. None of us had ever been there before. We were all the way at the top."

"How neat!" her mom said excitedly. "I've lived here so many years, and I've never been up there. Your father probably went up there when he was a little boy, for school trips. What's the view like?"

"Pretty amazing," Alice said.

Peggy squeezed her daughter's hand. "I am *really* proud of you, Alice. I know you're not a big fan of elevators. Or heights."

"Yeah. Well, today was kind of about conquering some fears."

Peggy sighed. "You're growing up so fast."

Faster than you know, thought Alice.

* * *

"So what did you do today?" Roz asked James. She sat on the couch, signing checks for the bills that had come in the mail that day. He was sitting on the living room floor, ostensibly watching "CSI" while his mind turned over the odd events of the day.

"You know," he said vaguely. "Stuff."

"Sounds thrilling," she said drily. She stuffed a check and a payment slip into an envelope, sealed it, stamped it, went on to the next bill.

"How do we rack up two-hundred dollar power bills?" Roz shook her head darkly. "I used to blame it on your dad and the wood shop, but he's off the hook this time. It *has* to be us. James, if you and Aiden aren't in a room, turn the lights off. And no more air conditioner. Use the fans. And whenever you're not using your computer or actually watching the TV, turn them off."

He made a noncommittal sound. *Did we make the right move, hiding the amulet?* he thought. *Are we putting Aidie in danger?*

"Did you hear me?" asked Roz.

"Sure, Mom. Use fans and turn out lights."

"I just want to be positive you're really hearing me."

"I am." He clicked the remote, turning of the television. "I'm beat," he said. "Have a good sleep, mom."

"Hmm?" She was engrossed in the next bill. "Oh. Good night, James."

* * *

In her little bungalow in Silver Lake, Alice thought she'd be too wired to sleep, but she was unconscious as soon as her head hit her pillow. She dropped instantly into a pitch-black, dreamless sleep …

She didn't know what woke her, but at 3 a.m. she sat bolt upright, senses alert. The fine hairs on the back of her neck were standing up.

She glanced at the glowing numerals of her digital clock, and then took in the rest of the room, which was dimly lit by the street lights streaming through her half-open blinds.

Everything looked normal in her small room.

Her closet door was closed – she'd always insisted that it be closed, from the time she was a toddler.

Her outfit for tomorrow was folded neatly over her chair; her books were stacked neatly on her desk, her DVDs and video games stacked neatly in her bookcase.

Her small vanity table with its mirror was scrupulously organized, lip glosses on the left, eye shadows on the right, perfumes and her tray of jewelry in the center.

Her laptop computer was on her nightstand, fully charged, judging by its solid red "Power" LED.

Everything *looked* perfectly normal – but it wasn't. Alice knew it in her gut.

Stealthily she slipped out of her bed and moved quietly to her bedroom door. It was shut tightly. She opened the door slowly, gently, so that it didn't creak.

She stepped silently into the hall, avoiding the floor board right in front of her door that always squeaked.

Alice listened. Peggy was snoring in the bedroom at the far end of the hall.

Across the hall, Alice heard the cold water faucet dripping in the bathroom sink. It had been dripping for months. Their landlord kept promising to fix it.

"It's no big deal," he told them whenever they called him. "I just need to replace the gasket. Won't take more than a couple of minutes." But somehow he never got around it.

At the other end of the hall was the living room-slash-kitchenette. It was silent except for the usual kitchen sounds, like the hum of the refrigerator, and the ticking of the big grandfather clock.

It was a little weird, Alice always thought, to have a big grandfather clock in such a tiny bungalow, but it was a family heirloom. Alice's mother had inherited it from *her* mother and it occupied a place of honor in one corner of the small living room.

Alice returned to her room, sat down on her bed. Everything *seemed* normal, but she couldn't shake the sensation that it wasn't.

On her night table, next to a pile of school books and fashion magazines and her sketch books, sat a photo of her and her father. Roberto was a big, dark-haired man with a blindingly happy smile. He was the one who always encouraged her to sketch as well as study.

"It's good to feed your brain," he'd tell her, "but you should draw, too. Your art comes from your soul …"

I miss him, thought Alice. *Why'd he have to go so far away to work?* None of it was fair. It was going to be a lousy summer. Spending all her time with James, and dealing with crazy faery people and quests, and not having her dad around to talk to about any of it …

Alice looked around her room again. Normal. One-hundred percent normal. Except …

The air felt … *heavy* was the only way Alice could describe it to herself. Heavy, and, now that she really thought about it, electric. As if the air were tingling, were silently singing.

Is there a lightning storm coming? Alice wondered.

It was then that she heard the voices, a soft, murmured argument. It seemed to be emanating from within her room. From her closet.

Alice froze for a moment. The closet – she'd never liked that closet.

She stood up and moved hesitantly toward the closet door.

It's all in my head, she told herself. *Got to be all in my head –*

She yanked open the closet door.

"Oh, pardon *us*, dearie," snarled the red-head.

Alice stumbled back several paces, almost falling over the little chair in front of her vanity.

The blonde and the red-head emerged from her closet, dusting themselves off, scattering little flakes of silvery powder and little flecks of silvery light with every movement.

The powder glimmered dully in the street light and moonlight washing through the blinds.

Ilwgyld! Alice had a name for them now. Hungry Ones. The bad guys. Otherwise known as Lou and Flo.

The blonde and red-head wore the same fantastic costumes they'd worn at Union Station, the same garish colors and fabrics.

"We was debatin'," said the blonde in a grating whisper, "how to best approach you without scarin' the livin' daylights outta ya, so ta speak. Which, you've gone and turned the tables by scarin' the livin' daylights outta *us*."

"She's such a clever, clever girl," sneered the red-head.

"Clever, clever, clever," agreed the blonde.

"I know who you are," Alice said accusingly.

"An't that lovely," whispered the blonde. "And who exactly might that be, duckie?"

Alice swallowed. Her mouth went dry as cotton.

She was alone, in her room, with these weirdos; her mom was fast asleep, her dad was in New Mexico, and James and Tariq might as well have been a million miles away. She decided this was no time to reveal how much she'd learned and start hurling accusations around.

"You're Lou," she whispered to the blonde, "and you're Flo," she whispered to the red-head. "You're running the *L.A. Magickal History Hunt*. And you're with the *Sircus of Impossible Magicks*."

Lou laughed a raspy, sandpaper laugh. "An't you clever? You *are* a clever girl."

"Told ya," sniffed Flo.

"We're with the *Sircus*, all right" Lou told Alice. "The *Sircus* is the whatsit that's sponsorin' the *Magickal History* competition. And we're here to give you the instructions for your next challenge. An't that excitin'?"

"Very," Alice managed, hoping she didn't look as terrified as she felt.

"Tomorrow, you're going to Lake Avenue. Do you know Lake Avenue, little lamb?"

"In Pasadena?"

"In Pasadena, yes. Well done. Well done! You're to go north on Lake Avenue until it ends – up, up, up in the foothills, duckie. And then you're to venture into the Haunted Forest. An't that lovely? The Haunted Forest!"

Alice had never heard of a "Haunted Forest" in Pasadena. Maybe it was part of Aelwyd. She was curious – but the last thing she wanted was a long conversation with these two. So she simply nodded.

"You'll be sure to do that little thing?" asked Lou. "You'll go to the Haunted Forest tomorrow? You shan't forget?"

"Sure," said Alice. "We'll go. We want to win the contest."

"'Course you do, gold fish. Be certain that you go *first* light tomorrow morning. And bring the older boy. And bring the little boy. Bring the protector and the trickster, lass."

"The little boy," Flo, the red-head said with a disturbing intensity. "You *must* bring him, or they'll be lots of trouble, like. Lots and *lots* of trouble, pet – oh, yes, indeed."

"When you wakes up," said Lou, "you're gonna think this was a dream, eh? But you're gonna go, notwithstandin'. You're gonna tell the older boy and the little boy and you're gonna go to the Haunted Forest. First light."

"I'll remember," said Alice. Their features were so terrifying in the dim light – sharp, lean, ravenously hungry. They made bird-like little gestures with their hands and heads.

These are our enemies. A giddy sensation of hysteria formed in Alice's throat, started to bubble up. Alice swallowed hard. *Leave, leave, leave, leave, leave my room,* she thought frantically.

"You quite well, dearie?" asked Lou, in a horrid caricature of concern. She tilted her blonde head, regarding Alice through shrewd eyes. "You looks, lass, like you ate somethin' what weren't quite-quite, if ya follows me."

"I, it was the ice cream," Alice said, putting a hand to her stomach. "It was the sundae, right before bed."

"Were it?" Flo sneered. "Can't stomach a sundae, can ya? Let's see how ya stomachs the Haunted Forest tomorra'!"

Lou chuckled and then Flo chuckled. It was an ugly sound.

"Now, before we goes," said Lou, "I believes you have a touchstone to deliver. So – " she snapped her fingers under Alice's nose, "give it here. Now."

Alice raised her fine dark eyebrows in surprise. "Now?"

"You 'eard 'er, pet – *now*," said Flo.

"But I don't have it," said Alice. "We hid it. Those are the contest rules: We give you all the touchstones at one time, *after* the competition concludes."

The blonde and the red-head made snarling and gnashing movements with their heavily painted mouths.

Alice took a step back.

"That's what the contract said," Alice said innocently. "You remember: 'We the undersigned do hereby agree to follow all rules of *L.A. Magickal History Hunt*, and relinquish all magickal objects obtained, *at the conclusion of the contest*, upon pain of – '"

"We know the contract, pet," said Flo, eyes blazing.

"An't no need for you to read it chapter and verse," rasped Lou.

If looks could kill, thought Alice, taking another step back.

"Well, then," said Alice, trying to sound much calmer than she felt, "you know we'll give you everything we find *after* the competition."

"What a dearie," said Lou, looking as if she wanted to pounce on Alice with her long fingernails. "What a *wise* little dearie. I *knew* she was a smart 'un – didn't I, Flo?"

"Indeed you did, Lou. A real little scholar. Reg'lar genius, she is."

Both the Ilwgyld looked around the dim room with darting, stealthy glances.

"It isn't here, of course," Alice said. "It's in a safe place."

The creatures hissed.

"'Nother place, is it?" asked Lou. "An where might this 'nother place be?"

Alice shrugged. "I don't know."

Lou took a deep, angry breath. Her bright, bird-like eyes bored into Alice's eyes. "She tells truth," the blonde muttered through a ghastly smile.

"She an't lyin," Flo agreed. "She don't know where the touchstone is.

"Well," said Lou. "Well, well, well, then. We shall see you after the *next* leg of the contest, lass."

"Yes indeed," said Flo, with a horrid grimace. "Yes indeed."

"And if you knows what's good for ya," said Lou, "you'll have the touchstones with you. Oh, yes, *that's* what you'll do, duckie!"

They lifted their arms and tossed great handfuls of silvery powder into the air.

The shining particles blinded Alice and made her sneeze.

She groped blindly for the vanity chair and sank down on it.

The clouds of powder wafted down, covering the floor in deep, glimmering drifts. Within a minute, the silvery particles evaporated like bubbles, with soft popping noises.

Alice looked around her room. One-hundred percent normal. Except the closet door was open. And in front of the closet door lay a purple high-heeled shoe.

Chapter Thirteen – The Haunted Forest
June 25th – Los Angeles

As soon as Roz left for work, Alice dug the purple shoe out of her backpack and slammed it on the kitchen counter in front of James.

"Hmm," he said. "This doesn't look like your style."

"Dumb shoe," said Aiden, eating his oatmeal at the counter.

"It's not *mine*, dork," Alice told James. "It's *Lou*'s. "Or Flo's. One of those *very* creepy *Sircus* chicks we met at Union Station."

"Where did you get it?"

"They paid me a visit, excuse me, a nightmare, last night." Alice shuddered. "They came in through my closet."

"*What*? Why didn't you call me?"

"I don't know. As soon as they left, I wanted to call, but then I just fell asleep."

"Post-hypnotic suggestion, again," James said.

"Maybe. Or maybe," said Alice, "it's that silver flash powder they use."

"Drugged?"

"Could be."

"More oatmeal for Aidie!" Aiden demanded.

James stood up and absently prepared Aiden's food, mind racing.

"When I woke up this morning, I almost thought their visit was a dream," Alice said. "It was all hazy and surreal. But then I saw this purple shoe, and it all came back to me."

"No one visited me," James said pensively.

"Be glad," said Alice, "be very, very glad. It's not fair! Why can't *you* be channeling guy instead of *me* being channeling girl?"

"Not my destiny, I guess."

"Well, I want a new destiny."

"I don't think it works that way."

"Well it stinks!"

The microwave beeped. James removed Aiden's oatmeal, set it on the counter.

"Eat now!" said Aiden fiercely.

"It has too cool, Aidie," said James. "We don't want you to get burned."

"Eat now!!"

"Hang on, Aidie, just a minute," said Alice, patting his shoulder. She looked at James. "He seems totally cranky. I wonder how *he* slept?"

James shivered. "They wouldn't bug *him*, would they? He's just a little guy. Like we talked about yesterday – they didn't even seem to pay him much attention at Union Station."

"Well, that's changed," said Alice. "They specifically said we *have* to bring him with us our quest today."

"Aidie want OATMEAL!" shouted Aiden.

"OK, Aidie, calm down, jeez – the oatmeal is cool now," said James. "Here you go." He slid the bowl in front of his little brother, who dug in like he hadn't eaten in a week.

"We're supposed to go to Lake Avenue this morning," said Alice. "Early. Like, we probably should already have left."

"Where the Borders bookstore was?" asked James.

"Yeah, I mean, that's the street," said Alice, "but we have to go north on Lake until it ends. *Way* up in the foothills. Then we go into some place called the Haunted Forest."

"Excuse me?"

"Hey, I don't come up with this stuff. That's what Lou and Flo said. 'Go into the Haunted Forest'."

"So, assuming we find this Haunted Forest, we go into it and do – what ?"

"I have no idea."

"OK." James nodded. "That's actually typical of quests, not being given a lot of information. Part of the quest is figuring out what the quest is."

"You can handle that, right?" asked Alice. "If *I* have to get the creepy visits in the middle of the night, *you* can be responsible for figuring out what the quests are."

"Seems fair," James said.

Alice's cell phone shrilled.

She rummaged through her backpack, found the phone, flipped it open and checked the caller ID.

"Penny!" Alice shouted into the phone. "How are you?"

"I'm fine, Allie-girl," said Penny. "Where *are* you? We totally asked the camp counselors and they totally told us it was none of our business. And we're like, 'We're her best friends!' and they were like 'Totally doesn't matter, go away.' Can you imagine?"

"Why didn't you call me sooner?" asked Alice. "Why didn't you text?"

"My dad, he was like, 'Don't bother your friend, maybe she had a family emergency, she'll call you when she wants to talk to you, blab blab blab.' You know my dad. He has no curiosity."

"Well, I actually *am* having kind of a family emergency, Penn. My dad went out to New Mexico to work with my uncle."

"No way!"

"Way. And my mom got this night job."

"No way!"

"Total way. And my dorky cousin has to babysit me all summer."

"Not James?"

"Yeah, James."

"No *way!*"

"Way!"

"But what about camp?"

"I can't go."

"That's devastating!"

"Tragic," Alice agreed.

"Well, we *all* miss you, Allie. Marisol and Lajuana and Su Lin and even Natasha."

"Natasha? But we totally hate her!"

"Totally. Total snake. But she says she misses you too."

"She just has to be part of whatever," said Alice, rolling her eyes.

"I know. Whatever."

"Whatever," Alice agreed.

"So there's nooooo way you can come to camp?"

"No, Penn. It sucks, totally, but there's no way."

"Total devastation."

"Totally," Alice said sadly. "Tell everyone I said 'Hi'."

"Absolutely."

"And I miss them."

"Of course."

"And I hope they have a good summer, and tell them to call me and text me. Except, don't tell Natasha."

"Perish the thought! Oh, dang, Chemistry's starting. We're working on sulfuric acids."

"Have fun, Penn," said Alice.

"You too, Allie-girl! I'll call you Saturday!"

Alice snapped her phone shut. She hurled it at the couch.

"Way to break your cell phone," said James.

"Way to be a dork!" said Alice.

"Hmm. Not one of your best."

Alice picked up her cell, inspected it. Luckily, it was intact. She zipped it into the front pocket of her backpack.

"You know, you're not the *only* one missing out on stuff this summer," said James.

"Don't care."

"What a brat."

"None of your business anyway." Alice sank down on the couch and subsided into a sulk.

James shrugged. Aiden had finished his oatmeal, announcing that he had completed his breakfast with a giant belch and a fit of merry laughter.

"Someone's feeling better," laughed James.

He took Aiden's bowl and spoon, washed them in the sink and set them on the wooden dish rack to dry.

"All right," said James, "sounds like we're already late, so we leave in T-minus five minutes. Everybody use the bathroom. I have a feeling there aren't any rest rooms in the Haunted Forest."

* * *

"Why don't you have a car?" Alice demanded. "I *hate* the Gold Line."

"Better than walking," said James. "And I'm sixteen, and our families are broke right now. Where am I getting a car?"

Alice sat against one window of the train, Aiden sitting on her lap, James sitting on the aisle, a barrier against any nut who might try to attack them. And there seemed to be plenty of nuts on this train this morning, but they all looked like run-of-the-mill L.A. characters – no faeries or Ilwgyld.

The children detrained at the Lake Station, a narrow platform that sat in the middle of the 210 Freeway. Cars and trucks and trailers and motorcycles roared past at full speed on either side of the median.

The noise was deafening. Alice put her hands over her ears. Aiden grinned.

"Aidie like *vrrooooom*!" the little boy shouted above the din.

They climbed the steep steps up to Lake Street, to the bridge which crossed the freeway below.

"North is to the right," said James. "See? We'll be walking up into the foothills – just like Lou and Flo told you."

"We walked, like, *thousands* of miles yesterday," Alice complained. "Isn't there a bus we can take? Look." She pointed triumphantly at a Metro Bus sign posted next to a bench. "Line 780 – no, that goes to Sierra Madre …. There, Line 20. No! Line 20.5. That's it. Lake Ave to East Alta Loma."

"Line 20.5? There's no such thing as a 'Line 20.5'," James objected.

"Well, there is today," Alice said, sitting on the bench. "It's on the sign. And, I can sense it."

"What do you mean, you can sense it?"

"20.5 is the right bus line for us. I can just feel it."

James shrugged and sat next to her. "If you say so. Do your super powers tell you how long we have to wait?"

"No. But I'm guessing not long."

At that instant, a small white bus with lavender and orange stripes pulled up to the curb with a squealing of brakes.

The tickertape crawl signs on its front and side read "Line 20.5 … East Alta Loma". The front door opened with a hiss of hydraulics.

"You three … get your scrawny little carcasses on the bus," grunted the driver.

He was slender, balding, with sharp, hungry features, and had a heavy case of five-o'clock shadow. His uniform was orange with lavender piping – not the usual LA Metro uniforms.

James glanced at Alice, who nodded.

"This is our ride," she said.

James stepped into the bus, Alice and Aiden right behind him.

"How much is it?" asked James.

"No charge," grunted the driver, "for the Chosen Ones".

The Chosen Ones, thought Alice. *And why do we have to be the Chosen Ones, anyway?*

James sat near the front of the bus, giving Alice the window seat as usual. The doors closed with another hydraulic hiss and a loud thud that Alice didn't like.

It's like we're sealed in here. Forever.

The ride was a blur. Literally. They cruised north on Lake at a terrifying speed.

Fast food restaurants and houses and gas stations and little parks zipped past the bus windows in a whirl of shapes and colors. The avenue tilted upward, growing steeper and steeper until it felt like they were driving up into the Rockies instead of the San Gabriel Mountains.

Soon the little businesses fell away; there were only houses along either side of Lake, large houses, Victorian mansions, set relatively far apart and separated from each other by vast expanses of green lawns and heavily wooded belts of trees. The driver really stepped on the gas, then, and everything outside the bus became a green haze.

Suddenly, without the slightest warning, the driver jammed on the brakes.

James pitched forward, almost smacking his forehead on a metal post.

Alice was glad she was holding Aiden tightly, or the child would've flown out of her arms.

The driver pulled a lever; the doors opened with an angry hiss.

"Last stop," he grunted. "Lake and East Loma Linda." And then, in case they didn't get the point, "Get out. Now."

James and Alice were happy to get out in one piece.

"Nice driving," Alice called up to the driver when they were safely on the sidewalk. "You might want to think about taking a lesson, someday."

The driver just stared at her. It was a very ugly stare. Alice took a step back, instinctively.

"Lou and Flo," grunted the driver, "'as got a soft spot for you three. They think we should treat you tender-like. But *I* an't got no soft spot, wretches. I'd as soon grind your bones to make me bread. Mark me, and mark me well – you 'ave them touchstones for Lou when she meets you."

He slammed the door shut – and the bus evaporated in a flash of silvery light.

"Wow!" shouted Aiden. "Bus go POOF!"

"*Why* do they have to *do* that?" Alice asked the universe at large.

James scanned their surroundings. They stood at the base of a heavily wooded hill where Lake Avenue ended. East Loma Linda wound into a heavily wooded and deserted looking area.

"If Tariq was here," James said, "he'd say this looks like the part in the horror movie where the stupid teenagers decide to go into the forest and end up getting attacked by demons."

"Where *is* Tariq, anyway?" asked Alice.

"He's at the hospital," said James. "His grandmother's sick."

"Oh. That sucks."

"Yeah," said James. "So, we're on our own today."

They stared at the foreboding woods.

"This seems like a bad day to be on our own," said Alice.

"Yup. But it can't be helped. Tariq said he'd call if his gram's feeling better later."

"Too bad they don't have cell coverage in Aelwyd."

"I know." James scanned the base of the wooded hill. "There's some kind of gate there," he said, pointing. "Alice, do you, you know, see any faery lights around there?"

Alice saw the gate, a space between two truncated stone walls.

"I don't see anything magical," she said. "But that must be the entrance. Yeah. I can sense it. That's it."

James walked toward the ruined walls, Alice and Aiden following him closely. It appeared as if the walls had once been beautiful, but they were crumbling now and filigreed with graffiti. Someone had spray-painted "Cobb Estate" on the wall in huge black letters. Ancient fencing stretched off in a westerly direction, eventually terminating, in the distance, at large fieldstone posts ...

"What *was* this place?" James wondered.

Alice put a hand to her forehead.

"OK, *ow*," she said closing her eyes, "major, major incoming. The, the Cobb Estate was built in 1858. Charles Cobb was a lumber tycoon who originally hailed from Maine." She winced as the data streamed into her mind. "It was 1916. Cobb and his wife bought a parcel of the Las Flores Ranch in Altadena and built a Spanish-style mansion. The estate survived a big fire in 1934. By 1959, 20 years after Cobb died, the beautiful mansion was in disrepair and was finally torn down."

"Allie smart," Aiden said admiringly.

"The area is now managed by the U.S. Forestry Service," Alice continued. "We're in the shadow of Echo Mountain. There are trails that lead to the top of Echo Mountain, where the Lowe Alpine Incline Railroad, the Echo Mountain House, the Lowe Observatory and the world's largest searchlight once towered over Altadena."

"Is that stuff still up there?" James asked curiously.

"No. It's all long gone." Alice clutched her temples. "In addition to botanists and hikers, the Cobb Estate, also known as the Haunted Forest, is popular with ghost hunters, many of whom claim to have captured evidence of spirits roaming the grounds. Ghost hunters report, among many phenomena, eerie lights, shadowy figures and the sounds of screaming."

"I'm sorry, I didn't catch that," James deadpanned. "Can you repeat it all – from the beginning?"

Alice punched his shoulder, and then held her head in both her hands. "Wow. That one *really* hurt," she said. "I feel sick."

"It's like they downloaded a whole terabyte into your skull," James said. "And it's not like there's much room in there to begin with."

She punched him again, a little harder this time.

"Seriously," James said, "what are we supposed to *do* with all that information? Is there going to be a test when we visit Aelwyd again?"

"Maybe," said Alice. "And if you fail, you get fed to a dragon – or something fantasy-geeky like that."

Aiden was studying the graffiti on the crumbling walls.

He put a small hand over a snarl of red spray-painted calligraphy. He patted the words. "Fuego," he said quietly.

James and Alice glanced over at Aiden, then at the graffiti he was patting.

Alice drew a sharp breath. The red graffiti read, "Fuego Wuz Here."

Alice knelt down next to Aiden. "Where is Fuego, sweetie?"

"Here," said Aiden, tapping the name.

Alice and James exchanged glances. Aside from recognizing and scribbling "Aiden" and "Mommy" and "Daddy" Aiden couldn't yet read or write. Besides which, as far as they could remember, Aiden had never been awake during their encounters with the Aelwyd warrior chieftain.

"You know who Fuego is, pal?" James asked.

Aiden's forehead crinkled. His dark eyebrows knit together, like when he was working on one of his little jigsaw puzzles. "Fuego is, Fuego is … *family*," Aiden said. He nodded to himself, satisfied with the word, but clearly feeling that it was somehow not *exactly* the word he wanted.

"*Our* family?" Alice asked.

"Yeah," Aiden said firmly.

"Cool," said James. They knew they were kin, somehow, to the Aelwyd folk, but to maybe be *directly* related to a heroic guy like Fuego was pretty awesome.

"*How* is he related to us?" Alice pressed.

Aiden's brow furrowed again. He shrugged.

"Aiden doesn't get what you're asking," James told Alice. "He's four, remember?"

"Well, how would you phrase it?" Alice asked. "You're about four. Mentally."

James knelt next to his brother and put a hand on his small shoulder. "Is Fuego an uncle?" he asked. Aiden shook his head. "Is Fuego a cousin?" Aiden shook his head again. James stood up. "Hmm," he said, "curiouser and curiouser."

"That's *my* line," objected Alice.

"I'm borrowing it. Sue me." James pointed at the graffiti. "I like that Fuego was here. It means that even though we can't trust those Ilwgyld witches, they sent us someplace Fuego's been. We can't be *totally* off track."

"Fuego good," Aiden said decisively. "Fuego very good. Fuego love James and Allie."

"That's comforting," Alice said drily. "I mean, all right, he *seemed* cool, but we don't really know any more about him than we do about the other nuts populating this nightmare, do we? Although, anyone who owns all those books *can't* be all bad." *I so totally would love a giant library like Fuego has …*

"Fuego good!" shouted Aiden. "Fuego love James and Allie." He kicked Alice's shin. Twice.

"Ow," she said, "and double-ow. This is a very painful adventure."

"Fuego good, Fuego family!" shouted Aiden. His eyes were glistening with angry tears.

"OK, OK, Fuego is very good," Alice said soothingly. She hugged Aiden and ruffled his dark curls. "Fuego is cool, right?"

Aiden laughed. "Cool!" he shouted. "Fuego cool!"

"That's better," she said. "Everything is OK, right Aidie?"

"Aidie cool!" yelled Aiden, laughing. He ran around in a circle a couple of times.

James and Alice laughed. James picked up Aiden and hoisted the little boy onto his shoulders.

"OK, Aidie, you hang on tight. You're going to be our scout, OK? But you've gotta be *very* quiet. Like the good little mouse. We're on a secret mission. If you see anything weird, you tug on my hair, OK? But not *too* hard."

Aiden nodded, and gave a little salute to his brother and his cousin.

They stepped through a gap in the walls. Alice drew a startled breath.

"Faery lights?" James guessed.

"Yeah," she said.

They were faint in the sunlight, but still visible to her, minute green-gold flecks hovering in cascades. They floated parallel to an overgrown drive that wound up the hill.

"We follow you, then," James said. "Don't worry. It's broad daylight and we're right behind you."

"What's to worry?" Alice murmured under her breath.

"You're welcome," said James. "You *did* just thank us, for having your back – right?"

She threw a sour smile over her shoulder, and then started up the drive.

* * *

James had always liked forests.

I miss dad, he thought, as they followed the overgrown drive deeper into the forest. *We should be planning our camping trip. Getting ready to fish and eat s'mores and shoot arrows …*

James pushed that thought out of his mind.

Forests soothed him. The lines of the trees, the pools of shadow, the shafts of green-gold light, the surprising splashes of color where flowers grew on the forest floor – when he was hiking, the world felt right.

Without thinking about it, James scanned the surroundings as they walked. It was like tuning in to different tracks of a piece of music. He registered the scurrying of small animals, the soft thud of falling acorns and the rustle of leaves in the breeze.

And it wasn't just sound. He was scanning the scents, too. He had learned when he was very small, on an early camping trip, that water has its own scent, a combination of the water itself and the minerals of the rocks and soil it flowed through. Dirt had a scent, and trees, leaves, moss and stone.

James scanned their surroundings as they walked. And after hiking up the drive to the ruined Cobb mansion, he knew that there was something wrong – very wrong – with the Haunted Forest.

It wasn't the forest itself. The place felt friendly, warm even. But there was something in it that didn't belong. There was an intruder in the forest. The animals and the birds sensed it too, James thought; that's why they were so quiet.

They found the ruins of the Cobb mansion relatively quickly, nothing to see but a graffiti-scarred foundation deeply overgrown with grass, plants and trees.

"Hmm," said Alice.

"Hmm, what?" asked James.

"The faery lights stop here. But," she looked around, "there's not really anything to see."

They strolled back and forth in front of the ruins, and then Alice sank down on the remains of the grand front steps.

"Did anyone think to bring any water on this escapade?" she asked. "I'm really thirsty."

"Aidie thirsty," said Aiden. "Aidie thirsty, Aidie thirsty!"

"Holy cow, all right," said James.

He opened his small backpack and drew out two juice boxes. "Here." He handed one to Aiden and one to Alice.

"That's *all* you brought?" she demanded incredulously. "Juice boxes?"

"Well it's more than *you* brought."

"I'm a *kid*! I shouldn't be worrying about provisions. *You're* the babysitter."

"And hey, check it out, *you're* the baby," he shot back.

James looked around him, taking in the ruins as if he were looking for something specific. "There must be an old well around here," James said thoughtfully, "that I can drop you into. A really deep well."

"You are *so* mean!"

"Don't worry. Aiden and I will get you on the way back. We wouldn't actually *leave* you here. Well, we *probably* wouldn't leave you here."

"On the way back from *where*?" she demanded. "*I'm* the only one who can see the faery lights. Without me you'd be *nowhere*."

"Brat!"

"Dork!"

"*ENOUGH*!!!" shouted a deep male voice.

James and Alice jumped.

A tall man in a dark, hooded cloak leaped up out of the ruined foundation.

Aiden shouted. Alice screamed. And Alice always insisted, later, that James screamed too. James always denied screamed. "I shouted in surprise," was how he characterized the sound he made.

The menacing figure marched toward the children. "Of all the pointless, time-wasting, ridiculous bickering!" he bellowed.

Aidie slumped, suddenly unconscious, and toppled off of James' shoulders. James scrambled to grab him, but Aiden fell. With a little cry Alice leaned forward and caught her tiny cousin before he hit the ground.

The figure swept back its hood with the swipe of one massive hand.

It was Fuego. His dark eyes flashed with irritation. His grim frown seemed carved of stone. His eyebrows were knit fiercely.

"It's *you*," Alice cried accusingly. "*You're* making Aiden fall asleep. Every time you're around …"

Fuego bowed deeply. "Guilty as charged," he said.

"But why?"

"Because they have a connection," James said, eyes narrowing. "That's how Aiden could 'read' Fuego's name on the wall. It's one of those time travel things, right? If Aiden meets you, the universe explodes or something."

"Or something," Fuego said.

"You're his grandson, from the future," guessed James.

"No."

"His great-grandson."

"No."

"His son-in-law?"

"No. Not a son-in-law. Aiden and I are blood relations."

"Then you're from the past," guessed James. "You're his great-great-great grandfather."

Fuego held up a large hand, effectively silencing the teen. "I'm not his great-anything. And, think upon it, James: as I am related to Aiden, I am related, also to Alice and to you, as well." He made a little bow to Alice. "But I'm not your grandfather, or your grandchild, or your uncle. I'm not your father – or your mother for that matter! It isn't of any blasted importance *who* I am in the context of your quest, and, in fact, it would hurt the mission if you realized my identity. So stop wasting time. You don't have all day to climb the mountain."

"The *mountain*?" asked Alice. She glanced at the thickly wooded land sweeping up from the ruins. "As in, we have to climb the whole *mountain*?"

"She can't be the *only* seer," James said to Fuego. "Isn't there a back up or something?"

"She's it," Fuego said grimly. "She's *the* seer. And you're *the* protector. And both of you must climb that mountain to complete your quest for the second touchstone. Which, as usual, the Ilwgyld have pushed you into too soon. Do you not recall my telling you to do nothing until after I saw you again?"

"Gee, I'm sorry," Alice said sarcastically, "but when two scary weirdos show up in your closet in the middle of the night – "

"SILENCE!" roared Fuego. "Don't take that tone with me, lass. All this bickering stops now. The fate of my people is on your shoulders – my people, and your family. And all you do is snipe. You," he jabbed a finger at Alice, "will show your cousin James the proper respect. And you," he pointed at James, "will remember that your cousin Alice is a child. She might sound like a grownup, and think like a grownup, but she's a sensitive little lass."

"I am not!" Alice protested.

"Yes you are!" shouted Fuego. He towered over her in his dark cloak.

She found herself pulling Aiden closer, contracting into herself.

"OK," Alice said in a small voice.

"Good." Fuego drew a deep breath. "The Ilwgyld damaged the faery lights here. That's why the trail of lights stopped. But if you head that way," he gestured toward the woods, "you'll pick them up again. Follow the trail until you see your ride."

"What ride?" asked James.

"You'll know it when you see it. But first, you must relinquish the touchstone you recovered."

"We don't have it," Alice said. "We didn't want to carry it, in case we were attacked by the Ilwgyld. We hid it, like you told us."

"I told you to hide it," Fuego said grimly, "and I also told you to return it to me for safe-keeping."

"How did we know when we would see you again?"

"You will always see me when you are questing. You will always see me shortly after you recover a touchstone."

"Oh."

"Was it the amulet?" Fuego asked? "The Corazon de Oro?"

"That means 'Heart of Gold'," James translated for Alice.

"I know, I know," she said. "My Spanish is at least as good as yours." She turned back to Fuego. "It *is* an amulet, and it *is* gold, and it *is* shaped like a heart. It has a panther symbol carved into it, and Mayan writing. We think – does it belong to James?"

Fuego nodded. "In the sense that James is the protector, the Corazon de Oro is his. It is an ancient touchstone of our tribe. It confers great power on the bearer – power for which James is by no means ready. The purer the protector's heart, the greater the power of the amulet."

"Here's where I get confused," said Alice. "Why does a faery tribe descended from Merlin have a *Mayan* talisman?" asked Alice.

"As I believe we told you," Fuego said somewhat reproachfully, "our tribe is a melting pot of bloodlines. We are Welsh, we are Mayan – we are many things. And we'll discuss all that over a lovely cup of bark tea some day or other. Today, I need that touchstone. And you need to get moving."

"But we don't have it with us," said James. "Alice and I decided it would be too risky to carry around on a quest, with the Ilwgyld popping up everywhere."

"And since they seem to have hypnotic powers," said Alice, "we didn't think it was safe for us to know where it was hidden. Even if the Ilwgyld couldn't steal it from us, they could maybe trick us into telling them where we hid it."

"So we gave it to Aiden to hide," said James. "We knew he'd hide it somewhere he'd remember, like his toy box, or some other place the Ilwgyld wouldn't think to search."

"And the Ilwgyld would never think to ask a little boy where such an important thing was hidden," Alice finished.

Fuego shook his head. "I'm impressed," he said, "and, also, grateful. Because if you gave it to Aiden to safeguard, he'll have had the right instinct. *He'll* have brought it with him. Check his questing kit."

"But Aiden wouldn't –"

"Check his kit!" bellowed Fuego.

"What a grouch," complained Alice. But she gently drew the sky-blue pouch from within the collar of Aiden's little polo shirt.

The pouch was much heavier than hers was. She opened the drawstrings, and removed the amulet; the Corazon de Oro flashed golden in the forest sunlight.

Fuego dexterously snatched it from her, his hand a blur; he tucked the amulet within his cloak.

"Hey!" Alice protested.

"Now you *really* won't know where it is," said Fuego. "Now it *truly* will be safe, reunited with the clan from which it was stolen so long ago."

"Stolen by whom?" Alice asked curiously.

"That," Fuego said firmly, "is a story for another time."

"Oh, *everything* is a story for another time," complained Alice. "Just once how about someone sits us down and takes the time to tell us something instead of rushing us from – "

"GO!" shouted Fuego. "Quickly!"

Fuego ran toward the ruins and leaped into one of its ink-black cavities.

"Is it my imagination," asked Alice, "or is he all bent out of shape today?"

"He was a lot friendlier yesterday," James agreed. "Today he's kind of … crabby."

Alice settled Aiden securely in her arms. He was still sleeping.

She headed in the direction where Fuego had said they'd find the faery lights.

Chapter Fourteen – Winter Quarters
June 25th – Aelwyd

After only five minutes of hiking, Alice saw the faery lights again.

"We've picked up the trail," she told James. "Just like Fuego said we would."

The lights stretched deep into the forest, up the mountain, in twinkling green-and-red strands. *Like Christmas lights*, Alice thought.

"How long will it take us to get to the top of the mountain?" asked James.

"How the heck should – *ow*!" Alice couldn't put her hands to her aching head, since she was holding Aiden, but she winced against the pain of the incoming information.

"Are you all right?" asked James.

"Do I *look* all right? It's this stupid channeling. I wish I could control it. To answer your question, it takes *hours* to hike up the mountain to the old ruins. But apparently we're getting a ride."

James looked around at the thick trees and brush, the steep hillside, the protruding slabs of granite. "A ride, huh? Not a car," he mused. "Motorbikes, maybe?"

"I have no idea," Alice said. "But with all these low branches, it seems like motorbikes would be 'hello, decapitation'."

"Gruesome thought," said James, "but true."

"Do you think Fuego's following us?" Alice asked. "Like, what do you call it, a rear guard or something?"

"I don't know. It looked more like he was waiting for someone. Laying a trap."

"Whatever he was doing, he was totally on edge. *No one*'s ever yelled at me like that."

"You seem to have survived," James said drily.

She pulled a face at him. They walked in silence for another five minutes.

"Getting cold," James murmured. His arms and legs were tingling. In the space of a few seconds his limbs felt suddenly freezing cold. His face felt cold too, almost numb. "Are you cold, Alice?"

"F-f-ff-freezing," she answered, teeth chattering.

James sniffed the air. It couldn't be *this* cold. In June?

"I think … I think I smell *snow*," James said. He had only smelled snow a couple of times before, when his dad took him up to Mammoth Mountain to ski and snowboard. Snow had a very specific crystalline scent which James had never forgotten.

Suddenly the world went grey, and misty. Tendrils of icy fog wrapped around them.

"The valence," James said.

"No k-k-kidding," Alice chattered.

And then, as quickly as they were in the valence, it was gone. They were back in the forest – but it had changed.

The trees were evergreens and birch but also redwoods – redwoods that stretched impossibly wide and towered impossibly high. The grand trees seemed to pierce the sky high above. Some of the trees were so wide at the base that it would have taken twenty people or so, James estimated, to surround them.

Snow blanketed the ground, here, and snow drifted down in large, soft flakes. The tree boughs were draped in pure white snow, and icicles hung from the low branches. The air was crisp, and scented with evergreens.

James and Alice shivered, but their eyes widened as they took in the beauty around them.

High above, among the tree boughs, white and green lanterns were hung.

"We're in Aelwyd," James said softly.

"Duh," said Alice, but without the usual sting.

"The valence is *really* thin here," James continued. "We were only in it, what, a couple of minutes? Things must slip back and forth between Aelwyd and the real world all the time. That's why people see and hear strange things, and think the forest is haunted."

Alice continued to follow the glimmering faery lights that only she could see. The pretty red and green lights grew brighter, coalescing in a blinding halo of red and green around a massive tree in the near distance.

Very softly, so softly James wondered if he was imagining it, a beautiful song began. It was a choral piece, a Christmas hymn, it sounded like, and the voices singing it, from the bass to the soprano, were perfect.

As the children walked, the song grew louder and louder.

"Hear that?" James asked. Alice nodded.

It was like angels singing.

Aiden stirred in Alice's arms. He woke, looking up at her with a drowsy little smile, and then smiled at his brother. "Merry Kistmas," he said drowsily, then fell asleep again.

"Christmas in June," Alice said in wonderment.

"Time – " James began, but his cousin interrupted.

"Yes, yes, time moves differently in Aelwyd," Alice said impatiently. "If *one more person* tells me that …"

Tall, lean figures in dark green cloaks detached themselves from tree trunks, from branches.

They were Aelwyd folk, and they were all singing. They smiled down at the children from boles and boughs high above, they lined the path that the children followed …

As the children passed, each faery bowed to them. James and Alice nodded at the faery folk. It was incredibly moving. Alice felt tears welling up in her eyes, and forced them back.

The first time she'd met the faery folk – *Was it just yesterday?* – she'd been so disoriented and a little frightened, she hadn't really appreciated their beauty. They were otherworldly and strange, with their enormous dark eyes, and the tiny motes of faery lights that swirled around them, and they had a grace that she envied.

These are Fuego's people, thought Alice. *And I guess, in a weird way, our people. They're depending on us to find the touchstones – and to keep the Ilwgyld from finding them.*

When the children reached the massive tree that was swarming with faery lights, they saw what could only be described as a welcoming committee, Tanwen at the head, with spry old Nain at her right hand, and a fierce-looking little fellow of about Alice's age standing to Tanwen's left.

As usual, Tanwen was cloaked in a veritable flock of glimmering faery lights.

Tanwen, thought Alice, *is somebody really powerful here. It's not just that she's Fuego's wife.*

Tanwen's green cloak, Alice noticed approvingly, was lined with a silver-green fur that looked warm as well as incredibly stylish.

Tanwen held up one hand, and instinctively James and Alice stopped. The faery chieftain's wife bowed deeply to them. They bowed back.

"Christmastide greetings, Chosen Ones" Tanwen said. "Fuego told us to expect you and to ensure your safe passage to the White City."

"Uh, Christmastide greetings to you too," said James.

Alice curtsied gracefully, managing not to drop Aiden. "Christmastide greetings," Alice said.

Tanwen seemed to be stifling a smile. "I see Fuego's little chat had an impact on your manners," she remarked cheerfully.

Alice scowled. "I don't need *anyone* to tell me about manners."

"Truly?" Tanwen raised an eyebrow. "As you like."

Tanwen placed her hand on the shoulder of the boy on her left. He scowled ferociously at James and Alice.

"This is Daith," said Tanwen, "my son, and Fuego's son. He is our great joy."

Daith glared up at his mother with an expression of anything but joy.

He carried an intricately carved long bow, like many of the other faeries, and he looked like he wanted to clonk his mother, or the Chosen Ones, over the head with it.

"Bow to the Chosen Ones, Daith," Tanwen said gently.

Daith folded his arms over his chest defiantly.

"Daith," Tanwen said sweetly, "we don't want our guests to think we're rude."

Daith ducked his head and glared at the snowy ground.

"*Daith!*" Tanwen's voice crackled.

Daith bowed briefly to James and Alice, then shot his mother a look of pure spite.

"Pleased to meet you," Alice told Daith, more amused than insulted. *So – the faeries might sing like angels,* thought Alice, *but they don't all act like angels.*

"Pleased to meet you," James told Daith.

Alice looked up at Tanwen. "That song you were all singing was beautiful. What is it called?"

"It's a Christmas carol," said Tanwen. "Welsh. Very old. Our ancestors carried it with them when they emigrated. Singing it every year is one of the ways we keep in touch with your world."

Yeah, that's a big top ten hit in our world, Alice thought wryly.

Daith kept glancing at Aiden, who was fast asleep in Alice's arms. Daith took a step toward Alice and her small cousin, but –

"Daith!" Tanwen's voice was like ice.

"I just want to see him," Daith sulked. "This is stupid!"

"Protecting the balance of the universe is *not* stupid," Tanwen said. "If you can't behave – "

"I can mother, I can." Daith shot a look of pure venom at Alice.

The young man's expression surprised her – *What the heck did* I *do*? But, *He's got spirit*, Alice thought.

"We must return to our Yuletide celebrations," said Tanwen, "but first we must send you on your way so that you can complete your second quest." She pointed to a carefully camouflaged stairway, made of branches and twigs, that spiraled up inside the tall, brilliantly lit tree. Up, and up, and up within the tree … hundreds of feet up.

Alice's stomach suddenly felt a little queasy.

"What, ah, er, what's up there?" Alice asked.

"These are our winter quarters," said Tanwen. "We have transport awaiting you above."

"And your transport consists of …"

"Zip lines," Daith said scornfully. "And canopy cars. Know you *nothing*?"

"You may leave now, Daith," Tanwen said firmly.

Daith glowered at his mother, turned on his heel, and disappeared into the vast tree.

"When your son says 'canopy cars'," said Alice, "does that mean, ah –"

"We have carved wooden enclosures," Tanwen explained, "gondolas, that travel on ropes throughout the canopy of the forest."

"So … that would be hundreds of feet above the ground."

"Hundreds of feet, yes. It is quite safe," Tanwen assured her. "And I know," she gave Alice a pointed look, "that the seer will not let her aversion to height forestall her from completing her quest."

"Of course she won't," said James. "Aiden and I will make sure Alice is OK."

"Sure," said Alice. "If I trip and fall out of the canopy car, you and Aiden can wish me a nice fall."

"You won't fall," James said firmly. "And you won't be scared. You'll be too focused on helping me keep Aiden safe."

Alice sighed. *Hundreds of feet in the air. Hundreds of feet.*

But James had a point. She'd be so focused on Aiden, and the mission, she might not even notice how insanely high they were above the forest floor.

"Just yesterday Tariq was dangling you over downtown L.A.," James said encouragingly.

Alice shuddered. That was a memory she was happy to suppress.

"James?"

"Yeah."

"Stop helping."

* * *

Tanwen and old Nain led the cousins into the interior of the towering tree, which had to be, James hazarded, about eight-hundred feet tall. Multiple stairways spiraled up through the interior, and a hive of walls, balconies, doors and windows hinted at a thriving community living within the vast tree.

As at the summer quarters along the brook, luminous blue mushrooms provided much of the light, here, but in celebration of the Yule season, the faery folk had strung thousands of white and green lanterns throughout their tree city.

"This way, if you will," Tanwen said politely.

She and Nain and a small complement of guards led the children to a stairwell that wound up along the tree's inner wall.

The company climbed in silence for many moments.

They passed windows bright with lights, and the scents of cooking, and murmured conversations. Some windows they passed were full of dark eyes, the occupants glancing outside curiously as their chieftain's wife and the Chosen Ones passed their home.

There were murmurs of "Tanwen" and "Chosen" and "The Protector" and "The Seer", and murmurs of "The Beloved One" which, Alice guessed, was probably a reference to adorable little Aiden, who was still fast asleep in her arms.

After they had climbed for ten minutes, Alice looked up. The top of the tree didn't seem any closer than it had when they'd started.

Are we walking all the way to the top? Alice wondered. She was curious how far they had managed to climb – but her fear of heights prevented her from looking down to see.

"We ride from here," Tanwen said, leading them onto a broad landing; the chieftain's wife stopped before a row of tightly woven baskets.

They look, thought James, *like the baskets of hot air balloons*.

Nain opened the gate of one of the baskets, and allowed Tanwen and the children to precede her inside. There was a great creaking, as of massive ropes stretching – ropes, Alice soon noted, that were made of vines and bark, and that instantly began pulling the basket up the inside of the tree.

Alice gasped. She pulled Aiden tighter against her.

"We are perfectly safe," Tanwen assured her.

The woman smiled tenderly at Aiden. "It is a credit to you," Tanwen told Alice, "that you care for the child so well. A credit to both of you," she added, nodding to James.

"Aiden's pretty important to us," James said.

"He is important to us, as well," said Tanwen.

"Aye!" old Nain said fervently.

"Tanwen – why does Aiden fall asleep whenever Fuego is around?" asked Alice.

Tanwen frowned.

"It's all right," Alice said hastily, "Fuego already admitted it's his presence that makes Aiden fall asleep."

"I see. But Fuego did not tell you *why*."

"He told us he's a blood relation, but he didn't tell us *who*. Whether he's an ancestor, or someone from our future, or, well, who he is. Somehow he's most closely tied to Aiden. I don't understand why he can't just tell us who he is."

"Fuego," said Tanwen, "always has a reason for the things he does, even when they seem to make little sense. He lives his life based on instinct and moment-by-moment calculations. If he chose not to tell you who he is, then there is a reason. As his wife, I will not betray that confidence. And, after all, you have more pressing matters to ponder than Fuego's identity. Your next quest, for instance."

"What is it?" James asked curiously.

"A brief sojourn in another time," said Tanwen. "Brief, and, we hope, pleasant."

James glanced down at his jeans and hoodie. "Uh – we aren't exactly dressed for sojourns in another time."

"We will provision you," said Tanwen. "Your attire shall not betray you. Your manners, however, and your speech, will not well align with the manners and speech of your destination. Hence, you must be very quick. You must find the touchstone and depart post-haste."

"Can you give us a clue, at least?" asked Alice. "What are we looking for?"

"You will know it when you see it."

"Terrific."

"Who stole the touchstones, anyway?" asked James. "And why can't Fuego get them? He's a warrior – you all seem to be warriors, *and* magical, too."

"The thief who hid the touchstones I cannot discuss," said Tanwen, pursing her lips in a sour expression. "As to why none of us can retrieve the touchstones, there was a spell placed upon them by the thief. The Ilwgyld cannot retrieve them, but neither can the faeries. *Only* the Chosen Ones can retrieve the touchstones."

"So let me be sure I get this," said Alice. "*Only* the Chosen Ones can retrieve them, because *only* the Chosen Ones can retrieve them."

"You're being glib," said Tanwen, "but, in a nutshell – yes. Only the Chosen Ones have the proper bloodlines and magick to be impervious to the spell. There were three talismans. You have restored the Corazon De Oro. Only two remain."

Alice shook her head. "What if we, I don't know, say 'No – we don't *want* to be the Chosen Ones'?"

Tanwen laughed, a short, barking sound.

"That's what I thought," said Alice.

The basket jolted to a stop at another broad landing.

Alice glanced up – the top of the great tree still seemed impossibly high above.

They followed Tanwen along a steeply sloping ramp, James, Alice and Aiden just behind Tanwen, Nain and the guards bringing up the rear.

"Here." Tanwen led them into a round corridor, bored deep into the tree's interior, with smaller corridors crossing it at random intervals. "This way, children."

Tanwen led them through labyrinthine passages, all lit by white and green lanterns and the luminous blue mushrooms with a scent like the sea. Tanwen finally halted in front of two low doors.

"Alice," said Tanwen, pointing to the door on the left, "you will find appropriate attire within. "James, Aiden," pointing to the door on the right, "your raiment is in there. The guards will remain outside your chambers until you are ready. They will then deliver you to the proper canopy cars for your journey."

"Thank you," said James, inclining his head. "Since we have to be mixed up in all this, we really do appreciate all of your help."

"Although more information would be appreciated," said Alice.

James shot her a look.

"What?" asked Alice. "Hey, I'm grateful for what Fuego and Tanwen are doing, but I'd like to know a lot more than anyone's told us so far. A lot more."

"And you shall," said Tanwen. "Another time."

With a regal turn and a flourish of her green cloak, Tanwen swept down the corridor. Her boots made no sound on the smooth wooden floor. She disappeared so rapidly, it was almost as if she had never been there …

In the tiny chamber on the left, Alice found a lovely white dress, circa the early 1900's. The material and cut were very fine, and, she was pleased to see, there was no abundance of fussy frills and bows. There was a pretty pattern, very subtle, worked into the snowy material. Someone had spent hours fashioning the garment by hand.

The dress fit perfectly. Alice neatly folded her own clothes, and placed them in a small green rucksack she found in one corner of the little room. Alice spun in front of the blurry mirror, admiring her new outfit.

Although, it *wasn't* a mirror, Alice saw, not a proper glass mirror. It was a sheet of water, suspended somehow – *faery magic*, she thought – in a beautifully carved wooden frame.

Her reflection was blurry, but Alice could see clearly enough to know that the white dress, and the white stockings and shoes, and the white cartwheel hat with little violets on it, all fit her to perfection. The outfit was very old-fashioned, but the fashionista in Alice recognized its stylishness.

When Alice finally stepped out into the corridor, green rucksack in her hand, James and Aiden were already waiting for her.

Alice burst out laughing.

"Shut up," James said.

"Now, now," said Alice, "is that how a little gentleman should speak to his cousin?"

"If the cousin is you – yes," said James.

James looked miserable in his outfit – white breeches, white stockings, white shirt with blue pin-stripes, white vest, and white tie. He wore a straw hat with a blue-and-red band around the crown.

"Gosh, you look dandy," laughed Alice.

"Drop it," James advised. He ran a finger around his collar. "I not only look like a dork, this thing hurts. How did people *wear* these things?"

"They weren't wimps," Alice said.

She knelt down and hugged Aiden, who was looking absolutely angelic in his white breeches, shirt, vest and stockings – an outfit identical to James', but cut to fit tiny Aiden, and with a softer collar and no tie. Aiden carried his small straw boater in one hand.

"Aiden wears it beautifully," said Alice, smoothing her younger cousin's dark curls. "This is what well-dressed young gentlemen wore at the end of the Victorian era."

"Where are we *going*?" James asked one of the sentries standing at silent attention in the corridor. "We're going to stand out like a bunch of weirdos."

"Not at the White City," said the guard on the left.

"What's the White City?" asked James.

"I did a report on it for school last year," Alice said. "Let me see if I can …" Alice closed her eyes and put a hand to her forehead, not channeling, but calling upon her nearly photographic memory. "The White City was the nickname for a grand hotel complex constructed by Thaddeus Lowe in the late 1800s. Visitors enjoyed gracious accommodations, a cog railway, even an observatory. Sadly, Echo Mountain House burned to the ground in 1900."

"Not sad for me," said James, "since I never saw it."

"You're such a philistine."

James rubbed the back of his neck, where the stiff collar was chafing. "Why do we have to get dressed up in costume to visit some burned out ruins?"

Alice turned to the sentry on the left. "Are we time-traveling somehow?"

The guard nodded curtly. "Faery time –" he began.

"Yes, yes, it's different than normal time," Alice said impatiently. "I get it. I mean, I thought I got it, but *now* I really get it. James, we're going to be able to see the White City! The way it was before it burned down. It will be *so* totally beautiful."

"Awesome," James said drily. "Still not worth wearing this outfit!"

"Aidie look good," Aiden said happily, patting his little white vest.

"Yes," said Alice, "Aidie *does* look good. Aidie will fit right in. *You* –" she told her older cousin, "should try not to talk much. Your horrible slang and your complete lack of manners will give you away."

"Well, *you* should fit right in," James told her irritably, wishing he could tear the itchy collar off his shirt. "*You* already seem like a snobby little Victorian know-it-all."

The sentries rolled their eyes.

"Chosen Ones, as usual, we do not have time for your squabbles," said the guard on the right. "We must leave now. We will escort you to the canopy cars."

Alice gulped.

The canopy cars. She had forgotten about them. *I wonder how high up they travel, exactly? If they're taking us all the way up to the White City, they must travel very high ...*

"Won't we freeze up there?" James asked the sentry. "Shouldn't we have jackets or coats or something to keep warm?"

And to cover up these dumb outfits! he thought. Alice and Aiden actually *did* look pretty good – but if any of James' friends could have seen him in those breeches and stockings ...

"It is summer in the White City," the guard explained. "It is the summer of 1899."

"A beautiful Victorian summer – frozen in time," Alice said admiringly. She considered the vintage photos she'd seen of Echo Mountain House, the lovely grand hotel, the visitors in white dresses and suits and parasols. It helped to take her mind off the canopy cars ...

The guards led them to another woven basket elevator, which rose up, up, up the interior wall of the vast tree.

"What, ah, what are we supposed to *do* in the White City?" asked Alice, to take her mind off how high they were climbing.

"As Tanwen explained," said one guard, "you are to seek the next touchstone."

"Is anyone going to give us a clue, though? About how to find it?"

The guard's eyebrows lifted. "You are the Chosen Ones."

"And?"

"You will find what you seek. Somehow. It is foretold."

"Oh, well – as long as it's foretold," said James. He shook his head. "And once we find it, how the heck do we get back? Back to our own time, and back to our own world?"

"You are the Chosen Ones," the guard repeated.

"Thanks," said James. "Big help. Much appreciated."

"I think my sarcasm is rubbing off on you," Alice said approvingly.

James scowled.

"I am so pleased," one guard said to another guard, "that I do not have any children."

"Disagreeable creatures," the other guard concurred. "Particularly mortal children."

"Yes."

"You're not supposed to insult us," complained Alice. "We're the Chosen Ones."

"Which is why," said the guard, "we don't simply drop you over the side."

Alice gasped. She didn't even want to *think* of how many hundreds of feet they were above the ground.

"That isn't funny," Alice said.

"It's sort of funny," James disagreed.

"But they aren't supposed to disrespect us like that," Alice objected.

"Why not? Everyone has a right to their own opinion."

"But we're the Chosen Ones. The *Chosen Ones*," Alice repeated. *Why doesn't James get what that should mean? These Aelwyd folk should practically be worshipping us.*

"Look, we just happen to be descendants of Jonathan Myrddin," said James. "We just happen to be the right kids in the right place at the right time. Or," he rubbed his neck again, where the collar was already scraping a painful red welt, "we're the right kids in the wrong place at the wrong time. We didn't ask for this, and it doesn't make us any more special than we were a few days ago, before we knew any of this."

"*Au contraire*," Alice said, "we are *way* more special. I was hanging over downtown L.A. getting a magical whatchamacallit off the Friendship Bell! Hanging over downtown L.A.!"

The guards looked like they were getting headaches.

"Sorry," James told them. "There's no 'off' button for my cousin."

"Well!" Alice said indignantly. She folded her slender arms, lifted her chin defiantly. "Of all the mean things to say!"

"James no be mean Allie," Aiden said fiercely. He gave his brother a kick on the shin.

"Ow!" said James. Aiden's 1899 shoes were heavier than his modern sneakers. "Aidie, come on. Don't kick me. That really hurt."

"Some Chosen One," said Alice. "Can't even handle a kick from a four-year-old."

"He's a really *strong* four-year-old," said James, stooping to rub his shin.

"He is," one of the guards agreed.

"I don't recall asking for *your* opinion," Alice told the guard. "If we weren't a million feet above the ground, I'd leave. I'd leave right now."

"Don't let us stop you," said the guard. "It is a free realm, lass."

"How can you *say* that to a little girl?" Alice demanded.

The guard shrugged.

"They must be getting to know you," James deadpanned.

Alice felt tears well up in her eyes. She and James were always bickering – it was second nature to them. But now, to have these strangers, these grown-ups, saying such mean things about her …

Aiden saw the tears in his cousin's eyes. He didn't understand them, but he knew they had something to do with what his brother and the guards were saying.

Aiden bunched his hands into little fists, shook them at James and the guards.

"No be mean to Allie!" he said ferociously.

Alice dashed one delicately patterned white sleeve across her eyes. She ruffled Aiden's curls. *No sense getting him all upset …*

"Allie is OK," she told Aiden. "Allie is fine. Shh. No need for Aidie to be mad."

Aiden hugged her.

"Aiden, you *are* better than any of us," Alice said. *James and I shouldn't fight so much. We should set a better example for Aiden. We should pay more attention to him …*

"And, here, I am most pleased to say, is your destination," said one of the guards.

He pulled a wooden lever, and the basket slowed and then halted.

"Everybody out," said the other guard. "Now."

James climbed out of the basket, onto a broad landing. Alice followed, holding Aiden's hand.

"That corridor," said a guard, pointing to a dimly lit tunnel.

"We'll find the canopy cars there?" asked Alice.

"Can't miss 'em," said the other guard. He grabbed the lever, threw it forward – and the elevator dropped away from the landing at rapid speed.

Don't look down, Alice told herself. *Don't look down.*

But something pulled her, almost hypnotically, to the edge of the landing. There was a slim wooden rail. She placed one hand on it, gripped firmly. She peered over the edge.

They were at least eight hundred feet up; below was the vast hive of the clan's winter quarters, balconies, stairways, elevators – an amazing city secreted within the great tree.

Alice swooned a bit.

"For crying out loud!"

That was James, sounding mean, as usual.

But he had grabbed her arm and was pulling her back from the rail, into the corridor that led to the canopy cars.

"Do you want to fall?" James demanded. "We're *all* the Chosen Ones, you know. Seems like it's a package deal. If you croak, I don't think Aiden and I can find the other two touchstones without you."

"Allie no croak," Aiden agreed.

James pulled Alice's arm and Aiden held her other hand as they navigated the narrow, dim tunnel. Alice felt too woozy from her near-faint to protest that James was practically pulling her arm out of its socket …

The guards had been correct; they could not miss the canopy cars. The tunnel dead-ended in a semi-circular room that contained only three things: the narrow platform upon which they stood; a thick, vine-like cable running over their heads; and, suspended on the cable at a distance of about five yards apart, a series of carved wooden gondolas.

The canopy cars were shaped like bubbles, perfectly round. There were low doors in them, on the side facing the platform, and small, circular windows. Inside, the vehicles glowed with the pale blue light of luminous mushrooms.

The vine made a high-pitched, ethereal singing sound as it rolled past over their heads, bearing the wooden cars. Alice saw clouds of faery lights sparking along the vine cable.

Magick, she thought. *Run by faery magick. Which makes me feel better … and safer … I think …*

The gondolas rolled toward them from the within the pitch-black depths of the chamber, and then sailed out of the tree through a massive hole in the trunk, out into the chill air peppered with snowflakes.

James looked at Alice.

"You'll be OK," he said firmly.

"Of course I will," Alice agreed. "Do you think I don't know I'll be OK?"

"Come on," James said, before Alice could start another argument. He grabbed the low door of the next gondola, swung it open. "Come on, come on. We should be in the same car. Aiden, give me your hand –"

Aiden ignored his brother's hand, took a running leap toward the canopy car, launched himself toward it.

Aiden was so small, instead of landing inside the vehicle, his fingers snagged the edge of the open door.

"Yay!" shouted Aiden.

James and Alice saw a blur of white cloth and dark curls as Aiden swung from the gondola door. He was several feet beyond the platform, with nothing below his feet but a pitch-black abyss ...

James' heart stopped for a moment.

"Aiden!" Alice screamed.

Aiden swung himself up into the gondola. He grinned at his brother and cousin from the safety of the canopy car interior.

"James, Allie – come on!" the little boy called cheerfully.

Alice felt her knees wobble. *He almost – Aiden almost fell ...*

James was muttering something darkly. He grabbed Alice's arm.

"Hey!" she said. "That hurts!"

James picked her up and all but tossed her into the gondola, swinging himself in immediately after her. Alice landed unceremoniously on her behind.

"Oof!" she said, the breath all but knocked out of her.

"Yay! Allie fly!" cheered Aiden.

"Allie broke her tailbone," Alice complained, struggling into a more dignified sitting position.

James closed the gondola door behind them. There was a simple wooden latch; he fastened it.

"Aiden," James said seriously, looking solemnly at his brother, "you *can't* do things like that. You could get hurt. You *have* to wait until James or Allie tell you it's OK to do things. Do you understand?"

Aiden spread his hands reasonably. "Aidie like fly," he said simply.

James sighed.

"Aiden … We *know* you like to fly, but it's dangerous. You could get hurt. We don't want you to get hurt. We don't' want you to get, you know, a really bad boo-boo."

"Boo-boo OK," said Aiden, holding out his arms, which bore a number of faint bruises, scabs and scrapes. Adventurous little Aiden's life was one long series of "boo-boos".

"You're wasting your breath," Alice told James. "Four-year-olds can't understand mortal danger. You're just going to have to do a better job of looking after him."

"*I'm* going to have to do a better job?"

"Fine. *We're* going to have to do a better job. Because he doesn't have any sense of what's at stake."

"Lucky him," James said ruefully, under his breath.

"I just wish," Alice settled herself more comfortably on the plain wooden floor of the vehicle, "they had given us a clue. *Any* clue. The White City was pretty big. I don't know where we should start looking."

"Never mind that 'till we get there in one piece," said James.

He moved to the front of the cramped car, where a large circular window revealed tree tops moving toward them and then passing them in the dark, cold night. Tiny motes of snow drifted down, some spinning through the window, landing on their hair and faces.

They shivered.

"I hope it really *is* summer in the White City," James said fervently.

This isn't so bad, thought Alice. It was OK to see the tree tops moving toward them and past them. It was too dark, and the windows were too small, for them to see how high up they were, how many hundreds and hundreds of feet above the forest floor. *Good thing this isn't a glass-bottomed gondola!* thought Alice. It made her queasy even to contemplate looking down at the winter woods, the ground so far below … She pushed that image away …

Aiden nestled against his brother, who remained looking out the front window, alert.

Something, James thought, *isn't right. Something …*

He heard a faint rustling sound. He felt a slight shift in the weight of the gondola …

"Well now!" said Lou, peering into the car through the side window, "an't this lovely!"

James shouted in surprise.

"Cozy-like," agreed Flo, peering into the car through the front window.

Alice screamed.

The Ilwgyld's bony arms, in their wildly flamboyant sleeves, had snaked into the car; their bony hands gripped the window frames.

Here in Aelwyd, the Ilwgyld looked even more terrifying than they did in the mortal world. Their sharp features, their hungry eyes, their claw-like hands, their sharp teeth.

The better to eat you with, though Alice, thinking of the wolf in "Little Red Riding Hood".

Lou's blonde hair whipped about her gaunt face. Flo's red hair streamed in the frosty wind.

Their large, luminous, greedy eyes gleamed in the moonlight, and in the pale blue light of the mushrooms that lit the gondola's interior.

Alice shrank closer to James, and put her arms protectively around Aiden. James circled both of them with his arms.

"Surprised you – didn't we?" gloated Lou. "Gave you a bit of a start – what?"

Not at all, Alice thought, reining in a hysterical laugh. *Psychos landing on the roof a thousand feet up – why would* that *be startling?*

"Now, no need to look like frightened geese," chided Lou. "We're here to protect you. An't we, Flo?"

"Protect 'em," Flo agreed, with a hungry gnashing of her teeth, and a mad light in her eye.

"See, those little tattoos what we gave you," said Lou, "in your kits, you know, those little marks lets us finds you when we needs to. But, those marks lets *other* things, what an't as kindly as we are, find you too."

Alice bit her lip. *Other things … things worse than the Ilwgyld …* It didn't bear thinking about.

Of course, thought James. He remembered how angry Tanwen had been when she found the Chose Ones had put on the tattoos.

"The tattoos," Tanwen had said, "are Ilwgyld markers. You are branded now. They will sense you wherever you are." And there wasn't any way to remove the tattoos. And the tattoos would attract more than the Ilwgyld. Tanwen had said, "They will call out to evil things …"

"We just couldn't bear it if anything 'appened to you three," said Flo.

Until we gather all the touchstones, James thought wryly. *Until you think you can steal them and kill us.*

"We've become quite fond of you," said Lou.

"Fond," Flo agreed, with an ugly smile.

"We've got quite tender-like feelins for you, now," said Lou. "Almost motherly-like. You three is almost like our own dear ones. We shan't let anythin' befall you. We shan't let the rath birds harm a hair of your heads. Not a single hair!"

There was a strange sound, outside the wooden gondola, indistinct at first, then louder.

It was a fluid rustling sound … as of thousands of wings …

"*Down!*" shouted Lou.

"*Down!*" shouted Flo.

Alice instinctively shielded Aiden, and James instinctively shielded them both.

The rustling was deafening, suddenly, and accompanied by blood-curdling shrieks.

Rath birds, thought Alice. *Whatever they are …* She squeezed her eyes shut.

James tightened his hold on Alice and Aiden. He did not close his eyes. He saw, through the windows of the canopy car, roiling clouds of wings, jet-black, and flashes of jet-black beaks, razor sharp, and flashes of razor-sharp talons.

The feathers beat and whispered, and the shrieking grew higher-pitched.

At first James thought the birds were shrieking – but the shrieks, he realized, were coming from Lou and Flo. They were shrieking like mad women. Each of them, with one arm, clung to the outside of the canopy car. With the other arm, each attacked the birds. The Ilwgylds' bony hands and sharp claws rent the air, and rent the rath birds. Feathers flew, and splatters of dark ichors – *the rath birds' blood*, thought James.

The Ilwgyld attacked with their hands and sharp fingernails and, James realized, with a sickening lurch of his stomach, they attacked with their gnashing teeth.

Flo's head whipped back and then forward; she spat out feathers; a trickle of dark ichors ran down her face.

Don't hurl, James told himself sternly. *Don't hurl ...*

After long, horrifying moments, the flock of rath birds receded.

Lou grinned gruesomely at James, feathers in her teeth.

"There, now," she said, "disaster averted. Why, me'n Flo is just like mothers to you three. We're almost kin, now."

James managed a sickly smile. "Thank you," he said, hoping he sounded sincere. *They saved our lives. They saved our lives. They need us right now ... And I guess we need them.*

"Don't mention it, pet," said Flo. The dark blood of the slain rath birds glimmered in her red hair.

"Our pleasure, quite," said Lou. "Now, you do your *very* best, duckies, to retrieve the next magickal object. Yes? And if you finds yourselves up against a wall, if you finds yourselves up against it, you should put on your rings."

"Our rings?" James asked curiously.

"Ah – the high-and-mighty faeries an't bothered to tell you that, has they? Yes, duckie –put your rings on when it's lookin' bleak. Do your best. Your *very* best. Cause, should you fail, my little dears, you'll think the rath birds had a peaceful time of it. Oh my, yes – a peaceful time ..."

Lou's last word was drawn out. She had released her hold on the gondola, and dropped away in the snowy darkness.

Flo gave James a most hideous wink, and then she dropped away too.

Ilwgyld can fly, thought James. *Interesting. Or, if not fly, they can float, or hover, or ride air currents, or something like that.*

"It's OK now," James told Alice, releasing her and Aiden.

"*OK*?" Alice demanded.

"Well, you know. Relatively speaking," James said.

"I'm not a baby, you know," said Alice. "You didn't have to protect me like that. You practically suffocated us."

"I was protecting *Aiden*," said James. "*You*, I think, would probably make a great addition to Lou and Flo's team."

Alice's eyes narrowed. "You take that back."

"What? I mean it. You three could form an evil singing group, or something."

"No fight," Aiden said, patting Alice's arm and his brother's arm.

Grey tendrils of mist rolled into the canopy car.

"The valence," said James. "We're almost there."

Alice peered through the front window of the vehicle. She could see little pinpricks of faery lights, leading the gondola and its cable into a pocket of pitch-black fog.

"When we get there," said Alice, "let *me* do the talking. *I'm* the one that did a report on the White City. I know the customs, and how to talk, and how to blend in."

"We're not going to *live* there," James told her. "We just have to get in, find the touchstone, and get out."

"Which could take who knows how long," said Alice. "There's a hotel, an observatory, a railway –"

"You need to follow your, your vision or whatever," said James. "We can't be checking *every* stupid building. This isn't a field trip. When you see those little lights you see, we'll just follow them to the touchstone."

Alice rolled her eyes. "So – now you're an expert on how this works? *I'm* the seer, James. You're the protector. Just protect us. Especially Aiden."

James opened his mouth to retort, but tendrils of black fog rolled into the gondola.

"Get ready," Alice said tersely. "We're almost there."

Chapter Fifteen – The White City
June 25th, 1899– Echo Mountain House

"We are *so* going to get caught," muttered Alice. "You can't possibly pull this off."

"Never mind the compliments," said James. "Do you see any faery lights?"

Alice shook her head.

"Well, is anything glowing?"

She shook her head again.

They stood in front of Echo Mountain House, at the base of the steps that swept up to the grand wrap-around porch, the four stories of Victorian elegance, the lovely dome. Flags atop tall flag poles rippled in the light breeze.

Men, women and children in pristine white summer clothes flowed up and down the steps. Some of them looked a trifle askance at the three young people gawking up at the hotel.

Alice nudged James in the ribs.

"Stop staring," she said. "Be cool."

"I'm cool."

"You look *way* too intense. We're rich kids on a summer outing – *not* on a mission of life-or-death."

"Except, my dear little cousin," he said tightly, "we *are* on a mission of life-and-death."

"Yeah, OK – but try not to *look* like it."

"You don't see *anything* glowing?"

"Nothing."

"Aidie thirsty," Aiden announced.

It was a glorious early summer day, sunny and bright, but a faint breeze brushed the mountain top, stirring the women's summer dresses and lacy parasols and the bits of ribbon on their straw hats.

"Aidie thirsty," Aiden said again. He tilted his head, smiling adorably at his brother and cousin.

"They should be serving lemonade on the porch," said Alice.

"Lemonade – yay!" said Aiden.

"Maybe this is a sign," James said hopefully. "Maybe we're being *led* to the porch. Look for glowing stuff."

"I know what to look for," said Alice.

She took one of Aiden's hands, and James took the other, and they climbed the grand steps that wended their way up to Echo Mountain House's grand wrap-around porch.

"People are staring at us," James told Alice out of the side of his mouth.

"Of course," she said imperturbably. "Aiden and I look stunning – and you look like a dork. And people aren't staring. That would be rude. They're just ... noticing us."

"Well, their noticing looks like staring to me."

"Only to the uncivilized, dorkish eye."

"Lemonade," said Aiden, keeping them focused on priorities.

At the top of the steps they could look left and right along the grand, pillared porch, where well-to-do Pasadenians strolled, taking in the fresh air and sunlight, or sat on plush chairs and divans, talking to each other in low, well-bred tones.

James rubbed the back of his neck. *This collar is driving me crazy! How could guys wear these all day?*

"Just think," said Alice, looking along the porch. "It's the last summer for this place. In February it will burn to the ground."

"What happened?" asked James.

"Kitchen fire."

"Huhn."

Not more than a few paces from where they were standing, James saw an elderly woman and a little girl, possibly her granddaughter – *Possibly her great-granddaughter*, James thought – smiling and talking quietly. The little girl was showing the old lady a china doll.

"Was anybody hurt in the fire?" asked James.

"No. Nobody died," said Alice. "But they never rebuilt this place. No insurance – no money to rebuild."

"At least no one was hurt," said James.

"Lemonade," said Aiden, starting to sound cranky.

Alice led them inside the grand hotel. "Isn't it beautiful?" she asked, gesturing to the magnificent carved wood and glass and sumptuous carpets and upholstery.

"It's pretty cool," James admitted grudgingly.

"*I* do the talking," said Alice.

"Fine by me."

She signaled to an immaculately attired bell boy.

"Pardon me," said Alice, "our father is not well. He is lying down, but he told us to lunch without him."

"Does your father require a physician?" the bellboy asked solicitously.

"No," said Alice. "Merely rest. But, we wonder, might you direct us to the restaurant?"

"Certainly, miss. You simply turn down that corridor, there …"

The restaurant was the prettiest place the children had ever seen. Light flowed through great glass windows and sparkled on the crystal chandeliers, the water glasses, the fine china and silverware. There were low vases of fresh flowers on each table. The table cloths and napkins were real linen.

"Your mom and dad would *love* this place," Alice said to James.

"Sure," said James, "they would. It's awesome. But we can't afford this. Unless you have some 1800's money stashed away in your giant hat."

"We don't need money," Alice said dismissively. "Our father is upstairs in room 303. He'll settle all the charges when we check out."

"But … that's stealing," objected James.

"Not really. It can't be stealing because, technically, this place no longer exists. We're visiting, well, I don't know what to call it. *You're* the video game geek – you should have some name for it. This is just a moment in history, playing over and over again."

"Temporal loop," said James.

"Sure, whatever. The people we're seeing are long gone. So we can't really steal from them – can we?"

"I guess not," James said doubtfully. "It still doesn't seem right."

"What's not right," said Alice, "is your etiquette. Put your napkin on your lap. Aidie, you too."

Aiden promptly placed his napkin on his head, and laughed hilariously.

Nearby diners glanced disapprovingly in their direction.

Alice gently took the napkin off Aiden's head, dropped it on his lap.

"Aiden," said Alice, "this is a time to be a good little mouse. OK?"

Aiden nodded cheerfully. "Aidie good," he assured her.

Alice gave their order to the waiter. It had been quite a while since any of them had eaten. Alice realized her stomach was growling.

"We'll begin with lemonade and punch," Alice told the waiter, reading from the menu, with its sketch of Echo Mountain House on the front. "Then celery, and cheese straws, and chicken croquettes, then the beef, then the Edam cheese with nuts, raisins, and chocolate cake. And milk with the cake."

"Certainly, miss. Your room, again?"

"Room 303," Alice said, without batting an eyelash ...

As it turned out, the boys were as hungry as Alice – even hungrier. Aiden downed glass after glass of lemonade and punch, and ate all of his chicken croquettes and beef and cheese, too happily focused on the delicious food to do anything mischievous.

"Wow," said James, finishing a second slice of chocolate cake, "they really knew how to eat in the old days."

"Milk good," Aiden said approvingly, drinking his third glass. He had acquired a little mustache and beard of chocolate frosting and chocolate cake crumbs. Alice gently cleaned his face with her napkin. "More cake Aidie," said Aiden.

"You've had two pieces," said Alice.

Aiden frowned.

"I'd give him a third piece," James suggested. "Unless you want to see a very un-Victorian nuclear melt-down."

"All right," sighed Alice. "One more piece, Aiden. You *have* been a very good little mouse."

Aiden nodded …

When they finished their meal, Alice signed the bill with a little silver pencil provided by the waiter. She signed her name with a flourish: "Alice Iztali" and next to her signature "Roberto Iztali, Room 303".

"You know," she said, as they strolled along the main corridor, past the gift store, and the barber shop, "I wish my dad really *was* upstairs, instead of off in New Mexico on that stupid construction job."

"That stupid construction job is paying your rent," said James. "And our mortgage."

"But – I miss him." It was an uncharacteristically vulnerable admission for Alice.

"Yeah, well," James shrugged, "Aiden and me miss our dad too. It basically sucks."

"'Aiden and I'" corrected Alice. "You say 'Aiden and I' not 'Aiden and me'. And the Victorians don't say things 'suck'."

"Who cares?" asked James. "Let's find the touchstone and get out of here. Anything glowing? Anything at all?"

"Not a thing."

"Where would it be hidden?" mused James.

"We'll just have to look around," said Alice.

"Are you *sure* you haven't seen anything glowing?" James asked thoughtfully.

"And what does *that* mean?" Alice snapped.

"It means, you totally like this place, and I just wanna be sure you're not making excuses for us to spend more time here."

"Well, you don't exactly seem to hate it here."

"I like the food," James agreed, "but I don't want to live here forever."

"Look, if I see something glowing, you'll be the first to know, dork. But I don't. So we're going to have to look around. Deal with it …"

They strolled through the lovely grounds, with its carefully tended plants and flowers, nodding politely to the other families they passed.

They allowed little Aiden to remove his shoes and stockings and wade in the children's wading pool. Alice was afraid the unpredictable little daredevil would plunge into the water and get soaked, but the genteel atmosphere seemed to be rubbing off even on Aiden; he waded like a perfect little gentleman, and raced paper boats, in a perfectly civilized manner, with another little boy.

They visited the observatory, with its impressive but – to the children – incomprehensible jigsaw puzzle of tubes and gears and cogs and lenses. A kindly old fellow with a droopy mustache explained to visitors about planets and stars and light years and how telescope lenses work.

James and Aiden listened to the old man, while Alice roamed about unobtrusively.

"Anything?" James whispered when she rejoined them.

The old man was on a roll, explaining meteors and comets to the small crowd of visitors.

"*Nada*," whispered Alice. "Nothing's glowing."

They visited the small zoo, where Aiden wanted to adopt the little black bear cub, and wanted to pat the snakes.

"The animals have to stay here," Alice explained to her cousin. "This is their house. And the snakes will be very sad if you pat them. They don't like to be patted."

"Baby bear likes Aidie," Aiden insisted.

"Now, Aiden," said Alice, "what if someone took you from your house? What if someone took you away from your mommy and your daddy and your brother?"

Aiden's eyes opened wide. "Sad," he said.

"Right," said Alice. "So we need to leave the baby bear right here."

"*And* the snakes," said James, shuddering.

Alice shot him a look. "James – you aren't afraid of snakes – are you?"

"Not afraid," he said. "I just don't like them much."

"Huh. Good to know."

As evening began to fall, they had searched most of the grounds and buildings.

"I think," said Alice, "we might have to go up the rest of the mountain, on the train. There's a little alpine house up there. Maybe that's where the touchstone is."

James shook his head. "If it was way up there, that's where the canopy car would have dropped us. No. It's around here somewhere; you just haven't spotted it yet. If they'd just given us some kind of clue. If they'd just …"

James trailed off, following something with his eyes.

Alice turned to see what James was looking at.

A girl – about sixteen or seventeen, about, James' age. With a mass of coppery hair piled under her straw hat. With very fair skin and very blue eyes.

Alice laughed.

"What a dork," she told her cousin.

"She's not a dork," James objected.

"Not the girl – *you*. That was like watching something in a stupid old movie. You got all quiet, and stared after her. Are you going to follow her and ask her to become Mrs. Dork?"

James moved forward, began following the young lady into the hotel's main lobby.

"Hey," called Alice. "I was just kidding."

She took Aiden's hand; they hurried to catch up to James.

James followed the young lady into the lobby, down a side corridor off of the lobby, and around several corners.

The young woman moved gracefully but with surprising speed. James barely kept her in sight. Alice and Aiden rushed to keep pace with James.

James finally halted in front of a door marked "Mechanical Wonders – Penny Arcade".

He looked to the left. He looked to the right.

"She's gone," he said, bewildered.

"Duh," said Alice, out of breath as she joined him. "She must be in the arcade."

"But I didn't hear the door open and close," he objected. "The girl turned the corner and then, 'poof' she was gone."

"People can't just vanish," said Alice. "Or, I guess they can, in these worlds, but she *looked* like a regular ordinary person. I'm telling you, she's in here."

Alice turned the heavy brass door knob, and opened the door to the room of "Mechanical Wonders".

It was dim inside the penny arcade, the gas lamps turned low in a large chamber filled with row upon row of machines fashioned from wood and brass and glass.

There were primitive pinball machines, and baseball machines. There were machines in which little puppets would dance if you put in a penny and pulled a lever. There were machines in which little birds would sing, and in which clowns would laugh.

James strode quickly up and down the rows.

"She's not here," he told Alice triumphantly. "I knew it. There was no way she had time to get in here. There's nobody in here but us."

"Yes," Alice agreed, "just us."

The air had a heaviness to it … It was oppressive.

Something creepy about this place, thought Alice. *And it's like we were led here. Maybe a trap?*

Aiden stopped in front of a glass panel behind which a little black bear of painted wood leaned against a carved pine tree.

"Give Aidie penny," Aiden told Alice. "Bear climb."

Alice dug a penny out of her rucksack. Would a 2012 penny work in an 1899 machine? The metal content, at the very least, would be different. But as long as the general size was the same …

Aiden fed the penny into the slot, pushed a little lever.

A faint growl – "Rowr!" – emanated from a speaker hidden in the wooden case.

The little black bear turned on its hind legs, first left, then right, and then began slowly climbing the pine tree in a herky-jerky fashion.

Aiden clapped his hands delightedly. "Bear climb!" he said.

Alice placed an affectionate hand on Aiden's shoulder. "Yes, Aiden. The bear climbs."

James had walked up and down the rows again.

"Why did she have to vanish?" he asked. It seemed to be a rhetorical question, addressed to the universe at large. "She was so pretty. Where did she go?"

"James, for all we know that was Lou or Flo in disguise," said Alice. "Probably Flo, with the red hair."

"No *way* that was Lou or Flo," said James. He shivered, remembering how the ravenous Ilwgyld had attacked the rath birds. "The girl *I* followed is was a nice, regular girl."

"She *looked* like a nice, regular girl," agreed Alice, "but normal girls don't usually vanish into thin air."

"She didn't vanish. There must be, I don't know," James looked around the shadowy chamber, "a hidden door or something. I feel like, I don't know why, but I feel like I need to find her."

"Sounds like a spell," Alice said skeptically.

"She's someone important," said James. "She has something to do with our quest."

"Or, much more likely, she's just part of a spell," Alice insisted. "Can you hear yourself, James? Since when are you all stupid and mushy about a random chick? We're on a mission here. The question we need to ask is *why* were we led in here? Is *this* where the touchstone is?"

James began tapping on one of the walls.

"What are you doing?" asked Alice.

"I told you. I'm looking for the hidden door."

Alice squeezed Aiden's hand. "I guess it's up to us, little guy."

Aiden nodded sagely.

While James moved along the walls, tapping them, and now and again pressing on the designs of the ornate, flocked wallpaper, Alice and Aiden walked up and down the rows of Victorian arcade games.

Alice didn't see any faery lights, and nothing seemed to be glowing.

Once in awhile Aiden would ask for a penny, if a game caught his fancy, and Alice would give him a penny from her rucksack. They watched ball bearings navigate mazes, listened to mechanical birds chirping opera arias, and saw mechanized Punch and Judy puppets bash each other with little wooden clubs.

And then …

"Robot!" Aiden crowed excitedly.

He and Alice stood before a glass case containing the carved wooden head and shoulders of a vaguely human figure. The head was bullet-shaped, the eyes square.

"It does kind of look like a robot," Alice told Aiden. "But it's an Automaton."

"Automa-what?" asked James joining them.

He looked miserable.

"No secret door?" asked Alice.

"No secret door," James said.

Aiden pressed his small fingers to the glass case, making little smudge marks.

"Robot," he said again. "Allie – make robot talk."

Alice dug another penny out of her rucksack. She handed it to the little boy.

"That's an Automaton, Aidie. It is *kind* of like a robot." She read the little plaque on the front of the machine aloud. "'Sopho – The Amazing Mechanical Marvel – Answers All Your Questions.' Huh. Maybe," she said to James, "Sopho can tell us where your little girlfriend disappeared to."

"Ha-ha," James said coldly.

"Or maybe it can tell us where the touchstone is," said Alice. "Go on, Aidie. Put in the penny."

Aiden dropped the coin into the slot. There was a click, and then a clatter as the penny rolled down a slide inside the wooden case, and then a whirring and clicking as the internal gears began to move. And then … silence.

"Well, *that* was a rip-off," said Alice.

Aiden hit the machine with one small fist. "Dumb Bozo – talk!" he commanded.

"It's 'Sopho'," Alice corrected. "Don't hurt your hand, Aiden. I guess it's just broken. Or, maybe it needs to be wound up."

Of course, she thought, stepping around the machine to examine the back of the wooden case. *Before electricity, the Victorians made all of these toys to work on purely mechanical power. You wind them up, with a key, to set them in motion.*

From the dusty back of the wooden case, a key handle protruded. It was a large, substantial key; it appeared to be made of iron.

And it was glowing.

Not just glowing – it was radiating waves of light so intense they almost hurt Alice's eyes.

And just below the keyhole, an inscription read, "Manufactured by Merlin Co., Sircus of Impossible Magicks, London, UK."

Alice inhaled sharply.

"You OK?" asked James. "Did you get a splinter?"

"No," she said.

Alice grasped the key handle gently, and turned it, over and over again, within the key hole, until it wouldn't turn any more. There was a loud click. She removed the key from the machine, and returned to her cousins.

"Whatever you did, the machine's working," said James.

Loud whirring and clicking and grinding sounds emanated from within the wooden case.

Sopho's head and shoulders contorted. Aiden watched the Automaton, mesmerized.

"I found the touchstone," Alice told James quietly.

She held up the iron key. It was heavy. It was shaped like a serpent with feather-like scales, and carved with minute symbols like those that adorned the Corazon De Oro amulet.

"Mayan hieroglyphs," said James. "Again."

"Yes," said Alice.

"Wish one of us could read it. You're *sure* this is the touchstone?"

"Yeah. If you could see how it's glowing – like a search light," Alice said.

"It's yours," said James, gazing at the serpent design. "The amulet for me, the key for you."

"Guess the third touchstone will be something for Aiden," said Alice. "Well," she looked around the game room, "we've got the touchstone. Time to hit the road."

James glanced ruefully around the room. "I just wish … well …"

"For crying out loud, dork, it was a spell," said Alice. "Just a way to lead us in here. And for all we know, it was an Ilwgyld spell."

"That girl was not evil," said James.

"That girl was probably an illusion," said Alice. "She probably doesn't even exist. And if she *does* exist, I mean, this is 1899. Whoever she is, she'd be long dead in our time."

"I just wish I could find her before I leave," James said helplessly.

Alice shook her head.

"Look! Bozo!" cried Aiden.

James and Alice turned to the Automaton, which now whirled and contorted at a seemingly impossible speed, a rotating blur within the glass case.

"Bozo *loco*!" said Aiden.

"Is Sopho supposed to do that?" Alice asked James.

"How would I know?"

"Boys are supposed to be mechanical. Is it, is it going to explode?" Alice took a step back.

"*You're* the one that knows all about the Victorian world," said James. "*You* tell *us*."

"Aiden," Alice said sharply, "get away from Sopho. Sopho is broken."

"Bozo go 'ka-pow'," Aiden said hopefully.

"That's what I'm worried about. Come here." Alice extended one hand.

Reluctantly, Aiden went to his cousin and took her hand, but his eyes remained fixed on the wildly spinning wooden Automaton.

"It didn't even answer any questions," James noted.

"Well – we didn't ask any," Alice said reasonably."

"True." James cleared his throat. "Sopho," he addressed the whirling figure in the glass case, "who was that girl I followed in here?"

"What a dork!" said Alice.

"Shut up," James told her.

There was a screeching sound, as of metal grating on metal, and Sopho's hinged mouth opened.

"She … is … she … is …," intoned Sopho, voice deep and metallic.

But before Sopho could tell them who or what the blue-eyed girl was, a blinding flash from the automaton's case dazzled all of them. It enveloped them in a pulse of blinding radiance.

James grabbed Alice's arm protectively, and she flung an arm around Aiden.

There was a pressure on their ear-drums, as if they were in an airplane at 30,000 feet.

And then the light and pressure faded, and they were in a grey, chill mist.

"The valence," said Alice. "Something transported us to the valence."

She squinted. Just ahead, she could distinguish a trail of sparkling faery lights. "I see a trail," she said. "I can lead us out. Guys – we *did* it! We found the second touchstone!"

"Go, us," James said wearily.

Aiden held out one hand. "Give key Aidie," he said.

Alice lifted her tiny cousin, handed him the key. She helped him to secure it in his sky-blue quest kit, tucked the kit under his white shirt again.

"Aiden," she said seriously, "if the bad people every ask for the key – "

"Aidie kick bad guys," Aiden said. "Ka-pow!"

"No, Aidie," said Alice. "If the bad people ever ask for the key, just give it to them. We don't think they'll ever ask you, but if they do, just let them have it."

Aiden smiled one of his winning smiles.

"Aiden," she said, "do you understand what Alice is telling you?"

Aiden nodded.

"OK. We're going home now," Alice said.

She turned to James; her older cousin was shivering in the chill of the valence, and looking sadly over his shoulder.

"What's your deal?" Alice asked him. "Come on. We did it. Let's go."

"That girl," he said. "Who was she?"

Chapter Sixteen – Battle
June 25th – Pasadena

When they finally emerged from the cold, murky mist of the valence, they found themselves at Pasadena's City Hall, a graceful building of red tiled roofs, a glorious Italianate dome, and statues of lions.

The children stood in the central courtyard, next to the massive fountain. The fountain's central spire was almost twenty feet tall. Water plashed in the basin. The scent of the courtyard's roses hung heavy in the warm night air.

James checked his cell phone.

"Ten o'clock!" he said. "At night! We are in *so* much trouble!"

"As usual," said Alice, "you're not getting the picture. *We*," she gestured to Aiden and herself, "are not in trouble. *You* are in trouble. You're supposed to be the responsible," she coughed, "teenager."

James ignored her. He checked his "Missed Calls" screen.

"Huhn," he said. "That's weird. Mom didn't call."

"At all?" asked Alice.

"At all," he said.

Alice pulled her cell phone out of her rucksack. She checked her "Missed Calls". Nothing. No missed calls. No voicemail messages.

"OK," said James, "this is good. They're probably been so busy working, they forgot to call us. If we catch a train now, we might get home before they do."

"*Your* mom might forget to call," said Alice, thinking of her brisk, business-like Aunt Roz. "But *my* mom always calls, at least once."

"Oh." James thought of his sweet, motherly Aunt Peggy. "Yeah. True."

"I hope they're OK," said Alice. A dark thought occurred to her. "James – you don't think the Ilwgyld would hurt our moms – do you?"

God – what a thought!

James tried hard to look nonchalant. "I'm sure they're fine," he said. "The Ilwgyld are too focused on *us* right now to bother my mother and Aunt Peggy. But we've got to get home – or my mother is gonna kill *all* of us!"

"We can't go like *this*," said Alice, pointing to her Victorian summer dress. "Or *that*," she said, gesturing to James and Aiden's Victorian attire.

"Oh. Yeah." James couldn't even imagine how embarrassing it would be if he ran into any of his friends on the train while he was wearing breeches and stockings! "Look, we're only a block from the Paseo," he said, referring to Pasadena's outdoor mall, "so let's go over there and change. Yeah?"

"OK," said Alice. "That's not a *completely* stupid plan."

"Thanks," he said drily.

"You're welcome."

"HEY!" barked a loud voice.

The three children were blinded by a bright flashlight beam.

Rapid footsteps crossed the dirt courtyard.

"HEY, YOU KIDS CAN'T BE HERE!"

Aiden shrank behind Alice and James, who squinted against the dazzle of the flashlight.

"THIS PROPERTY IS CLOSED!" boomed the man who was rushing toward them. He wore a dark uniform, with badges on the shoulders and pocket.

"Security guard," James whispered to Alice.

"Duh," she whispered back. "Let me handle this."

Alice threw a hand up over her face.

"Ow!" She said. "That light is hurting my eyes!"

The security guard lowered his flashlight. He looked young – maybe twenty or twenty-one; not that much older than James.

The young man regarded their Victorian clothing.

"What are you guys supposed to be?"

"We're in a play," Alice said smoothly. "At the Civic Center. For the Pasadena Historical Society."

"Then why are you wandering around here?"

"We're getting into our roles," said Alice. "We're soaking up atmosphere. It's a play about the Pasadena in the Victorian era."

"Well it's not safe here at night," said the guard. "You shouldn't be wandering around alone."

"We didn't realize how scary it would be," said Alice. "We thought there would be tourists, or an event, or something."

"Well there aren't." The guard looked around the courtyard. "You don't have parents with you? Where are your folks?"

"Over at the Civic Center," said Alice. "Waiting for us to perform."

"Then you better get back now," said the guard. "Go on, head back. Take Garfield Avenue," he pointed through the western arch of the courtyard. "Go south to the Paseo, and cut through to the Civic Center. That's the safest way. I'll watch from the steps to be sure no one hassles you."

"Thank you, sir," said Alice. She clasped her hands in a ladylike fashion. "That will make us feel much safer."

Oh, brother! thought James. *Alice can really ham it up.*

"I'll protect the kids," James told the security guard. "We'll be fine."

The guard frowned at James. "Would've been safer if you didn't bring them here in the first place. Not great judgment, kid."

James bristled at the word "kid". But before he could say anything –

"My cousin does his best," Alice said sweetly. "He's just not, well, he's not quite all there."

James ground his teeth to keep from blurting out the not-very-nice things he was thinking.

"*You* seem like a bright kid," the guard told Alice.

"Thank you," she said, modestly ducking her head.

"You make sure you *all* get back safely," the guard told her. "Go ahead. I'll stand right on the front steps, I'll watch to see you get safely past the –"

CRACK!

There was a crackle of lightning, and a blazing flash of light. The security guard crumpled to the ground.

James stepped toward the unconscious man, flinging out his arms to shield Alice and Aiden from whatever had hurt the guard.

There was a chuckling sound … a weird, gurgling laughter, as if someone not quite sane was laughing underwater.

Alice pointed with a trembling finger. "The statue," she said.

There was a horrible statue on the side of the tall fountain, a lunatic face with shaggy hair and horns. Water poured from its mouth. Alice had never been a big fan of that statue, but now it was a thousand times worse, because the face was *alive* somehow.

The eyes gleamed in the dim light, darting from Aiden to Alice to James and back again. The horrible mouth grinned. The awful, gurgling laughter was emanating from the statue's mouth.

With a terrible squelchy sound, like wet footsteps on stone, the face shifted and twisted. It pushed out from the side of the fountain, revealing a neck. The stone neck was attached to stone shoulders, to an entire stone figure that pushed itself out of the fountain's central column. The figure was draped in a toga.

Aiden and Alice and James took one giant step back.

The statue stretched, its stone toga rippling weirdly in the moonlight. It was, James hazarded, about fifteen feet tall. The creature shook its awful, shaggy, horned head. The face rippled again. With a dreadful slowness, like candle wax melting, the face transformed from a lunatic's face to Lou's face.

"That's better – an't it?" asked Lou. She grinned down at them. "'Allo, duckies. Pleasant night – what?"

James' arms remained flung wide, protecting Alice and Aiden. "Not exactly," said James. "What did you do to the security guard, Lou?"

The stone figure glanced disinterestedly at the unconscious guard. "Nothin' 'armful. Give 'im a little nap, is all."

"He's not dead?" asked Alice.

"Dead?" Lou's terrible stone face contorted as she laughed. "*Dead*? What does you thinks of me? Dead? I ask you!"

"So, he's *not* dead?" asked James, finding Lou's evasive remarks less than reassuring.

"Does I look like a doctor, lad? Shouldn't think he were dead. Only meant to give him a bit of a rest, like. Course, if his constitution an't strong enough – but, there, his 'ealth an't no concern of ours. We got bigger to fish to fry, don't we? We got important business what we got to conduct."

"What business would that be?" asked James.

"Why, the magick object, what you just found. I'm here to collects it, laddie."

Alice lifted a defiant chin. "We've already been through that," said Alice. "Remember the contract? 'We the undersigned do hereby agree to follow all rules of *L.A. Magickal History Hunt*, and relinquish all magickal objects obtained, *at the conclusion of the contest*.' And the contest hasn't concluded. We still have one more magic item to find."

The stone figure with Lou's face took one big step toward the children, its heavy feet sloshing through the basin of the fountain. With a dreadful grating of stone, it stepped up onto the stone ledge circling the fountain.

"Stay back!" James told the Lou. Lou in her regular form was disturbing enough. Lou inhabiting a fifteen-foot-tall statue was terrifying.

"Goodness me," said Lou. She looked about her, as if addressing an invisible audience. "The child thinks I mean to 'urt 'em. *Me!* Who loves children as much as if they were me very own." Lou's stone teeth gnashed, and her stone eyes rolled grotesquely in their stony sockets. "Does you know how *painful* it is to take on a form like this? Would I do this if you three little geese weren't dear to me as my own kin?"

The stone figure stepped down from the fountain's rim. It walked forward several paces, feet thudding on the dirt. It stepped over the crumpled security guard.

Lou gazed down at the children.

"Stay back!" James insisted.

"Or what?" asked Lou, with a nasty smile. "Don't appear to me you're in much of a position to negotiate – an't it? Now, my little geese, my little owls, my little ducklings, *where* is that key?"

With a screech of stone against stone, Lou's stone shoulders and torso bent forward, and her hideous face descended toward them.

The children each took a giant step back.

"I don't have the key," said Alice, heart pounding in her chest. "And if I did, I wouldn't give it to you. So there!" she added, mustering up more bravado than she felt.

"I don't have it either," said James. "It's safe with a friend. We have nothing to give you."

"Don't you, though, dearies?"

"No," James said firmly. "We don't."

"You'll just have to wait for the conclusion of the contest," said Alice.

"Will I, though, dearies?"

"Yes," said Alice. "You will."

"But I don't *care* to wait," said the horrid stone statue with Lou's face. "I'm terrible impatient that way. Real problem for me. Tragedy of my life. I gets impatient and rushes in and does unfortunate things what can't be put to rights. You know – 'all the king's 'orses, and all the king's men, can't never put it right again.'"

"Can't we *do* something?" Alice whispered to James.

He shook his head. "Not unless you suddenly have super-strength," he whispered. "Lou's created a kind of, like, avatar. The stone is from our world, so it's *real* stone – heavy, strong, unbreakable. Not much we can do against that."

Alice stamped the dirt in frustration.

"What are you talkin' about, duckies?" asked the statue. "What are you conferin' about, dears? Seein' sense, I hope. Tell your Auntie Lou where the key is, there's a good lad and lassie."

"We're discussing it," said Alice.

"Ah, there – *that's* sense, an' I'm sure. Takes your time, dears. Just make sure you make the right decision."

"Stone breaks," Alice mused, whispering to James.

"Sure," he said. "If we had Thor's hammer, and could lift it – no problem. We could smash the avatar into a million pieces. But we're not strong enough to break stone with our bare hands."

"It's too bad," Alice said thoughtfully, "the statue's so big. If it was, like, toy-sized, Aidie could break it."

"Aiden can break *anything*," James agreed, with an affectionate glance at his small brother.

Aidie nodded. "Aide break," he said.

"And 'ow is you doin', duckies?" called Lou. "Decided to tell me where to find the key, 'ave you?"

"Key!" shouted Aiden, rushing between James and Alice. "Aidie got key!"

Aiden leaped up onto one of the statue's massive feet and began hopping up and down. "Aidie got key! Aidie got key!" he chanted.

"Aiden!" James said sharply. "Get away from there!"

It was a terrify sight: Small, vulnerable Aiden, hopping up and down on that massive foot of stone …

"Aiden, get *back* here!" called Alice. She trembled. *What is Aiden doing? If anything happens to that little guy …*

"How, er, lovely," Lou said to Aiden, clearly torn between being annoyed at the child leaping up and down on her avatar's foot, and feeling ecstatic that someone was *finally* offering her the magic key. "Where is the key, Aiden, dearie? Give Auntie Lou the key, there's a sweet lad."

"No!" said Aiden. He threw back his curly head and laughed uproariously. "No! No! No!" he chanted.

"Aiden," called Alice, heart in her throat, "*please* don't upset nice Auntie Lou."

"Better listen to your cousin," Lou said, snarling down at the little boy.

"Auntie Lou *stupid*!" laughed Aiden. "Dumb-head Auntie Lou!"

"Well, well," said Lou. "An't he full of high spirits, like?"

"He doesn't mean it," Alice said desperately. "Don't hurt him, please."

"*Me*? 'urt a hair of this delightful little scamp's adorable head? Perish the thought. He can say what he likes – long as he gives me the key."

"Dumb-head, dumb-head!" sang Aiden.

He made a sudden, wild leap to the statue's other foot. "Dumb-head Auntie Lou!" he chanted.

"What is he *doing*?" Alice whispered to James.

"I don't know," James whispered helplessly. "Does he think he can break the statue by hopping up and down on it?"

"No key," sang Aiden. "No key, dumb-head Auntie Lou!"

Notwithstanding her many assertions of maternal affection, Lou's patience appeared to be wearing thin.

One of the great stone hands lifted, and swung down toward the little boy.

"Aiden!" yelled Alice. "Look out!"

James leaped toward his brother, to pull him out of harm's way.

But Aiden was already gone. With the agility of a monkey he somersaulted off of the stone foot and ran between the statue's feet.

James changed course at the last second, narrowly avoiding the great stone hand; it brushed his shoulder – *Ow!* – but didn't flatten him.

James crouched next to the statue's left foot. "Aiden," he called intently, "cut it out. Come here now."

Aiden shook his head, laughing. "Aidie break Auntie Lou!" said Aiden.

Somewhat awkwardly, Lou had turned the massive stone head so that she looked over her left shoulder, glaring down at the little boy, far below, who was dancing a victory jig.

"So, dearie – it's games you want, is it?" asked Lou. "Well, you shall have them. My, yes – you shall have them!"

Aiden stuck out his tongue, made a raspberry sound.

The statue turned, slowly – it took a certain amount of momentum and care for Lou to maneuver such a large object – and it lifted one giant foot, as if to squash the little boy.

"Aiden!" yelled James.

But Aiden needed no warning. He ran away from the statue, racing toward the east archway of the courtyard.

Lou's avatar gave chase.

The statue lumbered awkwardly, heavily. Each thud of its stone feet shook the ground. The little boy was much faster, much more agile ... but the statue covered ten paces with each single step.

"Aiden!" cried Alice. "Aiden – *no!*"

"Over here!" James called to the statue, trying to distract Lou. James waved his hands. "*I've* got the key, Lou! Come here! Leave my brother alone!"

Aiden darted suddenly into the long, arched colonnade along the east side of City Hall.

Lou's avatar followed the child, turning with a herky-jerky motion, almost over-balancing, but righting itself at the last instant.

Aiden wove back-and-forth among the columns, creating a zig-zagging, difficult-to-catch target.

He's so fast, marveled Alice.

James ran toward the statue, continuing to wave his arms wildly.

"Me!" yelled James. "Chase me, Lou! *I've* got the key."

But Lou would not be distracted.

Aiden disappeared from view when he dashed into the tower housing the southeast stairwell. The pounding of small shoes on marble steps could be heard.

"What's he *doing*?" wailed Alice.

"Taking the fight to the second floor," James said tersely. "Alice, can you channel some information? Is there *anything* about this place we can use to fight Lou?"

Alice closed her eyes. She frowned intently.

"Pasadena City Hall was completed in 1927. Based on the Italianate style of 1500's architect Andrea Palladio, this gracious, domed and arched building contains many symbolic features, including –"

"Fast forward," snapped James. "Something that can *help* us!"

"Including carvings of flowers, fruits, shells, flaming torches, lions, and artichokes."

Aiden appeared high above them, running fast as a bolt of lightning atop the wall of the second-floor walkway.

"Aiden!" yelled Alice. "Get *down* from there!"

Lou ran heavily along the east wall of the courtyard, glaring up at Aiden, trying to keep pace with him.

"Yes, Aiden," growled Lou. "Listen to your cousin. *Do* get down, there's a good fellow! I want to give you a hug."

With a horrible cracking sound, Lou tore an ornamental object from one of the railings. It appeared to be a lump of stone about the size of a human head.

"What is that?" asked James.

"Artichoke," Alice said dully. "Symbol of peace and hope."

Lou hurled the massive stone artichoke at Aiden as he raced past, high above.

"Aiden – *duck*!" shouted James.

Aiden laughed merrily. As if the child had eyes in the back of his head, he easily dodged the stone missile; it smashed to pieces in the corridor beyond him.

"*Get down here!*" shrieked Lou, losing all patience. She clenched her massive hands, with a horrible grinding sound.

Like a midget parkour expert, Aiden leaped from the bridge to the ledge of the northeast tower, gripping the edge of a medallion depicting a crown.

Aiden swung easily from the medallion to the statue of a flaming torch, turned a somersault in mid-air, and leaped through a narrow window into the darkness of the tower.

They heard his tiny footsteps pounding down the marble steps of the tower's spiral staircase. Aiden burst into view at the north end of the courtyard.

"*There* you are, duckie," growled Lou.

Aiden raced toward the west end of the plaza. He skidded to an abrupt halt at the north end of the colonnade. He turned on a dime, and raced back into the center of the courtyard.

Lou's statue grated to a sudden stop, almost overbalancing again, massive stone arms pinwheeling.

Fall! thought James. *Fall and break, you llwgyld witch!*

But Lou maintained the statue's balance. She righted it, turned, followed the child.

As Aiden raced past Alice, she tried to grab him, but he nimbly darted out of her reach.

"Aiden – *stop!*" Alice called.

Instead of stopping, Aiden ran clockwise around and around the central fountain, at astonishing speed. Around, around, around …

Lou's avatar gave chase.

The tight turns were difficult for the stone figure to execute; Lou's avatar began to list more and more to the right as it ran.

Aiden tightened the circles.

The stone figure stumbled, feet uncertain, its weight and the laws of physics pulling it precariously to the right, closer and closer to the ground. And then –

"Yay!" shouted Aiden, leaping onto the central spire of the fountain, clinging to it.

Lou toppled, made a final wild grab for the little boy. Aiden ducked easily under the clumsy stone hand.

"*No!*" cried Lou. The stone arms flailed. The stone legs took a couple of stumbling steps.

Down, down, down, the statue toppled, landing with a crash, half-sprawled across the fountain.

Its right leg shattered in two places.

Its right arm broke in half.

Its head cracked open … An enormous black-winged bird fluttered out of the crevice, and flew away, into the night sky …

"Yay!" Aiden cheered again.

He flung himself down from the fountain, raced around the broken statue, dancing a little victory dance.

"Aide break, Aidie break!" Aiden chanted triumphantly.

"You sure did," agreed Alice.

She and James examined the shattered stone figure. They nudged it gently.

"Is it … Is she …" Alice was uncertain how to phrase her question.

"I don't know," said James.

He walked cautiously to the statue's head. Lou's face was gone – it was the statue's normal stone face again, that lunatic face, with a mane of shaggy hair, and horns curling from the forehead.

"She's gone," said James. "That bird thing, I think … somehow that was her."

"She'll be back," said Alice.

"Yeah." James looked toward the dark night sky.

Aiden dashed to his brother and cousin, hugging first James and then Alice, and then throwing his arms around both of them.

"Aidie good?" Aiden asked hopefully. "Good Aidie?"

"Aidie is crazy," said Alice.

"You can say that again!" said James.

But they both knelt, and hugged the little boy with a ferocious, protective affection.

Chapter Seventeen – The Second Companion
June 25th– Pasadena

After ensuring that the security guard, though still unconscious, was otherwise unharmed, the children made a hasty retreat down Garfield and reached the Paseo without incident.

The Paseo was a pretty outdoor mall that had replaced a gloomy, fortress-like indoor mall. The children couldn't remember the old mall; it had been torn down before they were born. All they had ever known was the Paseo's lovely courtyards and shops.

They proceeded directly to the public rest rooms, where they changed into their regular outfits: jeans, t-shirts, hoodies and sneakers. They stowed their Victorian costumes in the rucksacks.

"We should keep the Victorian clothes," said James when they regrouped near the hot dog cart. "You never know when they could be useful. We might need to go back to the White City some time. On a mission. Or, you know, something."

"Right," Alice said skeptically. "On a mission. Not to find, gee, I don't know, a certain mysterious red-headed, blue-eyed girl, or anything."

James scowled at her.

They rested for a time in the Paseo's western courtyard. It was scattered with pretty little wrought iron chairs and tables. A fountain splashed. Tiny white lights strung around the elegant courtyard twinkled.

The stores surrounding the plaza were closed for the night, windows dark, faceless mannequins peering dimly through the glass, but the courtyard itself was still lively. A jazz band played Ellington tunes near the fountain, and a decent crowd, maybe thirty or forty people, sat near the stage, enjoying the music.

The hot dog cart, though it usually closed by nine p.m., had remained open to feed the concert crowd. James bought hot dogs for Alice, and Aiden, and himself, and they split a bottle of water.

"This quest is getting expensive," James complained. "*Five* dollars for a hot dog?"

"What a cheapskate," said Alice.

"*I'm* a cheapskate? What have *you* contributed?"

"How about that amazing lunch I got us today?"

"For free," James pointed out.

"Still – I arranged it."

"But it didn't last," said James. "Food from the past must be like Chinese food. An hour later, you're starving. It's like you never ate anything."

"Because the food was an illusion," Alice said. "Just like your red-headed girlfriend. But it was a great lunch while we ate it, and it was thanks to *me*."

"Aidie like cake," said Aiden, his mouth smeared with mustard. He took another big bite of the frankfurter. "More cake for Aidie," he suggested, mouth full.

"No more cake tonight," said James. He ruffled his little brother's hair. "You did a *great* job smashing that evil statue, Aidie."

"'Ka-pow'!" Aiden agreed.

Alice checked her cell phone. "*Still* no call from my mom," she said, sounding worried. "And *your* mom," she looked at James, "is going to kill all of us when we finally get in."

James shook his head. "No. I got through to my mother when you were changing."

"And?"

"And she and Aunt Peggy have to work night shifts. As in, all night."

"Since when?"

"Since tonight. So, you're staying at our house overnight, and I'm babysitting you."

"Huh."

"I know."

"You think ..."

"*Not* a coincidence," agreed James. "Someone, or something, arranged for our moms to work all night."

"That," said a deep voice, "would be me."

A tall, muscular figure in a black hoodie stepped from the shadows near the grand staircase – Fuego.

The strings of charming little lights over the courtyard made sizzling and popping sounds.

The well-dressed concert attendees sitting and standing in the plaza froze, like statues.

One woman had been talking to her companion; her mouth was frozen open mid-sentence. Whatever she'd been saying couldn't have been too interesting; her companion's expression was frozen mid-yawn.

Fuego sat down next to Aiden, who had slumped forward and fallen into a deep sleep with his head on the table.

"Nice of you to drop in," Alice said drily. "You know, since you're going to keep doing that, why don't you drop in when we *really* need you? Like a little while ago, when Lou almost massacred us?"

"You made quite a shambles of City Hall," said Fuego. "But you defeated that Ilwgyld harpy with great finesse. I remove the rubble, so your escapade will not appear in the local news. And you'll be pleased to know that I revived the security guard and erased his memory of the incident."

"But why didn't you *help* us?" Alice pressed. "When we were being attacked? You're a great warrior, right? Can't you do more than clean up the mess?"

"No, lass." Regretfully, Fuego shook his head. "Heroic quest – remember? The Chosen Ones *must* fight their own battles."

Fuego took the half-eaten frankfurter from Aiden. "Lovely lots of mustard," Fuego observed. He made short work of the frank.

"So – do you have an urgent message?" asked Alice. "Or are you just here to steal our food?"

Fuego threw back his head and laughed.

"You're really a dear," he told her fondly. "Though you can, at times, be quite trying."

"Hey!"

"I mean that in the kindest possible way," Fuego said.

"Well, that's not how it sounds!"

James had been studying the massive warrior during this exchange.

I just don't get it, thought James. Fuego was a chieftain, an accomplished fighter and leader of great importance; he radiated power and energy.

Yet, at every turn, he was personally involving himself in their quest, not able to assist them during battles or challenges, but giving them as much help as he was permitted to offer.

Why didn't Fuego delegate the babysitting to reliable lieutenants? After all, the chieftain had an entire elite faery guard at his disposal.

"Who are we to you?" James asked abruptly.

"The Chosen Ones," Fuego said.

"No. Who are we to you *personally*?" asked James.

"As Tanwen and I have both told you, we are relatives. We share bloodlines."

"But it's more than that," James said, eyes narrowing.

"Yes. And when the time is right, all shall be revealed, lad. Alas, the time is not at hand. You have much work yet to do this very night. That is why I arranged for your mothers to work the night shift."

Alice groaned. "I just want to go to sleep," she complained. "Can't we fight more bad guys tomorrow?"

"Would that it were so," Fuego said with uncharacteristic gentleness. "But you *must* obtain the final touchstone before dawn's first light. I believe," he extended one massive hand, "that you have something for me?"

James nodded. Wordlessly, he pulled the sky blue pouch from within Aiden's shirt, and removed the serpent key from it.

James handed the key to Fuego, who gave it a cursory glance and then whisked it into his hoodie pocket.

"We went to a lot of trouble to get that key," said Alice. "And to protect it. And you just stuff it in your pocket like it's a stupid candy bar or something!"

"Now that I have the Key of Wisdom," said Fuego, "I must return it immediately to Aelwyd for safekeeping."

"It's my key – isn't it?" asked Alice. "The amulet is James' and the key is mine."

"The Key of Wisdom belongs to the seer," said Fuego. "And you are the seer."

"What does it do?" Alice asked curiously.

"That is a conversation for another time."

"Oh, *everything* is a conversation for another time," complained Alice.

"The Chosen Ones must prepare for their final quest," Fuego said firmly. "Be ready to use the materials in your quest kits. At any rate, the powder and the potion. The rings, you are not sufficiently prepared to employ. Well, the girl is not."

"What does *that* mean?" Alice demanded, stung. "I can do anything the stupid boys can do."

"Calm yourself," said Fuego. "It is not because you are a girl, lass. It is because you have not mastered games the way James, and even Aiden, have mastered games. Proper control of the rings is akin to navigating one of the video games of this world. In your inexperience hands, Alice, your ring could prove extremely dangerous."

"Why do I have a *snake* ring, anyway?" asked Alice. She was feeling tired, and cranky, and she was annoyed at the way Fuego brushed off their questions. "Why a serpent ring, and a serpent key? Why not something beautiful? A swan, or a deer, or *anything* but a snake."

"In the Mayan culture, serpents are revered," explained Fuego, a shade of reproach in his voice. "Snakes are sacred and important creatures. They symbolize an ability to transform, and to travel in other realms. To communicate with the divine. You should be *honored* to be the bearer of that particular ring."

Makes sense, thought James. *Transformation, travel in other realms ... Alice is the one who can see the paths in and out of the faery world.*

"You should pay attention to the symbols you see around you," Fuego told Alice. "Serpents, or spirals, will have meaning for you. And once you are ready, your ring will be of *enormous* value to you. But for now – do not touch it."

"You're not the boss of me," said Alice. It sounded childish even to her own ears.

Fuego merely shrugged. He removed a small device from his hoodie pocket, began tapping at it.

"Are you – are you *texting*?" asked Alice.

Fuego grinned, continued tapping the tiny keys. "I only get reception in the mortal world," he said.

"So who are you texting?" asked James.

"Your friend Hisoka. I'm telling him to meet you here. For your next quest," Fuego hit the "Send" button, "you will need his assistance."

James lifted his hands. "Whoa. Hold up. If we have to finish the final quest tonight, then I guess we have to do it, but first we need a little rest. *Especially* Aiden. He just defeated Lou single-handed."

"Aiden *is* resting," said Fuego, nodding at the softly snoring little boy.

"He needs more than a few minutes' sleep," objected James.

Fuego smiled. "Your brother is far stronger, and more resilient, than you acknowledge."

"Aiden's still a little kid," said Alice. "None of us asked for this drama – especially Aiden. He should be at camp this summer, doing kid stuff. *I* should be at camp."

"Whine, whine, moan, moan," said Fuego, with a wave of one enormous hand. "You must release your self-pity, Alice. When *I* was a child *I* was learning how to hunt rath birds and fight Ilwgyld."

"But we're just kids," said Alice.

"No – you are *not*."

Fuego brought his palm down smartly on the table, with a terrible thud.

James and Alice glanced about, expecting that the loud noise would re-animate the frozen concert-goers, but they remained frozen like statues.

"You are the Chosen Ones," said Fuego. "*The* Chosen Ones. With all that you have seen, have experienced, have achieved in the last several days, one would *think* you would have begun to grasp your responsibilities."

"I don't *want* to be Chosen," said Alice.

"Immaterial!" said Fuego. "You are *not* the Volunteering Ones – you are the *Chosen* Ones. Forces far more powerful than any of us have selected you to save our worlds. Your petty wishes and complaints are of no concern to those forces. You must do what you must do."

"Or what?" Alice demanded. Fuego's mood swings never failed to annoy her. One moment he almost seemed like a cool guy, like a cool uncle, or something, but next thing you knew, he was yelling and being completely ungrateful for everything they were doing.

"What if we just say 'no'?" Alice continued, folding her arms. "What if we tell you and the Ilwgyld and your whole stupid world to take a hike?"

Fuego's nostrils flared, his face pale with anger. He spoke slowly, obviously controlling his temper. "If you do not retrieve the final touchstone, and deliver it to me, the Ilwgyld will launch a war upon my tribe. And if they win, they will gain control of the borderlands."

"Well what is that to us?" asked Alice. "What do we care about some stupid borderlands?"

"I think he means the valences," James said gravely.

"Precisely," said Fuego. "The Ilwgyld could come and go as they pleased in your mortal world."

"They seem to come and go as they please *now*!" said Alice. "We just want to be left alone!"

"If you hadn't donned the tattoos," said Fuego, keeping his temper, "the Ilwgyld couldn't track you so easily. But you did. So they can. What's done is done. They can find you and irritate you whenever they choose. It is not so easy for them to disturb *other* humans. And, presently, the Ilwgyld cannot remain long in this world, even when they inhabit shells, as Lou did this evening, when she inhabited that statue. The Ilwgyld are amphibious, so to speak, able to survive faery and mortal realms, but they can spend *very* little time here before they must return to their own world. Think of whales, or dolphins. They breathe air, but they must remain in the sea to survive. However, if the Ilwgyld obtain the touchstones, and take control of the borderlands ..."

"They'll be able to infiltrate our world," said James. "Whenever they like. And for however long. Got it." He shuddered at the thought.

"So, OK, that *is* a creepy thought," said Alice. "James and I will find the last touchstone. But we need to get Aiden out of this. We should hide him someplace. He could have been hurt tonight – he could have been *killed*, even." She turned to James. "Maybe that's how Hisoka could help. Could he watch Aiden? Or, could Tariq, maybe? Aidie really trusts Tariq."

"Aiden is crucial to your success," said Fuego.

"But – "

"*You cannot succeed without your cousin,*" roared Fuego. "*Each* of you plays your part, and *each* of you is vital to the success of your mission."

"Stop shouting at us!" yelled Alice.

"We'll do what we need to do," James said quietly.

"Whose side are *you* on?" Alice asked, turning to her older cousin.

"We don't have any choice," James told her. "You know we don't. It makes you mad. I know. It makes me mad too. But you know we have to do it."

Alice threw out her hands in complete exasperation.

"So tell us where to go," she told Fuego, "and what to do. Let's get it over with."

Fuego hesitated.

"So, you can't even tell us where to start?" Alice demanded. "You can't even give us *that*?"

He sighed. "I'll tell you, lass. But you must ... When I am short of temper, you must understand, I am angry at the situation, not you."

"Well, you could have fooled me!"

"I should try to remember," Fuego said, "what it's like to be thrown into the faery world. I was very young, you see, when it happened to me. It was such a long time ago when I first visited Aelwyd. I've almost forgotten what an adjustment it was. I didn't settle in Aelwyd by choice."

"What happened?" James asked curiously.

"My family lost me," Fuego said.

"How?" asked Alice.

"They just … lost me. They didn't intend it, but they became distracted and lost me in Aelwyd."

"There *are* a lot of distractions there," said Alice. "But you don't have to be so cranky with us just because you had a messed up childhood."

"I was terrifically homesick at first," Fuego mused, eyes far away. "What had begun as an adventure became tremendously sad. So be appreciative, lass, that when your quest concludes, you will spend some time again as normal children. Although …"

"Although what?" demanded Alice.

Fuego sighed again. "Never mind, lass." He glanced at the tower clock high above the courtyard. Although the people in the plaza had been frozen, the clock had continued to tick.

"Hisoka will arrive any moment, now," said the Aelwyd chieftain. His eyes had lost their far-away look and he was all business again. "Tell Hisoka to accompany you to the old terminal building on 4th and Hill. He's not to leave you alone for any reason. And you are all to go straight to the terminal building. You are not to permit *anything* to distract you."

"What's the old terminal building?" asked James.

"A gateway," said Fuego, standing up swiftly. "To the final battle ground of this quest."

"But – "

Without warning, before James could finish his question, Fuego leaped up onto the table.

"Hey!" cried Alice, startled.

Fuego leaped onto the nearby hot dog cart, where the server was frozen in the act of spooning chopped onions onto a frank, and then Fuego executed an amazing leap onto the grand staircase that swept up to the second level of the Paseo's west wing.

In a mere instant, Fuego melted into the shadows – and then he was gone.

There was a sudden murmur of conversation as the concert-goers were released from their frozen poses. The jazz band continued its tune as if it had never been interrupted.

"This is crazy," Alice said.

"Affirmative," agreed James.

Alice watched the people listening to the music in the courtyard, smiling, talking with each other, tapping their feet. "None of them have *any* idea they were frozen."

"Nope," agreed James. "I'm just glad this is almost over."

"Is it?" asked Alice. "What do you think the Ilwgyld are going to do after we give the last touchstone to Fuego? Do you think they're just going to laugh and say 'Oh, well, the kids gave the magic stuff we wanted to the good guys. How cute.'"

"Of course they'll be mad at us," said James, "but Fuego and his tribe will protect us. Fuego's warriors will have the touchstones – which must be massively powerful, or why is everyone going to all the trouble to try to get them? Fuego's army will have a showdown with the Ilwgyld. And the Ilwgyld *can't* win."

"So, I repeat," said Alice, "the Hungry Ones are going to be looking for our blood. *Especially* if they get their butts kicked by Fuego's tribe. Don't you think?"

"I guess." James rubbed his eyes with the heels of his hands. "I'm too tired to think that far ahead. Let's finish this quest, and then take it from there. Yeah?"

Alice made a noncommittal sound. "Do you know what's in the old terminal building?" she asked her cousin.

"No. Don't you? Didn't you write one of your ten million award-winning school reports on it?"

"Not that I remember. But – ow!" Alice pressed her hands to her head as a rush of information overtook her. "4th and Hill was a subway terminal building in downtown L.A. It was the hub of the original subway system – not the subways we have now. The terminal building opened in 1925, and closed in 1955 because by then everyone in L.A. had cars. There's an apartment building on the site now, but the subway tunnels are still there, underground, dark and abandoned."

"Super," said James. "Sounds like a really safe place to go at midnight."

"James, I can see, like, a picture of the tunnels in my head." She shuddered. "They're *really* creepy."

James shrugged. "As usual – these quests just gets better and better."

Aiden was waking up. He opened his eyes, blinked, stretched his small arms.

Aiden looked sleepily at the empty foil wrapper on the table in front of him. The foil had cradled half a mustard-smeared frankfurter when Aiden fell asleep.

The little boy scowled up at his brother. "James take Aidie's food!"

"It wasn't me," said James. "Fuego ate it."

"Oh." Aiden's scowl melted away; he actually smiled. "OK. Fuego good."

"Geez," said James. "You begrudge your own brother half a freakin' hot dog, that *I* bought, with my own money, but Fuego, who you never even met, can steal it, and that's OK."

Aiden nodded. "Fuego good."

"That's what you get," Alice told James, "for throwing Fuego under the bus. You're *such* a baby."

"He is a baby," agreed a quiet voice. "I'm glad I'm not the only one who's noticed it."

James and Alice jumped in their chairs, turning to face the newcomer who had somehow sat down at the table with them so quietly, so unobtrusively, that they didn't notice him until he spoke.

"Hisoka," said James, annoyed and relieved at the same time. "Some day you're gonna give me a heart attack."

Alice's eyes narrowed as she scrutinized her cousin's friend.

Hisoka didn't look anything like she'd expected. She'd figured he'd have spiky blue hair, like a character out of a Japanese comic book. That, she conceded mentally, would have been fashionable and cool. But she also expected him to be an annoying video-game geek, as dorkish as James, if not more so, wearing some T-shirt with a cartoon character on it, carrying a skateboard.

Instead, Hisoka had a neat crew-cut, and his face was set in a serious, calm expression. He looked like a young stock trader, in his dark suit and narrow dark tie and dark-framed Armani glasses.

"*You're* James' friend?" asked Alice.

Hisoka nodded.

"But you look *normal*," she said. "You even look cool."

Hisoka nodded again. "Video games are my hobby," he said , "but my main interest is international law."

"He starts USC in September," said James. "He graduated Blair early because he skipped a grade."

"Two grades," said Hisoka, not in a bragging tone, but the calm voice of someone setting the record straight. "Listen, why did you text me? I was right in the middle of a lecture on tariffs."

"Where?" asked James.

"Convention center," said Hisoka, tilting his head toward the south end of the plaza; the Pasadena Convention Center was directly across the street. "You're lucky I was in the neighborhood. So what do you want?"

"*I* didn't exactly text you," said James.

"Well who, exactly, did?"

"What did the text say?" asked James.

Hisoka lifted one eyebrow. "'Meet me hot dog cart Paseo. Urgent – James'. Not exactly a wealth of information."

"A friend of ours texted you," said James. "We're in this, well, we're kind of competing in, uh –"

How do I explain this to Hisoka? wondered James. *Tariq's always ready to believe anything. But Hisoka's a total skeptic. And we don't have time to tell him the whole story, let alone get him to believe it …*

Alice sensed a kindred, skeptical spirit in Hisoka.

All he needs right now, she thought, *are just the facts …*

"We're in a contest," Alice told Hisoka. "There's a big prize. It's like a scavenger hunt. We need your help."

"OK," said Hisoka. "But if I help you, I get a cut of the prize."

"Of course," said Alice. *The 'prize' will probably be being stalked by angry Ilwgyld*, she thought ruefully … *And Hisoka is definitely welcome to a cut of that!*

"I can't believe you're so cold," complained James. "We have to *bribe* you for your help?"

"If I have to miss the rest of the tariff lecture, yes, you have to bribe me," said Hisoka.

"Cold," said James.

Hisoka shrugged, a slight lift of his shoulders.

"Do we have a deal?" he asked.

"Whatever," James said grudgingly. "Tariq would just help to be a friend."

"Then I suggest you call Tariq, and I'll go back to the lecture."

"No – it's a deal," Alice said. *For whatever reason, Fuego wants us to have Hisoka on this mission – not Tariq.* "Whatever the prize is, we'll be sure you get a cut."

Hisoka peered over his dark-framed glasses at her, glanced at James. "She's authorized to make this deal?"

"Yeah, why not," said James. *It's all a bunch of boloney any way!*

"Where do we proceed?" asked Hisoka.

"4th and Hill," said Alice. "The old subway terminal."

"Fine. I suggest we take the Gold Line to Union Station, and then engage a taxi cab. Downtown L.A. is not a good place to roam after dark."

"Who's paying for the cab?" demanded James.

"Naturally, you," said Hisoka.

"We're splitting the prize, we're splitting the cab fare," said James.

Hisoka considered the logic. "Fair enough," he conceded.

Alice stood up, taking Aiden's hand.

"Let's catch the train at Del Mar," she said. "It's closer, and the Memorial Park station creeps me out."

"Sound plan," approved Hisoka. "Del Mar is better lit." He, too, stood up. "Just out of curiosity," he turned to James, "what does your mother think of this scavenger hunt? Does she approve?"

"What do you think?" scoffed James.

"I thought as much. I couldn't picture her allowing you to drag these children around downtown L.A. at night," Hisoka said.

"I'm not a child," complained Alice.

"Alice isn't a child," said James. "She's more like a cranky old lady."

Alice stuck out her tongue. "Says you," she said.

"Extremely mature," Hisoka said in his deadpan way.

As the children crossed the plaza, headed in the direction of the Del Mar Gold Line station, the jazz band segued from Duke Ellington to a song Alice recognized from her popular music class the previous year. It was an old song, from the 1940's – "Long Ago" – written by Jerome Kern and Ira Gershwin.

She would have bet twenty dollars that James had never heard it before – he only liked 80's music and skater bands, as far as she knew – but for some reason, the leisurely, haunting tune caught his attention.

James' footsteps slowed and he looked back over his shoulder toward the stage, the musicians, the concert-goers.

There was movement in the crowd – someone rising from their chair, heading toward the corridor of shops that ran west-to-east through the Paseo. A young woman, with a cap of bright red hair …

As if pulled by a magnet, James' path veered toward the young woman.

Alice groaned. Holding tightly to Aiden's hand, she hurried after James.

Hisoka, noticing no one was following him, turned and followed the other children.

"What gives?" he called to Alice.

"Long story," she said.

The shops along the two-block corridor were closed and dark. The expensively dressed and jeweled mannequins in the dim windows sent a shiver along Alice's spine. She hated mannequins, and in the dark, in this deserted part of the mall, they looked especially creepy.

"James," she called. "Forget it."

"But it's *her*," James said over his shoulder.

And it was her. Alice knew it as surely as James knew it. The red-haired young woman from the Echo Mountain House, now in jeans and a contemporary short hair cut rather than in a long white dress with a coil of red hair. Somehow, impossibly, she was the same young woman – although Alice was beginning to realize that, after all, very little was impossible.

Alice caught up to James, fell in step next to him.

Hisoka hung back, eyeing the mannequins in the window. Very few things unnerved Hisoka, but, like Alice, he was not a fan of mannequins.

"OK," Alice said quietly. "It's her, James. I agree. But this *isn't* the time to follow her."

"I have to talk to her," said her older cousin. "I don't know why, I just *have* to. Seeing her again means something. It's like a sign."

"It's not a sign," Alice disagreed carefully, not wanting to set off an argument. "It's a distraction. You remember what Fuego just said? We're supposed to go to the terminal building and complete our quest right away. No exceptions. Fuego was *really* clear about that."

From the courtyard at the other end of the plaza, lyrical strains of the song floated to them, muffled by the distance. *Long ago and far away, I dreamed a dream one day ...*

I wish this was all a dream, thought Alice.

James slowed, but didn't stop. The young red-head was about half a block ahead of them, strolling, seeming to be in no particular hurry, examining the shop windows as she passed.

"James you *know* I'm right," said Alice. "This is probably an Ilwgyld trick."

"But she led us, before," said James. "She led us to the room where we found the serpent key – what did Fuego call it? The Key of Wisdom. So she must be leading us *somewhere* now."

"She's leading us into the darkest, most deserted part of the Paseo, in the opposite direction of the train station. What part of that *doesn't* sound like a trap?"

Aiden slipped his hand from Alice's hand, grabbed his brother's wrist.

"Lady bad," Aiden said simply. He tugged the sleeve of James' hoodie, trying to draw him back toward the Paseo courtyard.

James faltered. He felt gravitationally, magnetically drawn to the red-haired young woman. But Alice was making logical sense. And Aiden's intuition about people was generally spot-on.

Alice saw the conflicting thoughts on her older cousin's face, pressed her advantage.

"Aiden's right," she said reasonably. "There's something bad about that girl. Come on, James. If you're meant to meet her, she'll pop up again some other time."

"Lady bad," Aiden repeated, nodding vehemently. He tugged harder at James' sleeve.

The red-head paused in front of Macy's expansive plate glass windows. It was difficult to tell from that distance, but she appeared to be watching their reflections in the glass.

James bit his lip. Part of him wanted to run to the girl. But in his gut, he knew he had to turn back ...

"OK, OK," he muttered irritably. "Let's get out of here. Come on. I don't know how long I can resist."

"It's awesome," said Alice, relieved, "when you listen to reason instead of being a complete idiot."

"Shut up," James grated.

Aiden pulled one of his sleeves and Alice pulled the other. He let them lead him, feeling like he was walking through quicksand as they drew him back toward the courtyard and the jazz band.

His feet felt heavy as lead. Lifting each foot, putting each one in front of the other; he felt like a sleepwalker trudging through a bog …

James could feel the red-head's eyes, watching him, boring into his back, just between the shoulder blades.

Come back … James … Come back …

Was he imaging it? It was a sweet voice, silvery. Was it all in his head?

"Why do you look kind of crazy?" Alice asked, glancing at her cousin. "I mean, more than usual."

"Shut up," he said. "Just keep pulling. Get me out of here."

"OK, since you're so *nice* about it," she said.

Hisoka, who had been bringing up the rear with his silent, graceful steps, took the lead now.

He gave James a quizzical look.

"So … How come I feel like you guys aren't telling me everything?"

"We'll explain it all later," James promised through gritted teeth.

"Are you on some sort of medication I should know about?" Hisoka asked.

"He's not," said Alice. "But he should be."

That's right, Alice, thought James. *Be mean*. Her comments were irritating him, distracting him from the feeling of those eyes boring into his back, that voice in his head.

James … Don't leave … said the voice …

Hisoka heard the noise first. He had ears like a wolf's. He heard a sort of subtle *sliding* noise. It was like the sound of a patio door being slid open quietly. *The way a burglar would open it*, he thought. *Stealthy*.

The sliding noise came from somewhere behind them, to the left. Then from behind them, to the right. Then from in front of them – both sides.

And then came the other noises; the faint rustling of clothing; the faint tapping of shoes on pavement …

Hisoka stopped cold in his tracks; Aiden and Alice actually walked into him.

"What – " Alice started to ask, but Hisoka held up one hand, and she fell silent.

In the shadowy corridor, a crowd was gathering in front of them. A crowd of figures creeping stealthily out of the stores. Figures in ravishingly expensive outfits. Figures without faces.

"I *hate* mannequins," whispered Hisoka.

"Get in line," whispered Alice.

The mannequins fanned out across the corridor, cutting off their return route to the jazz concert.

"Bad guys!" shouted Aiden, pointing.

James grabbed the back of Aiden's hood before Aiden could charge the mannequins and attack them like a one-boy army. James lifted Aiden into his arms.

"Aidie break bad guys!" said Aiden.

"Not this time," said James, holding his brother tightly.

Hisoka turned. As he had heard, as he had feared, mannequins had filed out of the shops behind them, too. These mannequins had formed several lines, like military troops, blocking any retreat.

Just beyond these mannequins, the red-head continued to stand in front of Macy's, staring into the plate glass windows. It was so dark, and she was so far away that it was difficult to tell, but Hisoka thought she was smiling.

Alice followed Hisoka's gaze.

No way forward, no way back, she thought. *Awesome*.

"If we don't survive this," Alice told James, "I just want you to know that I blame you completely for this."

"Duly noted," he said tightly.

"Uh, guys," said Hisoka, running a hand over his crew cut, "anything you want to share right now?"

"The scavenger hunt," said Alice, "is a *magic* scavenger hunt."

"I see." Hisoka absorbed that. "And, by any chance, are people trying to *kill* you to keep you from winning this scavenger hunt?"

"Seems like it," Alice agreed.

"That would have been a good thing to disclose before I said I'd help you."

"Live and learn," said Alice, shrugging.

"There better be a really, *really* big prize if we win," Hisoka said.

"Yeah. About that," said Alice.

"No prize?"

"No prize," agreed Alice. "Except our lives. Which *is* a really big prize, if you think about it. From a certain angle."

The mannequins, having blocked their paths, stood silently, gazing at the children with unnervingly blank faces, smooth as ostrich eggs.

"Aidie break," the little boy insisted, struggling to climb out of James' arms, but his older brother held him fast. James looked up and down the broad corridor, left and right, trying to discern any possible escape route. But they were penned into an area between the staircases and elevators, with no access to either.

"So ... What do we *do*?" Alice asked her cousin.

"Still thinking," he said.

"You're supposed to be a gaming genius. Pretend we're in a game – what do we do?"

"First, I tell you to shut up, so I can think."

Alice took a deep breath. Fighting with James wouldn't help, she realized.

"Did you guys slip me something?" Hisoka asked Alice. "Seriously. This can't be real."

"It's real. Deal with it," she said unsympathetically.

"But – "

"We're the Chosen Ones, it's this whole magical quest, and you're one of our Companions. Fuego got you into this, not us, so you can complain to him when you see him. If you see him."

"Alice," James said quietly, "is anything around here glowing? Do you see any doors out of here, you know, through a valence?"

Alice made a slow 360-degree turn, intently scanning their environment.

"Nothing," she said regretfully. "No magic exits."

James closed his eyes for a moment, slipping into that placid, Zen-like zone from which he played video games. When he opened his eyes, he examined the mannequins again, picturing them as hostile creatures in a game.

The mannequins stood in rows, not moving, blocking both sides of the corridor. Some of the mannequins were beige, some white, some a glossy aquamarine. They wore costly gowns, suits, and jewelry. Several of them wore fedoras on their egg-like heads.

They can't be very strong, individually, he thought. *Or there wouldn't have to be so many of them.*

It was like the early levels of a game, being attacked by a horde of the bosses' minions, each weak in their own right, their only advantage that there were so many of them.

Someone's playing puppeteer, he thought. *Lou … or Flo … one of the Ilwgyld … maybe the red-headed girl, even.*

If *one* individual was controlling the mannequins, they'd move like a pack, like a flock.

James pulled a couple of crumpled napkins from his hoodie pocket. He crushed them into one tight wad of paper.

He lifted the ball of paper over his head, waved it.

All of the mannequins turned their heads in unison, following the motion of his hand.

"Hey – don't get them upset," objected Alice.

James ignored her.

He pulled his arm back, pretended to throw the paper to his left.

All of the mannequins turned, stared at the spot where the ball should have landed.

James pulled his arm back again, pretended to toss the ball of paper to his right.

All of the mannequins swiveled, staring at the new place where the paper would have landed, had James actually thrown it.

"Flock mentality," Hisoka said.

"Yup," said James.

James handed Aiden to Alice. "Here. Don't let anything happen to him."

Aiden squirmed and tried to climb out of Alice's arms, but she held him securely.

"Aiden, be a good mouse," she coaxed. "You need to keep Allie safe."

"Aidie help Allie?" he asked.

"Yes."

"OK." Protecting his cousin was clearly more palatable to Aiden than being protected by her. Aiden clung to Alice, and glared at the mannequins in his line of sight.

"Hisoka," James called in a low voice, "you remember Level 9, Mortal Quest? When we double-timed the gargoyles?"

"Of course."

"That's how we're going to play this."

"OK. Which way do I break?"

"I go left, you go right, we plow through the other group of hostiles, then – "

"Then we bring it all together. Got it."

"What are you planning?" asked Alice. She hated feeling left out, and she didn't know what the boys were talking about. "What do you need me to do?"

"I just told you," said James. "You've got Aiden. And Aiden's got you. When it's time, you bring Aiden back to the concert and the crowd. The Ilwgyld won't do anything in front of a crowd. I don't think."

"And what are you guys doing?"

"We're going to take care of our new friends here," James said, with more bravado than he felt.

"How are you two going to handle hundreds of mannequins?" Alice asked skeptically.

"There aren't hundreds," James corrected her. "Fifty maybe. Maybe sixty."

"That's thirty apiece," said Alice. "How are you fighting *thirty* apiece?"

"This is a great pep talk," James said, "but we've got to get moving. On my signal, you just get Aiden back to the courtyard."

"But – "

"NOW!" shouted James.

He unceremoniously pushed Alice and Aiden into a narrow alcove in the wall. It was just a slight indentation in the concrete that had probably once housed a soft drink machine, but the alcove kept the younger children out of harm's way as James and Hisoka executed their plan.

James raced down the left side of the corridor, sneakers thudding on the concrete and tile.

Hisoka raced down the right side of the corridor, perfectly shined shoes as silent as if Hisoka were a ghost.

The mannequins blocking the route to the courtyard all lunged, in unison, like a flock of birds, and clattered after the young men.

The path to the concert was clear! Alice clutched Aiden tight, ran toward the twinkling lights and music of the jazz concert …

It's different, James thought, *fighting in the real world than it is fighting in a game.*

His lungs burned and his heart pounded as he ran.

Behind him, he heard mannequins rushing after him and Hisoka.

In front of him, the other group of mannequins stood their ground, blocking the entrance to Macy's, blocking the exit corridor to the street. The red-head was nowhere to be seen.

Just as well, thought James. *If she's gone she can't play any mind games, can't turn me against Hisoka or something …*

As James drew closer to the mannequins, he braced for impact.

Hope I'm right about this, he thought. *Five, four, three, two, one …*

SLAM!!

He plowed into the mannequins blocking the left side of the corridor.

Hisoka plowed into the mannequins on the right.

Ow! thought James. Some of the mannequins were light-weight – Styrofoam, maybe, he thought – and went flying as he barreled into them, but some were heavier, substantial, and although his impact pushed them aside, they bruised his shoulders, arms and ribs.

He glanced to his right; Hisoka had bowled over the mannequins on the other side of the corridor, scattering artificial arms and legs that detached when the mannequins hit the tiled floor.

James and Hisoka ran toward each other, meeting in the middle of the corridor, knocking over the few mannequins that were still standing.

The boys high-fived each other, then whirled to face the other group of mannequins which continued to rush toward them.

James and Hisoka each took up a fighting stance, fists clenched.

It had been easier barreling into the mannequins, James knew, than it would be when the mannequins slammed into *them*. This was *really* going to hurt.

James winced but stood his ground, fists raised. He braced for impact …

There was a sudden silence as the mannequins halted in their tracks.

The figures stood motionless, several rows deep, blocking the route to the courtyard.

Hisoka glanced at his friend.

"Their batteries run down?"

James shrugged.

Fuego said the Ilwgyld have limited powers in our world. Unless they get the touchstones ...

The mannequins' faces shimmered, shifted, seemed to melt, and then coalesced into the face of Lou. More than twenty Lou faces glared at the young men.

"'Allo, little gentlemen," sneered the mannequins. Lou's voice – in chorus.

Hisoka's eyebrows rose.

"She's one of the bad guys. Right?"

"Right," agreed James.

"Now, now, that an't any way to talk about Auntie Lou," said the mannequins. "*Bad* guy? I've got yer best interests in me 'eart, young gentlemen. I an't killed you yet – 'as I?"

"I'm guessing that's only a matter of time," said James.

"Not 'ardly," said the mannequins. "Now you listen, me lad, and you listen well – I'm one of your *only* advocates, where I hail from. D'you understand? It's down to me that you and your little friends are still breathin'."

"Sure," said James. "That's why you tried to kill my brother."

"Kill that little cherub? *Me*? Why, no such thing." Lou sounded offended. "I suppose you mean that wee unpleasantness at City Hall. Sure, I *might've* lost me temper a bit – but, you must admit, that little scamp could try the patience of a saint. And I an't no saint. Never said I were. All I'm tryin' ta do, in me way, is impress upon you the importance of bringing us those magickal whosawhatsises."

"We're trying to get the last one now," said James. "If you want the touchstones, you should let us go."

"Better to delay you, a mite, ducklings, than let you continue in your sorely misguided ways." The mannequins shook their heads in unison, made a "tisking" sound. "You're going to find the last touchstone tonight, dearie. And then you're going to give it to *us* – to me and Flo. And you're going to give us the other touchstones, too. You're going to take them from that, that, poxy, interfering *villain*, Fuego, and you're going to give them to me and Flo. Cause if you don't, piglets," there was a terrible plastic grinding sound as each mannequin clenched its hand, "we're going to take your mommies and daddies to a far-away place. Far, *far* away. And I *don't* mean never-never land, my chickens, my geese, my little rabbits."

James swallowed hard.

The thought of his mother, his father, being menaced by the Ilwgyld ...

"Ah! I sees that I'm gettin' through to you, at long last," chuckled the mannequins. Twenty horrid faced grinned at him.

I'm just glad Alice and Aiden aren't hearing this, thought James.

"So you goes on your merry way, like," said Lou. "You find that last magical thingamabob. And you bring it to Union Station with the amulet, and the key. D'you hear? Near the ticket windows, lad, right where we first made our acquaintance. Bring the touchstones – or you an't never, never, *never*, seein' your parents again."

The mannequins' mouths opened in the most malevolent of laughs.

And then their faces were wiped smooth, as if by invisible hands, and they were nothing more than mannequins again.

Hisoka removed his dark-framed glasses, cleaned them on his narrow tie.

"That really just happened. Right?"

James nodded absently.

Mom, he thought. *Dad ...*

He pictured Roz, so brisk, so business-like, but in no way ready for the nightmare creatures of the faery world.

He pictured Sam, so strong and capable, able to build anything, but not ready to grasp this magical reality.

With an angry shout, James charged the mannequins, punching one, whirling and kicking another.

The mannequins he struck toppled backward, thudded on the floor.

Their heads fell off and rolled along the tiles.

One of the heads rolled toward Hisoka. He stopped it with one perfectly polished black shoe.

"She's gone," Hisoka said reasonably. "You can't hurt her by doing that."

"So what?" snapped James. "It makes me feel better."

He kicked another mannequin. It swayed, but didn't fall over. He kicked it again. It fell; one of its arms shattered at the elbow.

"You're going to break your foot," observed Hisoka. "These are pretty substantial mannequins."

"I'm fine," lied James. His hand *did* ache, and his foot, too.

Hisoka bent over one of the fallen figures; it wore a black leather fedora.

Hisoka lifted the hat, placed it on his head, tilted it at a slightly rakish angle. He regarded his reflection in a dimly lit shop window.

"This one-hundred percent completes my outfit," Hisoka said approvingly.

"Great," said James. He kicked another mannequin. Now his foot *really* ached – it felt like he had bruised the instep. But it felt so satisfying when the mannequins toppled, when they hit the tile and shattered.

"You should know," Hisoka told his friend, "that since those dummies are no longer possessed, you are technically destroying property."

"Yeah? Well, you just looted that hat."

Hisoka shook his head. "I didn't loot. I did not enter any mercantile premises. I merely picked up an article of clothing that I found abandoned in a public space." He indicated the corridor between the shops.

James laughed. "You're really something, dude."

"I know."

"C'mon." James cradled his sore hand. He felt a little better after knocking over the mannequins, but his mother and father's faces still filled his inner vision. *How am I gonna protect them? How do I get the last touchstone to Fuego, without getting my parents hurt?*

And not just his parents, James realized as he and Hisoka walked toward the jazz concert. Alice's parents too. Uncle Roberto and Aunt Peggy …

James shook his head darkly. What could sweet, gentle Aunt Peggy do if she was confronted by the Ilwgyld? And even Uncle Roberto; he was a big, strong guy, but he had a kind soul. He was always so cheerful, seeing the best in everyone. *He'd probably try to make friends of the Ilwgyld!* James thought. *Uncle Roberto won't understand how evil the creatures are, until it's too late …*

Alice was sitting at a table, listening to the jazz music, and scribbling in a little sketch book. Aiden stood *on* the table, dancing to the music.

Concert-goers at other tables who had noticed Aiden's adorable, rather hilarious dance moves, were smiling at the little boy, and at Alice, whom they probably assumed, as most people did, was Aiden's sister.

James dropped into a chair next to Alice. Hisoka dropped into a chair across the table.

"So what happened?" Alice asked intently.

Up close, James could see that her smile, which she was wearing for the sake of the crowd around them, was totally phony. Alice's knuckles were white where she clutched her pencil and her sketch book.

"You're scared," said James.

"Duh," Alice said under her breath. "*Double*-duh. Of *course* I'm scared. What happened to the killer mannequins?"

"They weren't as tough as they looked," said Hisoka.

"I guess not, if you guys beat them," snarked Alice.

It was a mean thing to say, but, James realized, Alice was being mean as a way of releasing the terrible fear she'd been holding back. She was channeling her terror and frustration, as he had just done by knocking over the mannequins.

"It was Lou," James said. "She was playing puppeteer. As soon as she left, the mannequins just went back to being mannequins."

"What did Lou say?" asked Alice.

James shrugged. He tried to sound a lot more casual than he felt.

"Just, you know, dire warnings. We have to bring her the touchstones, or else."

"Or else what?" Alice demanded.

"Or else, they'll do horrible things to us," said James. "You know the drill."

Hisoka shot James a curious look.

James peered over Alice's shoulder, looked at her sketch book. She was drawing a map.

"What's that?" he asked, turning the subject.

Alice tapped the map with her pencil. "Trying to make a record of the valences, so we don't forget. Trying to make some kind of sense out of it. See, here –" she tapped a small oval, "this is the Sony Center. That's the valence that leads to Fuego's village Teulu. And this," she indicated a rectangle, "is L.A. City Hall, where the valence from Fuego's fortress leads."

James pointed to a triangular shape. "That's the Haunted Forest?"

"Right. The valence there leads to Fuego's winter quarters," which was designated by a tall set of parallel lines – the big tree, James realized – "and then there are those canopy cars into another valence, leading to the 1899 time loop, and then," she pointed to a hastily sketched dome, "there's Pasadena City Hall."

"What is a valence?" Hisoka asked James.

"We'll tell you later," said James, without looking up from the map. "We'll tell you the whole story on the train."

"I don't see any patterns," said Alice. "Yet. But at least we have a map of the valences we know about. And we can add the subway terminal building once we find out where that leads."

"I can hardly wait to find out," James said bitterly.

Alice glanced at her cousin.

Aiden, still dancing, seemed to hear something dark in his brother's voice. He flashed a big grin at his brother, gave him a quick hug.

"James dance," Aiden said encouragingly.

James shook his head. "Aidie dance," said James. "You can dance for all of us, little guy."

"OK." Aiden danced even more wildly, flailing his arms, making skipping motions with his feet.

An elderly gentleman at a nearby table leaned forward, addressing the older children.

"That's a very talented little fellow," the man said. "Absolutely adorable."

"Thanks," said James. "We hear that a lot."

"He must be a joy," said the man.

"He is," agreed James. *Except when he's drawing on the walls with crayons, or spilling stuff, or running around fighting giant stone statues that are trying to kill him ...*

"I run a talent agency in Culver City," the elderly man continued. "I very rarely do this, but I would like to give you my card."

"Sure," said James. *Why not? It wasn't any more surprising than anything else that had happened that week. Attacked by butterflies and birds and mannequins – and now Aiden was getting his big Hollywood break.*

The man pulled a business card out of his suit coat pocket. Alice took it and read it aloud.

"S. Kulkin, Talent Management" and a phone number in Culver City.

"What's your percentage?" asked Alice.

"Twelve," said Mr. Kulkin.

"Why not fifteen?" asked Hisoka, eyes narrowed.

"Incentive," explained Kulkin. "Only twelve percent, I'm motivated to get my clients bigger paydays. And I can steal talent from the vampires who take bigger cuts."

Alice and Hisoka nodded, satisfied with that response.

James grabbed the card from Alice, stuffed it in his hoodie pocket.

"Hey!" objected Alice.

"He's *my* brother," said James. "If anyone's signs him with a talent agency, it'll be me."

"And what's your name, son?" asked Kulkin.

"James."

"And your brother?"

"We call him Aidie."

"Aidie. Huhn. Kind of cute. We could work with that. He's five?"

"Four."

"Perfect, perfect. You keep that card. You show it to your parents and have them call me. That little kid has something. In fact," he swept all of them with a calculating glance, "you've *all* got something. You're a real beauty," he told Alice, "and you've got kind of a slacker teen vampire vibe," he told James, "and you've got that hipster chic," he told Hisoka. "Love the fedora."

"It's this new thing I'm trying," Hisoka said.

"Well, keep it."

The elderly woman at Kulkin's side tugged at his elbow.

"All right," said Kulkin. "My wife things I talk business too much. So, I'll let you kids enjoy the rest of the concert. But give my card to your parents. Make sure they call."

"Sure," said James.

"Great. Great." The elderly man turned to the stage.

"So," James said to Alice, "if you're done making Hollywood deals, we should *probably* head to the train station."

"Hey, *I* wanted to head to the train station, like, twenty minutes ago," she said indignantly. "If *you're* done following strange red-heads into traps, yeah, we should go."

James scowled.

"She has a point," Hisoka said quietly.

"No one asked you," said James.

"What if, if instead of fighting with each other, we catch a train?" Hisoka suggested. "And on the way, someone can explain to me all the strange things that are happening."

"Fine by me," said James. "Aiden – come here." He held out his arms. The little boy leaped into his brother's arms, still dancing.

"Aidie dance!" the little boy shouted happily.

"OK, but, Aidie needs to stop dancing now," said James, almost dropping the dancing child.

"Set him down," said Alice. "Let him dance while we walk. Why do you have to kill all the fun?"

"I can't kill *all* the fun," said James, setting Aiden down on the pavement. "There isn't any fun left after *you* kill it."

Hisoka shook his head.

"You told me you and your cousin don't get along," he said to James, "but I had *no* idea you both were so petty."

"Petty?" asked Alice.

"Petty?" asked James.

"Petty!" cried Aiden, dancing a jig. "Petty! Petty!" He didn't know what the word meant, but he liked to be included in whatever the older kids were discussing.

"Instead of sniping," said Hisoka, as they turned onto Green Street, "why don't you tell me what all this is about."

"It started a couple of days ago," said James.

"We met this weirdo on a train," said Alice. "But he turned out to be one of the good guys …"

Chapter Eighteen – Echoes
June 26th – Downtown Los Angeles

In the wee dark hours after midnight, a taxi cab pulled up in front of the elegant old building at 4th and Hill.

Four children emerged from the cab: two teens, a girl, and a small boy.

The young man in the natty dark suit and fedora begrudgingly gave the driver a ten-dollar bill.

"Since you're some sort of magical chosen one," Hisoka told James as they climbed the shallow steps to the building's front door, "why don't *you* conjure up some coin?"

"That's not how it works," said James. "We have magical ancestors and we can travel to these other realms, but it's not like *we're* magicians. We can't do magical stuff."

"Rotten deal," said Hisoka. "You're in deadly peril, and for what? You can't even conjure."

They stood in the ornate archway at the entrance to 417 South Hill. The former subway terminal building had been converted into luxury apartments. The heavy glass door was locked; a keypad discretely affixed near the door allowed residents to tap in a pass code to gain entry.

Through the door, the dimly lit lobby was an oasis of marble and brass, a glimpse of L.A.'s glamorous past restored.

"Fancy," Hisoka said approvingly, peering through the glass. "So, you can't conjure money – but how are you at breaking and entering?"

"We don't have to break in," Alice said confidently. She pressed a button marked "Doorman" on the keypad.

"Why would the doorman let us in?" asked James.

"Because Hisoka looks rich," said Alice. "And Aiden is adorable, and so am I. *You* should probably keep to the shadows."

A middle-aged man in a splendid uniform emerged from a door within the lobby. He strode purposefully to the entrance door, pressed an intercom button.

"Yes?" he asked, voice crackling through a hidden speaker. "How may I assist you?"

Alice tipped her head to one side, made her most appealing puppy dog face.

"We're sorry to bother you, sir, but we're looking for our parents."

"Are they residents here?" the doorman asked kindly.

"No, but they're at a party here. I can't remember the name of the people they're visiting. We have to find them, sir, because our nanny is sick. The ambulance came, and everything. Greta is in the hospital. We have to let our parents know."

Hisoka nudged James in the ribs. "She's pretty good," Hisoka whispered.

"She's OK," muttered James. "Don't give her a swelled head."

"We know this is an imposition – " Alice said apologetically.

"Not at all," said the doorman. He pressed a button; there was a buzzing noise, then a click, and the heavy glass door swung open.

Alice lifted Aiden into her arms, carried him into the beautiful lobby.

"Aiden," she whispered, "be very, very good. Don't be crazy. Be good, and I'll give you a candy bar later."

"No candy," whispered Aiden. "Read 'Good Little Mouse'."

"Sure," said Alice. "If you're good now, I'll read you the 'Good Little Mouse' later."

"OK." He laid his curly head against her shoulder. "Aidie good."

The four children milled about in the center of the lobby while the doorman went to a desk and consulted a large, leather-bound book.

"What are your parents' names?" he asked. "They'd have signed in. Should be easy to find out who they're visiting."

"Iztali," said Alice, at the same time James said "Jones."

The doorman looked questioningly at the children, eyebrows lifted.

What a bonehead! thought Alice. *James should know to let me do the talking!*

She smiled winningly at the doorman. "We're cousins," she said. Sometimes, she knew, the best line was the truth. "His mother is my aunt. I'm an Iztali, he's a Jones."

"So, your parents and your cousin's parents are visiting someone here?"

"Exactly. They might have signed in using Iztali, or Jones – or both."

"Got it." The doorman thumbed through the thick pages of the visitor book. "Hmm ... OK ... There's Izzard ... Imogen ... nope, no Iztali. Let's see if they used 'Jones'." He pored over the pages again.

James nudged Alice in the shoulder. She glanced at him.

Now what, genius? asked his expression.

Cool your jets, said hers.

"I'm sorry," the doorman said regretfully, "no one named Iztali or Jones has signed in this evening."

"But they must have," said Alice, sounding forlorn. "They said they were going to 417 South Hill. I'm *sure* they did."

"Don't worry," said the doorman, "we'll sort this out."

"Do you know who's hosting a party tonight?" Alice asked hopefully.

"No," said the doorman, "but residents don't always inform staff, unless it's gonna be a big party." He snapped his fingers. "You know what I can do?"

"What?" asked Alice.

"I can ask my staff to make a quick sweep of the building."

"That wouldn't be too much trouble?" asked Alice.

"Of course not." The doorman pulled a cell phone from his blazer pocket, pressed a button that put it in walkie-mode. "Ibo, Hector – come back," he said.

After a pause, there was a crackle of static.

"Ibo," said a deep voice.

"Hector," said another voice.

"Need you to sweep the building," said the doorman. "Ibo, you take the top half, Hector you take the bottom floors."

"What are looking for?" asked Ibo.

"Listen for a party," said the doorman. "Got some kids here in the lobby, their parents are at a party in the building. Name Iztali or Jones. Hear a party, knock on the door, find out if Iztali or Jones are there."

"OK. Got it," said Ibo.

"Got it," said Hector. "But what are we s'posed to do when we find 'em?"

"Tell them their nanny is ill. Tell them their kids are downstairs."

"Roger."

The doorman returned his cell phone to his pocket.

"There you go," said the doorman. "You kids take a seat, why don't you." He gestured to the comfortable-looking lobby chairs. "Ibo or Hector'll let us know if they find your folks."

"Thank you," Alice said sweetly. "I can't tell you how much we appreciate your help."

She sat on a chair, holding Aiden on her lap.

The little boy looked thoughtfully at the nicely upholstered furniture.

"Aidie jump?" Aiden asked his cousin hopefully.

"No," Alice said. "You can't jump on the furniture. You're being a good mouse – remember?"

Aiden sighed, but remained sitting in a civilized manner.

Hisoka sat on another chair. With his suit and fedora, with his poised manner, he looked perfectly at home in the elegant lobby.

James sat on the arm of one chair, fidgeting with the drawstring of his hoodie.

"So now what?" he asked Alice in a low voice. "It won't be long before they figure out you sent them on a wild goose chase."

"Patience, dork. Patience," said Alice.

Almost five minutes passed. Hisoka sat calmly, seemingly content with his own thoughts. Aiden closed his eyes, leaning sleepily against Alice. James continued to fidget with the drawstring of his hoodie. *When is Alice going to launch her plan? What's the hold up? Geez – is she falling asleep?*

Alice pretended to doze off, but she continued to watch the doorman from beneath lowered eyelids. *Too bad we have to trick him*, she thought. *He's a nice man.* The doorman was so kind and good-natured – he reminded her of her father. She wished, suddenly, that her father was there. She felt very small and young and alone. Even with her cousins there, she felt young and helpless. *None of this is fair …*

She pushed the helpless feeling away. *It is what it is*, she thought fatalistically. *And we're running out of time.* It was a large building, but it wouldn't be long before Ibo and Hector reported that they had been unable to find any visitors names Iztali or Jones.

Alice put a hand to her forehead, wincing in pain.

"Ow," she cried. "Oh, no. Not now."

The doorman was on his feet in an instant.

"What's the matter, kid?"

"It's … nothing …" she said with a martyred air, clutching her head with both hands.

Aiden stirred, frowned in concern, patted his cousin's hair. "Allie ouch?" he asked solicitously.

"Yes," she said feebly. "Allie ouch."

The doorman knelt next to her. "What's wrong?"

"Just … one of my migraines …" murmured Alice, head between her hands. "Don't mind me."

"You poor kid," said the doorman. "Tell me how I can help."

James rolled his eyes. *Oh, brother!* Alice *really* knew how to ham it up! But she was good. He had to admit it; she was good.

"Do you have any medicine?" asked the doorman.

"Yes … at home," Alice said ruefully. "It – *ow!*" She doubled over. "Goodness. This is … a bad one."

"My aunt gets migraines," said the doorman. "She always – "

"Lies down in a dark room," said Alice.

"Exactly," said the doorman. "I guess that's the common cure."

"It's … not a cure," Alice said. "But … it can … help."

"Here," said the man, offering Alice his arm, "let me show you kids to my office."

"Oh, I hate to be … any bother," said Alice, rubbing her head.

James managed not to laugh.

"That's OK," said the doorman. "I'll be sitting out here anyway. Won't be any bother at all. Come on …"

The doorman's office was a relatively small, stark room, with a desk, shelves and file cabinets. There was a swivel chair behind the desk and a swivel chair in front of it.

Alice sank into the chair in front of the desk.

"Here," said the man. He turned on a small goose-neck lamp on top of the shelves, turned off the overhead light. An amber dimness enveloped the chamber. "How's that, kid? Dark enough?"

"Much better," Alice said. "I think this will help."

Hisoka sat in the chair behind the desk. James sat on the edge of the desk, holding Aiden.

"You kids'll be all right in here – right?" asked the doorman. "You won't mess around with any of the files, or anything?"

Hisoka raised one eyebrow. "I can assure you," he said, "that we won't disturb any of your records."

"Of course. Sorry. I just have to say, you know – "

"Please don't … apologize," said Alice. She managed a brave smile, then laid her head down on the desk. "We're very grateful, sir. We appreciate your … hospitality and we … promise … not to touch anything."

"If you kids need anything, I'll be in the lobby," said the doorman. "I'll let you know as soon as the guys find your parents."

"Thank you," murmured Alice. She shaded her eyes with one small hand …

"OK, Meryl Streep – he's gone," said James.

Alice sat bolt upright.

"Let's go," she said.

"Go *where*?" asked James. "You've got us in a back room, without windows, and only – "

"I saw the door to the subway tunnels," said Alice.

"When?"

"We passed it on the way here. I figured the entrance would be somewhere out of the public eye. And, of course, I was right."

"She always this modest?" Hisoka asked James.

"Yeah."

Aiden tentatively touched his cousin's forehead. "Allie OK?"

"Allie is fine," Alice assured the little boy. "We're going to find some tunnels, Aiden."

"Tunnels!" Aiden said happily.

"Which door was it?" asked James.

"The third or fourth one we passed," Alice said. "It was somewhere between Forest and Hunter."

James looked confused.

"*Green*," Alice explained, as if he were hopeless. "It's a dark green door."

"Then just say so, why don't you?"

"I did. I can't help it if you don't know your basic colors."

"Was the door locked?"

"I don't know."

"You didn't see a padlock?"

She shook her head. "But even if it's locked, I can get us through it," she said confidently. "The door was *glowing*. It leads to a valence."

James extracted a pencil flashlight from his rucksack. "OK. Let's go."

"We should leave a note," said Hisoka. He pulled a silver pen from his inside blazer pocket.

"For who?" asked James.

"Whom," corrected Alice.

"Like grammar matters right now," scoffed James.

"For the doorman," said Hisoka. He tore a single sheet of paper off of a notepad on the desk. He wrote a couple of sentences in a neat, fluid hand. "There." He dropped the note on the desk, returned the pen to his pocket.

"What did you write?" Alice asked curiously.

"'Thank you for your hospitality,'" Hisoka quoted. "'Our parents called us. They went on to a party at the Biltmore.'"

"Nice," Alice said approvingly. "He won't raise any alarms."

"And he won't worry," said Hisoka. "Guy was nice to us. No need to freak him out."

"What's going to freak him out," James said tensely, "is if he sees us teleporting through a door. Let's go, already."

"What a crab," Alice said.

"Come on!"

"James is crab-head," laughed Aiden, furrowing his brow in a pretty good imitation of James' annoyed face …

The dark green door was heavy, but not locked.

"Is it really glowing?" asked James.

"Yeah," said Alice. And it was. It glowed with the intensity of a searchlight. "We're definitely supposed to go down there …"

Alice insisted on taking the lead, as only she would be able to see any glowing objects.

James followed her, Aiden riding piggy-back, ready to defend his brother or cousin as required.

Hisoka served as rear-guard, as he did whenever he, James and Tariq played Mortal Quest. Hisoka moved with silent stealth.

They followed a series of narrow, dank stairwells, feebly lit by caged light bulbs spaced far apart on the high ceilings.

The crumbling concrete and tiles, the puddles of water, the peeling strips of paint, all reminded James of the ghost hunting programs he watched.

"Place looks totally haunted," observed Hisoka, as if reading James' mind.

"Probably is," James agreed.

"Shut up," whispered Alice.

The stairs fed them into a vast underground chamber, even more ghostly than the staircases had been.

Legions of concrete pillars and arches marched off in different directions, into a distant darkness that was absolutely impenetrable. The air smelled musty and damp. Water trickled down columns, pooled in the parallel ruts that marked, here and there, places where train rails had been embedded.

Paint was peeling here, too, in long, wraith-like strips, and gritty bits of broken tile and concrete littered the floor.

But what was really eerie, Alice realized, wasn't that the subway terminal was falling apart – actually, for having closed in 1955, it didn't look half bad.

The spooky things were the items that looked fresh, that looked like the place had just closed yesterday – a sign with an arrow, "All Trains This Way"; brass letters on an office door, reading "Yard Foreman", the door's little window somehow still intact.

It's crazy, thought Alice. *But I can almost see them. I can almost hear them.* All those people, in the nineteen twenties, the thirties, the forties, crowding down here, like everyone crowds through Union Station. Everyone rushing to buy their ticket, to catch their train …

Motes of dust swirled, glowing with a silvery light. They spun and coalesced into ghostly forms – the shapes of men in boxy suits, the shapes of women in high-waisted dresses, the way they wore them in the 1920's, and in broad-shouldered blazers, like they wore in the 1940's …

The figures weren't distinct. They were silhouettes made up of hundreds of little pin-pricks of light.

They bustled past the children, up the staircases, down the abandoned corridors, even raced toward the tracks as if trying to catch trains that, in reality, had stopped running more than sixty years ago …

"Huhn," said James, brushing at his arm. "Felt a breeze."

"The air's dead calm," Hisoka said quietly.

"Guys – we're not alone," said Alice.

"Ilwgyld?" asked James, clenching his fists and scanning the massive space.

"I guess … ghosts," Alice said. "Not, like, I don't think they'll attack us or anything. Just … energy that keeps looping."

"I don't see anything," said James. "Where are they?"

"Everywhere."

Alice watched one particular blur of lights rush along the central platform. The shape was that of a woman in a 1940's blazer and skirt, with a 1940's pompadour.

The woman's figure bent down, and opened her arms, and a small shape ran into it – a little boy. A little boy in cap and short pants; the woman was welcoming him home from a journey …

Alice shivered.

"What's the matter?" asked James.

"Nothing." *I just wish*, she thought, *I didn't always see the things I can see now …*

Who had the woman been? Or the boy? Why was this particular action preserved here, imprinted like an eternal visual echo?

Emotions, thought Alice. *Strong emotions leave their mark on a place; but most people can't see them. Just lucky me. My abilities seem to be getting stronger …*

"I don't see anything," Hisoka said thoughtfully, "but I feel something. It's as if there are dozens of other people in here with us."

"Hundreds," corrected Alice.

"Are they a threat?" James asked, focusing on tactical concerns.

"No," said Alice. "They're just memories."

"Like the temporal loop at the Echo Mountain House," said James.

"No. That was stronger," said Alice. "That was so vivid we could walk around inside it, and interact with people, and even have the illusion of eating lunch. This is much simpler."

"Like a crowd of people coming and going," said Hisoka. "Some are happy, some are sad, some are worried. Their emotions are strong, but fleeting."

"No one ever stayed here long," said Alice. "It was just a gateway."

"Well, it's supposed to be our gateway, right now," said James. "Not to be a jerk, but I don't see anyone, or hear anyone, or feel anyone, and all I care about right now is *us*. Where do we go from here, Alice? Do you see a trail?"

"No. I feel like we're supposed to wait a while."

Hisoka nodded. "Places like this were designed for waiting."

James shook his head impatiently.

We've got to get that final touchstone. Got to figure out how to get it to Fuego, without putting Mom and Dad and Uncle Roberto and Aunt Peggy in danger ... If that's even possible ...

"Where did the trains take you?" Hisoka asked curiously.

Alice closed her eyes. She was getting used to information flooding into her mind on cue.

"L.A.'s Subway Terminal served lines for Glendale, Hollywood, and the San Fernando Valley," she recited.

"That's not so far," mused Hisoka. "But it was busy. You can *feel* it was busy."

"Downtown L.A. was crazy-busy, back then," said Alice. "There were movie theaters, department stores, drug stores, libraries, office buildings, lots of churches – "

"When does the history lesson end?" groaned James.

"My poor cousin," Alice said sarcastically. "We're making him feel like he's in school."

"Actually, you are," said James. "All we need to know is, which way do we go? Which tunnel do we follow?"

"James, don't you realize there's a reason we keep getting sent to these locations? I think we're supposed to be learning something."

James groaned again.

"I know," said Alice. "The word 'learning' gives you a rash."

"We keep getting sent to these places because the valences are thin there," said James. "That's all. It's not the places themselves. It's just, that's where the border between worlds is thin enough that stuff can slip through. Like ghosts, and faeries, and time loops."

"And us," said Alice.

"Yeah. And us."

"I think you're both correct," Hisoka said thoughtfully. "You're being sent to places where the border is porous ... but there's a *reason* the border is so fluid at those locations."

"I'll buy that," said Alice, nodding.

"I don't know what you just said," James told Hisoka, "and I don't really care. If a train doesn't pull up in the next ten seconds, I'm going to *really* start to lose it."

"The boundaries between worlds seem more fragile at places where lots of people gather," Alice told Hisoka, completely ignoring her cousin. "City halls. Train stations. And so on. Fuego's fortress connects to L.A. City Hall."

"That makes total sense," said Hisoka.

James kicked a chunk of concrete. He sent it flying a good ten feet, but hurt his foot, which still ached from kicking the mannequins.

"Ow!" he said.

Aiden patted his brother's shoulder.

"For crying out loud, watch out," said Alice. "Don't hurt Aidie."

"How is my kicking a rock going to hurt Aidie?" James demanded.

"Knowing you, it'll bounce back and hit Aiden. Or you'll drop him or something."

James kicked another chunk of concrete. It hurt his foot again, but the debris sailed a good twenty feet toward the center of the underground terminal.

"How did you wind up being friends with my dorky cousin?" Alice asked Hisoka.

Hisoka shrugged. "He's the finest gamer I've ever encountered. He immerses himself completely in the game environment. Even now, when he's behaving like a child, his senses are on full alert. James … buddy?"

"What?" snapped James.

"How many pillars are within the immediate area?"

"Eighteen," James said absently. He kicked another stone.

"How many staircases in the immediate area?"

"Three."

"Nope – only two," Alice said a little smugly.

"The one we walked down," said James, "the main one that's walled off, and that," he pointed over one shoulder.

Alice and Hisoka looked in the direction he'd pointed.

James was right; in addition to the two obvious staircases, there was a set of precariously leaning steps that led up to a manager's office.

"See what I mean?" Hisoka asked the little girl.

"Big deal," said Alice. "So he's aware of the environment. That's not as important as knowing things about it."

"I know things," said James, sounding a little stung.

"Like what?" his cousin asked skeptically.

"Like, I know there was supposed to be this tribe of lizard people living under Los Angeles," said James. "There were hundreds of tunnels underground between L.A. and Pasadena. The lizard people supposedly built them."

Alice lifted one eloquently scornful eyebrow. "*Lizard* people? What comic book did you get *that* out of?"

"It was on the news," said James. "They did an ultrasound on the downtown area, and found all these tunnels. It's a part of old L.A. folk lore."

"Huhn. Well," Alice looked around the dank, deserted terminal, "maybe a lizard person will be driving our train," she said drily.

"You think you're so smart," James said, kicking another stone. "It's not enough to *know* things. You can know ten million things, but so what? You have to be able to *do* something with what you know."

Like, they'll hurt our parents, James thought. *The Ilwgyld will hurt our parents if we don't turn over the touchstones. I know that ... But what can I do about it? Have to think of something fast ...*

"In a perfect world," Hisoka said reasonably, "people who *know* things work with people who *do* things. If you two would stop being brats, you could work very well together."

"We do work well together," admitted Alice. "We just hate it."

"Exactly," said James.

"Aidie want rock," Aiden told his brother, extending a small hand. "Aidie kick rock."

"Sorry," said James. "I'm not giving you a rock, Aidie."

Aiden scowled.

"See what a bad example you are?" Alice asked James.

James ignored her. He kicked yet another chunk of concrete; it shattered one of the few remaining panes of glass in the manager's office with a resounding crash.

Aiden clapped. "Aidie, too," Aiden insisted. "Aidie kick too."

"No kicking rocks," said Alice. "*Nobody*'s kicking any more rocks."

"I can kick rocks if I want," muttered James.

"How about something more useful," said Alice. "Since we don't know how long we're going to have to wait for a train. Why not try the rings?"

"The rings?"

"In our quest kits. Fuego said you're supposed to be good at using your ring because you're a gamer – whatever that means. Why don't you see if your geekiness is actually useful?"

"Huhn."

James pulled his questing bag from within his hoodie.

He reached inside and extracted the ring, which was plastic in the human world, and heavy silver in the faery lands.

He held the ring up to the feeble lights. The ring flashed faintly – metal. It didn't feel as heavy, or appear as richly jeweled, as it had in Aelwyd. But it was more substantial than the plastic ring it appeared to be in the purely mortal world.

"It changed," Alice noted simply.

James nodded.

"What *is* that?" Hisoka asked, staring at the ring and its unusual design. "Is that a cat?"

"Panther," Alice corrected. "We each have a ring."

"And what do they do?"

"We don't know yet."

James slipped the ring on the index finger of his right hand. It fit perfectly.

"Do you *feel* any different?" Alice asked.

James shook his head.

"Make it do something," she said impatiently. "If it has to do with games, is there, like, a little controller in it or something? Maybe the panther eyes are buttons?"

"Nah." The gems that formed the panther's eyes were much too small, James decided, to be control buttons.

"So how does it work?" asked Alice, frustrated. "Fuego said you were supposed to be amazing with the ring. Ha! Shows how much he knows about you!"

"Stop insulting James," advised Hisoka. "Let him focus. When James is in the zone, nothing can stop him."

"So I've heard," Alice said skeptically.

"He saved us from the mannequins," Hisoka said.

"What *did* happen with the mannequins?" asked Alice.

Hisoka shook his head. "Creepy. Plain creepy."

"Well, they couldn't have been *that* bad if you two escaped from them."

"A simple 'thanks' would be acceptable," said Hisoka.

Alice's insults seemed muffled and distant to James. He was, indeed, slipping into the zone. He gazed intently at the panther ring.

Don't overanalyze it, he thought. *Got to follow my instinct. A ring. You wear a ring. It becomes part of you. No. It's, like, an extension of you ...*

"Here – take Aiden," said James, handing his brother to Alice. "And stand back."

"Why should we – "

"Just do it," snapped James. He held his right hand out at arm's length, concentrating.

Alice stepped back, Aiden cradled in her arms.

"What's going to happen?" asked Alice.

"I don't know," said James. "Just, like, be quiet for now."

He continued to concentrate on the ring. The panther's jeweled eyes glinted in the muted light.

Alice gasped.

"What?" asked Hisoka, looking swiftly around the abandoned terminal, hands curling into fists.

"The, the energies," said Alice. "They're leaving."

"What do you mean, they're leaving?"

"I mean they're leaving."

Alice watched, unnerved, as the tiny motes of light, which had formed ghostly human figures, spun, scattered, flew away into the darkness that edged the vast terminal.

"Look at the ring," James told her. He was concentrating so hard, beads of sweat were forming on his forehead. "What do you see?"

"Nothing," said Alice. "The ring looks like a ring. *You* look like you're going to break your brain."

"I ... might ..." James said through gritted teeth.

His hand suddenly felt warm. It was like someone was holding a flame underneath his hand, beside it, above it. The ring itself began to burn.

"Wait," said Alice. "I see ... something. There's a light coming off the ring. Maroonish. It's, OK, now it's floating all around your hand."

"What else do you see?"

"Just the light."

James concentrated harder. He closed his eyes.

Maybe it's like a Wii ... The ring will transmit my motions somewhere, remotely ... and that will make something happen ...

James waved his hand to the left.

Alice gasped again. A pulse of deep maroon light – almost like blood, she thought – flowed from the ring to a point about ten feet in front of James' hand.

"What's happening?" he asked.

"The light's in front of you, now. To the left. Where you pointed."

"OK. Keep watching."

James waved his hand to the right.

Alice saw the stream of light ripple and leap to a point about ten feet to the right of James.

"Did the light move?" he asked.

"Yes," she confirmed.

James turned abruptly, moving his hand in an arc.

"The light followed," Alice said. "Wherever you point, that's where the light goes."

"I wish I could see it," said Hisoka.

"You're not missing much," said Alice. Now that her initial astonishment had passed, her analytical mind was kicking into full gear. "I mean – it's a murky red light. It's not like it's *doing* anything."

"Give me ... a sec," James said. He spun suddenly, waving his arm in a circle.

"Light's still following your hand," said Alice. "Wherever you gesture, that's where the light goes."

"Is it getting brighter?" he asked.

"No. But it's getting ... hm. Move it again."

James flung his arm toward the left.

Alice leaped back, Aiden held tightly in her arms.

"Watch it!" she said. "The light's expanding. At first it was a little ways from you, but when you make a stronger motion, the light gets further from you."

"But it's not any brighter?"

"No."

"So, if I'm getting this," said Hisoka, "James' ring creates a phantom light, and he can control where it goes by moving his hand."

Alice nodded.

"So ... Is it a laser?" wondered Hisoka. "What happens to something that gets caught in it?"

"You can count me out of testing!" said Alice. "You can count Aiden out, too."

"C'mon, Alice," said James, "step into the light. Let's see what happens."

"You'd better be kidding," she said. "That's so mean!"

"Well, *I'm* not testing it," said Hisoka. "*I* have an amazing, successful life ahead of me."

"If only there was an animal around," said James. He mopped at his forehead, but kept his focus on the ring. "If there was a rat or a cat or something we could test the light on it."

"Some poor, defenseless cat?" demanded Alice.

"Better to test it on a cat that on you or Aiden. Or, on Aiden, anyway."

"You think you're so –" Alice paused, mid-insult. "James?"

"Yeah?"

"The light is changing shape."

"It's getting bigger?"

"Yes. No. It's ... It's starting to look like something."

"Like what?"

Alice squinted. The murky red light was shifting, bunching up in shapes that looked like a head, shoulders, a long spine, limbs. The head was larger than a human head. The ears appeared to be pointed. The face appeared to have a muzzle ...

"James ... Stop whatever you're doing."

"Why?"

"Because I think this thing might be a demon."

James scoffed.

"I mean it," Alice insisted. She took several steps backward, toward the exit, pulling Aiden closer.

"What do you mean, a demon?" asked James. "We wouldn't have rings that can conjure anything evil."

"Why not? The Ilwgyld gave us the quest packs. They could've messed with the rings."

"No. Tanwen checked them out. She said the rings were OK."

"So, Tanwen can't make a mistake?"

"I don't know. She seems like someone who doesn't make mistakes –not many, anyway."

"Well, this could be one of them." Alice stared at the horrid dark shadow with the pointed ears, that only she could see. It was still shifting. It was crouching down on four limbs … It twitched a long, dangerous-looking tail …

Mrawr!!!

A shrieking roar, a roaring shriek – it split the air.

Hisoka jumped.

"What the freakin' freak?" he asked.

"You heard that?" Alice asked him.

"We all heard it," said James. "Alice – what is it?"

"I think it's a panther," she said, mouth dry. "A big panther. A *really* big panther."

The shadow of the great cat darkened, from deep red to an inky black. It became less shadow, more solid.

Hisoka stepped in front of Alice and Aiden.

"You see it now?" asked Alice.

Hisoka nodded.

The enormous cat glanced at Hisoka and the younger children behind him, but turned its full attention on James.

It's a beautiful panther, thought James. And it was. Glossy ink black fur. Regal bearing. Gleaming green eyes that seemed to look right through James' soul. *It's a beautiful panther – even though it looks like it's going to rip my throat out …*

James stood very still. He and the panther regarded each other silently.

The panther yawned.

Alice was the first to regain her composure.

"James – move your hand. Just a little bit," she added hastily.

Of course, thought James. *This is my panther. I control it.*

He moved his hand, ever so slightly, to the right, away from the other children.

The panther leaped gracefully several feet to the right.

OK. So far, so good.

James moved his hand gently to the left.

The panther stepped to the left.

It yawned, revealing great white fangs.

"Make it do something," said Alice.

"I need to ease into this," said James.

She rolled her eyes. "*These* are the amazing gamer skills I keep hearing about?"

"Any gamer worth his salt eases into a new character," Hisoka told her. "That's a *panther*. It's not a toy."

"It's not a toy, but it's, like, a weapon," she said. "James is in control of it."

"For now."

James lifted his hand and waved it to the right.

The panther sprang into the air with astonishing agility, landing twenty feet away.

"Good boy," said James. "Nicely done."

"I don't think you have to compliment it," called Alice. "It's just a stupid –"

The panther turned toward her voice, growled low in its throat.

Alice shrank back further, peeking around Hisoka's shoulder.

"Don't upset the panther," said James.

"But he's just ... Isn't he just a projection or something?" asked Alice.

"I don't know. Seems like he has a mind of his own. And he doesn't look too fond of you."

"That's *your* fault," accused Alice. "He can tell you hate me. He's picking up on all the mean things you think about me."

The panther growled again. Its brilliant green eyes glared at her.

"I don't *hate* you," said James. "I just want to send you far, far away. I think the panther feels like, it's kind of a loyalty thing," said James. "He won't like *anyone* who tries to hurt me. Which definitely includes you."

"Yeah? Well, I have a ring too, you know. Wait until I use my serpent ring. My snake is gonna bite your stupid panther."

The panther bared its teeth. *Mrawr!!* it shrieked again.

"Yes," Hisoka said drily, "this is extremely constructive. I'm so pleased we aren't wasting time with a lot of immature garbage."

James flicked his hand toward a distant line of pillars.

The panther sailed through the air in the blink of an eye, landed gracefully thirty yards away.

James drummed his fingers slowly, in the air.

The panther padded toward him, head lowered, moving with feline elegance.

"You're catching on fast," Hisoka said admiringly.

"Just like using a Wii," James said. "Well ... sort of like using a Wii. Same basic idea."

He turned his hand over, palm upwards.

The panther rolled onto its back, wriggled like a puppy. It even made a cheerful little mewling sound.

"If that thing doesn't chomp your head off, it's going to be an awesome pet," Hisoka predicted.

"Yeah. It feels like ..." James trailed off. He couldn't explain it. Alice and Aiden were going to understand once they used their rings. James felt a bond with the animal. It wasn't just a weapon, a tool against the bad guys. It was a guardian. It was maybe even a friend.

"Can you make it attack things?" asked Alice, peeking out from behind Hisoka. "And, before you try to be hilarious, no, I'm *not* volunteering. I'm being serious, James. Can you get it to attack the Ilwgyld?"

At the word "Ilwgyld" the great cat snarled and lifted a paw. The paw was as big as Alice's face. Razor-sharp claws sprang forth, and the panther made a slashing motion in the air.

"He seems to be on board with slicing and dicing the bad guys," observed Hisoka.

"Yeah," said James. He felt absurdly proud of the panther. It needed a name.

A word pushed itself into James' mind. The letters were deep red, edged in black. *Seebak*.

"His name is Seebak," said James.

"What kind of name is that?" asked Alice.

"I don't know," said James. "Google it. I just know it's his name."

"Seebak good cat," Aiden said approvingly. He seemed absolutely unafraid of the beast.

"Hi, Seebak," Hisoka said calmly. "Please don't devour us."

"He won't," said James. "He wants those Ilwgyld. Don't you, boy?"

Seebak snarled. Images danced in James' mind – sharp-featured, hungry-eyed Ilwgyld. They were fragments of Seebak's thoughts, James realized.

James gestured very carefully toward himself.

Seebak padded toward him, with the rolling, regal gait that only a great cat can achieve.

Seebak stopped in front of James.

"That is one tall cat," Hisoka said. Seebak's head was taller than James'. Even Seebak's shoulders were taller than James'.

Seebak inclined his great head to James as if acknowledging royalty.

Tentatively James stretched out a hand. Slowly he patted the glossy black head. It was solid. James could feel the heavy solidity of the skull under the panther's warm coat.

Seebak made that curiously gentle mewling.

"Don't domesticate it," warned Alice. "We need it to fight."

Seebak swung his dark head around, glaring at the girl.

"Ferocity doesn't appear to be a problem," Hisoka said. "So, you," he glanced back at Alice, "have a serpent ring?"

"Yeah."

"What about the little guy?"

"Monkey," said Alice.

Hisoka laughed. "Great. Just what we need – this little guy controlling a monkey!"

"Aidie use ring?" Aiden asked Alice hopefully.

She shook her head. "Not now, Aiden. Soon." *Like, maybe in ten years*, she thought. Hisoka was right; little Aiden trying to control a monkey would be complete chaos!

Seebak began to flicker, like a faulty holograph.

James' hand passed through Seebak's head as if it were water.

"He's fading," said James.

There was a flicker of murky light, and suddenly the ring on James' hand burned again. He muttered an indelicate phrase, shaking his hand, which hurt as if someone had pressed a burning torch against it.

"That," said Hisoka, "is probably the coolest thing I've ever seen. Seebak, I mean. When he was here. Not when he vanished."

"Maybe it's like the Ilwgyld," Alice said thoughtfully. "We can call up the animals with our rings, but they can only stay a little while. Longer in faery lands. This place," she gestured, "isn't totally mortal *or* totally faery land. I think your ring is only on partial power here."

James looked at his ring, which was not plastic, but was not the beautiful ring he had seen in Aelwyd. This was a betwixt-and-between ring.

Half power ... Imagine Seebak's power in Aelwyd! thought James. *Maybe with Seebak's help, maybe there's a way to make sure Fuego gets the touchstones, but still protect our parents ...*

James is hiding something, thought Alice. *He's worried. What happened with the mannequins?*

It was right on the tip of her tongue to ask, straight out, but she was distracted by a piercing whistle. If she hadn't been holding Aiden, Alice would have pressed her hands to her ears.

"Train whistle," said Hisoka. "Do you see the train?" he asked Alice.

She nodded. A flurry of lights at the far end of the massive room. There, where a tunnel had long been filled in, the blizzard of lights resolved themselves into the shape of a massive wooden train car. The lights concentrated in a great blinding head lamp.

James and Hisoka winced. Hisoka threw a hand in front of his eyes.

"OK. I see it now, too," James said.

The train car rolled up to them with a thunderous rumble that shook the concrete floor under their feet.

"How do these things seem so *real*?" asked Hisoka.

"Because they are," said Alice. "They are and they aren't."

Hisoka lifted an eyebrow.

"What's real in one realm is real in that realm – but not in another realm. *Except* where the worlds are close to each other."

"Bleed through."

"Yeah."

"OK." Hisoka nodded, satisfied. "I can work with that."

The train car rolled to a stop in front of them.

"Pacific Electric" was blazoned across the rail car. From its roof lifted a metal rod that connected to … nothing. There were no electric cables in the abandoned tunnel. But the tip of the metal rod sparked and crackled, powered by some mysterious, magical energy source.

"Santa Monica Pier" read the destination placard.

"That doesn't make sense," said Alice. "The subway trains *never* went to Santa Monica."

"Dorothy, we are *twelve million miles* west of Kansas, right now," Hisoka said. "Wherever the original subway went – "

"It wasn't far," said Alice. "The subway tracks connected with regular train lines out to Glendale, and Beverly Hills – never Santa Monica. I don't think. Maybe there was a bus that connected – "

"Alice, we can complain about the lack of historical accuracy *after* we get the final touchstone," said James.

"But this could be a trap," she said. "Fuego and Tanwen seem like they know history. This could be an Ilwgyld trap."

She peered into the front windows of the rail car, expecting to see the sharp, hungry face of the Ilwgyld man who drove the strange little bus to the top of Lake Avenue.

That was just yesterday, she thought. *Seems like a million years ago.*

No one drove the train car, Ilwgyld or otherwise. Just as the blazing blue energy powering the vehicle was a mystery with no obvious source, the vehicle seemed to be piloting itself.

"Fuego told us to come here," said James. "And this looks like our ride. Maybe it's a trap – but we've just got to chance it."

"Why chance things," asked Alice, "when we – some of us – have these things called 'brains' to think things through?"

James sighed.

"What is your brain telling you, Alice?"

"That it doesn't make sense, leaving for Santa Monica from here."

"We already know the maps don't match," said James. "Los Angeles and Rath Angeles aren't completely, completely …" he fumbled for the word.

"Congruent," said Alice. "I know. But still …"

"My gut is telling me this is our ride," said James. "And I don't see any other option." He swept his arm around the terminal. "It's not like I don't trust your brain. We'll keep our eyes open in case it's a trap. And now we've got Seebak to help."

Alice frowned. What her cousin was saying was fair – not that she felt any particular need to acknowledge that.

"I guess," she said sulkily. "But when we're being attacked by rath birds, don't say I didn't tell you so."

"Oh, I won't," said James. "I won't have to. The last words I'll probably hear are you telling me 'I told you so'."

"Probably," Alice agreed.

Hisoka leaped onto the running board of the old rail car. He doffed his fedora, bowing to the children.

"All aboard," he called. "Next stop, magical mayhem and destruction."

"Next stop, doom," Alice said darkly.

"Next stop, everyone be quiet so I can think," muttered James.

Chapter Nineteen – End of the Line
June 26th – Santa Monica

Alice would never forget the underground rail journey from the 4th street terminal to the Santa Monica Pier.

James sat quietly, holding Aiden, gazing thoughtfully at the panther ring on his finger, and obviously mulling over whatever it was he was keeping from Alice.

Hisoka had pulled an iPod and headphones from his blazer, and was listening quietly to music.

As they rolled through the dark, Alice gazed from time to time through the front windows, where the magic rail car's blazing headlight illuminated the rough-hewn stone tunnels through which they rolled. They were tunnels that mortal hand had never carved, she knew, based on the way they glowed and pulsed with vibrant faery lights.

Mainly, Alice's gaze was drawn upward.

Because somehow, thanks to the talent for perception that she had never asked for and did not particularly want, she was able to see up, through the roof of the rail car, through hundreds of feet of dirt and stone, to view many of the structures under which they passed.

Alice saw L.A.'s Central Library when they traveled underneath it. She saw it all, as if seeing blueprints picked out in little lights, the many, many levels of the library, its massive stacks of books, its pyramid roof and its Egyptian symbols.

The valence was *very* thin at the library, she realized. The valence was almost non-existent there. The symbols of the library – the sunbursts, the torches – crowded into her mind unbidden.

There was something magical there, Alice realized – and something very dark …

As they rolled under Figueroa Street, she looked up and saw, outlined in minute points of faery lights, *not* the massive skyscrapers – the banks and insurance companies – that now dominated Figueroa, but instead the Victorian mansions that had lined the sleepy street in the 1800's.

Again, there was something bright and inviting about the vision, yet a disturbing darkness, too.

Why does this matter? Alice wondered. *Why do I need to see these places?*

Briefly, as they travelled deep below the stadium where the *Sircus of Impossible Magicks* was performing, Alice got a heady sense of vertigo.

She saw and sensed *them*, high above her, limned in brilliant, purple-green light – the Ilwgyld who continued to carry on the old traditions of performance and evil magicks. And she could tell some of them sensed her, and James and Aiden, as they passed below.

Alice seemed to hear Lou's voice in her head. *Be seein' you soon, duckie. Almost time to pay the piper ...*

It was even worse as they glided under Wilshire Boulevard. Wilshire was, she knew from one of her history projects, the original grand concourse of Los Angeles. It had begun as rural fields, and ended as one of L.A.'s most glamorous, notorious and traffic-choked boulevards.

Alice's gaze was pulled upward; through the stone and dirt she saw lights outlining Wilshire's grand old buildings, many long razed or abandoned. The original Bullocks store was the most upsetting. So pretty ... but she could sense something so very, very evil crouching within it ...

I'm the seer, she thought. *I'm being given a map. James is the protector, so he gets a pet panther. I get a creepy mystical map. How fair is that?*

And why, she wondered, was she being shown these places *now*. If they were headed for the final part of their quest. All they had to do, in theory, was obtain the final touchstone and get it to Fuego. He and his faery soldiers would use the power of the three touchstones to push back the Ilwgyld. End of story – ideally.

So why show me all these creepy images? she demanded of the universe. *I'm finding the last touchstone and I'm done. Do you hear me? I'm done. We were chosen to find the touchstones. We're doing that. We're meeting our end of the bargain.*

Only, it wasn't a bargain, was it? A bargain was something two parties negotiated. This was a chore, a task that had been thrust upon them. Fuego had all but told them they would *never* lead normal lives again. *I don't accept that*, thought Alice. *Fuego isn't the boss of me ...*

The train car finally rolled to a halt inside a massive stone cave. It was a hollow within a hill, and no visible exit.

James leaped off the train first, ready to call Seebak from the ring at the first sign of attack.

Alice, holding Aiden, stepped out next, and then Hisoka, with his stealthy steps, brought up the rear.

"Don't see anyone," James said quietly. He looked at his cousin. "Where's the exit?"

"Dead ahead," Alice said, nudging her chin toward the rock wall, upon which she could see glowing, white-blue semi-circle.

"Do you think we're already at the pier?" James asked Hisoka. "Did we travel far enough?"

"We're here," Alice answered.

James looked at her curiously.

"How do you know?"

"I can *see* that we're here," she said. "My ability seems to be growing. I can see the pier through the door."

"It's glowing?"

"It's lit up like Christmas," Alice said, with a little shudder.

Aiden patted her shoulder. "No scared, Allie," he said kindly.

"Allie's not scared," she lied lightly. "We're going to the fun park, Aiden. What do you think of that? It's going to be lots of fun!"

"Don't tell him that," James said sharply. "Don't patronize him."

"James – he's four years old."

"Aidie four!" Aiden cried happily. "Aidie four!" He waved his arms.

"We don't know what we're walking into but it's probably not going to be fun," James said tensely. "Just don't tell him it's going to be *fun*."

"You get upset about the dumbest things," said Alice.

The boys followed her through the passage through the rock wall of the cave. It was cold and dark as they walked through solid rock.

Hisoka shuddered.

"This is so … weird," he said quietly.

"I forgot you're claustrophobic," James said sympathetically.

"Didn't the faeries ever think of drilling *actual* tunnels?" Hisoka wondered.

"Probably too much work," said James. "Why bother when they can just, you know, set up places to melt through stone."

"The faeries didn't make this passage," Alice said over her shoulder. "It was already here. The faeries just found it."

"Is this a valence?" asked James, looking around at the dense rock. He could understand why Hisoka was so uneasy. "Where's the fog, and all that stuff?"

"The valence is very thin here," said Alice. "Almost worn through. The real world and the faery world are super intertwined here."

"Define 'super intertwined'," said James.

"It's our world, *and* it's their world. So, the Ilwgyld can probably spend as long as they want here. And their power will probably be greater."

"But on the plus side," mused James, "we'll be able to use *our* powers more, too."

"Sure," said Alice. "Our brand new powers, that we don't even really understand and have barely had time to practice."

"I think I got a good handle on Seebak," said James. "And you seem to be getting really good with the seeing. I'll bet you spot the touchstone right away. And, you know, as soon as you see it, you have to tell me where it is. OK?"

"Of course. What did you think the plan was?"

Only question now, thought James, *is what do I do with the touchstone once I get it? Do I throw it to the Ilwgyld, and save our parents? Do I take a chance and keep it for Fuego? The faeries can use the touchstones to kick the Ilwgylds' butts. But Mom and Dad could be dead by then. Uncle Roberto and Aunt Peggy too ...*

They emerged from the cave just below the bridge that led to the Santa Monica Pier.

Hisoka sucked in a big lungful of sea air. He rubbed his eyes.

"I have never been so happy," he said, "to see the ocean before. Or the sky." He looked up at the dark night sky, brilliant with stars.

They had all been to the pier many times, with their parents and on school trips. They located the stairs up to the bridge with ease.

James gazed down the length of the pier. To him it looked dark and foreboding. The restaurants, the little shops, the 1920's carousel, the roller coaster and Ferris wheel and midway – everything was dark and padlocked in these wee early hours of the morning.

"So – see anything?" he asked her.

Alice shook her head. "We have to walk the pier," she said. "We have to – "

She was interrupted by a deafening "BOOM!" – like a transformer blowing.

Lights blazed on up and down the pier.

In the shops. In the restaurants. On the rides.

The Ferris wheel began turning.

The roller coaster car began racing along the sinuous steel track.

The old carousel began turning inside the carousel house; calliope music wafted to the children on the sea breeze.

James groaned. *Yes – this will make it easy for Alice to find the touchstone. With every single light in the place burning. And the music going. And the rides going …*

"Well, *this* is distracting," said Alice.

"Must be," said Hisoka.

"I think I should summon Seebak," said James. "If some big trap goes down, I don't want to be trying to summon him then."

"Plus," said Hisoka, "it's just crazy-cool to have a six-foot tall panther on an invisible leash."

James held his right hand out in front of him, stared at the panther ring, concentrating.

It happened much, *much* faster than the first time James had called Seebak from the ring.

Alice saw a surge of deep red light pulse from James' hand, and then Seebak appeared, standing a few feet in front of James.

"Hi, boy. We need your help."

Seebak graciously inclined his head.

James motioned forward, and Seebak began walking at a stately pace along the pier, toward the fun park.

James was not so much piloting the panther, Alice realized, as guiding the panther.

And, as she grudgingly admitted to herself, James was doing an excellent job. If a pack of blood-thirsty Ilwgyld leaped out of the shadows, Seebak would be on them before they could say one threatening word.

Alice shifted her attention from the beast, focusing her attention completely on the pier. Their shoes and sneakers thudded on the weathered boards. She could barely hear their footsteps above the carnival calliope music, the whirring of the rides … It was impossible, she knew, but she thought she smelled hot-buttered popcorn, and hot dogs, and hot fudge – all those summer scents that permeated the pier in the daytime.

Does everything we do leave a print? she wondered. *Like a tattoo. And in places where magic lives, we can sense those echoes. Sight, sound, taste, smell –*

They passed eateries and arcades and little shops. Everything was moving and alight, but there were no people anywhere.

"Anything, Alice?" asked James.

She shook her head. "Too bright, too loud," she said. "I can't see the trees for the forest."

"Where would it be hidden?" wondered James.

"Not on the Ferris wheel," said Hisoka. "You said they hid these touchstones a long time ago, right? Well, there was a Ferris wheel here forever, but then they replaced it. This one's pretty new."

"So, what's something here that's old – *really* old?" James wondered.

"Carousel," said Hisoka. "Oldest thing still out here, probably."

James looked over his shoulder. They'd already passed the famous carousel, which had been in numerous movies and television shows. It was housed in an old-fashioned wooden building.

Alice touched her forehead as the information flooded in, unbidden. "It's a 1922 carousel – a national landmark. Probably most famous for being in the movie 'The Sting' – whatever that is. But, guys, wouldn't that be a little obvious?" objected Alice. "Hide the touchstone in the *most* famous building on the pier? Right near the entrance?"

"Why not?" asked James.

"Because whoever hid the touchstones made it a *challenge*," said Alice. "I had to risk my life getting that stupid amulet off that stupid bell." Her palms broke out in a cold sweat at the mere recollection of Tariq holding her up over that railing, twenty-seven stories above L.A. "And we had to look all over Echo Mountain House to find the key. That was *really* hidden."

"According to that logic," Hisoka mused, "this magic object thing would be somewhere obscure. We should search all the little snack stands. And the game booths."

"Or the Ferris wheel," said Alice. "Since it's new, we wouldn't think to look there. But whoever hid the touchstones can move through space *and* time. Why couldn't the touchstone be hidden on something new?"

James groaned softly.

"James OK?" Aiden asked solicitously.

"We're hurting your brother's tiny brain with all this complicated talk," said Alice, smoothing Aiden's dark curls.

"I just want to find the touchstone," said James. "I just want to end this."

I'll give the touchstone to the Ilwgyld, he thought. *That could work. I give them the touchstone, but once I know our parents are OK, I sick Seebak on those witches. Lou and Flo won't know what hit them! And then I give the touchstone to Fuego ...*

"Look, Alice," said James, "your perception seems to be getting really sharp. Can't you just, like, clear your mind and reach out?"

Alice opened her mouth to make a sarcastic remark, but she took a deep breath instead.

This is no time to fight, she thought. As much as being mean to her cousin helped her to settle her nerves, the stakes were too high now.

Alice took a deep breath, held it, released it, took another deep breath.

She scanned the bright, loud, chaotic pier that surrounded them.

If I were a touchstone, where would I be hidden?

It would have helped, she thought, if Fuego had told them exactly what they were looking for.

She opened her senses; the lights, the din, the scents were almost overpowering. Everything flowed together. Nothing stood out.

We found the amulet, she thought. *The protector's amulet. And then the key. The seer's key. So the next item will be for Aiden, the trickster ...*

Alice raised her eyebrows.

"Got it," she said. "Maybe."

"What?" asked James.

"The next touchstone is something for Aiden."

James considered that. "OK. Makes sense. But *where* is it?"

An idea was circling at the edge of Alice's thoughts.

The bell at City Hall – a bell of friendship – that was *so* goody-goody James!

And the automaton, dispensing knowledge – that was *so* her.

Alice looked up and down the pier.

"What here makes you think of *Aiden*?" she asked James.

He looked up and down the pier, the food stands, the games, the rides. "All of it."

"But, specifically. He's your brother. What's his favorite thing here?"

"The arcade, maybe?"

"The arcade is *you*, James. What's something Aidie likes?"

James shrugged. "I mean, he likes all the rides, all the ones he's big enough to ride, and of course he wants to ride the crazy ones he's too little for, too."

"Aidie like traps!" Aiden said excitedly. He waved his tiny hands in an agitated manner. "Traps, traps – Aidie fly!"

"What does he mean?" Alice asked James.

James snapped his fingers. "Oh, yeah. The trapeze!"

"There's a trapeze? Since when is there a trapeze at the pier?"

"They give trapeze lessons near the fun park," explained James. "But Aiden's *way* too little. My mother and dad wouldn't let him try it the last time we were here, and he had a massive melt down."

"Aidie fly on traps!" bellowed Aiden.

"Kind of like that," said James.

Alice hugged Aiden. "Shh. Aidie, it's OK. We're bringing you to the trapeze."

"Hey," said James, "he really *is* way too small for the trapeze."

"*Aidie fly!*" bellowed his little brother.

Alice shot James a look. "If Aidie wants to go to the trapeze, we're bringing him to the trapeze."

"But it's too –"

"No one's gonna let anything happen to Aiden. There's a net, right? If they're giving trapeze lessons, there must be a net?"

"Yeah – I think so. But – "

"Aiden's been swinging around like a nut *without* a net all day. So he'll be fine."

James opened his mouth to object again, but Hisoka subtly shook his head.

"Let it go," Hisoka advised quietly. "We'll all make sure the kid's OK."

They found the trapeze school near the fun park.

"Huhn," said James.

"Huhn what?" asked Alice. "What's wrong?"

"This is – it's different. A lot taller. And no net," he said grimly.

As he recalled, the trapeze wasn't *too* far off the ground, and there was a net in case someone fell.

This was a whole different set up – because everything, he realized, was different when it crossed over into the faery realm.

Posts draped with rope ladders stretched up, up, up toward the night sky – at least eighty feet up. Rigging for trapezes stretched between the tall posts.

Below them, the ground – no net, no padding.

"Traps!" Aiden crowed happily. "Aidie fly!"

Seebak growled low in his throat, and padded toward the gate, effectively blocking it.

"James, will you move your dumb cat?" complained Alice. "You're totally over-reacting."

"I didn't move Seebak in front of the gate," said James.

"Excuse me?"

"I said I didn't move him."

"Seebak appears to be protecting Aiden of his own initiative," said Hisoka.

"So, this giant deadly panther is doing its own thing?" Alice asked James. "Way to control your animal totem!"

Seebak's massive head swung silently, as if on oiled hinges, toward Alice; its green eyes narrowed.

Alice's mouth went dry.

"Uh, we're sure this panther thing is one of the good guys – right?"

"Pretty sure," said James. "He doesn't seem to like you too much. That makes me think he's OK."

"Seriously," said Alice, "how can it be doing things on its own?"

"I think Seebak can key into my feelings," said James. "It *really* scares me, thinking of Aiden swinging around up there." James nodded trapeze rigging high above.

"Well, tell it to move," said Alice. "We have to get in there and find the touchstone."

Seebak growled at her again.

"And tell it I'm your cousin," said Alice. "Tell it not to bite my head off."

"Seebak," James said, "we need to get in there, boy."

Seebak lifted his magnificent head. He did not budge.

"We *have* to, Seebak," James insisted. "We won't let anything happen to Aiden."

Seebak made a skeptical snorting sound … But he reluctantly padded away from the gate.

"How about the part where you tell him not to bite me?" asked Alice.

James shrugged. "I don't want to be hasty. Let's see how this plays out."

Alice felt like throwing something at her cousin; but realizing that would probably bring Seebak leaping and snarling at her, she just made a face.

"Alice, do you see the touchstone?" asked Hisoka.

She looked up at the trapeze rigging, trying to ignore Seebak's green eyes boring into her.

Of course, she thought, *the touchstone will be up there. Everything has to do with heights, somehow. It's not fair …*

She gave the ground and the base of the posts a searching examination, hoping that she'd see a glowing touchstone at ground level, but …

Alice sighed. "OK. It must be up there, with the trapeze."

"I can look for it," offered Hisoka. "I'm a rock climber. I can shin up there in less than a minute."

"Wish you could," Alice said ruefully. "But it has to be me. I'm the only one that can spot the glow."

"Lucky you."

"Yes. Lucky, lucky me."

"I'll go with you, though," said Hisoka. "And we need," he reached for a cord coiled near one of the posts, "to rig some safety harnesses."

"It would be nice *not* to splat," Alice agreed, trying to sound flippant instead of terrified. Her palms were already sweating …

Hisoka and James fashioned a couple of safety lines that didn't look *too* fragile.

"How's that feel?" asked Hisoka.

"Uncomfortable," she said. "Tight. But if it keeps me from falling – "

"It will," Hisoka assured her. "You go up first. That way if you fall, I can help stop your fall."

"Unless she takes you out and you *both* fall," said James.

Alice glared at him.

"Just thinking through scenarios," James said innocently.

Like Alice, he was trying to be more flippant than he felt.

Take care of your cousin, his mother had told him. *Take care of your cousin.*

And here was Alice, looking so fragile and vulnerable, about to climb an eighty-foot tall post without a net ...

Seebak seemed to sense James' disquiet. The panther nudged James' shoulder with its head.

Look up, Alice told herself, over and over, as she climbed the post. It was encircled by slender metal rungs, barely wide enough, it seemed, to hold her small feet. Again and again it felt like the soles of her sneakers were going to slip off the rungs, but she always regained her balance. *Hold on. Look up ...*

Hisoka easily kept pace with her, several rungs below her every step of the way. She had no idea how he was keeping his grip and footing on the slender rungs. His dexterity was incredible.

Sooner than Alice liked, she reached to top of the post, and stepped, with great reluctance, onto a wooden platform that seemed as small as a postage stamp, and made terrifying creaking sounds when she put her weight on it. The platform shivered as if it were made of flimsy balsa wood, and was about to crack and fall away like the wing of a cheap toy airplane ...

"Stop," she told Hisoka, hearing him reach the top. "Don't step on the platform. I don't know if it'll hold you."

"Aye, aye," he said. "Standing by."

Alice examined her surroundings. The lights of the carousel, in the far distance, radiated through the windows of the old carousel house, along with faint, tinny calliope music. Much closer at hand, the Ferris wheel blazed and whirled, the roller coaster cars careened empty around the track. In the shadow of the Ferris wheel, the Scrambler spun and twirled. And beyond that, the dark, seemingly infinite Pacific Ocean stretched away ...

The platform upon which she stood towered above the coaster, but stood below the crest of the Ferris wheel.

Yeah ... we're about eighty feet up. Don't look down, Alice, she told herself.

There was a trapeze fastened to a hook on the post. It was secured there so that someone could grasp the trapeze and swing out, over all that yawning space, all the way to the other post. The thought made Alice giddy. The other post and platform looked so, so far away … Alice swayed a little.

"Hey – don't fall," Hisoka called.

"Thanks."

Alice could see another trapeze, secured to the other post.

"See the touchstone?" James called up.

"Not yet!" she called down.

There was, Alice noted, a long metal bar suspended halfway between the platforms. Alice had seen something like it at the Ringling Brothers circus one year.

It happened like this, she remembered: A lady swung out on one trapeze; a man swung out on another trapeze, from the opposite platform.

They met in the middle, at that long bar; they both released their trapezes – just the thought made and Alice feel ill – and then they grabbed the long bar suspended between platforms. They hung there, from that long bar, and did all sorts of acrobatics.

And then, finally, someone on each platform pushed a trapeze to each of the performers, and they leaped wildly into the air, and grabbed the trapezes, and swung back to the safety of the platforms …

How can people do that? Alice wondered, feeling ill. Watching that performance at Ringling Brothers last year had made her so queasy, she had almost hurled. *How can people swing through the air, and do acrobatics a million feet above the ground without a net, and …*

And, of course, the final touchstone was there, glowing brightly on the metal bar suspended eighty feet above the ground between the platforms.

"I see it," Alice said, voice unsteady. "It's on the center bar. There." She pointed.

"Son of a gun," Hisoka said soflty.

"Good work," James called up. "Alice, can you tell Hisoka where it is, so he can get it?"

"Hey," said Hisoka, "I'm a rock climber, James – not a circus freak. You don't expect me to actually swing out there?"

"Well Alice can't do it," said James. "She's afraid of heights, and I can't let anything happen to her."

"Nice to know I'm expendable, pal," Hisoka said drily.

"You're wearing a safety rig," said James. "You should be fine. Just be careful."

"Why don't *you* put on a rig, and come up here, and be careful?" Hisoka suggested.

Aiden wriggled in his brothers' arms.

"Aidie fly!" Aiden said impatiently. "Aidie go fly!"

"Not yet," James said soothingly. "This is Hisoka's turn. Hisoka is going to fly. He's going to do some funny tricks."

"Like falling," said Hisoka.

"No – Aidie!" insisted Aiden. "*Aidie* fly!"

"Aidie, you fly later," Alice called down to her cousin. She curled and uncurled her hands. She tried to remember that time in Phys. Ed. when she had to swing from one side of the monkey bars to the other. Like her parents, Alice wasn't too keen on athletics; she only worked hard at P.E. because she didn't want to drag down her grade point average.

It had been scary, swinging from rung to rung, going from one side of the monkey bars to the other.

It had hurt her hands, blistered them, and even though she was only dangling a couple of feet above the grass, she had been afraid of the height, nervous of falling, so her palms were sweating, she kept almost slipping off the bars …

But I did it. Alice had wanted the A for the class; she'd focused; she'd succeeded.

Alice grabbed the trapeze that was secured to the post, untied the cord that fastened it.

"Hey!" said Hisoka, "what are you doing?"

"I'm going to get the touchstone," said Alice.

Hisoka leaned over the platform, cupped his hand over his mouth as he yelled down to his friend.

"James, Alice is going to swing for the touchstone."

"Well, *stop* her," yelled James. "She's gonna kill herself."

"You stink!" Alice yelled down to him.

"Alice – don't do it!" James shouted up. "Hisoka will get it."

"I will," Hisoka told her earnestly. "I don't want to, but I'm stronger, kid. I'm more agile. I've got way longer arms."

Alice lifted the trapeze. It felt solid, not flimsy. And it was wrapped with fabric. If her hands *did* sweat, the fabric would wick the perspiration, keep her from slipping. *I hope …*

Alice stood on her tip-toes, held the trapeze bar above her head.

It's just physics, she told herself. *I hold my arms straight; I leap out; gravity pulls me down at thirty-two-feet-per-second squared –* her stomach did an unhappy little flip at that thought – *I'll hold on to the trapeze, and I'll arc up toward that long bar, and I'll grab the touchstone, and swing right back to the platform –*

"Alice, I swear to God, let go of that trapeze," yelled James. "I'll climb up. I'll get the touchstone."

"Aidie get stone!" shouted Aiden. "Aidie stone. *Aidie!*"

Alice tiptoed to the very edge of the platform, trapeze held above and behind her head. *I can do this. I can do this.*

"Stop her!" James shouted to Hisoka.

"Can't," Hisoka called. "The platform's too weak."

"Then get down. I'm going up!"

"Alice," Hisoka told the girl, "James is coming up. Let him do this."

"Tell James to stay down there," said Alice. "I'll throw the touchstone to him. He needs to protect it, and keep it safe for Aiden."

I can do this … I can do this …

The touchstone looked so far away. It was some kind of little box.

"Why aren't you *stopping* her?" James called to Hisoka.

"This seems important to her," Hisoka said.

"Falling to her death?"

"Getting the touchstone," said Hisoka.

James tried to set Aiden on a bench near the post, but Aiden clung to his brother, digging his fingernails into James' shoulders.

"Ow! Aiden, listen – I need you to be a good little guy. I have to help Allie. You stay right here. *Right* here."

Aiden kicked his brother's ribs, pulled James' hair.

"Hey! Cut it out!" James managed to untangle his little brother's hands from his hair.

"Aidie fly!" Aiden kicked James again.

James had never seen his brother so out of control. Aiden was willful, and he could be mischievous, even a pain, but he wasn't purposely violent.

"Aiden, I know this whole thing is really confusing and crazy, but I need you to be cool. Can you do that? Can you be cool?"

"*My* stone," said Aiden. "*My* stone!"

Maybe he feels some kind of connection with it, thought James. *Maybe the touchstone is calling him ...*

"We'll give you the touchstone," said James. "I'll bring it down – "

"No!"

Aiden suddenly did something he had never done in his four short years – he bit his brother.

James cried out as Aiden's teeth sank into his left hand.

Aiden tore free of James' grasp, leaped for the post, grabbed the rungs, started scrambling up the ladder.

James hissed in pain. Aiden had bit deeply; the mark was bleeding, James could smell the coppery scent of blood.

Aiden's footsteps clanged up the metal rungs.

James ran to the post, began climbing, injured hand aching every time he grabbed a rung.

"Aiden's coming up," Hisoka reported to Alice.

"Is James with him?"

"Right behind him."

Alice nodded. She flexed up and down on her tip-toes.

"Hisoka?"

"Yes?"

"Tell James to get down there. He should be the one to catch the touchstone."

She gripped the trapeze firmly, and pushed off.

"*Alice!*" cried Hisoka.

"*Alice!*" cried James.

"*Allie!*" cried Aiden, halfway up the post, startled to see his cousin sailing through the air high above, clinging to a trapeze.

It does feel like flying, thought Alice. She swung gracefully through the air, holding on for dear life. The brilliant lights of the fun park flashed past her. *It's really sort of beautiful ...*

She focused on the bar suspended between the platforms, and the box fastened to it. It was growing closer and closer ...

Just have to grab the box. Grab it box and throw it down to James.

"Get *down*!" Hisoka called to James. "Get down so she can throw it to you!"

"But Aiden – "

"I've got Aiden," said Hisoka. "Aiden, come on – you're almost here."

James clambered down the ladder.

Alice reached the top of her arc, just as the box was within her range. *Grab the box, swing back to the platform. Grab the box, swing back to the platform.* In her head, she repeated the phrase like a mantra that could keep her safe.

She stretched out one hand, to grab the box. But –

Alice cried out.

Releasing one arm had thrown her off balance. The trapeze tilted dramatically to one side – Alice felt her hand slipping ...

Alice cried out again as her other hand slid off the trapeze.

The safety rope James and Hisoka had wrapped around her snapped, and fell away.

It fell down into the darkness, twisting like an albino snake.

I'm gonna fall ... I'm gonna die ...

Alice grabbed desperately for the long bar as she fell past it.

She felt cool metal under her hands. She grasped it, held on for dear life. Stopping her fall so suddenly wrenched her shoulders. Her hands, damp with fear-sweat, slipped on the smooth surface of the bar.

No! I'm not going to fall.

An image came to Alice, a memory from when she was very small, hanging from the monkey bars by her legs. It had been her Dad's idea. Most of the silly, fun things she had ever done had been her Dad's idea. *You can't always be serious, Allie. You have to have some fun.*

If her hands were slipping, Alice would have to hold on by her legs, too. Alice swung her legs up over the metal bar.

Shifting her weight wrenched her shoulders again, but she held on. She clung to the metal rail with one arm and both legs, and fumbled to grab the little glowing box …

James slid down the final rungs of the post, looked upward. Alice was clinging for dear life to the bar. Aiden had reached the platform; Hisoka was holding the little boy.

"Careful!" yelled James. "Don't drop him!"

Almost got it, thought Alice, fingertips within a hair's breadth of the glowing box. It was small, about the size of an ice cube, she thought.

Her fingers closed around the box.

Yes!

Alice didn't allow herself look down. She knew that if she looked down, she'd lose her nerve, and her grip, and then fall.

She looked at the little box instead. Yes – this was Aiden's. It had minute monkeys carved on it, and minute Mayan hieroglyphics.

"James," she called down, "are you ready?"

"Yeah," he said. "Throw it down. But don't let go of the bar."

"Thanks, yeah, I was totally planning to let go of the bar, but if you say I shouldn't – "

"Just drop the box, Allie."

Look out below, she thought. She released the box.

James saw a tiny cube tumbling through the night air. He cupped his hands, judged the direction and velocity to a nicety …

The small wooden box landed in his hands with a stinging *smack.*

"Got it!" he yelled excitedly. "Got it!"

Thank God, thought Alice.

Her arms and legs ached from clinging to the bar. She wrapped her legs tighter around it.

I want to be at camp, she thought, *with Penny and Marisol and Lajuana and Su Lin. With all my friends. Even with evil Natasha. I want to be mixing acids and designing historical dioramas, and painting each other's nails, and making fun of Natasha's terrible ensembles …*

"Guard the box with your *life*," Alice called to James. "Your *life*." *Since I just risked my own life to get it.*

Alice glanced over to the platform where Hisoka was holding Aiden. The little boy glared stormily at his cousin.

"Aidie box!" Aiden shouted.

"James is guarding it," explained Alice. "The bad people want it."

"*Aide* box," insisted Aiden. "Give Aidie box!"

"I'll bring you to James," Hisoka promised the child. "Calm down, pal."

"No!" Alice called sharply. "Not yet, Hisoka. The Ilwgyld could attack James for the touchstone. Keep Aiden up here 'till we know it's safe."

James turned in a full circle, making a wary recon of the area.

His senses were on full alert; he felt like he could hear a moth land on a flower. But he didn't hear or see anything unusual. No giant statues or evil mannequins. No sign of Lou or Flo.

They trust me, he thought. *Lou and Flo trust me to give them the touchstone; they know I don't want anything bad to happen to our parents.*

He held up the tiny box, regarded it curiously. It was a wooden box, inlaid with decorative strips of wood. Marquetry, he knew. His dad and his uncle made marquetry furniture. Uncle Roberto designed it, and his dad crafted it. The box was decorated with little monkeys, and Mayan hieroglyphics. *Have to learn some Mayan,* James thought.

The box didn't seem to have a lid. James turned the object over in his hands. *OK … I get it … Puzzle box.*

Opening it would require finding a pressure point, or a hidden latch.

Seems like a pretty complicated thing for a little kid like Aiden. Of course, we were supposed to be older when we started the quest.

James shook the box. It felt heavy, like there was something inside, but he didn't hear anything rattle.

So, here it is. The final touchstone. My gut says give it to Fuego. But what happens to my Mom and Dad if I do? And what happens to all of us if I don't?

On the platform, Aiden squirmed impatiently in Hisoka's grasp.

"Aidie get box!" the little boy insisted, elbowing Hisoka's chest.

"Ow. Aiden, kid – come on. Don't hurt big brother's friend," pleaded Hisoka.

Whoever gets here first gets the box, James decided. *If the Ilwgyld get here first, I give it to them, then tell Fuego they have it. He can take his elite guard and steal it back. And if Fuego gets here first, I give him the box, but he* has *to make sure our parents are safe …*

Neither solution, James realized, was very good. *Why do I have to make this decision? Why me?*

Alice twisted, getting a surer grip on the metal bar. Her arms felt like they were on fire. *Come on, stupid Fuego. Come get the box, and get me down from here …*

"Are you OK up there?" James called to Alice.

"Do I *look* like I'm OK?"

"If Hisoka pushes the trapeze back to you, do you think you can grab it and swing back?"

Alice thought about flying through the air again, an eighty-foot drop below her sneakers. "Forget it," she said decisively.

"But you must be getting tired up there."

"Of course I am. But don't *say* that! Don't make me think about it."

"But you – "

"Oh my God, will you just be quiet? If I fall and die, it's totally your fault." Alice wriggled again, keeping her precarious purchase on the bar. "Can't your dumb cat do something to help?"

James glanced at Seebak, who had been standing quietly at his side.

"Cats can't climb ladders," James said doubtfully.

"They can't swing on a flying trapeze, either," said Alice. "I'm not saying send him up here. I'm saying, Seebak is part of the faery world – right? Does he have any, like, magic connection? I mean, is there some way he can help us signal Fuego?"

"Huhn." James considered that suggestion. "Fuego seems to pop in and out whenever he feels like it, Alice. I don't know if we can call him to us."

"Well can we *try*?" Alice hooked her arms tighter around the bar.

She was so tired; her arms were aching more every minute. *P.E. class will never seem like a big deal again …*

James turned to Seebak. The panther regarded the young man with what seemed like a friendly air. *How can I assist you?* said the look.

"Do you … Is there a way you can contact Fuego?" James asked, feeling idiotic. *Right. Seebak is going to whip out a magic cell phone and call faery land …*

Seebak's eyes closed. He shook his head, so gently that James thought perhaps he imagined it.

"Sorry," James called to Alice. "Looks like no-go."

Aiden finally broke free from Hisoka.

"Hey!" Hisoka lunged, but his hands caught only empty air. Aiden grabbed the trapeze and flung himself into the air, sailing one-handed toward Alice.

Alice turned at Hisoka's exclamation.

Her small cousin rocketed toward her on the trapeze, dark curls blown back by the breeze.

Alice's heart dropped.

"Aiden – what are you *doing*?" she cried. *Don't let him fall! God, universe, Fuego – whoever's listening – don't let him fall!*

Aiden released the trapeze, swung his arms, and grabbed the metal bar.

With an uncanny agility he pulled himself up into a sitting position, balancing easily several feet from where Alice was clumsily clinging for dear life.

"Aidie help Allie?" the child asked kindly.

"Allie is OK," Alice said.

Aiden pressed a small hand to Alice's face. "Allie get Aidie box?" he asked, tilting his head winningly.

"No, Aiden. Allie can't get your box right now. Allie's kind of twisted up like a pretzel ."

"Ha! Pretzel." Aiden laughed. Then, growing serious, he pointed down at James. "Allie get Aidie box?" Aiden asked. "Please?"

That box must really be calling out to him, thought Alice.

"Aidie, the bad people want the box. James is protecting it. OK? He's going to give it to Fuego."

"Fuego?"

"Yeah. Fuego will take care of it."

Aiden closed one eye, considering what his cousin had said.

It still trips me out, thought Alice, *how Aiden seems to know about Fuego, even though he's asleep whenever Fuego appears.*

"Fuego good," said Aiden.

"Yeah. He can be weird, and annoying, but he's good," agreed Alice.

"Fuego get Aidie box."

"That's the plan, Aidie."

"OK." Aiden nodded, satisfied.

"What are you talking about up there?" called James.

"Never mind what we're talking about up here," Alice said waspishly. "What are *you* doing down there to get us down, or to call Fuego?"

James pulled his quest kit from within his hoodie. *Maybe there's an answer in here. Maybe there's something we can use ...*

He regarded the slim silver flask, the small silver box. In mortal L.A., they were just a vial of water and a box of sand. But what were they here, where the mortal and magical worlds overlapped?

"Do you want me to swing out and get you guys?" Hisoka asked Alice and Aiden.

"*No!*" Alice said sharply. "You could end up crashing into us. You could knock us to our deaths."

"If I were really careful about it – "

"No!" she repeated. "What about a ladder? Are there any ladders around here? Or maybe you guys could make a net, or something. Can someone do *something* for us?"

"Ladder. Net. Got it." Hisoka tipped his fedora at them, and began climbing down the post.

James opened the silver flask. Liquid gurgled inside.

He sniffed it. No scent.

It was probably a healing potion, James realized. In every game that he'd ever played, the novice heroes had access to some kind of healing potion or med kit.

Of course, this isn't a game. For all I know, there's poison in this flask.

He secured the lid, slid the flask back into the pouch.

He opened the silver box. Inside was a little mound of silvery powder; it glittered prettily in the dim light.

"What's that?" asked Hisoka.

James jumped. It was downright supernatural, how quietly Hisoka moved.

"Don't know," said James. "Part of our quest kits."

"Looks like pixie dust," said Hisoka. "Sprinkle some on your head, see if you can fly."

James shot his friend a look. "You're a laugh a minute, Hisoka."

"True. Look, never mind the pixie dust, we have to find a ladder or something and get the kids down."

"What do you think I'm *trying* to do?" asked James. He pinched some of the silvery powder between his fingers. The little grains made the faintest, prettiest of tinkling sounds as they moved, like distant bells.

"Kind of *sounds* like pixie dust," said Hisoka. "Maybe it *can* make you fly."

"No. But I think I know what it is." James grabbed Hisoka's fedora, threw it on the ground.

"Hey!" objected Hisoka. "My hat!" He reached down to snatch up the fedora, but Seebak took a menacing step toward him, growling.

"It's not your hat," said James. "You stole it."

"I acquired it," corrected Hisoka, warily eyeing Seebak. "It was on public property when I found it after the battle. It was a trophy of war."

"Whatever. Still not your hat."

James rubbed the silvery powder between his fingers, listening to the faint, silvery music; it reminded him of the wind chimes his mother had hung on the porch.

James tossed the powder at the fedora.

There was a bright flash of silver light, the crash of a mirror breaking, and then a waterfall of twinkling silver particles, thick as smoke, roiled around the fedora.

When the silvery haze faded, James and Hisoka regarded the patch of ground where the fedora had sat.

The hat was gone.

"What happened?" asked Hisoka.

"Teleported," said James.

"Where?"

"That, I don't know," James admitted. "Probably to somewhere in the faery realm."

"But you don't know."

"No."

"So, how does this help the kids?"

"I don't know," James admitted. "But now we know what the powder does. Sort of."

"So, we can't help the kids, and my awesome fedora is in faery land."

"Yeah."

"Will you two losers get us *down* from here?" Alice called.

"Yes, dearie," said Lou. The fierce-eyed blonde materialized at James' elbow without warning.

James and Hisoka jumped.

Seebak growled at Lou; the dark fur stood up on the back of his neck.

"Now, now, apologies for startling you, like," said Lou.

She wore her bizarre, colorful circus outfit – the one she had worn when they first met her at Union Station.

"Did I miss anythin'?" asked Flo.

The fierce-eyed redhead materialized at James' other elbow. She, like Lou, wore her circus costume.

"Not a thing, not a thing," Lou assured the other Ilwgyld. "I arrived only a tic afore you, Flo."

Lou looked upward, gave Alice and Aiden a cheery little wave. "'Allo, pets. 'Allo, me little owlets, me little piglets, me little geese."

Alice's heart sank. *Where is Fuego?* Even with Seebak, James and Hisoka were probably no match for Lou and Flo. *At least Aiden and I are safe up here*, she thought. *Well … relatively safe …*

"Leave the kids alone," James told Lou.

The blonde laughed. It was an ugly sound – like frogs croaking, like a rusty door groaning.

"Now, now, *that* ain't the proper manner – is it, Flo?"

"T'ain't," Flo agreed.

"We're here all friendly like," said Lou. "You an' Flo and me got business, James Jones. An't we? You gives us what you promised, and we'll uphold our end o' the bargain."

"Can't speak fairer than that," Flo said, with a vicious grin.

Lou extended one bony arm, opened her claw-like hand, palm upward.

"Come on now, there's a good lad," she coaxed. "Give us the magickal whatsawhosit. There's a wise and likely lad, who knows what's good for 'im."

James drew a deep breath. He glanced at the little puzzle box in his hand. He glanced at the silver box of teleporting powder in the other hand. He glanced at Seebak, who was growling very low.

"Now, now, now," said Lou, waving one bony finger like an evil caricature of a school mistress. "I can see some of them horrid little thoughts tumblin' through your tiny little brain, James Jones. You don't want to do anythin' stupid – does ye? Think on your mother. Think on your father. And your uncle. And your aunt. You send us back to Aelwyd," she nudged her sharp chin at the silver box, "or loose that beast on us," she nudged her chin at Seebak, "and you won't *never* see your family again."

"Not *alive*, no how," Flo added, with a hideous grin.

High above, Alice could see Aiden becoming more and more agitated. Although the child probably couldn't understand all of the nuances of the conversation below, he knew that the bad guys were threatening his family. And it would be just like Aiden to do something reckless to try to help …

"Aiden," Alice said, forcing herself to sound calm, "hold on tight to this bar. Do you understand, Aiden? Hold on tight, and don't let go. No matter what. James and Hisoka will take care of the bad guys."

"Aidie kick dumb Lou!" said Aiden.

"No!" said Alice, and then, more calmly, "No, Aiden. Aidie has to be a good little mouse."

"Good mouse dumb!" Aiden said rebelliously.

Eighty feet below them, Flo yawned. "Gettin' weary of waitin'," she told Lou. "When can we shred 'em?"

James felt an icy finger of terror along his spine.

"There, *that's* right," Lou told him approvingly. "You *should* be afraid. We're the thing in the closet, dearie. We're the thing under the bed. We're the thing in the shadow, when you're pedalin' home of a dark night, and you thinks you sees somethin', somethin' terrifyin', just out the corner of your eye." She held her hand closer. "Gives us the magickal thingabob, duckie. Here, now. You do that little thing, and we won't touch a hair of your head. Or your family's."

James swallowed hard. "You ... do you *promise*?" he asked.

Flo cackled as if she had never heard anything so hilarious.

Lou gave him a smile as cold and thin as a shard of ice.

"Not a hair of your head, gosling. Promise. Me word's me bond. Just give me that box," she stretched her hand even closer. Her bony fingertips almost brushed his hand ...

"Don't do it!" shouted Alice. "James – wait for Fuego!"

Flo hissed, threw a look of pure venom at Alice.

Lou's smile soured, but she ignored the little girl.

"Think hard, boy," she told James. "Think on our powers, lad."

Lou snapped her fingers.

The lights of the fun park blazed brighter. The music swelled until it was almost deafening.

The Ferris wheel turned faster. And faster.

The coaster cars raced up and down the track at insane speeds.

James cleared his throat.

"That's nothing," he said, with more bravado than he felt. "You're just doing a parlor trick."

"Truly?" snarled Lou. "What an intelligent lad it is. What a bright fellow it is."

"Too bright," snarled Flo.

"Too bright," Lou agreed.

"Show it something else," suggested Flo.

"Shall I?" asked Lou. "Yes. Yes. I'll show our lad here what happens to them what don't do as we ask – 'specially when we've asked so nice-like."

The blonde turned suddenly toward Hisoka.

Startled, Hisoka took a step back.

Lou flicked her wrist with an almost indifferent elegance.

Hisoka's dark necktie was pulled up, as if by an invisible hand.

"*Ggghhrggh!*" said Hisoka, choking, as he was dragged up onto his tiptoes.

"Let him go!" shouted Alice. "Let him go, you witch!"

"*You'll* do well to keep a civil tongue in your head," Lou called to Alice.

The blonde Ilwgyld lifted her hand.

Hisoka was pulled up higher, several feet off the ground, choking and gagging and clawing at his tie.

"Now," Lou said to James, "do you see your way clear, gosling, to giving me that magick box?"

James kept his temper with great difficulty. He tried to ignore the image of one of his best friends, dangling above the ground, choking.

"You know what I notice?" James asked Lou, keeping his voice steady.

"No, pet? What do you notice – asides, that is, that I'm stranglin' your dear chum, here?"

"I notice," said James, "that you're always *threatening* us, but you never actually *hurt* us. Me and Alice and Aiden, I mean."

Flo hissed at him.

"Like when you were chasing Aiden at City Hall," said James. "I know he's fast, but you could've crushed him if you really wanted to."

"Yes. Yes, a *very* bright fellow," Lou said with an acid smile.

She closed her hand; Hisoka gurgled pitifully, clawing at his tie and collar.

"Is it that you don't want to hurt us," asked James, "or that you can't?"

"Give you one guess, dearie," sneered Lou.

"That's what I thought," said James. "You haven't just been protecting us so we can get the touchstones; you totally *can't* hurt us."

"We *can*," Lou said bitterly. "But the Dark 'Un won't allow us."

"Won't let us touch a hair of your horrid little heads," growled Flo.

"I see." James held up the puzzle box. "So even if I give this to Fuego …"

"That's right, pet. We can't harm you," admitted Lou. "But as I keeps tellin' you, and tellin' you – we an't threatenin' *you*. We can do whatever we wants to your *parents*. Your *friends*."

Lou squeezed her hand into a fist.

Hisoka gave one final gurgle; his head slumped to the right.

Lou opened her hand.

Hisoka fell to the ground in a heap, and did not move.

Keep it together, thought James, *keep it together, keep it together –*

"*Soka!*" yelled Aiden. "*Soka!*"

"Shh. It's OK," Alice told her little cousin. "Hisoka is taking a nap. Hisoka is sleepy."

"*Bad* ladies!" yelled Aiden. He pulled a handful of pebbles from his hoodie pocket, threw them at the Ilwgyld below.

Aiden's aim was, as always, impeccable.

Flo and Lou's heads snapped back as they were struck by the stones.

"Brat!" spat Flo, casting a vitriolic look high above.

"He needs a lesson," seethed Lou. "And someday, we'll mete it out, dearies, oh, yes, we'll mete it out, and when we do – "

"Yes, that's all very threatening," said James, "but the fact is that right now, at this moment, you aren't allowed to hurt the Chosen Ones. Interesting."

Hisoka, James saw, though unconscious, was alive. Though the young man lay crumpled in a heap, Hisoka's chest rose and fell as he breathed.

Hang on, buddy, thought James.

"Now you listen to me, lad," said Lou, leaning forward intently. "This is the *last* chance for us to settle this civil-like. You give me that magical thingamajig this instant, or we'll throw your parents to the rath birds, *and* the rath bears, and then whatever's left of them will be dropped into the Pit of Night."

James thought of his mother Roz, her grim beauty, the way she held the household together. He thought of his father's open, kind face, his quiet confidence. He thought of sweet, sensitive Aunt Peggy, and Uncle Roberto, always quick with a joke.

James leaned toward Lou, until he was almost touching her forehead.

Startled, she shrank back.

"Now you listen to me, you hag," James said quietly.

He took a step forward.

Lou took a step back.

"If you threaten our parents again," said James, "I'll have Seebak bite off your head."

Lou glanced at the great black panther. Seebak stared at her, licking his chops.

"Now, let's not be *hasty*, duckie," said Lou.

"I don't want to be hasty," said James. "I want us to think this through very carefully."

He took another step forward.

Lou took another step back.

"I'm giving this last touchstone to Fuego," James said. "Not to you. And if *anything* happens to *any* of our family, or *any* of our friends, we're going to go to Fuego, and we're *all* going to hunt you down."

Lou raised her claw-like hands.

"Let's be reasonable, lad," she said in a wheedling, whining tone.

"Seebak bite lady!" Aiden yelled impatiently, from aloft.

"Just have your dumb cat decapitate them, already," shouted Alice.

James smiled.

"See – I *am* the reasonable one," James told Lou. "You can take my deal, or you can deal with my brother and cousin."

Lou clenched and unclenched her hands. She clearly wished she were allowed to tear James limb from limb.

"If you gives Fuego that touchstone," she said in a strangled voice, "his clan will drive us from the forest, my gosling, my gooseling, my little duck. They'll drive us out of Aelwyd."

"How terrible," James deadpanned.

"You don't know what you're about," Lou whispered. "You only *think* you know."

"I know you're leaving now," said James.

He took yet another step forward.

Lou stepped back, gnashing her teeth at him.

"Unless," said James, "you want to wait around for Fuego."

Beaten, enraged, Lou lifted her hands to the night sky. She shouted, she shrieked – horrible, inarticulate cries, more bird-like than human.

Aiden covered his small ears against the inhuman cries.

"It's OK, Aidie," Alice said soothingly. "Hold on. The bad ladies are almost gone …"

Flo began to shriek, even louder and fiercer than Lou.

The red-head pointed at the roller coaster – a section of track exploded, raining bits of shrapnel and massive metal chunks on the ground below.

The racing coaster cars plunged off the shattered track, bursting into fireballs as they struck the ground.

The red-head pointed at the Ferris wheel – there was a deafening groan of tearing metal, and the wheel tore off its hub, bounced on the asphalt, and then rolled forward with a loud rumble.

It rolled over the Scrambler, crushing the Scrambler cars, and several of the metal arms.

The Ferris wheel rolled through the fence, and into the Pacific Ocean. It bobbed for a few seconds, and then sank into the water like a great stone.

"You won't be protected forever," screamed Flo. "We'll feed your livers to the rath birds! We'll feed your hearts to the orth magru!"

Lou fixed James with a look he would never forget. It was a look of the deepest hatred, corrosive and pitiless.

He knew in that moment that Lou would never rest until either he or she had been destroyed.

The air around Lou and Flo wavered, rippling like hot dessert winds. The Ilwgyld were engulfed in dark shadows that fluttered and rustled like the feathers of a great crow.

Lou never broke her gaze. James' heart hammered in his chest, but he didn't drop his eyes.

And then, with wild gusts, like the beating of enormous wings, Lou and Flo melted away.

Chapter Twenty – Home
June 26th – Los Angeles

"Yay, James!" yelled Aiden. "Bad ladies go!"

He danced a little jig on the bar.

Alice's heart stopped, watching Aiden dance so recklessly eighty feet above the ground.

"Aidie, hold the bar," she said. "Hold on tight. With *both* hands. Don't let go."

On the ground, James crouched, checked his friend's pulse.

Hisoka was already stirring. There were nasty bruises forming on his throat. But his main concern as he regained consciousness and sat up was –

"My tie," groaned Hisoka, voice raspy. He held up his once-natty dark tie, which was in shreds. "This tie cost me forty dollars!"

"Glad your priorities are straight," said James.

"Hey, now. Talking about priorities," Hisoka said, voice hoarse, "way to let those psychos almost kill me!"

"Sorry," James said sincerely. "But I wasn't sure how I was going to play it, or what they could do. And, you know, you're like a brother to me, but Aiden – "

"Yeah, I get it." Hisoka rubbed his bruised throat. "Aiden actually *is* your brother. And you three are the Chosen Ones, and all that, and I'm just a totally expendable quest Companion. I'm like the guy in the red uniform on 'Star Trek'."

"Totally not even," objected James.

"But even lowly quest Companions should get hazard pay," said Hisoka. "Maybe enough for a new tie?"

"This isn't really a paying gig."

"Uh, excuse me," called Alice, "but is anyone *ever* going to get us down from here?"

Hisoka rose to his feet. He staggered a bit, but didn't fall.

"Yeah, I'll find that ladder, or net, or something," he called to Alice. "Sorry, kid, I got distracted, being choked and unconscious and everything."

"Never mind," said Fuego.

They all looked in the direction of the deep voice.

Fuego stood on the trapeze platform, dark cloak whipped by the early morning breezes.

"Finally!" complained Alice. "Are you *ever* going to help us when we're in deadly peril?"

Fuego shook his head.

"Are you *ever* going to realize," he countered, "that you don't need my assistance, lass?"

"We sure could have used it tonight," she said. "Way to almost let us die. If you – *Aidie!*" she screamed.

Because, as always happened whenever Fuego appeared, Aiden had fallen into a deep sleep. His fingers had slipped; he toppled off of the metal bar.

Alice flung one arm wildly, trying to grab Aiden's hood, but she was too late.

The little boy fell in what seemed to Alice like nightmarish slow-motion, falling, falling, falling toward the ground.

"*Aiden!*" James shouted.

He and Hisoka raced to the spot on the ground directly under the long bar, arms outstretched, prepared to catch the little boy. It was completely illogical, trying to catch a tiny child falling eight stories, but they weren't thinking, they were acting on instinct …

Fuego pushed off the platform, one arm wrapped around the trapeze, the other outstretched.

He snagged Aiden's hood.

"Don't drop him," yelled Alice. "Don't drop him, Fuego."

When the trapeze reached the end of its arc, it sailed back to the platform.

Fuego leaped easily onto the platform, insanely graceful for such a hulking warrior, carrying Aiden as if the child were as light as a goose down pillow.

James put a fist to his mouth. He felt like he might be sick. Watching his brother tumble through the air, knowing he probably couldn't save him …

"It's OK, pal," Hisoka said. "It turned out OK."

James nodded. Yeah. Fuego had saved Aiden. But if Fuego hadn't been there to catch him …

On the other hand, thought James, *if Fuego hadn't been here, Aiden wouldn't have fallen.*

Fuego climbed down the rungs at supernatural speed, Aiden under one arm.

The chieftain carried the sleeping child to James.

James took Aiden, held his brother tightly. Aiden slept peacefully. He looked angelic, as usual, while he slept. His heart beat was even; there was no shadow on his face.

"Is there any way around it?" James asked.

"No," said Fuego, understanding what James was asking. "Aiden will always slumber whenever I visit you."

"And you're not going to tell us why."

"No. Not yet, lad," Fuego agreed.

James shifted Aiden to one shoulder, handed the small wooden puzzle box to Fuego.

"Here," James said ungraciously. "The last touchstone. We almost died for it. Even Hisoka."

"*Even* me?" asked Hisoka. "There's some gratitude."

Fuego gave the box a cursory examination, then tucked it into his dark cloak.

"You almost perished," Fuego said. "But you recovered the Box of Mystery. And you lived to fight another day." He clapped James on the shoulder. "You did well, James. You did very well."

"What about me?" demanded Alice.

Fuego looked up, where Alice was still clinging to the metal bar.

"You did well too, Alice. *All* of you." Fuego clapped Hisoka on the shoulder, including him in the praise. "You're all yet in battle shock. You do not realize how much you achieved, this night. But you can all be proud. Yes. Quite proud."

"I don't want to be proud," called Alice. "I want to get down from here."

She knew she was whining. She hated whining, but she couldn't help it. Her arms ached from hanging onto the bar, she was shivering in the early morning ocean breezes, and she was tired, very tired, of being brave.

"Get me down," Alice called plaintively.

"Ah. About that," said Fuego. "Alice, you have one more task to perform."

"Great," she muttered. "So – let me have it. What is it?"

"Let go," said Fuego.

"Excuse me?"

"Let go."

"Of this bar?"

"Of that bar."

"Are you *crazy*?" She wrapped her arms and legs tighter around the metal bar.

"Your arms must needs be so very weary," said Fuego. "You cannot hold on forever, lass."

"Says you! Watch me!"

But Fuego was right. Her arms ached so badly they burned like fire. Her legs were nearly numb from clinging to the bar so long …

"Let go, Alice."

She sighed.

"This is a magic thing – right?" she called. "I'm going to float down like a feather – right?"

"No," said Fuego. "You're going to fall. But I'll catch you."

"Ha!"

"Can you really catch her?" James whispered to Fuego.

"Do you doubt it?" asked Fuego. "Have you not seen my feats of strength and agility? The question is not whether I can catch her, but whether she can let go. She must do this. She must face this fear."

"You can do this, Alice," James shouted encouragingly.

"Come on, kid," called Hisoka, "you'll be fine."

Fine! Right! thought Alice. *Dropping at thirty-two-feet-per-second squared. Fine? I'll totally splat!*

"Five," said Fuego.

I can't do this, thought Alice.

"Four," said Fuego.

"Come on, Alice," said James.

"Three," said Fuego.

Alice took a deep breath. Slowly, she let go of the bar.

"Two," said Fuego.

Alice fell back, hanging upside down by her legs. She swung giddily, forward and backward.

My God! The ground is so far below!

Fuego and James and Hisoka looked like tiny bugs.

"One," said Fuego.

Here goes nothing ...

Alice straightened her legs, releasing her grip on the bar.

She stretched her arms out straight below her, like a diver.

She plunged down, down, down, eyes fixed on Fuego's dark cloak.

James held his breath, as his cousin plunged eight stories.

Catch her, Fuego. Catch her ...

It must have been his imagination, James would think later, but it appeared, for a moment, as if Fuego lifted off of the ground, flew up into the air several feet as easily as a swimmer pushes up from the bottom of a pool.

Whatever happened, Alice was falling and then, suddenly, Fuego was holding her. She was so small compared to him that he cradled her like a toddler.

Gently, Fuego set Alice on her feet.

"There," he grinned. "Told you I'd catch you, lass."

Alice smiled. Like swinging on the trapeze, as terrifying as falling had been, it felt strangely beautiful, strangely poetic.

I jumped eight stories. I am now officially, totally, insane ...

"You OK?" James asked his cousin.

"Yeah," she said. She touched Aiden's dark curls. "How's the little guy?"

"Seems to be all right," said James. He turned to Fuego.

"What happens next?" James asked the chieftain.

Fuego shrugged. "You go home."

"Yeah, but I mean – "

"You go home," Fuego repeated. "Your mothers will be home by eight in the morning. Rest until that time. Certainly, you deserve some hours of peace."

"But, I mean, in the future," said James. "What are you going to do with the touchstones? And what are the Ilwgyld going to do to us? I'm glad I stood up to them, and it worked, for now, but I'm worried – "

"About your family," said Fuego. "Aye, lad. I understand."

"And what about me?" demanded Alice. "Has anyone else here had Lou and Flo materialize in their *closet* in the middle of the night? I don't think I can possibly sleep in my room ever again!"

James shook his head. "That's right, Alice. Make it all about you."

"It's not all about me," said Alice, "but it sure is *partly* about me. Tell you what – after the Ilwgyld pop into *your* closet in the middle of the night, then you tell me how it makes *you* feel."

"The Ilwgyld will not disturb you for a time," Fuego said firmly. "Any of you. Of that, I shall make sure and certain. With the touchstones, my people in Aelwyd can drive the Ilwgyld into the darklands. Of course, as you have ascertained, the touchstones are your property. And they will be returned to you at the proper time."

"You can keep them," said Alice. "Really. Keep them forever if you want."

Fuego lifted one dark eyebrow.

"Hey, I'll sign the Key of Wisdom over to you right now," said Alice. "Have any paper on you? Hisoka's got a pen."

"Alice," Fuego said kindly, "one cannot sign over one's destiny."

"There's always a loophole," she said confidently.

"Who hid the touchstones?" James asked, trying to catch Fuego off guard.

Fuego bit his lip. "That ... I am not permitted to share that information."

"Let me guess," Alice said wryly. "Whoever hid the touchstones was related to us, and all of space-and-time will blow up if we know who it was."

"Something like that," Fuego conceded.

"Do we *ever* get to learn more about them?" asked James. "These ancestors of ours?"

"In time," said Fuego. "In time, you will learn more than you ever wished to know. And now," he clapped James and Alice on the shoulders, "you must rest. Dawn is nearing. And I have – " he glanced at the demolished roller coaster, the flattened Scrambler, the shattered pedestal that had anchored the Ferris wheel until Flo tore it loose, "I have rather a mess to clear up," he said.

"But I have so many questions," objected James. "Who is that red-headed girl? Is she good, or evil? What is that liquid in our quest kits? And that teleportation powder – where does it send things?"

"I'd like to know the answer to that, too," said Hisoka. "Fuego, sir, if you see a *really* cool fedora lying around somewhere in magic land, send it my way, would you?"

"All will be answered – in its time," Fuego told James.

"Come on – 'All will be answered in time'?" complained James. "That's totally one of those wizard cop-outs. You're a *warrior*, Fuego. Can't you just be straight with us?"

"I'm a warrior *and* a wizard," Fuego had said. "And now – you are truly beginning to try my patience. Get thee hence. Do not call me – I will call you. And above all, take care of each other. Even with the Ilwgyld driven to the darklands, your totem tattoos can still call dark things down upon you."

"Wait. Hold up," said Alice. "Our tattoos can *still* call dark things down upon us? We need details. *What* dark things? Are you talking rath birds? Or that orth magru thing Flo mentioned? You can't just drop something like that and then disappear."

"*I* am not going to disappear," Fuego said. "*You* are going to disappear."

"But – "

Fuego waved his hand.

The familiar blinding flash, and sound of a shattering mirror, then the sparkling lights and silvery chiming of teleportation powder enveloped the children.

Alice squinted.

Twinkling particles roiled about her amidst a silvery music.

She stretched out her hands, found an arm, grabbed it blindly …

It was only a few seconds later that the powder dispersed.

She and James stood on the front lawn of James' house, James carrying little Aiden.

Aiden stirred, lifted his drowsy head.

The lovely Victorian house was silhouetted against a sky stained pink with the coming dawn.

Alice thought she had never been so happy to see her cousins' house.

"Sun," Aiden said happily, pointing to the dawn sky.

They climbed the steps to the porch and sat for a moment on the porch swing. No one said anything for awhile.

James handed Aiden to Alice. The little boy settled against her, fell asleep again.

"Did all that really happen?" Alice asked.

"Yeah," said James.

"Where did Hisoka go?"

"Maybe Fuego teleported him to wherever his fedora went."

"I'm serious."

"So am I. You never know, with Fuego." James yawned. "Don't worry about Hisoka. Fuego must've sent him to his house. I'll text him in a bit, make sure he's OK."

Alice tousled Aiden's dark curls. "Do you think he'll be, like, traumatized by any of this?"

"Aiden? No way," James said firmly. "Me – probably. You – I don't know. That was *really* cool, when you let go of the bar."

"That was cool," agreed Alice.

"I think it increased your confidence," said James. "Probably your arrogance, too. Because you weren't confident and arrogant enough before."

Alice kicked his shin.

James laughed.

"What if Aiden tells your mother?" Alice asked thoughtfully. "Or my mom?"

"About what?"

"About *any* of it. Fuego, the Ilwgyld, Aelwyd – "

"You've met my mother – right?" asked James. "If Aiden starts talking about crazy adventures, she'll just tell me to stop letting him watch my video games."

"True. Aunt Roz *is* totally practical."

"*Your* mom might believe him," James mused. "Aunt Peggy has a great imagination."

"She'll just think he's telling a story, I guess," said Alice. "I'm just glad he's safe. James – if Fuego or the Ilwgyld ever come back, we *have* to keep Aidie out of it."

"Agreed. Agreed we should *try*. I don't know if we can …"

When Roz and Peggy arrived at the house, yawning, with dark circles under their eyes after their night shifts, they found the children getting along surprisingly well.

James had connected his game controller to the living room flat screen, and was playing Mortal Quest online, with a couple of friends named, as Roz saw by the tags onscreen, *thadude1055* and *rockemsockem99*.

"Turn that down," said Roz, dropping her keys and purse on the kitchen counter.

"OK," said James.

Alice was sitting on the floor near James, Aiden sitting on her lap. She was reading to Aiden from a book with an adorable little mouse on the cover.

"Hi, sweetie," Peggy said to Alice. "Did you have a good time?"

"It was OK," said Alice.

Roz opened the refrigerator. "Juice?" she called to Peggy.

"Sure. If it's not too much trouble," Peggy said in her sweet, high-pitched voice.

"No trouble." Roz took a bottle of orange juice from the refrigerator, opened a cabinet, rummaged around for a couple of glasses.

"James – why aren't there any clean glasses in this cabinet?"

"Sorry," called James. "Forgot to wash any."

Roz glanced at the sink, which was piled high with dishes, glasses and silver ware. "James, what do you *do* all day? Is it too much to ask you to wash some dishes?"

"Maybe he was busy watching the kids," said Peggy. "Alice can be a real handful."

"Thanks, mom," said Alice, rolling her eyes.

"It takes five minutes to wash dishes," said Roz. "James – are you listening to me? Why didn't you wash the dishes?"

"We, you know, we were kind of busy yesterday," he said, eyes still on the screen as he maneuvered his warrior through a swamp laced with pools of bubbling lava.

"Nice one, dude!" Tariq's voice rumbled from the flat screen's speaker.

"Don't get over-confident," warned Hisoka's voice.

"James, you're not *just* watching the kids," said Roz. "You're watching the house, too. I put you in charge of everything. I've put a lot of trust in you. Don't let me down."

"I'll try not to," he said. He maneuvered his warrior along one of the lava pools.

"James is actually doing a pretty good job of watching us," said Alice.

"Really?" asked Roz, startled. It was rarer than rare for Alice to say *anything* nice about her older cousin.

"Really," said Alice. "He's very protective. Aidie – turn the page now."

Aiden turned the page.

Alice read aloud.

"'Oh, no – I'm in a real pickle now,' said the Good Little Mouse. 'Whatever shall I do?'"

"Good mouse is baby," said Aiden. "Good mouse dumb. C'mon, Allie – read Aidie 'bout Fuego. Pow! Ka-pow!" Aiden made punching and karate chop moves.

Roz found paper cups in one of the cupboards, poured out orange juice for herself and for Peggy.

"Alice, I hope you aren't reading Aiden any violent books," said Roz. "He gets hyper enough as it is."

"Aunt Roz, swear to God, I haven't read Aiden anything but 'The Good Little Mouse' since I've been here."

Roz sipped her orange juice. "Well – probably something he saw on TV. If you could keep it tuned to PBS – "

"Whatever you say, Aunt Roz."

Peggy smiled. Alice sounded so polite this morning – so grown up.

Maybe, Peggy thought, *all the challenges of the summer, all the time with her cousins, will be good for her …*

Later, when Peggy and Alice had left, and Aiden was napping, James went to the sink and washed the dishes.

Roz sat at the kitchen counter, tapping numbers into a calculator and sorting through bills.

"Is it too much to ask," asked Roz, "that you don't spend so much time on the computer? This wireless bill is crazy. James – I need you to be responsible."

James was silent.

He rinsed the dish he was washing and set it on the rack to dry. He dunked another dish in the warm water.

"And what's up with this cell phone bill?" asked Roz. "You'd think we were calling Russia! I called your dad twice last month – *just* twice – and those calls alone are fifty dollars!"

James rinsed the dish. He set it in the drying rack. He grabbed a bowl encrusted with oatmeal – Aiden's bowl, he saw. He ran it under the hot water tap.

"Mom?" said James.

"What?" Roz didn't look up from the Macy's bill she was examining.

"Thank you for everything you're doing."

"What am I doing?" she asked. She tossed the Macy's bill onto the little pile of bills on her right. She opened the gas bill.

"I know it's tough with dad gone," said James. "I know you miss him. And it's all on you. You've got hold it all together. Even with Aunt Peggy. You're helping her be strong, too."

Roz was silent. She smoothed the gas bill on the counter.

"I just want you to know I appreciate you," said James.

Roz took a pen from the little pen-and-pencil holder on the counter. It was a lopsided Mayan temple, fashioned from clay; James had sculpted it for her in his fourth grade art class.

Roz wrote the date on a check. She filled in the amount, made it payable to "L.A. Gas Co."

James used a sponge to scrape at the oatmeal on the bowl.

"James," said Roz, not looking up from her checkbook.

"Yeah, Mom?"

"You're doing good with the kids."

"Thanks."

She tore the check out of the checkbook, placed it in the envelope, sealed it.

"I'm going to keep being hard on you, James."

"I know."

"Life isn't a hayride."

Where does she get these expressions? James wondered. But he knew what she meant …

When Alice got home, there was a message from her father on the answering machine. She and Peggy played it a couple of times; Roberto's cheerful, deep voice filled the room.

He told them he missed them. He was sorry he had to work so far away. "It can be a real bear, being grown up, Alice," he said. "A dad's gotta do what a dad's gotta do. I hope you're sketching, Allie. I hope you're being silly. You only get to be a kid once. Enjoy it all you can …"

Alice napped for awhile, and then sketched the afternoon away.

She drew the Ilwgyld, and the faery folk, and Fuego.

She drew City Hall, and the beautiful Echo Mountain House, and the eerie subway terminal.

She drew the massive Santa Monica Ferris wheel as it rolled and bounced crazily toward the Pacific Ocean …

Alice and Peggy ate supper in front of the television, sandwiches on paper plates.

"Are we gonna lose the house, Mom?"

"I don't think so," said Peggy. Her eyes welled with tears, but she held them back. "I hope not, Alice. We're doing everything we can to keep it."

Alice nodded. She squeezed her mother's plump hand.

Alice didn't say "It'll be OK, Mom," because maybe it wouldn't. But, "I'm really proud of you, Mom," she said. "It must be scary, working these new jobs."

"Kind of," said Peggy, "but I'll be all right." She hugged her daughter. "Alice, you know your dad and I will do anything for you. For you, for us, for the family …"

* * *

James and Alice saw the news report at the same time, in their separate houses.

They were both tuned to the Channel 3 evening news.

Alice was sketching again; James was playing toy soldiers with Aiden.

"Sony Stadium has apologized to ticket holders for the 'Sircus of Impossible Magicks'," reported the news anchor, "and has promised full refunds. The circus troupe, based in London, was scheduled to perform at Sony Stadium through next week. According to stadium spokespersons, the circus troupe left town last night *without* notifying stadium officials. The whereabouts of the circus is presently unknown ..."

312

Appendix – Glossary By Alice Iztali

Aelwyd. Faery realm in California.

Borderlands. Non-space between the mortal and faerie worlds.

Box of Mystery. Touchstone. Puzzle box. Associated with the Trickster.

Chosen Ones. Three descendants of Jonathan Myrddin, a member of the original *Sircus of Impossible Magicks*. The Protector, the Seer, and the Trickster are destined to return three stolen touchstones to Fuego and his clan.

Companions. Heroes fated to help the Chosen Ones. Tariq and Hisoka.

Corazon de Oro. Touchstone. Amulet. Associated with the Protector.

Daith. Fuego's son.

Darklands. Where Fuego will banish the Ilwgyld by using the touchstones.

Dark One. Somebody (something?) that really scares Lou and Flo!

Faeries. Creatures with magical and warrior abilities – seem human except for height, eyes, and magic.

Flo. Ilwgyld woman; member of *Sircus of Impossible Magicks*.

Fuego. Warrior, magician, chieftain of Teulu village. Somehow related to the Chosen Ones.

Hungry Ones. Ilwgyld. Evil faeries.

Ilwgyld. Evil faeries. Descendants of original *Sircus of Impossible Magicks*. Want the touchstones to take control of the Borderlands. Seem to be part bird.

Iztali Family. Roberto, Peggy, and Alice (Seer). Live in Silver Lake.

Jonathan Myrddin. Member of the original *Sircus of Impossible Magicks*. Fled London after the Great Fire, when his *Sircus* membership was exposed, and settled in Massachusetts. Disagreed with the deadly methods and greedy goals of the *Sircus*. Ancestor of the Chosen Ones.

Jones Family. Sam, Roz, James (Protector) and Aiden (Trickster). Live in South Pasadena.

Key of Wisdom. Touchstone. Serpent Key. Associated with the Seer.

Lou. Ilwgyld woman; member of *Sircus of Impossible Magicks*.

Merlin. Legendary wizard of King Arthur's court. Supposedly founded the *Sircus of Impossible Magicks*. Possible ancestor of Jonathan Myrddin.

Orth Magru. Monster. Details unknown.

Protector. One of the Chosen Ones.

Rath Angeles. Part of Aelwyd interwoven with mortal Los Angeles.

Rath Birds. Vicious, dark-winged birds in Aelwyd.

Seebak. Panther. James' animal totem.

Seer. One of the Chosen Ones.

Sircus of Impossible Magicks. Troupe of faery magicians supposedly founded by the wizard Merlin of King Arthur's Court. "Good" *Sircus* branch broke off and moved to the United States.

Tanwen. Fuego's wife.

Teulu. Fuego's clan village in Aelwyd.

Trickster. One of the Chosen Ones.

Valences. Borderlands between faerie and mortal worlds.

Acknowledgements

Sircus of Impossible Magicks: Chosen would not have been possible had I not enjoyed a childhood in which there was an abundance of unstructured time to play outdoors, to watch fireworks, to read, to invent games, to write stories, to see movies, to climb trees – to inhabit a "world of children" where my siblings and our friends learned about life together, and created imaginary worlds. So, I thank **my mother and my father**, who gave us that invaluable gift of freedom.

Thank you **Craig and Amy**, comrades on many childhood journeys, real and imaginary.

Thank you **Julia** for reading the first draft of *Sircus*, and providing invaluable insight.

Thank you **my friends**, and **my family (especially the aunts)**, for your constant encouragement. Writing is a cloistered business; authors don't survive those long, solitary hours inside their heads without knowing that there are wonderful people who believe in them, who have faith that the authors will succeed in translating imagination into the written word.

Thank you **Los Angeles, California**, which became my home twenty years ago, for being such a fascinating and mysterious place, with a history more fantastic than anything anyone could invent. If you would like to learn more about the locations mentioned in this book, I strongly encourage visits to your local library, local bookstore, and the Internet.

Thank you **Starbucks** for crafting the salted caramel mochas that fueled my editing sessions.

Thank you **my readers**, a loyal and discerning lot.

Most of all, thank you **my nieces and nephews**, who are lovely human beings, and constant inspirations. Their presence in our lives is a gift, a grace we can never repay.

More Books By Leslie Le Mon

Sircus of Impossible Magicks: Apprentice

The second book in the *Sircus of Impossible Magicks* series

COMING 2013 – 2014 to Amazon.com

Cold Dark Harbor and Other Tales of Ghosts and Monsters

Ten chilling New England tales where things go bump in the night

Digital and Paperback. Available at Amazon.com

The Disneyland Book of Secrets 2013: One Local's Unauthorized, Rapturous, and Indispensable Guide to the Happiest Place on Earth

The newest edition in the "engaging ... must-read" series includes chapters on Cars Land, Buena Vista Street – *all* the new attractions and *all* of the material from the prior editions. 1,000+ pages. It's a vacation in a book!

Digital. Available at Amazon.com

About the Author

Leslie Le Mon is a graduate of Mount Holyoke College. She grew up in Germany and New England, and has lived in Los Angeles since 1992.

For more about the author, her books, and the worlds about which she writes, visit:

www.leslielemonauthor.com

Comments and questions can be sent to:

les.lemon.author@gmail.com

Although Leslie cannot respond to every message, she reads – and appreciates – all of them.

Copyrights

All content of *The Sircus of Impossible Magicks: Chosen*, including all text, photos, illustrations, and cover art:

© Leslie Le Mon, 2012

Made in the USA
Monee, IL
08 December 2022